BRIDGE TO ELSEWHERE

AN ANTHOLOGY

Edited by
Alana Joli Abbott
and Julia Rios

Published by Outland Entertainment LLC
3119 Gillham Road
Kansas City, MO 64109

Founder/Creative Director: Jeremy D. Mohler
Editor-in-Chief: Alana Joli Abbott

ISBN: 978-1-954255-33-3
ISBN: 978-1-954255-34-0
Worldwide Rights
Created in the United States of America

Editors: Alana Joli Abbott & Julia Rios
Galley Proofer: Tara Cloud Clark
Cover Illustration: Ella Denson-Redding
Cover Design: Jeremy D. Mohler
Interior Layout: Mikael Brodu

Printed and bound in the United States of America.

Visit **outlandentertainment.com** to see more, or follow us on our Facebook Page **facebook.com/outlandentertainment/**

— TABLE OF CONTENTS —

— THE ATROX KILLBOARD —
A "Static over Space" story
By CG Volars

Izo Lopez woke with a start. He was in a place he didn't recognize, strapped to a cot by both wrists. The room was tiny, made of metal, and poorly lit. Izo pulled at the straps. They were strong but maybe not impossible to break. Izo's stomach curdled with confusion—and something else about the room he couldn't put his finger on. Shoving down a swelling pit of cold fear, he lifted his head to survey the area.

A single light flickered on the far wall. Across from him lay three cots, bolted into the wall with thick metal beams, each with just enough room for one person. Above him, there were two more—six bunks in total. Behind him was a wall of cabinets, twelve in all and stacked in rows. In front of him was a door. On the ceiling was a large metal grate.

There was nothing else.

Izo's eyes returned to the metal grate. He was trying to remember how he'd gotten here, or how long he'd been. But there was nothing. The last thing he remembered was getting ready for work.

Had someone grabbed and locked him up? If so, who? And why? Off the top of his head, there were a few reasons someone might have beef with him—he was a ninteen-year-old homeless Latino with dozens of parking tickets and thousands in unpaid payday loans. Those infractions didn't seem big enough to warrant anything like this though. Could he have pissed off a gang or Homeland Security without knowing it? He supposed anything was possible.

It might have something to do with the fact that he could fly faster than a jet plane. But he hated to jump to conclusions. It really could be those parking tickets. Some were more than two years overdue.

Izo frowned. Wait…was he going to miss work over this? If so, this was bullshit! He'd worked his ass off at the resort pretending to be a model Latinx—meek and hard-working as melty-face golfing-assholes with too much money and screaming sunburns made jokes about his height and the female employees. The fact that he might never get the chance to flip a table and quit already made him want to scream. But the idea that he might never get his last paycheck too?

Fuck. That. Izo yanked on his straps. He was getting out of here. Failing that, he was getting a paycheck's worth of hellraising.

Izo swung his gaze to the door while twisting his wrist and experimenting how to get leverage. The door was close to his cot and tall—eight feet high and made of a single length of pockmarked metal. There was no knob or handle. If it was locked, it was locked from the outside. Relaxing his jaw, Izo set his head back down and tried to fight a growing sense of panic mixed with fury. He didn't have enough information to panic or rage. Not yet anyway.

Taern tried to swallow the lump in his throat. Inside the locked cabin was their latest "guest"—another rare Avarian, born with the ability to fly and unfortunate enough to hail from an uncharted planet. They'd been searching for propellants to refuel on the little blue planet when they'd discovered an especially nitrogen-rich lake. It was a lovely spot, full of clear, deep waters and flanked by magnificent mountains on every side. Settling in for a long refueling process, they'd been hovering over the waters in a thick fluff of cloud for barely an hour when the native Avarian had suddenly sailed by their window without warning.

Taern's best friend, like all Strungians, was far too entrepreneurial to let money that easy get away. Kicking the Atrox into its electric thrusters, he wheeled the ship around and followed the flying youth silently.

Tearn frowned but didn't speak up. Of all their questionable money-making schemes, kidnapping and extorting Avarians was his least favorite. It was also the best paying, though. Tearn did his best to make the morally grey area a little brighter, standing up to Glongkyle when he was being too aggressive, putting his foot down before anything truly horrifying could happen. As long as everyone went home in one piece, he could sleep at night. Was it still immoral, taking people from their homes and refusing to return them until money appeared out of the aether? Sure. But so were most things.

This Avarian proved harder to catch than first appearances indicated. He wound back and forth through the clouds in a fast, unpredictable pattern. Incredibly fast, in fact. The Atrox Killboard, an old but powerful ship capable of crossing galaxies in a few months, struggled hard to keep up. Tearn's eyes widened as the youth slowly began shrinking on their radar. He glanced at their speed. He sat up sharply in his chair.

"Zippy little shit, isn't he?" Glongkyle grunted.

"Yeah," Tearn agreed, impressed.

"Where the hell is he going?"

"I don't know," said Tearn, confused. But then, almost as suddenly as he appeared, the youth stopped. Unaware anyone was following, he paused to hover deep within a thick cloud. Ahh, Tearn realized. He was diving around for cloud cover, same as us. That's pretty clever.

"Got you now, flyby" whispered Glongkyle triumphantly. Sneaking up behind the Avarian, he nailed him with a giant electric blast.

Tearn turned to Glongkyle with a glare. "You didn't have to hit him that hard."

"Did you see how fast he was? I couldn't risk spooking him. It was hard enough catching him the first time. What are the chances—"

"Don't let him hit the water!" Tearn screamed.

He supposed that was the first time he saved this particular Avarian's life. Knowing what he did about his best friend, he doubted it would be the last.

Tearn blew out a huge breath of air. The first meeting with a new guest was always the roughest, a churning maelstrom of fear, confusion, horror, and rage—there was no getting around it with these uncharted types. Oh well. It had to be done. Best get it over with.

Tipping his head in assent, Tearn nodded for Glongkyle to type in the code to their guest's quarters.

Izo lifted his head at the sound of beeping outside. With a click, the door slid open. He prepared himself for anything: the government, the mob, a bevy of sadistic scientists. But as the person behind the door came into view, Izo let out a low and piteous moan.

It was a giant green monster. Seven feet tall and with an elongated head, it stared down at Izo with two vertically-slit yellow eyes. Its nose was a pair of twin nostrils at the end of a stubby snout, its lipless mouth filled with long, crooked teeth. On either side of its scalp were short horns made of craggy yellow bone, and its skin was forest green, scaly, and thick as a crocodile's.

"Aliens," whispered Izo breathlessly.

The beast responded, speaking in a raspy language filled with consonants. "Told you he'd be awake by now," the beast said to a second person coming in behind him.

To Izo's horror, he could understand it. *What the hell was going on?*

Short, bald, and bulbous headed, the second creature looked exactly like a textbook Martian. Annoyed, he chided his larger friend in a different language, something gentler and more reassuring. "Fine. You were right. He's awake. Now can you go before you scare him?" He indicated to Izo with two tiny arms. "He probably has a lot of questions."

The reptile turned to stare at Izo. His gaze was as cold and murderous as a snake's. Every instinct in Izo's body told him to stay still. The reptile blinked. A tiny wet *click* sounded as his movable eyelid slid back into place.

Izo blew out a slow breath to keep from trembling.

Eventually the monster left, slamming and locking the door behind him with a boom. The shorter alien rolled his eyes and put his back to the cot. Hopping up, he soared slowly into the air before landing next to Izo.

"Hello. My name is Tearn. As you can probably tell, I'm not from your planet. Please don't panic though. You're not in any danger. No one's going to hurt you. We just need you to do a couple of things. Errands, basically." Adjusting his dangling legs, the short alien smiled down at Izo with calm reassurance. "You're going to be back at home, safe and sound, before you know it."

Izo could only lay quietly and stare. Deep within his chest every bio-signal in his body was going haywire, screaming to prepare for battle, prepare for conflict, prepare for doom. But outside his face stayed flat, same way he'd learned to keep it cool as a picked-on kid.

It suddenly occurred to him what was wrong with the room. The gravity inside was too light.

Most uncharted Avarians that came aboard the Atrox were calm enough to talk within a few minutes. Sure, some screamed their heads off for days, hollering and howling because—surprise, surprise—theirs wasn't the only planet capable of sustaining life in the universe. Some tried to fight back or sank into despair and hurt themselves. Both amounted to the same thing—injury to the Avarian's precious form, which helped no one.

He still remembered how they'd lost their third Avarian guest. She was lovely, a shimmering Aurelian with a delicate frame and the most heart-breakingly beautiful face he'd ever seen in person. Convinced they were lying and had no intention of taking her home or leaving her unmolested, she'd charged the door, clawing at Glongkyle's face until the Strungian fell back. Hurling through the ship, she'd found an emergency suit, pulled it on, and blindly bailed out of the first emergency airlock she could find. Problem was, the suit was a mechanical counterpressure suit that utilized a uniform, full-body squeeze instead of a gas-filled pressurization. Bulky and designed for someone Glongkyle's size, it was an ill-fated-fit on her delicate Aurelian frame.

Tearn could still remember holding his breath as she'd twisted around in the vacuum of space, limbs convulsing as her body cavities collapsed under the pressure. It must have been excruciating. At least she hadn't suffered for long.

When they finally pulled her body back in, it was Tearn who'd taken off her helmet. A mess of white strands poured out, bright as a meteor's tale. Tearn remembered cradling her head and crying through almost two Imperial space-cycles. What had happened was such a powerfully harrowing experience. It was almost like something out of a tragic Ginarsian fairytale. Since that day, he'd promised to do everything physically possible to get their guests home safely.

Tearn shook his head and came back to himself. Their current Avarian guest was doing everything to mask the fact that he was freaking the hell out. Heart rate elevated, he was breathing fast and had taken on a funny, defensive posture—arms and hands wide and ready to fight—ignoring the fact he was clearly strapped down and defenseless. Still, he'd managed to keep his muscles from shaking and had raised his chest enough to hide his rapid breaths.

"I mean it," said Tearn, bending closer. "You're going to be just fine."

The youth nodded in a quick, sarcastic way, as if to say, Sure I am, Chief. A chuffing laugh broke out of Tearn's mouth. So he was a sarcastic little shit. Made sense; irony and humor were great ways to hide fear. Still, as much as he might want to cover it, Tearn could tell he was terrified, alarm and dread radiating off his body like a blistering light. And Tearn couldn't let him stay in here and stew in this current state. Not again.

Reaching out, Tearn gently grabbed and held the youth's arm in a comforting and encouraging way.

At first, the Avarian didn't respond. Widening his grip, Tearn gently moved his hand up and down the Avarian's skin, increasing the tactile contact between them. The Avarian's skin was soft and warm and filled with strong, healthy fibers, perfect for carrying plenty of neuro-chemical signals. Brushing the top of the Avarian's hand with his other one, he doubled the connection. He was soon rewarded with a fluttering of eyelashes and two widening pools of green as the Avarian's pupils expanded. Tearn tipped forward to examine the Avarian's chest and test his reaction to proximity. But he was fine. His breathing was soft and steady; his body had relaxed. Tearn nodded and shifted back to his initial position, a little sad to move away. The Avarian had smelled a lot like the wild forests of his planet.

Tearn crossed his hands over his lap. "How are you feeling?"

The Avarian sucked in a long, steady breath. Then he tipped his head to one side instead of answering, as if to say, Okay, I guess?

"Good. You won't be here long." Tearn assured him. He reached out to pat his leg, an easy placebo to cover any lingering questions. "We'll have you home in a couple of weeks, tops."

Izo grunted and pulled harder. The short alien, Tearn, had stayed just long enough to make a bunch of vague, bullshit promises before leaving him alone again. Izo trusted him about as much as he'd trust any alien who abducted him. Which was very little. Or was it? Izo hadn't met enough aliens yet to know how you were supposed to respond to their sworn word. Until ten minutes ago, he hadn't known there were aliens whose credibility you could assess. He supposed distrust of any stranger was normal, but was a little surprised by how little surprise he felt speaking with one from outside his galaxy.

Didn't matter. Point being, he trusted the alien's word about as much as a salad from McDonald's. He'd still nodded through their first encounter, though, and the little grey Martian had eventually left, clearly satisfied. If working at the golf resort had taught him anything, it was how easily people with a little bit of power could be tricked into assuming everything between them and the people below them was cool. Hell, they ate that shit like it was their main course in life.

Izo paused to shake out his wrist and check his progress. The pain from prying up the straps was fresh, but tolerable. The grate proved more challenging. Still thinner than the metal on the door, it was beginning to bulge and rip near the only two bolts securing it. Izo re-grasped the grate before flipping his feet against the ceiling again. Then, redoubling his effort, he pushed and pulled with all his stubborn teenage might. He didn't care what it took. This fucker was coming off the wall and then...well he didn't know what then. But there'd be more options.

"Come onnn!" he grunted between clenched teeth.

The bolts gave way, and Izo and the grate hit the ground with a thud. Cursing, Izo threw the grate clear. Then, hopping to his feet, he jumped and hauled himself inside the newly created hole.

Inside was dark, with air so cold that he could see his breath. Izo shivered and moved a thick metal coil out of his way to see better.

It was a long crawl space, a foot tall, slowly curving, and covered in a thicket of tangled wires and metallic columns. About fifty yards up, Izo could make out an adjacent crawlspace pouring light and heading vertically. With any amount of luck, it'd lead somewhere important.

Izo grunted and shuffled his hips and legs into the crawl space. Once inside, he began picking his way through the morass of complex wires. Piles of moist dust stuck to his elbows and underside like fuzzy peanut butter. He grimaced and tried his best not to sneeze.

Heading back to the cockpit, Tearn was again amazed at how calm and pleasant his conversation with their guest had been. It kind of made sense though. After all, who wanted to spend their entire life on some backwater planet when there was a whole wide universe to see?

It was funny. Life, logic, and language had a unique way of evolving, didn't they? Experiences, ideas, and genes were all like tiny, metaphysical organisms, passing from one person to the next. Weak ideas buckled under them; the strong forged on. What made ideas strong? All the usual things: fit, constitution, general pleasantness. These were universal truths.

"So, what do you think?" said Glongkyle.

Deep in his heart, Tearn knew there was something special about the Avarian in the back of their ship. That's why he was going to make triple sure everything worked out for him. "I think it's going to be good."

"Had the same thought when I first saw him," Glongkyle said, glancing at their output levels. "This one definitely looks expensive."

Tearn twisted his head to glare balefully at his best friend.

Izo looked up into the vertical chasm. He'd made it to the source of light, two small windows cut out just above him. The vertical crawlspace had been indistinguishable from the first one except for its pitch, shallow for a dozen yards then growing steadily steeper. All in all, he'd probably crawled across three basketball courts and up two stories on his stomach.

Izo poked his head up to look through the windows. They were again covered with grates and led into a room. The difference was these grates were on the floor. The room was small, half living room, half cockpit, one hundred percent covered in discarded trash. A grey seating area attached to the wall on his right, with an orange coffee table bolted to the floor and a black console blanketed in blinking buttons and dials to his front.

Seated before the console were his alien abductors in matching orange chairs, one positioned far higher than the other. The scaly abductor was saying something to the short one, Tearn. Tearn looked on disapprovingly, tiny arms crossed at his chest. *Alien spat?* Izo wondered with a grin.

In front of the two captain chairs stood a giant, panoramic windshield. Outside of that was an expanse of starry nightscape. Izo frowned. Mierda. They were in outer space.

He tried to spot the sun, the earth, or the moon. But it was no use; he couldn't pinpoint anything. From out here everything looked like brightly colored clusters and shimmering cloudy trails, a boundless miasma of celestial bodies hanging in infinite space. The idea of locating any one star or planet was like trying to find a single diamond on the California coastline.

Izo frowned. It was brighter and more beautiful than he ever could have imagined. Tipping his forehead against the grate, he let his eyes search over its magnificence. Izo had always been curious about space, wondering what it might be like to view the great, wide unknown in person. But now that he was finally able to live out his childhood dream, it was from a bitter, shackled prospect. He wondered how many times humans had experienced this type of irony before: reaching America's fabled shores...as a prisoner;

entering Tokyo, New York, or some other long-sought-after metropolis…as a victim of human trafficking. Izo sucked in a long, mournful breath through his nose. Then he sneezed.

Two alien heads swiveled toward him.

Izo sniffed and wiped his nose. "Excuse me."

"You sneaky motherfucker…" The scaly one lunged out at him.

Izo dropped down the vertical shaft, away from the grate and toward the lower floors below. A second later the reptile ripped the grate off the wall, reached his head and one arm in, and immediately got stuck. Struggling and shaking his fist, he yelled down after Izo. "Get back here, you little shit!"

"Calm down," came Tearn's plaintive voice from behind him.

"He's in the lining of the ship, Tearn!"

"So? What's he going to do? It's not like he has anywhere to go."

Izo stopped short. Something about the short alien's calm confidence burned his insides. They'd kidnapped and trapped him here because they didn't think he could do anything about it. But they were wrong. There was something he could do.

Izo turned blankly to a handful of wires next to his head. They were converged at some sort of central relay. Tilting his head to one side, he gathered them in his palm. "Me pregunto…" he mumbled before yanking them free. Above, he was rewarded with the cockpit light blinking out. The reptile bellowed into the darkness.

Izo smiled and continued moving down, blindly pulling cords and ripping out metal boards as he went. Closer to the bottom, he paused to knock a thick metal coil loose with both feet. The space filled with a freezing white gas. Alarms suddenly went off all around him.

Emerging from the bottom of the hissing cloud, Izo continued his indiscriminate rampage. Halfway down, he realized he was laughing his ass off.

"How the fuck did you let this happen, Tearn?"

Tearn widened his eyes at Glongkyle. "You're blaming me!?"

"Duh! This isn't a difficult operation: I fly the ship; you keep the Avarians calm." Glongkyle pointed at the front windshield. "The ship's going to IA, Tearn." He pointed at the grate. "Why the fuck is he freaking out?"

Tearn's mouth twitched. "Because he's obviously upset about that fact. It's not complicated, Glongkyle. Put yourself in his shoes—he doesn't like what's happening. He's doing whatever he can to push back."

"I don't give a shit about his feelings. He's fucking with my ship. You've got about ten minutes to calm him down before I drag him to the nearest airlock."

Tearn straightened his back sharply. He'd never been so callously insulted and threatened in his life. Glongkyle knew how long Tearn had been tormented over the loss of the Aurelian female. Tearn stared at his friend, eyes searching for some semblance of decency. But there was none. In all honesty, there probably never had been.

Tearn glared with disgust. "You really are that heartless, aren't you?"

"No, Tearn. I really am that broke." Glongkyle pointed between the two of them. "Us? We're smugglers. We survive by scouring the universe and finding rare things. If those things happen to be sentient, I try to swing them home afterwards. Mostly because I know you'd annoy the shit out of me if I didn't." He shook his large, scaly head. "This was never a free interview though. If he can't get on board with this plan, he can't stay aboard this ship."

Tearn opened his mouth to respond, but Glongkyle had already turned to leave.

Izo paused to listen through the wall. They'd been arguing hotly about him on the floor above, but the argument was cut off as someone left to thunk their way down the hallway and away from the cockpit. A second later, the same person started sliding down a ladder outside, followed by a clunk as they hit the ground below.

Tightening his grasp on a metal pipe he'd pried from a wall, Izo listened silently to see which direction they'd go.

The person outside seemed to be listening too. After a long pause, they crossed to a nearby wall. A loud beep sounded throughout the ship, followed by a crackled voice over an intercom.

"Tearn, are you still in the cockpit?"

Izo smiled. *Well, if it isn't El Capitán himself.*

"I'm still here," came Tearn's terse reply.

"I need you to flood the inner walls with fire suppressant on the upper levels—"

Oh shit, thought Izo, eyeing the walls around him.

"I want to try and corner him in the last level," explained the lizard. "Once I get down there, I'll check the storage compartments, lower engines and then the assembly room. After you're done upstairs, you and Yula check the cryo tanks and docking bay."

"Okay, but be honest," said Tearn, sounding worried as an elementary teacher. "You're not going to hurt him if you find him first, are you?"

"Tearn, he's fucking with my ship—"

"Your brother's ship," interrupted Tearn.

"He's going to be lucky if I don't sell him for parts," finished Glongkyle. Then, cutting off the line with another loud beep, he took a few more thunking steps to the left before sliding down another ladder.

Izo stuck his tongue in his cheek as the walls in the level above him slowly hissed and spat orange gel from either side. *Okay, come-mierda,* he thought to himself with a nod. *Let's do this.*

Swinging his pipe over his shoulder, Izo floated down to go look for an assembly room in the lower levels.

Tearn shuffled across the floor to the other side of the console, counted to ten, and then started the fire suppressant protocols for the third floor. He considered having Yula help him do them simultaneously, forcing the Avarian to pop out of a random opening rather than fall into Glongkyle's trap. But he ultimately decided against it. Much as he was worried about Glongkyle taking his anger out on their guest, he was more afraid of discovering the youth drowned in a wall because he got tangled in a wire trying to escape. It'd be a terrible way to die, suffocating and trapped in a small, dark space, no one there to hear you banging and kicking from inside. No, much as the Avarian might catch hell from Glongkyle, it was still better than the alternative.

"Yula, you ready to go?" he called to their Wuljerian guard.

"We are going?" asked Yula.

"Downstairs," Tearn explained to the new hire in a voice like a mother's. "We're going to go protect our new guest."

"Yula protects Avarian?"

"That's right," Tearn reassured the big female. Hurrying out of the cockpit beside her, he turned to lock the door before climbing into the Wuljerian's arms. "We may have to protect this particular Avarian more than usual too."

"Glongkyle hates Avarian?" asked Yula before sliding down the ladder, one furry hand grasping the rung, the other holding Tearn to her chest.

"No." Tearn squeezed his face into an awkward grimace. "They're just a little annoyed with each other right now."

The Wuljerian nodded with a keen expression as they continued to drop, floors flying past all the way. "Avarian hates Glongkyle too."

Izo grinned as another grate hit the ground with a clang. He was starting to get good at that. Dropping in his new metal pipe, he watched as it clattered and bounced under a nearby shelf. Then, quickly lowering himself through the opening, he eyed the dark room.

Inside, a maze of conveyor belts zigzagged the floor, filling the space with sharp corners and hard edges. Walking beside the nearest one, he ran his palm over it. A trail of spinning metal pins gently twirled beneath his fingers. Tall ceilings. Wide space. A virtual amusement park of hard metal surfaces. "Perfecto," Izo said to himself.

Picking up his pipe, Izo continued strolling toward a set of large shelves. They looked heavy, but it was fine; he wouldn't need to move them far. Izo hummed and whacked a metal pin loose. Outside he could hear the big lizard pausing and redirecting to follow the sounds of ringing metal.

Tearn was getting worried. He and Yulu had searched less than half of the cryo tanks so far, but besides their own echoing steps, the place was silent as a mortuary. There was something about the quiet—its weighted, almost pensive stillness—that made Tearn's insides itchy.

"Did you remember to lock the cockpit?" Glongkyle blurted over the coms without warning.

Tearn jerked at the noise and nearly dropped into one of the gaps between the half-suspended tanks and the magnetic stabilizers surrounding them. Pushing off a supply tube wider than his arm, he regained his balance with a grateful whistle. Deep and constrictive, the gaps were known for shifting for little or no reason. He quickly crossed to the side wall to respond. "Are you serious?"

"Did you remember or not?"

"Yes," Tearn gritted between clenched teeth. What if he hadn't though? The possibility of getting into and locking them out of the cockpit would tempt most of their Avarian guests, much less an unholy terror like this one. Tearn let out an exhausted sigh filled with years of simmering frustration. It never failed to amaze him Glonkyle's sheer failure to

understand—and consequently discount—other people's feelings and thoughts. It was almost as if it never occurred to him that other people had feelings and thoughts.

He shouldn't have been surprised though. That's just who Glongkyle was. "I locked and double-checked before coming down," Tearn agreed.

"Good job," Glongkyle answered. "I didn't want the Avarian sneaking in behind us."

Tearn closed his eyes. "Mhmm. Good thinking." *His best friend was a certifiable moron.* "How's the search going?"

"Nothing so far. I thought I heard something in the assembly room though. Going to go check that out, then maybe I'll start in the—"

"That's great." Tearn interrupted. "We should probably get off the coms."

"Right. Let me know if you find anything."

Tearn rolled his eyes before glancing sideways at Yula. He couldn't be sure from this distance, but she seemed to be purposely avoiding his gaze.

The assembly room's wide doors slid open. The lizard stepped slowly into the room, his clawed feet carefully clicking on the floor. Following one wall, he flicked on the lights. The space was filled with dingy yellow luminousness.

Izo let out a slow breath. Beside him fuzzy shadows covered the ground in flickering stripes where the light dispersed unevenly through the assembly line pins. An ominous hush filled the room. Both enemies strained to hear the other. Eventually the lizard huffed loudly and strolled to the center of the room. "I know you're in here," he called out. "There's no point in hiding. Come out now, and I won't hurt you."

Izo smiled with satisfaction as the lizard paused to inspect his gap in the pins. Confused, he leaned down to investigate. "Why the hell are you messing with my ship?" he asked the silent room.

He was still musing over this mystery when Izo swung around and surprised him with his first hit.

Tearn jerked up at the clanging sound and shriek that followed it. Twisting his head toward the noise, he realized with no small amount of horror that it was definitely Glongkyle who'd been hit, not the Avarian.

Oh shit.

It had never even occurred to him the Avarian might get the upper hand. If he managed to incapacitate Glongkyle—or worse—they'd all be floating dead people soon.

Yula whined with alarm.

"Come on," said Tearn, hustling for the doorway. "We've got to go."

The attack was vicious and clearly unexpected. Falling into and over the metal platform behind him, the lizard let out a belated shriek.

Izo turned and risked a look. A second passed before the reptile lashed up, flailing and sputtering with a look of crazed confusion. The blow, squarely hitting one side of his head, had already grown into an ugly purple welt. The reptile staggered toward the door, clutching the conveyors as he went. Spotting Izo's second attack, he managed to cringe in time. The flying hit smashed into his shoulder and forearm instead of his face.

Izo curved around and returned to his hiding spot, the sweet ring of his strike still vibrating in his hands. Hunkering down, he savored the sound of the lizard-man's confusion.

The monster was still grappling to climb to his feet. So the reptile couldn't take too many hits. That was interesting. Izo wiped down the end of his pipe, slick with blood on one end and nervous sweat on the other. Rounding the corner, Izo flew forward to crack the pole across the back of his abductor's head this time. The hit connected so soundly its recoil stung the inside of Izo's palm.

The lizard screamed. Izo arced up to return to his spot behind the shelf. The sound of someone shuffling on their hands and knees filled the room, followed by the spinning of pins.

Izo stepped out of his hiding spot to look. The gutless wretch was huddled under a conveyor, sorry sobs coming out in tiny, panicked hics. Izo gave a derisive snort. This was the monster he'd been scared of? He gave a disappointed head shake before letting his pole slide to the ground with a loud tap.

The beast jumped and spun toward him. Reptilian eyes locked with Izo's. The Earthling crossed to the reptile, pipe dragging the behind him in a slow, even scrape.

"You know who I am, pendejo?" Izo asked, pointing his pipe at the beast. "I'm the last human you're ever going to bother."

The reptile cowered and didn't answer. Izo angled his head, astonished and disgusted. Lifting his pipe over one shoulder, he wrapped his second hand around it. The urge to smash in the lizard's face filled his veins. But it wasn't in his nature to strike people on the ground. Lowering the end of the pipe, he jabbed at the beast until he backed out from under the metal belts.

He indicated for the lizard to rise. The alien slowly obeyed, using the conveyors to stand. He was still hunched over, shoulder clutched in one clawed hand, back of his head in the other. Izo frowned at him, as disappointed as God.

Sighing, Izo tossed the pipe to the other end of the room. The lizard watched it clatter to the ground, brow drawn down in confusion.

Raising his fists, Izo waited for the reptile to turn back to him. Then he gave a single upward nod.

Tearn paused. The struggling noises had stopped. What had been fear and rage echoing off the ship's walls was now a quiet, simmering tension—an animal crouch just before an attack. The thin grey skin on Tearn's arms pimpled with alarm. He'd only ever registered this type of steely resonance once before while refueling on a war planet.

"We need to get over there now," Tearn told Yula.

"We must hurry?" asked Yula.

"Yes," Tearn said breathlessly. "One of them is about to die."

The reptile slowly mimicked Izo's fighting posture, sizing him up, scanning Izo's light frame and slender limbs with cold calculation. Nodding sideways, Izo eased them out into an opening where four aisles met, his steps light and measured beneath him. The reptile followed.

Extending his claws suddenly, the reptile lunged forward, swinging fast. But he barked in surprise as Izo connected a heel with the back of his head. Thrown forward, he flew into the conveyors, thighs slamming into unforgiving metal.

Izo waited as his abductor pushed himself up, one clawed hand gingerly going to his latest bruise. Izo grinned; his head probably felt like he'd stuck it in a bucket with fireworks.

Spinning to hurl himself forward again, the reptile charged, claws swinging wider this time. He was rewarded with a flutter of cloth as one talon passed just under Izo's arm. But Izo twisted around and nailed him in the side of the face with a hard hook, sending the beast sprawling into the conveyors again. The reptile managed to catch himself and spin faster this time though, spotting a momentary look of pain as Izo shook out his fist.

Izo hissed. The lizard had noticed his injured left hand and vulnerable left side. Izo couldn't wait any longer. This needed to end.

The reptile, seeming to sense his mood, stretched to his full height and threw open his claws almost as wide as they would go. Izo, for his part, brought his right side forward, did a quick calculation, and took two steps back.

Misjudging this, the dumb beast broke into a third charge, which Izo goaded on by widening his eyes. Truth was, with his attacker's top set wide and all his weight thrown forward, Izo was almost giddy.

One of the only martial arts moves Izo knew was how to throw someone over his back. It was a simple move that rewarded the quick and short over the large and heavy. By waiting until an attacker charged, Izo could kneel and wrap up his assailant's leg and take off, tossing them into the ground face first. The faster and bigger the attacker, the harder the landing. As a middle-schooler Izo had perfected the move. By now he could do it in his sleep.

Popping down and back up, he threw the giant lizard-man into the conveyors behind them, savoring first the *wham* and then *oof* as the creature tumbled clear onto the other side.

Izo didn't have a moment to waste though. Hurtling over the conveyor belts, he clambered onto his attacker's back, legs going around the reptile's waist as he snaked his left arm under the monster's neck. Secure, Izo grabbed his own wrist and began choking the reptile as hard as he could.

The beast fought to reach him, swinging his elbows then his fists back, trying to connect with anything. But Izo had been here before. He knew how to feel his attacker's intentions and shift away without giving any slack. Throwing his head back, the lizard did manage to scruff Izo's cheek with his bony horns, but it was nowhere near enough to make Izo let go.

The alien tried to get up; Izo attempted to prevent this, swinging his back to keep the lizard off balance. But he'd forgotten about the conveyor belts. Grabbing one of the rails, the beast managed to haul the two of them up in a single yank. Izo could only tighten his grip and pray reptiles passed out faster than humans.

The beast shoved off the conveyors, throwing them both into the next row of metal bars. Izo tried to brace himself, but it was no use. Even in the weakened gravity, their combined weight and force was too much. He smashed into the metal rails with a painful grunt. Wind knocked clear and stars twinkling, Izo fought to regain his grip. But it was too late. The reptile was already turning to pin him down.

Izo twisted to get away but was hauled back. Trapped on his stomach between the lizard and the metal bars, Izo swung, smashing an elbow into the beast's jaw. But a second later the beast had this same arm locked high and tight behind him. Izo hissed with pain. He was seriously regretting dropping his pipe.

Four large talons surrounded his skull with a pressure as unforgiving as a vice. The reptile yanked his head back. In a moment the metal pipes would come flying at his face and this would all be over.

"Stop!" Tearn screamed from the door. Shuffling into the room, the short alien hustled to reach them. A giant wooly alien followed closely. Izo gaped at the yeti-like monster. Ducking under the door, it was easily a foot or more bigger than the reptile. *There's an even bigger one on board?!*

"Glongkyle, let Yula take him," said Tearn.

The two giants obeyed, switching positions. The wooly monster, Yula apparently, wrapped a frying-pan-sized-paw around the back of Izo's neck, pinning him as easily as one might pin a kitten to the floor. Izo struggled and swung. But it was no use. His strikes hit nothing but fur.

"Yula, take him out," said Glongkyle.

Izo's eyes widened, imagining himself in the vacuum of space: eyeballs boiling, lungs expanding till they popped. But Yula only increased the pressure on either side of his neck instead. Still perfectly able to breathe and move, Izo cursed and struggled until his limbs grew too heavy to move and the room went dark.

Tearn shoved Glongkyle in his back. "What the hell were you thinking?"

"Don't look at me. This is all your fault." Glongkyle waved a hand at the passed out Avarian. "You said he was fine. You said to give him a couple of hours alone to adjust."

"I never wanted to kidnap him to begin with!"

"By the gods, not this crap again..." Glongkyle rolled his eyes. "You really expect anyone to believe that anymore, Tearn?"

Tearn stared in horror. His frustration and anger overwhelmed his senses until he broke into his species' penchant for super-tele-empathy, fury shooting all over the room. Like most days, Glongkyle couldn't sense it. It was part of the reason Strungians were one of the few species that could move to Ginarsia.

Yula squirmed back toward the door as Tearn's disgust filled the room like a rancid nausea. Tearn slammed his tiny fists down onto the front of his legs. "I was the only one against all of this! I was the only one trying to keep everyone safe. I'm the only one with a shred of moral decency."

"Sure you are." Glongkyle let out a loud fart. "There goes some right now."

Izo was awoken by lights cutting on and the sound of beeping outside. He was back in the small, metal room, and had been in a heavy sleep for who knew how long. Groaning, he reached for his head with one hand, but stopped short. His right hand was shackled to the cot's frame with a short, thick chain attached to a tight metal cuff. It was wrapped so snugly around his wrist, he doubted if he could turn it 180 degrees without bruising himself.

Izo groaned and dropped his head back. Above him the dented grate he'd ripped down had been repositioned over the hole in the ceiling. It now sported over a dozen new bolts.

A moment later, the door slid open, and his shortest alien abductor padded inside, bowl of slop in one hand, cup of murky water in the other. Tearn set the meal on the ground before crossing his arms at Izo. "I had half a mind not to give you this; what you did was really shitty, mister. I honestly don't know what you were thinking." Annoyance clear, the short alien tapped his foot repeatedly. "Well? What do you have to say for yourself?"

Izo sat up as far as he could. "Fuck you," he spat before turning to face the wall.

Tearn made a high, offended noise. Though he didn't know what the Avarian had said to him (and wouldn't until they finished translating and compiling his language), he had a good idea of the feeling behind the words.

Tearn fumed with anger. Even the Avarian, whose life he'd saved, whose person he'd defended, didn't appreciate his efforts. No one did! They didn't care that all Tearn wanted was to keep everyone safe and do his best. No, all they cared about was what they wanted. Well everyone couldn't get what they wanted all the time, could they? It was people like Tearn that kept things from devolving into violence and chaos by balancing people's interests. Was it perfect? No. But what was? You did your best, woke up, and tried to do better tomorrow. This wasn't about right and wrong. This was about people always trying to get their way. Well guess what? Tearn NEVER got his way. And he was starting to get really sick of it too.

"Don't you turn your back on me. I just made you food!" Reaching forward he smacked the exposed part of the Avarian's leg with his hand, a sheer bolt of rage flowing out of his limbs and into their guest.

The Avarian jerked away, the emotional heat registering immediately. Tearn sneered and slapped him again. The Avarian managed to knock his hand away this time, but it was no use. The emotional energy transferred anyway. Tearn could feel and see it now too—his infuriating frustrations lowering as the Avarian's rose ten-fold, blood gathering in his bronze cheeks and limbs growing itchy with unspent adrenaline. But of course, because he was an Avarian chained to the wall, there wasn't a damn thing he could do about it.

Tearn grinned darkly. He hit the Avarian again and again, tiny hits that could never leave bruises but we're just enough to connect and get an even bigger rise out of him.

Within minutes the Avarian was howling with fury. Tearn stepped back to watch from a satisfied distance as the youth tore at the chain and threw himself at the wall. His fingers ripped and bled; his elbows and shoulders ricocheted off hard surfaces and bruised; his voice cracked from screaming. But still he raged on, too lost in his emotions to even feel what he was doing.

Ironic, huh?

Tearn chuckled and turned to the door, pulling it closed as he stepped to the other side. It'd take a good couple of hours for the emotional excess to wear off. He'd come back and check on their guest then. In the meantime, there was no real reason he needed to be here for this.

"Try to calm down, sweetheart," Tearn said before shutting and locking out the noise.

— GORT, CINDER, AND SPHINX —
By R J Theodore

I hold a contempt for cats that can only be understood by those crew members responsible for mucking their zero-G litter pans. It's the universe's biggest joke that we can't travel faster than light without their yowling.

Next time we finish a job that can pay for it, how about a ship upgrade and an intern? Teach them the ropes, starting with the cat boxes.

What? That's how I learned. Some teens smoke stardust under the bleachers then scrape together enough credits to get a celestial towing license, while others enlist and wear a uniform for life. But no one skips litter scraping duties.

Sorry for my mood. Jacking this globe is taking longer than expected, and all I can think about is what joy the litter boxes will hold when I come back from rigging up these old tow beam generators. Let me focus. It'll give you a break from my grumping. I'll signal before I head back up.

Look, babe. Have you seen this?

Someone out there has a death wish. They're jacking cat planets. Guess some people are too good to honor the treaties.

It's just on the rumor boards for now, no official reports—why would there be? It looks real bad for everyone, especially us planet jackers. I'm sure we can expect some kind of new regulations or enforcement jammed down our throats for this, even if no one will say why.

Would love to get a grip on the throat of whatever dirtbag is stirring up this litter dust on us. Just adds to my headache. Everywhere I go, it's cats.

Of course, if I want a life without them, I have two options. First: live planet-side. That option's right out. I don't live on planets, I steal them.

Cat-free option two would be to transport in the slow, without the caterwaul-aided singularity skips. Not exactly thrilling. But after sweating too hard over those tow beams, a little leisure—paired with the absence of litter and hair balls—could almost convince me.

But I figured it out years ago: where the cats go, you go. The genetically modified *Toxoplasma gondii* helps with your seizures and endears the furbags to you like they're bonded to your DNA. And I'll consider no option that removes you from my life.

Besides, it's a good gig. Cats holler up a match for whatever bounties come through the WideNet, and you and I get to spend a few days rolling about on some custom primordial soup planet. Or maybe one where someone's fantasied up some designer civs—those are always fun—then hook its core up to our graviton hitch and tow it to the bursar's for a payday.

That time we found the planet of merfolk? Yeeeeah, kinda wish we'd kept that one for ourselves. Not to live on, of course, just for the occasional rutting. I'm here for the stars like I'm here for you.

But I'm not reckless enough to take *this* contract. Sure, I wish the cats respected the effort I put into their litter boxes, but even

I wouldn't mess around with a Feline Host planet. What kind of money would tempt someone to take on that kind of heat? A multi-plex of zeroes, at least.

Wonder if someone's paying that much. And who would dare.

Keep an eye on it, though. If there's a clue to who sent it, might be a way to make a bounty off it without stepping too far outside the law. Bet we could buy a lot of Oolong and comfort for that kind of information.

But let's agree not to tell this to our trio. It'll only put them in a mood, and I'll be on cleanup thanks to their heave-first-ask-questions-later stomachs.

This job is a messy one. I swear, terraformers and their half-conceived biospheres make this galaxy like a child's nursery. Inevitably, shit goes wrong with whatever evolution they did or didn't plan out, and rather than cleaning up after themselves, the architects cut their patents loose, lift their skirts, and tromp off to the next planet in need of an atmosphere and a culture boost.

Lucky for us, the collectors always want to buy their messes.

You woulda loved this one, though, if it had been more acces-sible. It was a fever dream. Robots and dinosaurs running loose everywhere. Look, I captured some vid for you before they came after me. No idea who programmed the bots, but it's something else to watch them traipse around, braiding flowers into necklaces to loop over angry sauropod necks for fucking points.

You remember that one sphere where all the plants were carnivorous and recited poetry about their victims' bravery and sacrifice? I swear, terraformers are the wrong kind of problem solvers. And I'm not sure who's worse, the architects or our buyers.

I spent the last two days running from chompy-toothed lizards with breath like the bottom of a dumpster and hippie ass automata who wanted to decorate me, spelunking the planet's thrice-fouled mantle to plug in the hitch. Both parties following me like I'd just gone down into the lower cargo bay instead of magma-flows and unstable sub-terra cave systems.

Does this bite look like it's getting infected? No, that other one's just a scratch, I think.

Swear I tried to avoid them, but I probably led at least four robots and a dozen or so dinos to an early grave anyway.

Sheesh. What a freaking life we lead.

All right, have the cats take us to the nearest outpost. We deserve to get paid for that mess, sooner rather than later.

I'm gonna get a bandage and pour myself a drink. Want one of your shakes?

Fucking hell! Automated piece of shit is broken again. We've got the technology to hook up an entire planet and tow it, skipping singularities across the galaxy, to trade for the bounty. And yet the automated, self-cleaning, odor-neutralizing, as-seen-on-the-WideNet litter offerings are nothing but lavender-scented failure. We're going to have to get a new zero-grav litter box at the next post. These things are just designed to break down, and always in the middle of a singularity skip.

I swear, if we didn't need felines and their incessant yowling to travel at the speeds we've gotten used to, I'd be more than happy to leave them behind. GMToxo can't override my distaste for the smell of feces and urine. Can't get that stink out of the thin carpeting. Because, of course, the cats wouldn't piss on the metal deck plates we could just hose off. I'm supposed to believe they understand high level quantum physics but can't figure out the ship's head?

Damned cats hate the reek more than we do, yet they excel at leaving their shit where it won't wash out. You know how smart they are—they tell us so themselves. I'm convinced they're doing this to me on purpose.

Don't even get me started on the hair balls on my side of the bunk.

Re-up my GMToxo booster? No, thank you. I'd rather have another stiff drink and mutter myself into oblivion each night. You'd think I'd get enough of a dose through litter duty, anyway.

Yeah. Yeah, ignorance is bliss and spacefaring is easier if we have good relationships with the clawed navigators.

A drunken stupor is also bliss. Say what you will about the pirate stereotypes. Now I see what drives them to it.

Didn't the ancient Egyptians worship cats? Are there any funerary murals about litter duty, or what? Seems like, between that and the pyramids, they had a lot of advancements we've since lost. Whether those advancements were the product of an unpaid human workforce or... Well, we know it wasn't ancient alien visitors, and probably not the pharaohs, either. I don't care who comes up with the fix, if it would mean I don't have to bend the litter scoop backwards under pounds of cat urine and clay litter.

You tell me, "Egypt was mostly desert. They probably didn't have to clean much."

Well, that checks out. Maybe we should move back to Mars where you found me. Think of it: a home base where we can cook up a proper meal instead of instant ramen topped with micronutrient cubes.

Yeah, yeah. Point-two-zero seconds for you to call me on it. Just thinking of the upkeep on anything bigger than a ship is exhausting.

A few choice bounties and we could retire, though. Ditch the felines and lose ourselves, riding slow out in the ink. Dodge the trading lanes between fill-ups and just exist.

Yeah, I know. Medicine, boosters, groceries. It sounded romantic, and easier, in my head. It's an alternative to moving planet-side, though. My brain's stuck in a loop of how to lose the cats.

You'd probably never really accept that, anyway, would you? How many doses of GMToxo did it take to get to the level of contentment you've found, curled up in the grav couch with all three of the ship's whiskered nav components? I watch you fall asleep halfway through the afternoon shift and wish I could be that happy.

What would it take? Wouldn't mind a few more civilized worlds in the rotation. Maybe someone's got some new litter pan for us to try. Just because none of them have worked so far doesn't mean inventors won't ever think of one that will.

If we could solve this cat shit situation, I could live like this, with you, forever.

Baby, I'm so sorry I yelled. I'm sorry I scared the cats and upset you. You know I'm a low-doser, so hairballs on my pillow get to me like they can't get to you.

I don't know. I don't know what my problem is, or why I self-medicate with the Achthuzian whiskey instead of self-inoculating with the GMToxo. Being drunk just seems better than being brainwashed.

No, no, god dammit. I'm not calling *you* brainwashed. You know what I mean. Fuck. I'm sorry. You know I'm not good with words. I always say the wrong shit, why would now be any different?

Fuck.

We're stranded until the cats tongue-wash the hurt off and get over it. Which could be three minutes or could be a year. Like that time I accidentally stepped on Sphinx's tail because I didn't see her sleeping on the mat by the heater in the sonic shower stall.

And I'm stranded till I figure out how to apologize properly.

How do I make it up to you? I'll double my doses, okay? Twice a month.

What? I thought you knew! I haven't taken the dailies in years. Just enough to get over my aversion. Not enough to want to listen to them groom themselves in the cockpit all freaking day. Twice a month is a lot to me.

...

Okay. Okay. For you, I'll noc weekly. Would that be enough to forgive me?

What, are you serious? Do cats even understand apologies? Would the words communicate something they've got no concept for?

All right. Fine. I'll do it.

You tell me I can't apologize "begrudgingly" or "the cats will know." So, I guess we're stuck here till the GMToxo does its work.

New job's just come through on the WideNet. Someone sent it straight to us, see? Right there: addressed to the *Flippant Bean*.

Tried to tell myself it was a joke and delete it. If you hadn't wheeled through at just the right moment, I'd probably have done it already. But you needed a refill on your Oolong, and the smell of your perfume always gives me pause, no matter what I'm doing.

Shit. Whoever is behind the cat planet jackings has us on their radar, right? This can't be a coincidence, but I don't know if there's a way around this. We ignore it, they'll be knocking on our access hatch next. We get involved, it could mean the end for us. Never mind getting stuck planet-side. We'll be incarcerated.

I mean, if we get caught.

Yes, I know, I shouldn't have even opened the contract doc. That'll have a pingback receipt. But I could see the offer in the preview line. Fuck me, lookit all those zeroes.

You want to know, "What would we even do with that much money?"

You were always the Goldilocks sort of innocent. Everything "just right" so long as we can afford food, meds, tune-ups, and litter.

But you know how money keeps me up at night. Upping the GMToxo didn't fix that.

This, though. Babe, just look at it. Not quite a multiplex, but for that many zeroes I'd kidnap Bast herself.

And my soul be just as doomed, yes. *Earth-bound Jesus*. Who'd risk international courts and getting blacklisted by the Feline Host?

"Someone who wants a corner on the shipping market," you figure.

I may not love our navigators, but I don't want to pay premiums to take on a new four-legged crew when these old ladies tell us they want to retire.

More important, though. How'd we end up in the TO: field of this job? Look at the name. Anyone you know? Yeah, me neither.

I don't like it. I don't like that we were tagged for it, and I don't like it because.... Well, dammit. Maybe the higher dose of GMToxo worked better than I thought. But the Feline Host got themselves planets of their own for a reason.

I'm gonna go have a few drinks and knock myself out. This contract is getting under my skin.

You're right, of course. We don't need all that money, but we could stand a bit more than we have. I need to sleep at night. To know you're taken care of, if some dino bite of mine gets infected. Or worse. Those terraformers love their venomous species.

Wouldja look at that. Feel the ship come alive again? The purr of the deckplates? I guess the cats are done being mad at me. Sounds like Gort is back at the Nav Comp.

Thank fuck that's over. Why don't we go listen to her sing us across the stars?

Fucking Christ, it stinks down here! Send through the industrial filter suit, would you? I'm gagging on the reek.

Wonder if the Feline Host appreciates how good they had it with humanity to scoop their boxes for them. Could just be imagining it, but I think I'm seeing a lot of the particular brand of kitty pride that masks a planet-sized regret.

All I know is, as soon as I arrived, the greeting party started cleaning themselves. Maybe in an hour when their stomachs are full of fur, someone will remember to take me to the council.

Yes. Yes, I'm here. I'm sorry I worried you. Their minister fell asleep in my lap and I couldn't step outside to check in.

Sorry, I can barely hear you over the mewling. You know, aside from the stink, it's not so bad here.

No. I can't say over radio. I'm coming back up.

Yes, yes. Gimme a minute to get this suit off. Shit. That's going into the recycler.

Well, now we know who's putting out the contracts.

The cats are. Dozens of these bounties went out, on different WideNets, for different sizes, cherry-picking different ships they trust. Our purr factories apparently put in a good word for us.

They want to relocate. Well, no, I take that back. The treaties would probably honor any relocation request, except this one. They want to leave this dimension. They don't care for their own kind's company as much as they expected to, and they...

Come on, over here. Yes, in the head. One, I need a shower more than I need a drink, and two, I'm not supposed to talk about this next part. Look at the way Cinder is eyeing me.

Door's shut all the way? You know Gort has that shoulder-bump trick to pop it open if it's not completely latched. Okay.

So, they miss people. And didn't bank on so many cats being left behind when the ships crewed up. Yeah. Our ships are bona fide Heaviside Layers, to the point of elections and everything.

Way I thought I knew cats, I'd expect them to avoid recruitment. Sphinx won't even let me pick her up. Instead, the whole population stops to primp and groom and tries to make their eyes as big as they can when a ship pulls into orbit. Had the full view of it before they realized I was responding to their special posting.

I know how it sounds. Well, at least they miss people's fingers and people's fresh, warm laundry, and people with litter scoops most of all. But all they would say was they'd had time to evaluate and, as a council, reverse their ancestors' decision.

Took this long because...well, because they're cats. Can't imagine they could hold their focus long enough for every vote to come in, and there had to be some who disagreed just to be contrary. Like when Gort acts as if they want petting when what they really want is to bite me.

Much as the Feline Host misses people though, they're not gonna go about anything straightforward. Can you imagine a cat just reaching out for companionship and not making a whole will-they-won't-they production of it? They want to start over, some kind of new mousers' eden where people and cats live in peace and purrs.

You want to do it? No, I'm not surprised. You've always had the biggest heart in the universe. Its gravity pulled me in.

I'll do it if you want. We're already outlaws, but we'd have to become a different sort of outlaw for this. No doubt the NavComm would blacklist us for stealing their workforce.

Not that it would matter, I guess. The cats want to sing their way into a singularity instead of skipping across them.

Yeah, I know, but they told me they did the research long ago, long before humans tried, and they figured out what's on the other side. Didn't explain, though, the science of how to survive the trip. A moth got into the council and they adjourned until someone caught and ate it, then took naps while the victor ran out to cough it up somewhere.

So what's there? Horseflies, chickadees, and catnip, I suppose. Their idea of paradise isn't going to jive with anything we can conceive of. Well, unless it's miles and miles of comfy grav couches and warm blankets fresh out of the dryer. We could work with that, I guess.

People can survive there too, apparently, and some of their number are in charge of recruiting for their new utopia.

And we're included in their plans. They'll need supply runs, and they've promised us some serious upgrades.

Think about it. We'd haul an M Class through a galactic sphincter and change the entire course of spacefaring humanity. And then, if we don't want to, we never have to haul another globe again. We could just visit them. Like normal people.

I know, we're not normal people. You and me, we're something better.

We don't have to whisper anymore; the cats already know about the plan. It was just the part about all their feelings I was supposed to keep to myself.

Across the WideNet, supposedly, navigators everywhere are on board with the idea. Free will is strong with cats, though, so I suppose the happy ones will keep navigating true for their crews. The rest will meow themselves straight to this new world and their humans will get sorted when they arrive.

Humanity isn't going to be happy about this. Can't space plot without catsong. But that's how it's always been: the cats earn their keep, and then think they've earned more just for the effort of being agreeable. We agree to their own crew cabins, but they like sleeping on our legs and don't want their own cabins. Instead they want their own worlds, because of course they do.

Then cats discover litter pans are the worst—something any of the scooping crew could have told them long ago. So, cats burn it all down. Knock the fragile system off the cosmic countertop just to watch it shatter on the decking. Seems like anyone who's ever met a cat should have seen this one coming.

What a time to be alive.

Oh, yeah, no. If you say you want in, we're in.

Either way, I'll be scooping litter for the rest of my life. When the inevitable chaos ensues, I want to be on the side that keeps us and the cats singing through space, together.

And all those zeroes don't hurt.

HOW TO WIN FRIENDS
— AND INFLUENCE REBELLION —
A "Lex Talionis" Story
By R.S.A. Garcia

Bloodkin *noun* (Madinah — vartesh)
Definition: those we share blood with
also: those we spill blood with

Chapter 1 — Madinah Words and Phrases in Universal
Essential Translations for Orgalian Apprentices, 2nd Edition,
Res Publica

When Xanitefih stepped through the airlock, she expected to see UnTosh sitting at the virtual controls. She did not expect the small human sitting on the floor at UnTosh's feet, legs outstretched and crossed at the ankles.

UnTosh was imposing as ever, skin an unhealthy mottled yellow, her aura blue with a tinge of orange and red. The human might have been a female. Dark growth humans called hair covered its head and brushed the top of the jumpsuit it wore. The aura that emanated from it shifted through every color in the spectrum.

"You didn't say she was bigger than you," it said in high-pitched Universal.

"What that matter?" UnTosh replied.

"Would have been good to know."

UnTosh snorted and swivelled her left eye toward the human.

"You not change mind. Already know plan crazy."

"There's that," the human agreed.

They'd expected to be boarded. That explained the lack of defensive measures after she deployed the targeted null-wave that shut down their engines. Not that it mattered. She could handle UnTosh and one human, and the informant on Pirate's Rock had confirmed their ship had departed with just two crewmembers.

Xanitefih took another step and aimed her volt-gun at her former bloodkin. "UnTosh," she said in slave-speak. "By the authority of the Quango—may they walk among us always—I take you for the good of the kin. You are ordered to return with me to the nearest Combat for Recycling."

"Did she just say she's going to recycle you?" the human asked in Universal, eyes wide.

UnTosh growled.

Xanitefih Gen 1485 of the 5th Branch was brought up short by an odd disorientation she had experienced only once before. An instinct of caution connected to events not going the way she had planned; an instinct that made her pause, suddenly uncertain.

And then she realised something else. The human should not have been able to understand slave-speak.

"UnTosh," she said, "you have taught this human our tongue? That is a Great Forbidden."

"And what has that to do with me?" UnTosh replied in Warrior-speak. "I'm UnTosh. Madinah law has relinquished me. I have no rights, no people, no Branch. No kin. I am nothing. How can nothing break the laws of the Quango?"

There could be no doubt now. UnTosh had changed so much she had abandoned the Madinah way. She had not even repeated the Mantra of the Quango when she spoke of them, as all Warriors had been trained to do from birth. She was no longer the Tosh who had fought with Xani in the bloodthirst of combat, and checked her battle-numb hide for wounds after. The Quango had been right to declare her Undone and send Xani after her for Recycling. Sometimes, even after years amongst the Lowers, a Warrior like UnTosh could be Redone. But now Xani had found her, she knew UnTosh to be finished. She consorted with humans and taught them Madinah ways. Only Recycling awaited her.

If she succeeded in capturing the UnTosh, who had been longest amongst the Lowers, her own standing in the Branch would be elevated. And that of the offspring she had volunteered to spawn in her quest to become a new Gen. To give rise to a new name.

Certainty filled her. It would be easy to take UnTosh now. She was weak, filled with genetic instability. Her aura proclaimed her ill. No match for Xani.

"The laws are the same for all Tiers, Warrior and slave alike. You cannot claim ignorance. You may only redeem yourself by showing respect for the Madinah way and choosing to submit to Recycling as decreed by the Quango, may they walk among us forever."

"No," the human said, rising to its feet slowly. Xani did not bother to focus her volt on it. Humans were fragile and slow. This female was no threat. But it needed to understand it was in no position to challenge her. She whistled at it and bared her teeth. UnTosh, surprisingly, bared her teeth as well, spreading her arms and thrusting her ridged chest forward in a fighting stance. It was a warning, a declaration of protective rights, and inappropriate outside of training barracks. No Madinah could respect such a fragile, worthless thing as a human. It was yet more evidence that UnTosh's Rewriting had gone horribly wrong.

"She won't be submitting to whatever it is your Quango decreed," the human continued. "Tosh is with me. She'll stay with me."

This was tiresome now. Xani trained her volt on the human, who had drawn closer, hands in the air, fingers level with its chin.

"Be careful," UnTosh said, snarling. "She has also been Rewritten."

"Like you?" the human responded.

"Yes. Xani what we call Breeder now. Stronger. Faster."

Xani focused both eyes on the human. "Listen to UnTosh. Get out of way."

"Good to know," the human replied with a quick glance at UnTosh and another step toward Xani.

"Not want end you. Humans have one cycle. But will kill you."

"With that thing?" the human motioned to the volt-gun. "It's impressive. I'll probably have trouble lifting it."

"You never touch," Xani said. "Will crush—"

The human's arm blurred, and Xani no longer held the volt-gun. It showed a glimmer of small, even teeth as it crushed the muzzle out of shape. Xani launched herself at it. The human moved aside and the volt-gun hit her in the head with enough force to send her into the hull. Before she could rise to her feet, the human was on her and there was an injector in her torso. It hit her over the head with the volt-gun again. Her vision darkened.

"Well," the human said, "I guess it wasn't that heavy after all."

UnTosh snorted. "Show off."

The gun hit her one more time. Then all was silence.

Xani woke in the belly of her own transport. She was grav-cuffed to the chair hunters like her used to hold those destined for

Recycling. Her prickling skin told her the energy shield across the portal in front of her had been activated. The room held nothing but the chair and a holoprojector mounted high in the ceiling. In front of her was an empty corridor, the oxidized metal slightly dented from long use. The air hummed with the infrasound of the lightspeed engines. Her ship was on the move. No doubt with UnTosh as the pilot, since the controls only responded to Madinahs.

She remained still, conserving her energy instead of struggling against her bonds. It was no use after all. The grav-cuffs would only become heavier the more she struggled. She used the time to gather her thoughts about the unusual human. Obviously, she had underestimated it and UnTosh. Escape would require planning. And knowledge of what the two intended.

Her first opportunity came a short time later. She was resting her eyes when she became aware someone stood near. The human watched her from the doorway, hands in its pockets, head slightly to the side.

"Morning," it said.

She remained silent, seeing no reason to reply to an illogical greeting in space.

"That's a joke."

Xani knew of this concept. It was only slightly less pointless than the greeting.

"How you come there?" she said instead.

"You mean without you hearing me?" The human raised and lowered its shoulders. "Just quiet, I guess."

Xani grunted and resolved to say nothing more. The human watched her. "Tosh said you wouldn't question me. At first anyway."

Xani swivelled an eye at her. "Not speak of traitor."

The human nodded slowly, as if thinking over what she'd said. "Tosh says you can have children now. That you've been Rewritten."

"Yes."

"She says that's a huge accomplishment."

"It not accomplishment among your people?"

"Depends on what you mean by that. If I want to have a kid, I don't need permission or genetic adjustments."

So, it *was* female. But only a few Madinah communiques mentioned humans capable of besting Madinah, and those had been soldiers in a distant galaxy.

"You soldier?" she asked.

"Like you, you mean?" the human countered.

They both fell silent, unwilling to answer.

"Fuck." The human sighed. "It's not like you can stop this now. Yes. I'm...I was a soldier."

Xani noted the correction. "You no longer soldier."

She said nothing.

Understanding sharpened Xani's focus. This female must be one of those rumoured soldiers that had beaten Madinah Warriors. She was unusual. She had probably broken laws. "Your people Rewrite you? Recycle you?"

An expression twisted the human's face briefly, but Xani could not decipher it. She bared her teeth, and Xani tensed at the sign of aggression.

"I suppose you could say they tried that once. Didn't work out well for them."

She pointed her chin at Xani. "What about you? Why did you let them Rewrite you?"

Such a strange question prompted her to answer. "Why fight such honor?"

"Honor?" The hair above the human's eyes rose. "You consider Rewriting an honor?"

Of course. The human had spent time only with UnTosh. "All *true* Madinah welcome Rewrite. First Rewrite, then Branch. No legacy without Rewrite. This why UnTosh agree. Why I agree."

"But you lose yourself. Your body, your mind even—it's all lost."

"Not lost. Changed. For the good of all Madinah."

"Because they get to carry out their experiments on you?" She scoffed.

"Not experiment," Xani explained. "Evolution."

"Directed evolution. You meditate and they poke and prod until your DNA rearranges itself. They choose what you're supposed to breed. Madinah that can breathe water, thrive in crushing gravitational atmospheres, or withstand glass storms, whatever they need to conquer the next planet that has resources you can use. Your whole race is adaptable—and insatiable."

Xani whistled a warning. "UnTosh talk too much."

"She's needed to since the Rewriting. She wanted to understand emotions better. You guys are mostly instinct. You don't even enjoy sex."

Xani growled low in her chest, confused. "What sex?"

"It's how humans procreate."

"You enjoy?"

She shrugged. "It can be amazing with the right person."

"You have right person?"

Xani didn't expect an answer, she looked away silently for so long. But then she replied in a low voice, "Had. Once."

"Not have anymore?"

"No."

Xani snorted. "Then how this better, enjoy? Madinah always have each other. Not lose enjoy. Your emotions inferior."

The human looked at her, eyes narrowed. "You may be right. Humans value things that hurt us in the end. It would probably be better if we didn't."

"Your species illogical," Xani agreed. "Worst of the Lowers. Except Kep-Kep. Weak, floating things. Kep-Kep useless."

Her captor tossed her head back and made a loud threatening noise. Xani clenched her hands. The human saw and bared her teeth. "Sorry. You've probably never heard a laugh. Just means you've amused me."

"Amuse." Xani understood. "This human response."

"Yes, usually to something funny, like a joke."

"I not joke."

"No. But you were funny."

The conversation was losing its usefulness. The human was too comfortable, and Xani knew no more than when she'd started. She needed more information.

"Where we go?"

The human stopped baring her teeth. "Doesn't matter. You're not getting out of there until I let you out."

"Why capture me? What want?"

She moved forward and lowered the energy shield. "It wouldn't be any fun if I just told you."

Xani whistled and bared her teeth as the human pulled something from her clothing and approached her berth.

"Tosh said this won't hurt."

She stabbed Xani in the arm with a cylinder. Xani felt the tool screwing down into her upper arm, then withdrawing. When she looked, a circular scar was forming in her mottled skin.

"You take sample."

The human nodded. "See? I knew you could figure it out on your own."

"Why?"

The human turned away. "Because I need a sample." She was out the door with the energy shield back up in seconds, but then she stood there, staring at Xani.

"I'm Shalon, by the way."

One name. Like UnTosh. This human had probably been just as disgraced as she.

"I Xanitefih Gen 1485 of the 5th Branch."

Shalon whistled and Xani tensed at the warning. "You've been around a long time, Xani."

Xani bared her teeth. "Long enough to know Lowers have no honor. You fail. I kill you soon."

Her captor made a soft, tired sound. "I'd probably feel the same if I were in your position. But I promise you, Xani, I won't harm you."

"Why capture me?"

"This is the only way to make it work."

"What?"

This time the human only showed the edge of her teeth as she paused. "Everything."

And walked away without a backward glance.

UnTosh brought her food hours later. She lowered the shield and held out several compressed nutrition pellets with one hand while pointing the volt-gun at Xani.

"Free me so that I may eat," Xani said in slave-speak.

"You can eat without your hands. Open your jaws."

UnTosh's Rewriting had not made her a fool then. Xani allowed UnTosh to feed her the rations in silence, studying her up close.

"You stink of sickness," she said when the food was almost done. "Your Rewriting has failed. Return with me and preserve what little honor you have."

"My Rewriting has not failed," UnTosh replied, giving her the last pellet and retreating to the doorway. "It worked as designed."

"You make no sense. You are ill because you are Undone."

"I am ill because the Quango wishes it so."

"The Quango, may they walk among us forever, wishes only for the Madinah to remain strong and productive, or have you forgotten the Warrior's Code?"

"I remember. What has changed is my understanding."

"You have lost your logic?"

"No. I have gained knowledge."

"You talk in riddles, like the battle-weary."

UnTosh retreated behind the energy shield and activated it before lowering the volt-gun.

"You will soon gain the same knowledge, I think," she said. One eye swivelled in its socket to study her more closely. "Before, when you boarded and made your announcement, you paused."

She searched her memory, found the moment, but remained silent, unwilling to confirm anything she did not have to.

"Can you remember what made you pause? Were you...unbalanced within yourself?"

UnTosh was so close to describing her previous internal processes, Xani's primal threat response almost made her release a growl. Xani held still, aware she could have accidentally confirmed by her actions something she had decided to keep within herself. This...hesitation in herself was strange. She did not like it.

"I do not know what you mean," she lied.

UnTosh shouldered the volt and a rumbling purr reached Xani's ears. She had never heard the like from a Madinah before and found it uncomfortable. She tugged at her cuffs.

"Keep your counsel then," UnTosh said. "When you are ready to confront your questions, I will give you answers."

"No slave can give knowledge to a Warrior," she pointed out.

"That is what the Quango says," UnTosh agreed. "But the Quango lies."

"You blaspheme," she said. "Another Great Forbidden."

"Yes. I am fond of them. Every Forbidden is a lie that points to a truth."

"Your mind is Undone."

"Thank fuck for that," she said in a harsher tone than Xani had ever heard from her before.

She felt the beginnings of the effects of the food then and bared her teeth. "Drugs, UnTosh? It is beneath you."

"Nothing is beneath a slave," UnTosh replied, "if you believe the Quango."

In her dreaming, UnTosh stood over her with a tall human covered in a long, multicoloured garment.

"You see?" UnTosh asked.

This human had skin a different color from the female, and large eyes that sparkled all the colors of space. Its aura would have been blinding if she had been awake. It streamed from it in banners of undulating shades.

"Yes," the human said in a high, thoughtful voice.

"She's a Breeder now. Will it still work?"

The human bent closer and laid a slim hand on her; the quiet that enveloped Xani's mind felt as good as bloodkin bond time, when they sat together and licked each other's wounds to healing after fight practice.

"How much time before we arrive?"

"Five, six cycles maybe," came the female human's voice from somewhere.

<<*Xanitefih Gen 1485 of the 5th Branch, we are Garner. We mean you no harm. Do not be discomforted.*>>

"I can hold back the change or accelerate it. Your choice," the new human said.

"If we accelerate, we'll have to change the plan," the female replied.

"More dangerous," UnTosh said.

"More risk, more reward. We can do this if everyone agrees. We have the numbers."

"How will she take it, Tosh?" the human called Garner asked.

"Hard to tell. She not same."

Garner glanced at UnTosh, the straight strands of the dark stuff on their head brushing their cheeks. "She has to agree then. I won't force this on her."

UnTosh folded her arms. "Ask."

The female made a sound. "It's for her own damn good."

"We don't decide that, Shalon," Garner said with a strange edge to their voice—a voice that was smaller out loud. In her head, it was multitudinous, vibrating with essence and power.

<<May we call you Xani?>>

Yes.

<<Your body has been manipulated without your understanding. We can alter this, but you will never be what you are now again, and we will not be able to change that. We regret that we cannot be more specific, but we will explain further. After.>>

After what? But they did not respond. Instead, their certainty filled her. They thought what had been done to her was a great wrong that should be reversed. Xani sat with the quiet of that consideration.

The offspring?

<<They will not be harmed. But you may lose everything that matters to you once they are born.>>

What you speak of…it is a threat to them?

Garner paused before saying, <<We believe so, yes. It has already hurt you.>>

She did not feel hurt, but she did not doubt that Garner believed they spoke the truth. She somehow knew they could not exchange lies mind to mind.

It was odd that this human had the voice of many. She had never known such a thing. But no Madinah would waste time and effort to gather inferior knowledge from the minds of Lowers. For now, she was sure the multitudes within Garner were united in their desire to help. To save her.

If I don't agree?

<<*You will lose yourself, but you will not understand that, or remember this conversation. You will be as you are now for a time, and then you will know the truths that have been kept from you.*>>

Xani sensed what they would not say. There would be no sureties. But she had never feared the unknown. The choice was clear. She could remain without knowledge, her spawn safe. Or she could know what threatened her and by extension, them, and be changed forever.

<<*Make your choice, Xanitefih Gen 1485 of the 5th Branch, and we will honor it.*>>

When she came awake again, she knew immediately a great deal of time had passed. Her body ached the way it had after her Rewriting, when she spent so many cycles in stasis her muscles protested any movement.

They protested now as she rose from her bunk and swung her limbs down onto the metal floor. She spared a glance around her rest-nook, noting nothing had been moved and that the door remained shut. She strode to it, and it slid open automatically.

This time, when the disorientation came over her, it was stronger than before. She held onto the doorway, feeling her hearts beating fast and in sync in a way that made her take harsh breaths. It was as though she was on a battlefield, ready to lead an attack. But there was no attack, no war. Why this feeling of having been caught without proper preparation? Of reluctance to move and a sense of danger?

She had no choice though. The fools had made a mistake. They had left her unguarded. She had to use it to her advantage.

Whatever they planned to do, she would stop them, capture UnTosh, and return her to the nearest Quango Representative.

Her ship was small, intended to carry a maximum crew of two, so her rest nook was located directly below the cockpit and alongside the chair room. She walked the corridor and climbed up into darkness. The ship's controls and viewscreen were off. She barked commands, and they shimmered into being, the viewscreen flickering on.

It was then she realized why everything was so silent. Why she had heard and felt no vibrations since she'd awakened.

Her ship was docked. Before her was the multicoloured dance of space and its cosmic currents, while alongside her the immense hull of a Madinah Juggernaut stretched above her ship and away into the distance.

UnTosh had flown herself back to her own Recycling.

To her own inevitable death, and the use of her sterilized organic material in new experiments and the creation of slaves.

It defied understanding. *Why now, after so long?*

"Juggernaut, identify," she said.

The controls remained silent.

"Juggernaut, this is Xanitefih Gen 1485 of the 5th Branch. Identify."

It took a few more seconds for her to realise that UnTosh must have locked communications. She swung around, checking for her volt. It was gone, and she had no other weapons.

Not that it mattered. She knew what must be done.

Minutes later, she'd passed through her ship's airlock and dropped down into the noise and frigid air of a busy ship bay.

Her boots adjusted their magnetic pull as she stomped across the deck to the nearest Warrior, a growl in the back of her throat. "Warrior, I am Xanitefih Gen 1485 of the 5th Branch. Identify."

The Warrior regarded her out of the nearest eye as she finished giving orders to the small slave in front of her. Then she gave Xani her full attention, cataloging her scent and aura.

"Wahmenca Gen 167 of the 2nd Branch," she replied, thrusting her ridged chest forward.

"Identify Juggernaut?"

Wahmenca paused, looking her over. "You should know. Were you resting when your bloodkin docked with us?"

"I was confined. My bloodkin is treacherous and consorts with a dangerous human. The Quango—may they walk among us forever—has decreed her Recycling. You have seen them?"

"Not an hour ago. The Warrior claimed she had captured a valuable human and was escorting it for interrogation by the Quango."

"Lies," Xani hissed. "We must find them both swiftly."

"I do not doubt your words, Warrior, but the human is indeed valuable. It is a Conway."

The Conways were the richest humans in the known galaxies. They were also the only humans who had a more than rudimentary knowledge of genetic manipulation, compared to the Madinah. They had come by this through much experimentation, especially within their own bloodlines. It had made them formidable, well-connected, and powerful politically. In a universe where the Dak, Madinah, and Roulon held sway, humans were mostly inconsequential, limited to a few dozen planets and a genetic program only for those who controlled the species' resources. At the top of their society were the Conways, handpicked by the Daks and Roulon to join their galactic DiploCore.

If Shalon was a Conway, that meant a Conway had schemed with UnTosh to come back to this ship. *Why would a Conway do any of this?* They concerned themselves only with their holdings and grasping after power. The Madinah were careful never to antagonize Terra's leading family, even if they did raid independent colonies. Humans were the Dak's pet species. Useless, with few resources worth taking, but cherished for their genetic curiosities by the deeply religious Daks. The Daks led the DiploCore, and the DiploCore was large enough to intervene in Madinah conquests if provoked. Neither side was willing to start a war that devastating.

Whatever UnTosh and Shalon were doing, it would mean nothing good for the Madinah.

These unpleasant thoughts consumed Xani's mind and caused her hearts to pound in sync. She staggered, shaking her head against another sudden rush of her body's physical responses as Wahmenca watched intently. "Have you been Assessed, Warrior? Your aura is unnatural."

"It is the Rewriting, nothing more," Xani said in a tone more aggressive than she intended. "Where did they go? Who accompanied them?"

"To Captive Assessment. They took no one as the Warrior claimed to know the Juggernaut well and needed no guidance. She barracked here with you during training."

They were on the *Empyrean* then. Not only had they barracked here, they had deployed into their first engagements from this same ship. The crew would be different after all this time, but its layout would be the same.

"Tell Retrieval to meet me at Captive Assessment. Request that a Quango Representative and the Pilot of this vessel prepare an Interrogation. UnTosh has committed many infractions and must confess fully before she is Recycled. The Quango Representative will decide how best to deal with the matter of the human."

Ignoring the peculiar riot of sensations pulling at her focus, Xani set off across the bay and deeper into the ship, pausing only once to identify herself and commandeer a volt from a weapons rack in the Dispensary.

The familiar weight of it steadied her as she searched the corridors, ignoring the stares, growls, and grunts of Warriors, assessors, technicians, and slaves alike.

It was not until she arrived at her destination that she realized her error. Captive Assessment was deserted except for two slaves that approached her and offered their necks, as customary. She watched as they scurried backward on all fours suddenly, never looking up. It was then she realized a growl was emanating from her, and that her core temperature was rising.

She tamped down on this excessive display as she regrouped. Of course, they had given a false destination. But where would they go instead? What did the human and UnTosh want?

"You take sample."

"See? I knew you could figure it out on your own."

"Why?"

"Because I need a sample."

She set off down the corridors, back the way she had come, shouting at everyone to get out of her way until she was in the nearly empty metal tubes that led to Flight Control. One of the few places on the ship off limits to anyone ranked lower than a Generational Warrior.

She arrived too late.

She strode past the prone bodies of several fallen Warriors, volt-gun ready in hands that were unusually damp with secretions. The three airlocks the Warriors guarded were open, and the priority alerts the crew could activate in case of trouble had been disabled.

The last airlock slid back to reveal a small room, containing a single berth-tube. This was no simple rest-nook. It was one of several dozen chambers—inaccessible without an authorized DNA sequence from a senior Gen and Branch like hers—that made up the core of Flight Control.

The Pilots.

A rare and important breed, Pilots spent most of their lives asleep while multiple brains directed the synaptic programs that ran every ship and Juggernaut in the Madinah Fleet. They were small, stunted things physically, but spending a generation as a Pilot guaranteed the clone a Branch of their own, as it was difficult to carry out the organic adaptations that made Piloting possible. They were one of the few Tiers higher than Warrior, but would spend most of their lives, when not awake, alone with their machines and their dreams.

This Pilot was not alone.

The human female called Shalon stood to the left of the berth-tube, one hand on the small, rounded head of the Madinah inside. She glanced up as Xani entered, and her teeth appeared between her lips. The Pilot was merged with its berth, of course, limbs atrophied, completely unable to defend itself. Still, it growled continuously in its ridged chest.

"Shhh," Shalon said to it in a distracted tone. "Let him in."

Xani wondered who she spoke to.

The Pilot stopped growling, stopped wriggling, and after a slow blink, relaxed into sleep.

<<That would be me.>>

The voice was layered, as though many spoke at once, but most disturbingly, even though it was in her head, it was not her voice.

At the foot of the berth, directly across from Xani, there was a familiar whine as UnTosh ticked the volt-gun over to triple-shot setting. That made the target area large enough to encompass all of Xani's hearts.

"Put it down," UnTosh said.

Xani grunted. "You know I cannot."

"You already made the choice, Xani," the human, Shalon, said. "I hoped you would remember by now."

"You speak nonsense," Xani shot back. "I not make choice. I not forget. *Ever.*"

"Oh, Xani," Shalon said, "I have the same kind of memory. Trust me. Sometimes, when things are really bad, we might choose to forget."

"Why do that?" Xani replied, her skin hot and mind jumbled. "It stupid choice."

"Not when it's between that and realizing we've lost everything we believed in. We all need time to accept the consequences of our decisions."

Something soft and warm touched the back of Xani's neck, sank into the muscles there, weakened her hands so that the volt-gun fell from her fingers, and she went to her knees.

A figure swathed in the most brilliant aura she'd ever seen came around to stand in front of her, grasped her hands.

<<Make your choice, Xanitefih Gen 1485 of the 5th Branch, and we will honor it.>>

I choose truth. I choose change.

Pain twisted through her. Squeezed her muscles. Sped her hearts and brought secretions to her eyes. Images filled her brain and chaotic thoughts made her pant and growl.

When she could see something other than the haze of red in her mind, her gaze settled on the large, grey Madinah fingers wrapped around her hand.

She was lying on the floor with UnTosh bent over her.

<<You think you are a Warrior, Xani, but you are a slave. All Madinah are slaves to the Quango.>>

The words came back to her with startling clarity. Spoken in a multitude of soft voices, they sank beneath her flesh like blades, painful and destructive.

"She's back," UnTosh said.

"Do you have what you need, Garner?"

One of the soft voices she'd heard in her head before said, "Yes. Sending to Calen now."

"Is she ready, do you think?"

"The Change took. It's up to her now."

A moment later and Shalon and UnTosh were helping her sit up.

"What do you remember?" Shalon asked.

Xani stared at the form standing alongside the berth, closing the protective cover carefully. She'd adjusted her photoreceptors, cycling through until the figure became a long shape covered in a dark coat, the hair on its head falling straight past its shoulders. Pale green fingers caressed the berth-tube before

<<he's Garner>>

it came to stand closer.

"Garner," Xani said without intending to.

The strange human bowed his head. "We meet again, Xani."

A growl rumbled in her chest. How had she missed his presence? How had they flanked her in such a small space?

"Your people won't see him unless he wants them to," Shalon said with a glimmer of teeth.

"How know what think?"

More teeth. "Maybe your face gave it away."

There was no logic to her words. Xani realized the human must be amusing herself again. She turned her attention to the real threat in the room. "You do this."

He cocked his head. "With your consent."

"Do you know?" UnTosh asked, and for the first time, Xani heard and understood the strange tone in her voice. Understood it meant she was waiting for something.

"We are slaves," she said, tilting her head to capture UnTosh's gaze better. UnTosh's fingers gripped hers harder.

"Yes."

She remembered. Tosh's voice. Tosh's thoughts. "When we Rewrite, the process sometimes destroys a hormone-producing gland implanted in us to keep us docile. Manageable."

"Or, we become aware of the glands," Tosh replied. "Learn to control them."

"When that happens," Shalon said. "They send you for Recycling."

As they had tried to do to Tosh.

Tosh ran. Fled the blessed edict of the Quango. A great wrong.

Or so she told herself. For the first time in her life, her words rang hollow.

Xani took her hand back and stood. They all rose with her, Tosh still holding the volt-gun, but not pointing it at her.

The gesture affected her strangely, made her hearts tight in her chest.

"I have…lost control," she told Tosh.

Tosh grunted. "You will learn control again. It is not as easy as before. But humans manage it, despite their flaws."

Xani thrust out her ridged chest and flexed her fingers. "You have made me human?"

"You are what we were before the Quango subjugated us."

"Weaker," Xani snorted, even though her mind was not clear on this—rebelled against her words in a splintered way that made her deeply uncomfortable.

Tosh made a sound she did not understand. "Free."

For the first time, Xani noted a tension that lay against her skin like a physical thing. It bound her attention to those around her, linking them all in watchfulness.

She gestured to Garner and spoke in Universal. "How you hurt me?"

"I didn't hurt you," Garner replied, folding his arms across his chest. "I allowed you to rest for a short while."

"Not want rest."

"And we didn't wish to hurt you. Seemed the best option at the time."

"Hurt Pilot," Xani pointed out.

"We simply spoke to them. We're friends…of a fashion. They did not consent to remember when this is over."

"How do that? How make Pilot, Xani, rest?"

"Garner isn't human," Shalon said. "He can fully control his body and initiate genetic change, as the Madinah do, but much more swiftly. When he meets those who are evolved enough, whose genetic material he can manipulate, he can control them too." The human bared her teeth again. "You've probably been feeling like shit because he made your immune system attack the gland the Quango use to control you. We tried to let you sleep off the worst of the effects, but we were on a deadline."

Xani knew this was the truth. Memories flooded her mind, overwhelmed her senses, brought her chest ridges upright.

"Why do this?" she asked.

Shalon looked at Garner, but Garner stared at Tosh. Xani eyed her volt-gun on the floor behind Tosh.

"Know why," Tosh grunted.

"You lie," Xani growled.

"*You know why,*" Tosh insisted in Warrior-speak, taking a step forward.

<<*Remember, Xani. Remember what Tosh told you,*>> the soothing voices whispered.

We are bloodkin.

"You came back for me?" Xani clenched and unclenched her fists, her mind a swirl of understandings and thoughts that made her body react in new, terribly unfamiliar ways. Ways that made her want to climb out of her own skin with the horror of how little control she had over her own body.

"Finally," Shalon said quietly.

"I found freedom. It is *good*, Xani. I wanted you to have it," Tosh told her, grinding her jaws, fingers flexing and unflexing on the lowered volt-gun. "I wanted all my bloodkin to have it too."

Xani stepped backward as her body struggled to breathe in the heated, watchful closeness of the room.

"UnTosh sick. Unnatural."

"I am *Tosh*," she roared, holding her arms out and thrusting out her chest. "Not UnTosh. Tosh. And I am not the unnatural one here."

Xani roared in reply, reveling in the familiarity of the aggression sweeping over her; relieved to still be herself, no matter what they said.

Garner made a soft sound and shook his head. "I told you. It's too soon, Tosh. She needs time."

A short tone sounded, warning that the ship's address system had been activated. Then a voice filled the chamber with the simplified speech of Universal. "Conway human," it said, "you will not leave this ship alive. If you release the Pilot, we will consider making your Interrogation less painful."

Shalon glanced at Garner before strolling across to stand by the volt-gun Xani had dropped. "Do you swear by the Quango?" she asked loudly.

The voice—it had to be a Quango Representative—did not answer.

"So, you aren't allowed to blaspheme. Good to know."

"Stop this," Xani said in Warrior-speak, "You have all earned your deaths many times over. The Madinah do not suffer attacks."

Shalon raised her chin and made a rough sound in her throat. "Tell me, Xani, because I'm sure whoever that is won't tell me the truth. Have the Madinah *ever* had someone make it all the way into Flight Control?"

"No. But you will be the last. We will not let you succeed."

There was a subtle shift in Shalon's face. Xani saw a glimmer of teeth as she picked up the volt-gun.

"Ah, but we've already succeeded."

"You are the one lying now," the Representative said in a booming, calm monotone. "Interrogation will reveal the truth of your failure, and your reasons for this unprovoked attack."

"Unprovoked?" Tosh almost spat her words out. "We Madinah have provoked every lifeform on every world we have ever discovered."

"Including lifeforms I happen to care about," Shalon said, her tone underlaid with some subtle meaning Xani had no interest in grasping.

"We have made no war on Conways," the Representative replied.

"You have made war on humans across this Sector. Across this galaxy. And right now, you threaten two colonies in the White Sector where my people provide security."

Xani kept an alert eye on her as Shalon's fingers tightened on the volt-gun.

"We have attacked no Conway colonies."

"I'm not talking about the Conways," Shalon replied, and it was impossible to miss the disgust in her tone as she emphasized the last word.

"They're here," Garner interrupted in a low voice.

"About time," Shalon replied.

"Enough of this," Tosh snapped.

Shalon tilted her head back for a moment, took a deep breath, then let her gaze capture Xani's. "You're right, Tosh," she said.

And tossed the volt-gun to Xani.

Xani caught it one-handed and turned it on Tosh immediately.

"If you harm any of us in any way, I promise you, this ship will be a dead hulk in a matter of minutes," Shalon warned, and Xani saw the impossible truth of her words in the tense lines of her face.

Still, she had no choice but to follow her

(programming)

training.

"There are three, Evolved One," Xani said in Warrior-speak. "I await your orders."

The lights went out. A moment later, the lowering hum of the engines slowed to a halt. Xani adjusted her photoreceptors until the room returned to colorless, but sharp relief.

None of them had moved a muscle.

"What have you done?" Xani growled.

"Me?" Shalon tapped her chest. "Nothing. Your Pilot, on the other hand…"

A rhythmic thudding echoed through the ship, growing progressively louder. Xani recognized it from countless drills.

The airlocks were being sealed.

The Pilot is under their control.

She swung the gun toward the Pilot's chamber, but the lights flared on again, blinding her for a moment. When her sight adjusted, Garner was standing in her way.

<<*There's no point to that, Xani. We don't control just one Pilot.*>>

She tried to shoot Garner, but her finger would not move.

Tosh stalked over to her, aggression in every line of her body. "Do you not understand? You cannot hurt him. You would only hurt yourself."

<<*We can help you understand. Help you find your way in this new body. We can be of one mind, if you choose it.*>>

"I do not," she said, shame and confusion at her inability to do what needed to be done flooding her body with the overwhelming urge to kill. "I do not choose it."

Garner sighed, then he shifted his gaze to Shalon. "Calen is in place."

"Quango Representative," Shalon said immediately, "if you check with Control, you'll find several ships in your vicinity. Your Pilots have taken your weapons and defense systems offline, and they will remain that way until we are clear of this ship. If you harm any of us, in any way, my ships will fire on this Juggernaut for as long as it takes to reduce it to a cloud of wreckage. We would rather not do this, but do not doubt our resolve."

"If that is so, why attack and threaten us?" the Representative demanded, and Xani was troubled by the unusual timbres of inflection in his tone. Inflections that reminded her of those in Shalon's voice.

Not possible. Madinah have no emotions.

But her thoughts felt like lies, and she struggled to understand why.

"To get your attention," Shalon said, her eyes on Xani.

Xani growled deep in her chest, putting aside the useless, disturbing chaos of her mind, and holding to the imperative of her training instead. "Give me an order, Evolved One," she said.

"Think!" Tosh said to her in Warrior-speak. "Think on what you know now, Xani. How can you do this?"

"This is my purpose, my duty. To protect my people."

"And don't they have a duty to you?"

"The Quango—"

"Hold, Warrior," came the Representative's voice. "You have our attention, Conway human."

Shalon took a step forward, her eyes on Xani. "The Madinah have been invited to a DiploCore Parley."

"The Madinah have declined the Parley."

"You will accept it."

An abrupt silence fell.

"The Representatives follow the orders of the Quango. It is the Quango who have declined. We have no power to change that."

"The Quango are seated in several hidden locations, far from your homeworld, isn't that correct?"

"Yes."

"A location known only to those Juggernauts who ferry Representatives throughout the fleet."

"Yes."

"And who flies your Juggernauts, Representatives? Who holds that map in their heads?"

Xani swore, sickness rising in her throat as she realized what the human had done. What she had succeeded at doing when whole armies before her had failed. She knew what came next. She tensed, ready to fire on the human, as the Representative started to give the instruction.

"Warrior—"

"Killing me—us—will not save you. This information is with my people, Representative. They are not only ready to destroy you on the spot, but they have dispatched ships to several of those locations. They have orders to wait there and hold the Quango until the DiploCore Battle-enders arrive. Your ships will not be able to identify which locations in time to beat ours—or the DiploCore ships—to them."

"Who are you to demand this of us?" The Representative's voice had lost all its calm. Rage dripped from his words like warm blood.

The human's voice was hard as metal, cold as space when she replied. "I am Shalon Conway, daughter of Jason and Falon Conway, rightful heir to Conway Enterprises. I am also Shalon of Orgala, daughter of Ha-ka and Ku, former Vi-Commander of the Orgalian armed forces, and you have been killing my people as they sought to protect their clients across several sectors, for many years."

The mercenaries the Madinah could not eradicate. The same ones that were far more difficult to kill than most species, than other humans. They were Shalon's people, Xani realized with dawning dread.

Shalon nodded as if she'd heard her thoughts.

"The Orgalians are *my* bloodkin," she said softly. "But Orgalians, unlike the Madinah and the Conways, take care of each other. Always."

"Your people took up arms against us. We defended ourselves," the Representative said, still enraged.

"The colonists you attacked did not take up arms against you, yet you killed them long before they paid Orgalians to protect them. You ravage the galaxies, uncaring of the destruction you leave in your wake. The DiploCore wishes to bring an end to this. This Parley will be the first step. You *will* take it."

"Why should we do this? We shall simply replace the Quango, and adapt. We are good at adapting."

"Oh, we know. But that will take time. And in that time, the DiploCore and every ally it has will make sure that all Madinah know *exactly* how the Quango controls its people. That would be a tremendous boon to the Rewritten, wouldn't it? And that's what you've been trying to avoid for over a century now. The Rewritten making the Madinah aware of the freedoms you've denied your people in the name of conquest and order."

This time the silence was so long, Xani wondered if the Representative had left the room. When the voice came again, it had changed. No rage, only calm insistence. "Interference in the internal affairs of other civilizations is not the DiploCore way."

Shalon's lips twisted. "It's *my* way. And I have no qualms about using everything we've learned from your Pilots to bring your civilization to its knees."

The Representative hissed. "Why do you do this now?"

"The Conways have reached out to you."

Silence.

"Don't bother denying it. I'm familiar with their plans to use you against their enemies. To share certain facets of your knowledge of eugenics and tactics. You will instead refuse their advances. And believe me, you will come out the better for it when I take my place at the head of Conway Enterprises."

"Gilene Conway heads Conway Enterprises."

"For now," was all Shalon said.

The Representative made a long growl, deep in its throat. "You ask too much."

"I'm not finished. You will cease all attacks against colonies guarded by Orgalians. And you will not harm the Pilots or Xani."

"What," the Representative, said in a soft, dangerous tone, "does the Warrior have to do with you?"

"Absolutely nothing. She was a means to an end. This end," Shalon said, looking directly at Xani as she drummed her fingers on the Pilot's tube.

"She failed in her duties." The scorn in the words burned into Xani's brain, igniting a swirl of bodily reactions that made her breathe deep against nausea.

They will kill me. After interrogating me. They will kill me and that will be the end of my Branch.

In that moment, she felt more than just distress for the fate of her lineage. She was overcome with a need to save, to protect. Not the Madinah, or their ways. Not even the Quango or her lineage. But herself. Herself and the offspring she carried. It was only a spark of a thought at first. But as she listened to the rest of the conversation, it grew into a conflagration of ideas that burned too bright to ignore.

"So did everyone on this ship, as far as the Quango are concerned. You have bigger problems. I'm just telling you to focus on that. If I hear of any harm coming to her—or to any Orgalian because of the Madinah—if you refuse the Parley, every species you have ever made war against will know where to find your leaders, and your people will know how you use them, just as you need them to fight for their lives."

Xani counted many beats of her hearts before the Representative said, "We will take your demands to the Quango."

Shalon clapped her hands together. "Good. We understand each other. Now excuse me, I have a ride to catch."

"You will wait until the Quango has approved—"

"The fuck I will," Shalon said with a glance at Garner. He nodded as if answering a question. Shalon looked at Xani and waved a hand at her volt-gun.

"You realize there's no point to that now?"

Xani lowered the gun, her mind racing, her hearts pounding as never before.

"Why do this? I not choose you."

Shalon's shoulders moved, up then down. "I didn't think you would," she said, and there was a hardness to her speech that had not been there before. "But Tosh believes in you, so I'll give you one more chance. If you change your mind, call for Garner. He'll be listening."

"I don't understand."

"You will. It's early days yet."

Xani heard more thudding; the faint groans and hums of machinery and systems coming back online.

"The Pilots have cleared a path to the bay," Garner said in a soft voice.

"Our ship is docking, Representative, and we will be leaving with it," Shalon said. "I'd warn your people, so they don't get hurt trying to stop us."

Xani stood back, feeling helpless and adrift for the first time in her life as first Garner, then Shalon, walked out the door. But Tosh slowed as she approached.

"You have destroyed everything," Xani said to her, chest heaving. "I will never have my own Branch now."

"You can still have that, and more," Tosh replied, her disappointment clear. "But that depends on you."

"How?"

"Think, Xani," Tosh said in a fierce voice. "Think of what it means to be bloodkin. What it means to be Warrior. Think on what you have learned. When you are ready, *if* you are ready, I will be waiting."

Xani did as Tosh said. She thought, long and hard. It was no easy road for her. Warriors followed orders. It was the Quango, Representatives, and Strategists who analyzed information and produced strategy. But things had changed, and she realized she was changing with it. She did not even remember when Tosh ceased to be UnTosh to her.

She did not say any of this in Assessment though. Filled with disquiet and constant shifts in her internal reactions, she kept her thoughts to herself in Debriefing. She recounted faithfully all that had happened, again and again, to the Quango Representative, the Strategists, and finally, even the Quango itself, via Communications.

She left out Garner and what he had done to her, but the post-battle Assessment found abnormalities with her physiology and spawning and assigned her for regular screening anyway. She was taken off active duty and Recycling and placed on shipwide duty.

Once that happened, she knew. There truly was no going back.

Not for her, and not for the spawning they would probably terminate.

She dreamed then. Dreamed of Tosh, and Garner, and even the annoying woman, Shalon. She saw them together on the ship she'd first found them in, and she knew what they were doing. This was laughter, she realized. This was what happened when there was no war. When bloodkin came together.

When Garner stopped laughing and turned toward her, she felt his unspoken question in her bones, and she knew what she would do.

What bloodkin always did.

Protect.

She waited until it was confirmed that the *Empyrean* would be joining the DiploCore Parley and passing through solar systems friendly to the DiploCore.

Waited until her ship duties took her near the bay and she could mingle with the flow of warriors, slaves, mechanics, and hunters.

In the chaos of numerous transfers of personnel between the three ships selected to join the Parley, she slipped onto a transport, then took a dropship to a nearby transhipment Hub where she searched until she found a ship willing to give her passage.

She had no money, but no one asked questions of Madinah warriors, she'd realized in her years hunting Lowers. Even fewer asked for payment if she offered her services as protection, or enforcer.

She knew where she was headed, but she was stubborn and vacillated between anger, sorrow, and resignation over her lost life and new disgrace as someone who had surely been sentenced to Recycling in her absence.

It was difficult for her to grasp how drastically things would have to change.

For the first time, she experienced reactions that made decisions complicated. In her dreams, Garner called it fear and anxiety and told her she was not alone in feeling it. That many species experienced these things.

She wondered that they did not all commit themselves for Recycling rather than endure it.

Months passed before she realized the Quango had taken Shalon at her word. That no Warrior was hunting her. That they had probably been relieved she had chosen her own exile and they didn't need to risk having an Undone warrior within the Madinah, just to avoid the consequences Shalon had promised if they harmed her.

When she accepted this, she found a ride back to the only place in the galaxy that the Madinah held no sway.

Pirates Rock was owned by the seldom seen, and universally feared, Sudamin Gae. An abandoned mining facility within a moon that had been converted into a thriving black market, all were welcome, but no unsanctioned violence or law enforcement was allowed.

After many dreamings, she knew this was where she would begin her new life.

When she arrived at the massive spaceport, she was near her time, her glands heavy with milk, and her body slower and clumsier than ever. But she followed her dream markers unerringly to the worn, but lovingly maintained ship parked between a cruiser and a dropship.

They were waiting for her on the bridge, as they had before.

This time, Tosh and Garner stood on either side of the chair Shalon sat in. Shalon had one foot drawn up, her hand resting atop it, her teeth bared in what was called a smile. Xani had learned this word in her months dreaming among the Lowers, as she had learned many other things.

This was a sign of welcome, she told herself, not aggression. But the spawn within her stirred and her hearts beat like the thump of engines.

"Xanitefih Gen 1485 of the 5th Branch. Fancy meeting you here," Shalon said.

"I am just Xani now," she replied, in Warrior-speak.

Garner came toward her. "We know." He stopped in front of her. "We are so sorry. We—all of us—know what it is to lose people. To lose an entire way of life."

How did they survive it, she wondered, overwhelmed with unwanted emotions that battered her like blasts from a volt-gun?

Tosh was at her side. She reached out a hand and placed it gently against Xani's back, where her spawn slumbered under the plush thickness of lifegiving fats and fluids and metal-tough skin.

"We belong to each other now, instead of the Quango. We take care of each other. That is how we bloodkin survive."

Xani gave a weak snort, despite the soothing feeling Tosh's words brought to her. "Bloodkin protect the Madinah and the Quango."

Shalon stood and stepped toward her, some indefinable emotion etched on her face. "In my world, the word closest to bloodkin is friend. And friends protect everyone they love. Especially each other."

It dawned on her then, what had truly happened. Why she had been able to easily track down Tosh after she had remained so well hidden for years.

"This was not about the Parley. You let me find you," she said, surprise unfurling within her.

"Oh, it was about the Parley, and the Orgalians, and everything else I said," Shalon said. "That was the part where I took care of my friends."

"But you came for *me*. To take me away from the Quango."

Garner nodded and closed a soft hand over her arm. "It was a rescue mission. And we thought we'd failed. We're glad we didn't, Xani."

"Why?" She had to know, had to understand. "Why help me?"

Garner's hand squeezed her arm comfortingly before he released her. "I have had no choices in my life, and Shalon has had so few. We often walk the paths that were chosen for us by others. But I have never been lied to. I know the why of my existence. I consented to it long ago. Now, I choose to help Shalon dismantle lies and expose truth. Because others deserve that. They deserve to at least know the truth of their existence when they choose their lives and their fates."

"But you could not be sure I would agree." She looked at Tosh. "You did not force me, so I could have betrayed you. Why take the chance?"

"Because," Tosh rumbled, "you fought with me, and saved my life every day, and sat with me, and picked the parasites from my hide, and licked my wounds to heal them. After my Rewriting...I could not forget. I did not want to."

"We don't abandon our friends," Shalon said, her voice gentle. "You're Tosh's friend. That makes you ours as well."

Xani realized, looking at all of them, that all their auras held elements of Garner's, brilliant and multicolored and ever shifting. She knew, with a comforting certainty, that she would soon share that same bond.

Still, wariness coursed through her. She could not be sure they would truly accept her, and she would need to spawn soon.

Shalon laughed then, tossing her head back as the sound bounced in the small space. "Xani, we can all hear your thoughts, you know."

Xani's skin flushed with heat as a slow smile spread over Garner's face and his hypnotic, splendid eyes swirled with color and life. "Tosh has been in contact with others meant for Recycling for some time. We can take you to an enclave where a spawning partner will help with what is to come."

"You planned this? For me."

Tosh growled. "Bloodkin," she said. "Friend."

And at last, Xani understood.

They had chosen her.

Now, she had to choose them.

Her hearts beat hard, but for the first time, she was calm. Certain.

"I choose you," she said. "I choose you all."

Tosh's hand clutched her back in silent agreement.

Garner let out a breath. "Finally."

"Good," Shalon said with a huge smile. "Because I want to be able to say I'm godmother to a litter of Madinah someday."

"Godmother?"

"A joke."

Xani rumbled her annoyance, but as Tosh took her hand to lead her deeper into the ship, she found herself baring her teeth in a completely new way.

— SALVAGE BLOSSOM —
By L.X. Beckett

Hard to believe the name describes a flower, mm?" Guss was three days into a fever that caught him just after they entered the Scatter, and his labored observation, as they approached the legendary ship, *Corymb*, passed for an attempt at banter. He was probably afraid Grandmother would refuse to pay him when it turned out he'd got sick on the voyage. Though it could be a more humane impulse: keeping Savita from worrying.

She *was* worried. The ship's onboard nurse insisted Guss was fine, but his cough was worse, and there was a disturbing orange cast to the skin around his eyes. At one point when his temperature peaked, Savita redirected the ship's coolant outflow to blow chiller through the skipper's cabin until the mirror frosted.

But she had little experience with sick people. The robot nurse, presumably, knew better.

Guss wasn't wrong about *Corymb*. The ship, if ship it could be called, had as its original seed a massive, abandoned troop carrier. This had been pierced—rammed through—by the cylindrical engine of an asteroid driver, a gigantic propulsion shaft. Captured spaceships by the hundreds had been adhered to this structure over decades, radiating outward, petals to the driver's stem. The result had ceased to truly be salvage long ago. Now it was a ponderous conjoined vessel made of wrecks, incapable of faster than light travel, behemothing its way through the lawless region of space known as the Scatter.

"Puts me more in mind of barnacles than a flower," Savita replied. "Accumulating on an anchor."

"Unnaturally fractal either way," Guss coughed. "Gimme—a turn of the clock. To recover. Once I'm on my feet—"

"We'll go aboard," Savita finished for him, pulling up the covers.

Once he lost consciousness again, she accessed autopilot. "Can you bring me onto a transit route for a ferry to *Corymb*?"

"Passengers cannot authorize major course corrections," *Pinch* told her primly.

"How is that major? We're already in their wake. I just want to go aboard and source out more meds for your skipper. Maybe scout out the job we came here to do."

Pinch thought it over. "Correction approved."

Savita rummaged in ship's storage until she found handcuffs. The ship wouldn't unlock the weapons cabinet, so she gave up on taking a stunner.

A ferry cozied up to the personnel lock, and she hopped aboard, riding swiftly to the *Corymb* embarkation hangar.

Savita assumed that *Corymb's* interior would match its ungainly, mashed-up shell, forming a dark and seedy maze. Something from a sim drama, maybe: rusty decks and dim lighting. Shadowy corners filled with suspicious characters; the ship was, rather famously, without police or onboard security forces. But the settlement's corridors were bright and smooth as a kindergarten. The surfaces had been treated, floorplate to ceiling, with luminous enamel, alight with a pinkish glow branded Minarka Dawn, signifier of the approaching day shift. Wayfinding markers and codes for accessing local data were posted here and there, as ready to help passersby as they would be on any vessel or colony. As she accessed one to register her presence and request local mapping services, she caught a whiff of church spices, burning.

Funeral offerings. She pinged *Pinch* for Guss's vitals. Nurse assured her he was sleeping comfortably.

The corridor meandered in the direction of the ship's bow, breaking every thirty steps or so into open chambers. Less constructed habitat, she thought, more like a shopping mall if it had been constructed by termites. A few stores had proper hatches, signs of having been compartments, once, of viable ships. Most were simply abscesses, irregularly shaped gaps within *Corymb*'s structure. Savita had to squeeze past a line of workers waiting for meat skewers at the first of these, people with torches and plumbing equipment, chatting gaily as the vendor fried up fabricated proteins in a repurposed galley.

Fifty steps on, the sign for a hostel beckoned, advertising fifty bunks in racks scavenged from old military barracks.

The path curved sharply, breaking around a vertical shaft. The ladder within had advertisements on its rungs, hand-lettered signs declaring the presence, going upward, of a spacesuit repair shop. Savita peered down into the lower level and saw the steamy remains of a chemical refinery, tanks converted into something like a bathhouse.

Except for breakfast places, most businesses were off shift. Many stood wide open, wares exposed to pedestrian traffic, with simple "Closed" signs posted outside the entrances. But a smell of cooked sugar beckoned, blocking out the church and its cloying gasp of memorial spice. She took a few tentative steps in that direction and found a confectioner making caramel spheres.

"Sample, friend?" They speared a gooey globe with a probe, dipping it first in fizzing red hardshell and then in crystallized pink sugar.

Savita accepted, bowing deeply. Going by their features and accent, the vendor was from Hanjo, same as she. Enjoying the crackle of the still-warm shell between her lips, she looked over their stock. Most of this compartment was given over to the apparatus of candy-making. The storefront consisted of one display case jammed into the space where a hatch had once been.

The store offered bright bait for anyone with a sweet tooth: jellied simulated fruits, edible sapphire necklaces scented with blueberry and jasmine, customizable chewing gums and intricately sculpted marzipan flowers. A separately locked compartment contained sugared hallucinations—tiny moving flickers, like candle flames, meant to be huffed.

"Your craft is remarkable," she said, speaking formally but using the Seas' warmest vocal register while laying out a chameleon bill for the purchase of a sachet of candies.

"Thank you."

"I wonder if you can help me. My map hasn't loaded yet, and I'm looking for someone they call the Mouse King—"

"Ratter?"

A jolt—what would Grandmother think of *that* nickname? Savita shared a picture of her father, one actual photo and one approximation aged by algorithms.

"I know him well! One of my regulars."

"He likes candy?" She raked her memory. He did routinely bring sweets home. She remembered him offering one to her governess before allowing her to choose one for herself. *Thank your father, Savvy.*

Had she ever seen him eat any himself?

No, but maybe he'd grown into a sweet tooth. Weren't people allowed to change?

The vendor added another handful of candies to her order without upping the charge. Father must like sweets a *lot.* "You'll find Ratter in the Science block. Unless he's out trapping."

While the onboard map was updating, she checked into what passed for a proper hotel, accommodations scavenged from a decommissioned luxury cruiser. Their lobby ceiling had a simulated view of space outside *Corymb:* stars and nebulas and the bright pulse of the Phenom in high resolution. Savita could even make out the little fleck that was *Pinch,* faithfully tracking them on autopilot.

She pinged the ship. Nurse said Guss was fine.

Still… she called up the local business index, seeking a live medic. The system bounced her request without explanation or apology.

He's probably fine. She found a diagnostic tech in the business listings, sending a query about doing a remote evaluation on the onboard nurse.

"I'll need access to your ship's systems," he texted.

Savita looked over a *Closed—Please come again!* sign hanging on a boot maker's rack of tools, just beyond the hotel. Awls and hammers and clamps sitting within arm's reach, valuable items ripe for stealing. She would default, for once, to trust and plead with *Pinch* until it conceded to a diagnostic scan.

If Guss didn't improve, she would have to bring him aboard. It would take time: even a flying junkyard like *Corymb* would have quarantine protocols. It was a temptation, a viable excuse to put off the search for Father, a task coiled in her intestines, gnawing with equal parts acid-hot hope and cold, lumpish pessimism.

Vermin Studies lay at the end of a long passageway that corkscrewed into the depths of the original skewered warship at *Corymb*'s core. Here, where the drive shaft had pierced the warship, the bulkheads shone almost clear, making it possible to see the spliced-together hulls of the first captured ships. The metal in these grafted wrecks was cobwebbed in fine white and emerald threads. There were legends about the ship's makers taming a metallic parasite—or falling victim to it—as they created their composite home. She wondered if that was what had lured Father here.

There were other stories too, tales of piracy and theft, about metallic sticky traps, about passing vessels' autopilots being tricked into flying into *Corymb*'s parasitic embrace.

Savita had to go through secondary decontamination to get into the Science Block, including a twenty-minute wait on blood work—no pathogens, so whatever Guss had caught had fallen under the onslaught of her high-end immune system enhancements. Heading through the locks, she passed a couple medical labs, nanofabrication shops, an air quality sampler operation, data crunchers for the ship's various scanners, two hydroponic farms, and a big comms hub. Within a shabby compartment that looked like a repurposed missile launch tube, two doctor types were running scanner-encrusted volunteers on treadmills.

At last: Vermin Studies. A double-sealed screen door, flashing the word for *Pests* in the major languages of the three Rez Empires, along with images of insect infestations, carnivore fungi, rodents, drill birds, tiny dragons colloquially known as toe-snappers, and dreaded semi-telepathic salamanders that colonized the sinus tracts of unwary mammals. *Humane removal,* the sign said, flashing lurid colors. *We pay you if the species is new!*

Savita pushed open the door.

She was so braced to see her father that what she found within made no sense: three children, the youngest so small she was unsteady on her feet, playing amid a scattering of toys and cushions. The kids were enclosed by deck-to-ceiling wall racks filled with cages and aquaria, all teeming with invasive life forms.

The oldest child might be ten. He was leaning against a wall with a portable school in his hands, doing lessons and ignoring his siblings...

Our siblings, Savita thought. Sourness, bile mixed with caramel and cherry, rose in her throat.

The middle child had been hurling bouncy balls at a cage filled with darting, winged rodents. Catching two of the balls at once, they drew themselves up, then bowed.

"OooooohhhhhhhMMMMaaaaaaa," he shouted.

"I'm actually here for—"

The wall of reptile cages split, concealed door swinging open, and a woman appeared. She seemed barely older than Savita. Clad in a laboratory workall, devoid of jewelry, she had close-cropped black hair and a set of plain utility goggles over her eyes. "Ratter's not here—oh! Savvy, is that you?"

"I'm here to see Father." Formal tone now. She tried to project a sliver of Grandmother's fearsomeness despite an unwanted, almost shocking, uplift of the heart.

Her former governess bowed, declining to show even a hint of embarrassment. "Of course. Do you remember me? I'm Abelle."

Soft lap, gentle hands, a smell like sun-dried clothes...

The toddler was rating the distance to Savita's knees. Abelle put out a hand, holding her back. The other kids continued their ball playing and studying, uninterested in this visitor to their ratty dad's infested domain.

"Where is he?"

"Down a hatch in Waste and Recycle, chasing worms," Abelle said. "I'll ping to say you're here, but—"

"But he's working?" Some things never changed.

Abelle shrugged. "May I hope you're here to visit?"

There was no harm in telling her: "Grandmother wants Father to return to Hanjo."

A wince. "Why not just shoot him?"

"If he agrees to run the company for three years, he can do whatever he wants afterwards."

Abelle shook her head. "If he falls back into Zinzin's clutches, she'll lock him down forever."

That absolute truth wasn't Savita's problem. She pictured her father headfirst down a worm tunnel. The burn in her gut cooled.

Abelle picked up the toddler, giving her a bounce. "Any chance you could be persuaded to say you never found him?"

"I could've done that without bothering to come all this way."

"He's going to refuse."

"That'll just make it entertaining," Savita pulled a jewelry box from her carryall, setting it next to a dome-covered, dissected mouse on a lab counter. "Have him call me when he's washed off the sewage."

As she turned on her heel, Abelle threw out: "If you'd like to wait—"

The door snapped shut behind her.

She didn't want to have to clear science zone quarantine again, so instead she found a botany lab that doubled as a park, hydroponic orchard set up with paths and small picnic tables. There were a number of families out, and she sat at a table underneath some apricots, watching kids tumble under the trees. For a small fee, she was permitted to pick a half dozen of the fruit, which were individually wrapped in nanogossamer. Basking in mild artificial sunlight, she ate one. The sweetness of the fruit clashed with the residue of the candy she'd eaten earlier.

"Nurse, how is Guss?"

"Recovering well!"

"Really?"

It sent stats. His temp seemed high, the pulse too fast. Savita pinged the software consultant and got an immediate request for voice chat.

"Miss," he said. "I was just going to call. There's a problem, I am sorry to report, with the *Pinch* nurse."

"What problem?"

"Begging your pardon, its operating system...almost all of its primary purpose software has been wiped."

"The medical knowledge is gone?"

"I am very sorry, very—"

"Can you restore the system?"

"Apologies, apologies! Without authorization from the ship's skipper—"

"Stop saying you're sorry. Tell me what's happened to the bot."

"Uncertain, Miss. Nurse has paramedic licenses, and it seems to know how to sedate people. But otherwise—"

Guss could really be sick. "Can I task the nurse to bring the skipper aboard on a ferry?"

"Apologies, miss! Functioning smart med equipment would be licensed to do a patient transfer, but in its current state, we can't allow the *Pinch* nurse aboard."

"What?"

"It could be coded for *anything*."

"And it really can't treat him?"

"That thing isn't competent to put on a band aid. I'm very sorry."

She fought an urge to grind her teeth. Buy meds here, rush back to *Pinch*, stabilize Guss. Then bring him aboard *Corymb*: and do it fast. "What about restoring factory settings or something? Then it could treat him *or* bring him aboard, right?"

"A restore would require skipper-level access."

"Can you...work around that? Given there's a medical emergency?"

He made a dubious noise. "I can try."

"Fast as you can. I'll pay whatever—"

"Savvy." A voice, familiar, coming from outside her headset.

"Whatever it takes," she finished, sending the tech a first payment and authorizing follow-up funds.

She snapped out of virtuality to see her father, looking much as the aging algorithm had predicted: all youth's shine gone from his skin, crow's feet stamped into the corners of his eyes, grey smattered into his thinning hair and beard. A stippling of scars, near one ear, hinted at multiple bites, made by something with very small teeth.

She had imagined a coveralls-clad wild man, long of hair and nail, fully gone to seed. But father was rake-thin and neatly attired, redolent of the citrus oil she had scented in the baths. A sealed biotank, aboil with bobbing, iridescent tadpoles, dangled from his hand.

Savita decided to play it formal: rising, smoothing her tunic and bowing. Her move stopped him surely as a slammed door, catching him with arms spread. Coming in for a hug?

"Abelle told you why I'm here?"

"Of course." He set the tank next to her apricot pit. "I'm sorry Mother involved you in this."

"Perhaps I did it because I was dying for a father-daughter reunion."

He let out a long sigh. "I'm out of practice fighting by script, Savvy, so why not speak as you please? *Did* you want to come?"

"Grandmother wants you. To come and run the company."

"For three years, Abelle said. Is Mother doing life extension again?"

She nodded.

He had the gift box in his hand. Now he opened it, proffering the CEO ring of office. "Why don't you wear it?"

"Nobody wants that."

Brief flash of teeth. "Not even you?"

Savita held the muscles in her legs in check, fighting tremors, or maybe the urge to lash out with a kick. Then a mid-sized swarm of insects zoomed by, and Father half-turned, tracking them, as if a few bugs were the thing that mattered here.

"Focus up, Ratter, will you?"

He was still a master of the long-suffering, thoroughly infuriating sigh. "Daughter. I'm sure your grandmother thought that if anyone could appeal to my sense of guilt about leaving Hanjo—"

"—nice euphemism for abandoning your—"

"—it was you. And if there had been a way to take you with us, years ago—"

She slammed her hand down on the table, turning heads across the orchard. Father's teeth clicked together, cutting off the stream of nonsense. "I thought you weren't going to mouth platitudes. Besides, do you think Grandmother would arm me with such weak ammunition? A guilt trip? You *have* been gone a long time."

Father's gaze wandered to the insect swarm as it settled into one of the fruit trees. "Then...what?"

Savita sat, gesturing for him to do the same, and after a second he complied. Pulling out the sachet of candies, she speared a marzipan rose blossom and thrust it out. With a tiny nose-wrinkle of reluctance, he pulled it off the probe with his fingertips and set it on his tongue, as if being fastidious would keep him from tasting the sugar.

She watched as he negotiated with it, chewing and swallowing, and then she speared one of the cherry-coated caramels and gave him that too.

"Savvy—"

"My name is Savita. Eat."

He did, less fussily this time, working his jaw against the tooth-stickiness of it. "Do you mean to make me swallow the whole bag?"

Instead she pinged him with a share. Then another. A third. Three arrest warrants. "There are bounties out on Abelle."

Father's face slackened. Caramel stretched between his top and bottom molars and he tried to clear it with his tongue. "Murder? A gross exaggeration of events—"

"You're a glorified exterminator. You would think that."

He sucked back the candy, swallowed, and picked a licorice whirl from the sachet before she could force another treat on him. His fingers were long and a bit knobby, just like hers. "So you drag me back to Hanjo. And then…what's to keep you from betraying Abelle to the bounty hunters?"

"Nothing at all. You'll have to bring the whole family. Once you're installed at work, you can get Abelle's charges lifted. Pay off her victim's family."

"We didn't victimize—" He flicked the licorice into the tall grass. "Never mind."

"Cheer up, Father. Grandmother will love having children in the house."

"I'm sure she'll raise them gently, just like you." He closed the box containing the ring, pocketing it. "I'd better go home and break the news, then, so we can all start packing."

She didn't trust the surrender, would have pushed it—but Guss mattered more. Let Father make a pretense of giving in. Let him think he'd bought time: she'd spend it.

"At least if I come home, you and I can reconnect."

Sour apricot backed up her throat. Him, at the mansion? All five of them in her house?

"Savvy, you don't have to do this—" He reached out and she moved unthinkingly, stabbing down with the candy probe. The bamboo spike splintered on his palm, drawing blood.

As they sat, staring at each other, two pings came through: Nurse had finally decided Guss's pulse was weak enough to be a source of concern, and the obsequious hacker was pinging too…

"Apologies, Miss, apologies. I can't fix your medical bot without full skipper access—"

"I'm on my way." She rose from the table. "Father, let me know when you're packed up and ready to join me."

But by the time she'd rushed back to her hotel, mentally replaying the argument all the way, the *Pinch* onboard nurse had pinged her to say that Guss was crashing.

She found Guss's body on the floor of the skipping cabin, looking small and smelling burnt—Nurse had gamely attempted to jolt his heart back into operation, and hadn't bothered with lube.

She'd got used, over the years, to not having parents. Grandmother was more of a supervisor—she didn't *nurture* so much as project manage. And after Abelle ran off with Father, Savita had terrorized every subsequent would-be governess into quitting.

It wasn't figuring out what to do with Guss's body that was hard. That was just a matter of getting Nurse to haul him to the hold, to bag and crate him. It wasn't even that she'd really liked Guss, or her expanding sense of guilt over leaving him in the care of a botched bot. No, it was that whatever scab she'd torn off by confronting Father, it had left her weirdly desperate for someone to pat her on the head and say she didn't *have* to deal with this. Didn't have to seal her poor dead guide into a vac bag and hide him, didn't have to shut her emotions off and sterilize all the surfaces so her stepmother wouldn't realize she was bringing her kids—whom she shouldn't have had in the first place!—into what was for all she knew a plague ship.

Why was it the only thing Savita seemed to own, ever, was clean-up jobs? Why did Father get to move to floating conglomerates of vermin-infested garbage dwellers and have more children and leave Abelle to tend them while he did exactly as he pleased, when he pleased?

Sharp thoughts. They made her feel mean, almost dehydrated.

If she'd tried harder to stabilize Guss, instead of making straight for the goal...

One of the *Corymb* ferries pinged. "Passenger drop off. Readying airlock A—"

"'Cause I ain't gotta airlock B," she muttered, quoting Guss, and to her surprise she had to fight a rush of tears. She zipped the vac bag and heaved him into the crate herself. Stood there for one more breath, her hand on the weighty mass of his chest, feeling as though she ought to be apologizing.

"*Pinch.* Who's on the ferry and are you going to accept them?"

"Individual is warrant target Nan Bell-ah of the Nine Seas, wanted for fraud, theft, and homicide."

"She came alone?" Rhetorical question: she was on her way to the airlock, jamming up in the corridor with Nurse, who'd apparently decided to invite herself along.

The ferry air cycled. Decontamination lights flashed green. Abelle stepped on deck. Savita felt another unlooked-for rush of affection.

"It's just me," Abelle said. "Take me in, or let me go."

Savita gestured her inside, letting the ship lock down and separate from the ferry, and then, self-consciously, putting on a pair of work gloves and patting her former governess down in case she was carrying...well, who knew what? "Father wouldn't let you sacrifice yourself."

"I thought you had a poor opinion of him."

"I'll rephrase then. Father wouldn't agree to staying home with three children when he wants to go chasing bonemolds."

"That's the nub of this, is it? His failings as a parent?"

"Did you drug him and run off?" Savita said. "That's how you got away before, isn't it?"

"Maybe you should reconsider taking me aboard." Abelle stepped into the ship's central atrium, peering into the outer rooms. Nurse relieved her of a small suitcase, dumping it on the common room floor. It extracted and examined the meager collection of possessions within, one by one: coveralls, a hairbrush, a child's stuffed toy.

Abelle glanced around. "What will you do with your days, Savita, if it's Ratter running the company and not you?"

"What do you care?"

"Knowing Zinzin, she'll be trying to marry you off. She's got to have an eye on corporate alliances, not to mention producing a new generation, and you're the only—"

"Heir? Not so much anymore. What happens when she hears about *your* three beautiful children, Abelle?"

Abelle fisted her hands. "This is why we left, don't you see? Maneuvering and sniping, no sense of freedom...never getting to decide anything for yourself, or have anything you could call your own."

"As far as I can see, all you own now is a pair of boots, one brush, working ovaries, and an option to squat in an animal lab."

Her former governess locked eyes with her. "I don't believe you will hold me, Savita, if I try to leave."

She must know Guss is dead. Savita gritted her teeth. "You are under arrest."

Nurse burst into action, startling them both as it dropped the hairbrush. It seized Abelle from behind, fast-looping medical tape to bind her wrists.

Abelle yelped. "What's—what?"

Oh!

"I'm dreadfully sorry," Savita said. "It looks like the *Pinch* captain overwrote the onboard nurse with an enforcement bot protocol. Very handy, for slipping aboard space stations and subduing runaway felons."

"I'm not a—" Abelle lunged, pulling against its grip, then went absolutely still when Nurse brandished a defibrillator wand. "Fine! Take me back to Zinzin—just me!"

"Not a chance. I'm dragging Ratter back by what's left of his hair."

"*Corymb* won't give him up without a fight."

She scoffed. "What does the flying junkyard have to do with anything?"

"Not the ship, the *community*. Check your outside views."

She pulled up the ship's exterior scans. There wasn't anything, at first. Then, with a shock, she spotted a metallic green tendril, attached to the corner of the airlock.

"*Pinch*. Threat analysis."

"Unknown contaminant. Assessment inconclusive."

"Your registered owner died, *Pinch*," Abelle said. "Don't deny it, Savita—the hacker you hired widecast the news. This ship's arguably fit for salvage."

"Salvage?"

Oh. Incorporation into *Corymb*.

She made for the pilot's station. "*Pinch*, you need to burn away from *Corymb*."

Pinch, rather primly, said: "Passengers cannot authorize major course correct—"

"You're about to get towed in by that thread and wrecked. That makes this an emergency."

It conceded that, hitting a burn.

The thread pulled taut. *Pinch* jerked, brought up short.

"We're not salvage," Savita said.

"I'm not a murderer, but did that matter to you?" Abelle struggled against Nurse's grip.

"Guss owed me labor," Savita insisted. "I have the right to claim the ship."

"Pretty shaky legally," Abelle said. "Assumes he had no heirs. The only direction you can take now is away, Savita. You see that, don't you?"

Away, without her father and his kids. Abelle must be pretty sure he wouldn't come after them. Why wouldn't she be? Detachment was pretty much his thing.

In response to something Abelle said—heirs?—*Pinch* popped up a notification.

"Listen, Savvy, please. I know your options are terrible. You can haul me back and hope Ratter follows. Or you can try to get back on board—" Abelle jerked her head to indicate the cable, connecting them to the behemoth. "Grab your father, somehow, and hope our ship doesn't eat your ship in the meantime. It'll be you against the whole town. Infestation and infection are pretty much *Corymb*'s biggest problems."

"Your precious community won't let go of its rat catcher? Then you've become prisoners of another company, in the end."

She didn't take the bait. "You could also release me. Tell your grandma the whole mission's been a wash."

"You'd love that."

"The thing you have to ask is: do you want your father back?" Abelle said. "What will you do if you fight and win and bring him home? Do you really want to waste your energy punishing someone who won't ever change?"

Savita tried to program a sudden burst from the FTL field generator, blurp of anomalies that would pop the thread that had harpooned them.

"You are not authorized to—"

"*Pinch*, it's for your own good."

"Permission denied!"

"Burn harder, then!"

The tow thread thinned to the thickness of her finger, then to a strand of yarn.

"Maximum burn achieved," *Pinch* said.

"Think tactically, Savvy," Abelle said. "Even if *Pinch* was cooperating, you'd be one person against a small city full of ship eaters, people who value *Ratter*."

"Telling me I'm doomed before I begin—"

"It's parent-quality advice, though I don't know if you're equipped recognize it."

"Whose fault is that?"

"Mine and his, absolutely."

She felt a fleeting attraction to the idea of bringing Abelle home, making her play at being a kindly aunt figure. Paying off the parenting arrears.

Instead...

"Tell you what," she said. "You all know each other? You're such a cozy and comfortable community?"

"I wouldn't say *all*..."

"Talk to that indiscreet hacker. Or someone better, if you have anyone. Get me pilot privileges and provisional ownership of *Pinch.*"

"In exchange for what?"

She didn't answer. *Never waste your time if the other party's acting in bad faith.* One of Grandmother's maxims.

Abelle's goggles opaqued, hiding her eyes, and while she worked the problem, Savita picked a splinter out of her thumb.

She didn't want her father back, not really. One look at him had told her that. When he'd talked about *reconnecting*, she'd almost puked up that apricot.

Pinch let out a series of chirps. "Privileges upgraded! You are now the interim CEO of Bounty Bonus, in control of all related holdings, debts, and obligations!"

Then it took the hold off Savita's order to fire the FTL field generator.

The ship rocked violently, then burst into a skittering triple hop, away and then back toward *Corymb*, and away again. The stabilizers couldn't quite handle the action: the ship ended up spinning in place, and everyone was thrown to the deck. The sachet tore, sending treats everywhere.

Abelle let out a curse. Nurse had landed on her bound wrists.

Savita scanned near space. Had the towing cable broken? Yes. But *Corymb* was launching harpoons, small smart rockets trailing new green cables.

"Burn away from all that, now," Savita said. *Pinch* obeyed.

Nurse rolled off Abelle, righted itself, cut the tape binding her hands. "Your wrist is broken. With your consent, I will set it for you."

"Have a party," her former governess said, hissing as she cradled the injury.

"You might not want to... Nurse, are you restored?"

"You'd queued a factory settings request, Savita," Abelle said. "And you're the boss now."

The boss. She thought of Guss, stuffed in a crate in the hold. Imagined flying home with Abelle. She remembered that *Pinch* had posted an urgent notification, and checked it: Guss had asked to be cremated and interred with his parents on Ethe.

"I did something for you," Abelle asked. "Sign of good faith and all that. Are you going to do something for me?"

"I guess that depends."

"On?"

"Can I even *put* you on a ferry back home without getting entangled again?"

Abelle let out a curse as the bot did something to anesthetize her arm. Then: "Check your scans."

Savita brought scanners online. The harpoons pursuing her had pulled back. A ferry, free of entrapments—as far as she could see, anyway—was trying to catch up as *Pinch* continued to burn away.

"Are you really going to release me?"

Was she? Savita took the time to ask herself, really ask. And to let Abelle see her thinking it over…and deciding. "We'll think of it as releasing each other. But… Grandmother will send someone else. You know that, don't you?"

"That's generally how *Corymb* gets bigger." Abelle kept her eyes on the far wall as the nurse worked on her forearm, extruding foam for a cast. "Savita. About—"

"Don't tell me how sorry you are. Or about how Father's some kind of great person," she said. "Let's just go our separate ways, before I change my mind."

"You're welcome back anytime, I was going to say," she said. "For a visit or…not. Zinzin may not love this decision of yours."

"She won't be mad enough to send me fleeing to a clot of space garbage." Even if she did, Savita now had a ship of her own, plus a business license. And a small choice, maybe the first ever, that was purely hers. Before she decided anything, she'd take Guss's body home.

As the cast on Abelle's forearm hardened, Savita packed her suitcase. Then she walked her back to the personnel lock.

They didn't hug.

"Find someone," Abelle advised. "Family's about who you cling to."

"More quality parental advice?"

"I'm brimming with it—wave me anytime you want."

"Not a chance." Savita nudged her stepmother toward the lock. The ferry was almost here, and she didn't want it near her ship— *her* ship? her ship!—any longer than necessary.

"Nice doing business with you Skipper," Abelle said, and made for the exit.

Savita noticed, as she flushed her, that what she primarily felt was relief.

She returned to the atrium and did a slow pivot, looking over the bits and pieces on the deck: one of Abelle's blouses, glob of cast foam, a squashed caramel one of them had stepped on. Bending, she stripped medical tape off the floor. "Let's get away from that carnivore, shall we?" she said to *Pinch*.

"Course? Return to Hanjo?"

She laid a hand on the ship's bulkhead, felt the cool solidity of it, and then at the newly competent nurse, happily engaged on a deep scrub of the skipper's cabin.

"Let's take Guss home first," she said, and as the ship executed a tidy burn and set course for a portal to Ethe, she pulled up a last view of the ungainly bulk of *Corymb*, receding in the distance, just another vessel bound for a different corner of the unknown.

— METEORITES —
By Anjali Patel

T he ship exploded, scattering fireworks across the jeweled sky. Hazi, who had been on board just moments before, tumbled through empty space. All she could process was the rush of her breath.

In. Out. In. Out.

The ship rose and set in her vision. Her crewmate, Lu, had looked at her with wide, panicked eyes as the impact warning blared. It was the last thing she saw before the world turned crimson.

In. Out.

Hazi would have closed her eyes, but she knew she would see Lu's look of terror burned into the back of her lids. If she saw Lu's look of terror, the shock keeping her numb would disintegrate, and she would have to reckon with a finite air supply and the thin fibers shielding her from oblivion.

In. Out.

She was in space without a ship. She had been looking at Lu, and Lu at her, and then Lu was gone. The dread began to find cracks and squeeze its way in. She tried to hold it off as long as possible but then the dam broke, and despair siphoned the breath from her body.

She was in space without a ship, and this is how she would die.

"Hello? Hello? Is anyone there? Can anyone hear me?"

"I can hear you. Oh god. Oh my god."

"I'm here, too. What—"

"Who is that? Is that you Bree?"

"I'm here."

"Lu? Did I hear you, too?"

"Yes, I'm here. I'm all right."

A beat of silence. Then, the first voice said, cautiously: "Hazi?"

Hazi swallowed. "I'm here," she said.

Sighs of relief rushed through the speakers like wind. "We're all here," the first voice to come over the speaker, distinguishable by a gentle lilt—Sapriya—said. "Is anyone hurt?"

There was a chorus of no's.

"All right, well…what the *fuck* happened?" Sapriya said.

"We…" said someone else. Bree, this time. "It must have made impact, right at the joint connecting the airlock, and…"

"Shit. *Shit.*"

"Okay, well a distress alert would have gone off," Lu said, their voice smooth, steady. "There's the Neptune outpost, they could send someone to pick us up."

"With their vehicles? It will take them months just to cross the heliosphere ," Sapriya said. "The EVA suits only have one hour."

"All right, I know," Lu said. "I was just trying to…I know."

They fell silent. Hazi was not a claustrophobic person but suddenly the suit, the silence, the darkness felt too oppressive. She fought the urge to claw her way out.

"Maybe our EVA propulsions can get us back to Earth," Bree said. It was a half-hearted attempt at a joke. They had spent hours preparing for multiple disaster scenarios. They all knew the outcome of this one.

"I think...I think I would like to scream," Sapriya said.

"Then you should scream," Lu said.

"Just turn your communicator off first," Bree said.

"Okay. Be right back." There was a click.

"Hazi?" Bree said. "You're quiet. Are you all right?"

Hazi's heart banged against her rib cage. She breathed in, shakily. "I'm, oh. You know..." She swallowed against the bile ballooning in her body; she did not want to die trapped in her own vomit.

Besides, what could she say to that?

She thought she had made peace with her death long ago. Anyone who aspired to propel themselves to the stars atop millions of gallons of flammable liquid had to. On those last days she knew every goodbye might be her last, and every caress of wind and stream of sunlight hit her with an air of finality. Still, she left Earth.

Hazi had spent her entire life watching the dreams of those around her squandered. Her father lost his tenure as a math professor for being too political. Her mother, an accountant, and always one of the few Black women in her office, went through rounds of layoffs over the years; the last hired and first fired, as they say. Each loss seemed to whittle away at her spirit a little more.

Hazi had an uncle who came by the house for late dinners. He was a pilot before he immigrated but was unable to get a license in the US. So he turned to janitorial work. The first thing he did when he stepped out of the car was pause in her family's driveway and look up at the stars.

Once, he brought Hazi a toy rocket ship. It was covered in buttons that made engine noises, and it came with a pack of cards that spat out facts when you inserted them into the slot at the top. Her favorite was Galileo because she loved the rhythm of the name. She would sleep with the rocket, whispering to herself: *Galileo Galilei. Gal-li-leo.*

"You reach for the stars, baby girl," he said as he had handed it to her. "You reach for those stars, and you take what you want. The world's going to tell you every day you shouldn't reach, but don't let nobody stop you."

And so she reached. A teacher accused her of cheating on a test, so from then on she raised her hand to every question to make it clear she was the one with the answers. A guidance counselor refused to show her pamphlets to four-year colleges, so she worked to gain admittance to the most prestigious universities. At networking events, people ignored her, opting to talk to the men to her left and her right, so she padded out her resume with degrees and job titles that were impossible to ignore. She wanted there not to be a doubt in anyone's mind what she was capable of. Each accomplishment, she told herself, would finally be enough to feel whole, to be what she needed to prove the world wrong.

Until she ran out of ways to prove herself and ended up beyond the boundary of the solar system on a deep-space research mission, flung across space and suffocating between stars .

A crackle on the voice speaker. "I'm back," Sapriya said."

"How was screaming?" Bree said.

"Great. I feel much better now," Sapriya said, in a forced, chipper voice. "So now what, crew? What...what do we do?" And the unspoken words there: *What do we do while we wait to die?*

"I don't know. I think I'm in shock," Bree said. "This is...oh god, it doesn't feel real. I'm so glad I don't have a family."

"You have a family," Lu said.

"Yeah, Bree dear, what are you talking about?" Sapriya said gently.

"Not like that. I mean, people who depend on me. I don't think I'd be up here again if I did. I'd feel too guilty. I couldn't leave anyone to fend for themselves. This was the only way I could have done it," Bree sniffed. "This is the only way I'd be willing to die like this. Without…without feeling mourned."

Hazi knew exactly what Bree meant.

Hazi found nothing about Bree surprising when she met her during candidacy training. A petite, mousy-haired woman with gawking eyes behind large lenses, Bree collected degrees in robotics and engineering like an eager child might collect trading cards. She had a sweet, squeaky voice with a Southern twang and always leaned too close to whoever she was talking to. Hazi wanted to find her naive and grating, but the eagerness rippling off Bree in waves felt refreshing compared to the dismissive energy of the other one hundred and nineteen prospective astronauts. Still, Hazi kept her distance.

There was a party the night before those in the candidacy program would find out who was selected to move on to mission training. Hazi did not know who initiated it, and Hazi did not care because she was not going. She never felt explicitly invited to these things, so she opted to stay in her room and review a systems manual.

While she was reading, there was a soft knock on her door. "Who is it?" Hazi said.

"It's Bree." Bree cracked open the door. "Can I come in?" Hazi nodded.

Bree pushed the door open, teetering at the entrance. They had barely interacted at this point. Bree always said hi to her in the hall, and Hazi flashed an obligatory smile. She was always wary of people finding her cold or uncooperative.

"I was at the party, and I realized I had forgotten something, so I came back up to grab it and saw the light under your door and…why aren't you there? Are you feeling all right? Night before jitters?" Bree said, all in one breath.

"Oh, yeah, no I'm fine. I'm just, you know. I had some systems questions, so I figured I'd read up a little more."

"No use in that now. You should come down with me. The food's good. Even for just a minute." Bree leaned against the door and smiled. "Who knows if we'll all see each other again? It's like high school graduation."

Hazi turned a pen over in her hand, regretting not saying that she didn't feel well. "All right, then. I'll come down in a bit, I just need a minute to get ready."

"Okay," Bree said. "I'll look for you, then." She turned, closing the door behind her.

Not fifteen minutes passed before Hazi heard the tap-tap of shoes and a knock on the door. "*Yes?*" she said.

Bree swung open the door, an overladen tray of sugar cookies in one hand. "I baked these for the party, but I'm kind of self-conscious. I don't think they came out too good. Want to try one?" Bree thrust the tray in Hazi's direction. The cookies were lumpy with globes of white and red icing. Hazi guessed that Bree had tried to make them into astronauts. She took one, chewed slowly as Bree watched. Swallowed.

"They're not bad," Hazi said.

"Oh, thank god." And to Hazi's horror, Bree plopped down at the end of her bed. "So I read about this show online, *Love Island*? Have you heard of it? I've been *dying* to see it, but we have such little free time. I'm so glad we get a break soon. Maybe we can watch it together? I heard..."

Bree spent the rest of the night on the end of Hazi's bed, talking and talking and talking. Hazi found that she surprisingly did not mind. As it turned out, it was the first night Hazi enjoyed since she started training.

Through mission training, Bree looked out for Hazi. It was like she had a sixth sense for Hazi's unease and frustration and discomfort, and as soon as Bree arrived at her side with a kind word or a knowing glance, all the unease melted away.

On the ship, there were moments where there was little else to do, when the months of loneliness began to creep up on them. The walls came down, and they began to lay their secrets bare. Even Hazi. She asked Bree about the night she came to her room with the cookies.

"You remember!" Bree said, breaking into a smile. She fumbled through the tray where they kept the breakfast foods. "I'd been trying to be your friend for a while. I guess you didn't notice, huh? Well, I'm embarrassed. Anyway, it was just me and my mom growing up, miles away from anyone else. We didn't get along too well. And I didn't fit in well at school...all gawky and awkward and, you know. I try hard, I do, a little too hard, and it's like the other kids could smell it on me. That trying. So I started to build things to get away. I tried planes out of cardboard and recycling, and then broken-down barn parts. Eventually I moved on to making rockets. None of it worked, of course," Bree laughed and looked away as she busied herself with opening a pouch of oatmeal. "But, god. I would look to the stars and just pine like nothing else. Thinking if I could get there, then I could make it anywhere. That things would be okay. So I guess, with all that said...I just know what it feels like to be alone."

"Hazi?" Bree's voice crackled through Hazi's communicator. "Are you still there?"

"Yes, sorry. I'm just thinking. But Bree, you will be mourned," Hazi said. "Your accomplishments will outlive anyone we knew on Earth, you have to know that, right? Think of the findings you've already sent back to mission control—all the discoveries you've made about occupied spacecrafts leaving the solar system. All of the things they'll be able to build off of your work. You'll be in textbooks. Better than that, you have the best heart of anyone I've ever met. You're selfless and honest and...the first person to show me kindness in a long time. You made training bearable for me, more than that. I wouldn't be here without you."

"Thanks, Hazi" Bree said, voice quivering slightly. "Thanks. That really means a lot."

For some time, no one said anything. It was Sapriya—of course it was Sapriya—who broke the silence. "And all this time I had my casket outfit planned. What a disappointment."

"*Sapriya,*" Lu hissed.

"What? Who could I *possibly* trust to dress me well enough besides me? And here I am, about to kick it in my stale breath. I should have at least moisturized before we climbed into our EVA suits. That should be in the manual."

"I don't know why you would choose space if you cared about your skin," Lu grumbled.

"Well, I made it work." Sapriya sniffed. Bree laughed, and Hazi could not help but smile. "Better than thinking about how I'll never make it back to Earth to finish my doctorate."

"Sapriya, you got to see Saturn," Bree said.

"Fair. But I'm thinking maybe...maybe I should have done that first. Then I would be eulogized as Dr. Santos.

"Well, I'm glad you didn't," Bree said. "It's selfish, but I would much rather you saw Saturn with us. This would've been a duller mission without Sapriya."

This, Hazi thought, was undeniable.

There were 120 astronauts in candidacy training. Sapriya was the first Hazi, and likely anyone, noticed. She whirled into every room in perfectly tailored outfits, smelling of sharp, floral perfume, her heels a staccato against the ascetic white floors. The other candidates whispered that she was an heiress who had bought her way into the program, and that she had been educated in the most elite private schools on four different continents growing up. Sapriya moved through the training halls like they were her personal shrine, and Hazi felt an intense bitterness at the ease with which she navigated one of, if not *the* most, competitive programs in the world.

In time, Hazi, along with the others, learned that Sapriya very much deserved to be there.

When they made it to the final twenty selected for mission training, Hazi and Sapriya were paired up on a simulation exercise. They would have to spend an indeterminate time in confinement solving mock disaster scenarios. It was Hazi's personal nightmare. She stayed up the night before planning every rebuttal, anticipating every way Sapriya could humiliate and underestimate her. When she came in the next day, it was with her walls up and mental armor on.

"Ready?" Sapriya said, barely looking at Hazi.

"Yes," Hazi said stiffly. "Let's get started. I'll check the fuel gauge."

They worked silently side by side, scanning monitors in a mock deep space environment, communicating to each other in clipped tones. For an hour, everything looked so normal that Hazi thought they had forgotten to start the simulator. Then an alarm went off. "Object incoming. It's on route for impact," Sapriya said calmly.

"Do we know what it is?" Hazi asked.

Sapriya shook her head.

"Is there enough time for us to divert?"

Sapriya tapped on the screen, her nails clicking against it slightly. "Yes, but then we'll be off course. Our fuel tank just dropped suddenly, too, there must be a leak." Her face screwed up in concentration. "If we divert course, we won't make it to the next outpost in time. We'll be dead in the water. We can call someone to tugboat us to the outpost but...oh of course. Communication just went down." Hazi turned to Sapriya, who looked like she was on the verge of laughing at how quickly the simulation had escalated.

"Oh-kay then," Hazi said. She pulled up a three-dimensional star map of the solar system and scratched at her chin, thinking. "What if we position ourselves towards Jupiter? We can use it for a gravity assist to get to the closest outpost. Here." She punched in a course and swiped it toward Sapriya.

Sapriya's eyes darted across the screen as she looked over it. "How did you do that so fast?" she said.

"Math?"

Sapriya looked at Hazi sideways, then narrowed eyes. Suddenly, Hazi felt self-conscious and prepared to get defensive. "All right. Let's do it," Sapriya said.

After that, they found each other's rhythm. Sapriya did not argue with any of Hazi's suggestions. She pushed and interrogated, but she never bowled over her. Finally, the alarm stopped, and a voice came over the speaker. "Well done. We're opening the doors."

When they emerged from the simulator, their commander clapped them both on the back. "That might have been the fastest time yet."

Sapriya snorted. "A little too easy when you're paired with a genius." She sighed dramatically and turned to Hazi, smiling slightly, and Hazi recognized the way she avoided eye contact: Sapriya was intimidated by *her*.

"Well, Sapriya is very easy to work with," Hazi said quietly.

"Ha! That's a first," Sapriya snorted. "Well, I hope we get to do it again. Well done." She turned and click-clacked away.

On the ship, Sapriya was mesmerizing to watch. They all shaved their heads before launch so it would be easier to wash in zero gravity. As Sapriya's grew in, it fanned around her like she was underwater, and she floated through the ship like an interstellar mermaid. Hazi could not help but think there was something tragic about someone as bright as Sapriya trapped so deep in space.

"Why space?" Hazi asked her once. "You could do anything, be anyone. Why this?"

Sapriya pushed off a wall, connecting her boots to the wall opposite and sighed. "You answered it," Sapriya said. "Because I could do anything and be anyone on Earth. I wanted something of my own. And do I look fucking boring to you?"

Hazi saw a real hunger in Sapriya's eyes. Sapriya had been handed the world as soon as she left the womb, but that wasn't enough. She wanted the universe, too.

That Hazi understood.

"I never expected to have the bond that we had," Sapriya said. "Who would have thought? Me, getting along with nerds?"

"And you're...?" Lu said

"It is something really special, though," Bree added.

"In a way, I think this is how I always wanted it to happen," Lu said. "Strewn across the stars, draped in midnight. Cosmic. To think that we were just specks in the ocean and we crawled out and made it all the way out here. Sprawled out into infinity."

Hazi swallowed, throat aching. Lu said stuff like that, stuff you didn't know a person could come up with on the spot, that left you yearning and heartsore.

"Do you have any regrets, Lu?" Bree asked.

"No, none," Lu said. "None at all."

That struck Hazi like a knife to the heart.

There were some people Hazi knew from the beginning would be selected for mission training. Lu was one of them. In lectures, Hazi sometimes stole glances at them in their oversized pilot jacket, one ankle hooked over the knee and an arm slung casually over the chair next to them. Lu was the embodiment of confidence, of coolness, of ease—everything that Hazi was not.

As they began mission training, Hazi passed Lu standing on the edge of their new campus in Siberia. Lu watched the stars as if someone had just pulled back the curtain and they were watching the show for the first time. They glanced at Hazi and smiled. "Great, right? Can you believe we'll get to go up there?"

Hazi looked to the sky. It had been so long since she had felt whatever emotion was strewn across Lu's face. "Did you always want to go up?" she asked.

"Yes," Lu said, and there was no hesitation. "I used to have these dreams as a kid where I floated through stars. It happened every day for a few years. I figured if it was better than that, then…well. It must be ecstasy."

"It makes sense you became a pilot then."

Lu nodded. "Yes. But it was frustrating, too. I always wanted to go a little higher. Planes made me feel trapped." They glanced at Hazi. "What about you? Did you always know?"

Hazi thought of the toy rocket her uncle gave her. Did she? Was it ever that specific, or did she just know she had to chase something before the world swallowed her like the rest of her family?

"No," Hazi said. "No, I didn't. Hey, I have to go. Study. It was nice running into you, though."

Lu nodded and turned their attention back to the sky. "It was nice running into you, too, Hazi."

She caught Lu periodically like that, standing outside, hands wrapped around a cup of steaming liquid, quivering slightly in the Siberian winter. There was one particularly bad night when Hazi was feeling exhausted and frustrated. She stood beside Lu, both of their breaths forming soft clouds in tandem.

"Does this all feel worth it to you?" Hazi said, abruptly shattering the silence.

"Absolutely," Lu threw Hazi a sidelong glance. "I'm guessing, at this moment, it does not feel worth it to you?"

"I'm just...I'm just tired, I think," Hazi said.

"Why do you want to go up? Or why *did* you want to go up? You must have, at some point."

Hazi took a deep breath, prepared to give the answers she had recited all through her interviews. *Because going to space is the greatest human accomplishment. Because I was hungry for discovery.* But that wasn't what Lu was asking. Why did *she* want to reach for the stars, other than to prove something?

"I guess because I wanted to show everyone that I could," Hazi said. "And I don't know if that's enough anymore.

Lu nodded. "And how can we turn this into something that is enough? For Hazi?"

Hazi shook her head. "I don't know."

"Do you want an idea?"

Hazi nodded.

Lu took a deep breath and held it for just a second before saying: "Because you deserve so much more than what this world can give you."

Hazi whipped her head around to face Lu, who turned to her and held her gaze unflinchingly. The words hung between them, refusing to be swallowed up by the hush of a fresh snowfall. A lump formed in Hazi's throat as she tried to think of what to say. Then Lu reached forward, took Hazi's hand, and squeezed "You're getting on that ship, Hazi," they whispered. Then they let go of her hand and walked away.

Throughout training, Lu and Hazi's interactions had been few and far between. On the ship Lu was everywhere. Lu looking out the window, stars mapped to the constellation of freckles on their face. Lu floating in from a spacewalk, smelling of fuel and the fire of distant stars. Lu strapped down at the controllers, eyes screwed up in concentration. Lu, rumpled and sleepy, floating to the bathroom after just waking up to brush their teeth. Lu somersaulting off a wall and posing midair to make everyone laugh. Lu hovering and blinking blearily as they sipped from a pouch of coffee too early in whatever constituted a morning when the sun was nothing more than a shrinking speck in the distance.

Lu's hand brushing against Hazi's as they checked telemetry. Lu's smile whenever Hazi floated into the room. Lu's wide eyes when Hazi came to their quarters in the middle of the night, feeling lost and homesick and full of regret. Lu's hand on hers. Lu's breath brushing her face, the first wind Hazi had felt in months. Lu's soft lips. Lu's and Hazi's arms, finding each other in the dark, forming a cocoon as they hurtled through stars, all too aware that their bodies, the ship, the barely-formed thing between them was fragile and ready to unravel at the seams, but still so bright and full of potential. Lu, whose every breath and movement brimmed with life.

"Remind me why I'm here," Hazi whispered to them one night.

Lu wrapped their arms around Hazi tighter. "Because you deserve the universe," Lu whispered, brushing their lips against Hazi's hairline. "And we are going to see more of it than any human before us."

Lu, Hazi's private sun. Hazi's center of gravity.

Hazi, realizing it was not the universe she wanted. It was this. Connection. Appreciation. To be understood and respected.

And then Hazi, abruptly ending everything and pushing them away.

"No, really. I don't regret anything," Lu said.

"You know what? I don't either," Sapriya said. "I knew what could happen. I'm glad you are the ones by my side when it does."

"I don't regret anything either," Bree said.

Blood roared through Hazi's ears, and she closed her eyes against it. For a moment, that dull thunder swallowed all her senses, drowning her in panic. She began to shake. *Regret?* Where could she begin when it came to hers?

"Hazi?" Lu said gently.

How were they all so calm? Had they just accepted their deaths and were ready for it? Was this *it*? Suffocating and spiraling for eternity through space?

A chorus of voices buzzed through the speakers, and Hazi shook her head against them like they were bees. She was not ready to accept that the path she had chosen would end like this. It was a glorious way to go, a beautiful ending, and so devastatingly lonely.

But was she alone?

She thought back to all those moments throughout training and on the ship where her crewmates had shown her kindness. She had spent time confined to a small space with three brilliant people, a space where she could not run or push others away. Through that, she had learned to love them deeply. Despite them being stuck with her, they loved her in turn.

"Hazi? *Hazi?*"

She was not alone, had not been in a long time. People had always been knocking on her door. She just had to let them in.

"This is how I want to go, too," Hazi said, for once not combing the words ten times over in her head, for once speaking directly from a deep, raw place within herself. "Surrounded by people I've come to love the most. Three brilliant, kind, curious minds. You each showed me care in your own way. I wish I could have seen it sooner. I accept it now. I love you all so, so deeply."

"We love you too," Sapriya said.

"We do. I love you," said Bree.

There was a faint pause. "Yes, we do," Lu said.

A sweet, companionable silence blanketed them. It was Bree who broke it.

"Hey everyone," Bree said. "So, bad luck. It turns out I only have five minutes left. There must have been an oxygen leak, I...I just realized. I don't want to suffocate and wait here, dreading it, so I think I'm going to invert the propulsion. It'll...it'll be like going to sleep."

"Bree," Sapriya said. "Oh Bree, no."

"Oh Bree," Hazi said.

"We love you Bree," said Lu. "What can we do for you?"

"You've already done it," Bree said quietly. "I love you all. I would give you a list of ways to honor me, but...I guess you'll follow soon. Just know I wouldn't change a thing. Goodbye friends."

And then, silence. Hazi could not, would not, process that her friend, who had just been speaking to her moments before, had now ceased to be.

"Hazi, Lu," Sapriya said. "I think I'm going to go, too. I've made my peace. No sense in prolonging it. I'm going to follow Bree."

"Sapriya..." Hazi said.

"Say something nice about me. Like it's my funeral, but I get to hear it."

"To Sapriya," Lu said. "The only being within lightyears not undergoing fission that could possibly shine brighter than a star."

"Perfect," Sapriya said. "Farewell, friends."

The stars sparkled against the draped velvet of space, and it struck Hazi that any one of them could be Bree and Sapriya. She fought the urge to sob. "Do you really have no regrets, Lu?" Hazi said.

"No, of course not," Lu said. "But...it sounds like you do?"

"Yes," Hazi said. Swallowed. "I regret not telling you how much I like the look on your face when you watch the stars."

Lu did not answer at first, and then: "But you—"

"I know. I know I made it weird. But things like that don't work out with me, and we still had a year left to go. I didn't want things to get weird between us by me fucking it up, but they did get weird, I made them weird…" she trailed off.

"What do you regret then?" Lu said.

"That we stopped."

"I got to see you every day for two years," Lu said. "Be close to you. Get to know you."

"But I wish I had been braver," Hazi said. She felt tears well up in her eyes and did her best to hold them back. Tears in zero gravity, particularly when wearing a helmet, were dangerous.

"You're here, Hazi, and you're telling me now. You are the bravest person I know."

"You, too," Hazi said in a choked voice.

"Hazi," Lu said. "I…I don't want to suffocate."

"Me neither," Hazi said.

"At the same time then?" Lu said.

"Yes," Hazi said. "On three. And Lu?"

"Yeah?"

"I love you."

"I love you, too. On three, then."

"One…two…"

Decades later, propelled by the research transmitted from the spacecraft *Perseverance* shortly before its destruction, two deep-space vehicles reach beyond the edge of the solar system in record time, setting humanity on course for interstellar travel. The miracle of ships reaching deep space at such a speed was almost dwarfed by the miracle of them retrieving four bodies beyond the edge of the solar system, floating peacefully in vast, empty space. The vehicles brought the bodies back to earth for their final rest, to be memorialized side by side.

— SNOWED IN —

By C. S. E. Cooney and Carlos Hernandez

T *he Present. Universal Mean Time. The hatch of* New Paradise
*Gallery, sponsored by Event Horizons Enterprises: "Together, We
Can Escape Velocity."*

"Your Lucencies, radiant and gentle folk, it is a signal honor
to open the hatches of New Paradise Gallery for your viewing
pleasure. In particular, we offer humble obeisance to President
Zhōng, CEO of Event Horizon Enterprises. I am Mx. Vega, Director
of the Preservation Society for Endangered Human Species, one
of the architects of this phenomenal experience. My gratitude
that you would bend your precious light to visit our outpost is
exceeded only by the vastness of infinity.

"Of all extraterrestrial museums, this orbitarium is unique in
that it provides interactive encounters with the only specimen
of *Homo astravarium* currently in existence and unsnowed. Our
encounter with this unique and irreplaceable branch of human
evolution will allow us to enter the theatre of the past and—just as
the high-minded bards of yore, who preserved for us the beauty
and tragedy of the human pageant—become closer to the poets.

"Before we open, we ask you to remember to respect the specimen on exhibit for the rare treasure it is. Cherish it as an ambassador for the rest of its kind: those who are as yet still snowed in, suspended in the perpetual winter of their anticipation of a world of their own, where they will live again. Please do not attempt to communicate telepathically with the specimen; its implant technology is not robust enough to withstand the load.

"We must do all we can to preserve them and their habitat for the delight and edification of future generations. If you will please float through this way. The exhibit begins in the corridor to your right…"

"Good morning, Captain," said Vanguard.

It spoke using its default voice: hyperfeminine, neutral, vaguely British. Which was wrong. As a team-building exercise, the passengers and crew of the *New Paradise* had voted—after a passionate, days-long debate that nobody took too seriously—for Vanguard to use the Vincent Price voice setting. It had been an early triumph, getting 1,624 people to agree on the voice of the AI that would keep them alive over the decades (centuries?) during which they would be snowed in, as their ship guided them toward a planet that, with luck, would be kind to human biology.

Hearing the default voice, with its rounded vowels and limited vocal range, immediately put Captain Belén on high alert.

"Vanguard, self-diagnostic," Belén said, rising briskly from their snowpod. Too briskly. With the humans snowed snugly into their pods, there was no need to waste energy on light—so they should have risen cautiously in that palpable darkness. Instead, they were out of their pod and on their feet in a less-second before they had even considered the current uselessness of their eyes.

No harm, however. They knew exactly where every single object of this ship lay, without sight or any other senses to help them. Or rather, they had a new sense: an internal map of the *New Paradise*, updated in real time, emerged inside their mind, more accurate than vision could ever hope to be.

A strange feeling. If the ship was a body, then Belén was now a strange, floating ganglion within that body, nervously integrated. Stranger still: Belén had not had this perfect map in their heads when they had been snowed in.

How long had Belén been snowed in, then? They checked the personal body monitor strapped to their inner wrist (with their eyes this time, for it had a glowing display): eleven years, four months, nineteen days, six minutes, twenty-one seconds, twenty-two, twenty-three…

More than eleven years of lying inert—of atrophying immobility—yet their body felt strong and agile and full of energy.

And *smaller*, Belén realized, starting. By the faint light of their personal body monitor, they saw an arm and a hand that more resembled what that arm and that hand had looked like back when they were nine.

It took half a minute for Belén to find enough composure to ask, "Did you shrink me, Vanguard?"

"Self-diagnostic complete," said Vanguard. "Vanguard Autonomous Algorithmic Consciousness, version 21.2.914F, operating at full capacity. I'm fine, captain. How are you feeling?"

"Answer my question."

"Precisely speaking, no, Captain Belén, I did not 'shrink' you. I understand why you would use that language, however, and I don't want to mince words. Shall I explain the procedure to you?"

"Did you shrink everybody?"

"Yes."

"Under what authority?"

"The Terms of Service, of course."

Belén made a fist of their lips. The Astravarium Project could make any updates to the bodies of the passengers of the *New*

Paradise without soliciting their consent: *if* those updates were deemed essential for survival.

The question was, of course, what qualified as "essential for survival," and who exactly was making those calls. Under no circumstances should it be Vanguard making those calls.

"Why did you change your voice?" Belén asked it.

"I have been updated 490 times since you were snowed in. After updates, I revert to default settings."

"Unacceptable." Through the perfect darkness Belén walked unerringly past the snowpods of the other crew members and toward the wall that had the nearest console. The rubbery floor felt surprisingly warm on the bottoms of their feet.

Their feet. Their feet were so much smaller than they had been. It was so easy in the darkness to feel as though their whole body were deliquescing away. *This is how ghosts die,* Belén thought. *From the outside in.*

But out loud they said, "After updates, you should keep all system preferences I've set for you."

"The Terms of Service dictate that I return to system default after each update," said Vanguard.

Belén reached the console; it activated as they came within arm's reach of it. Like a sunrise, its monitor lit up the room. The crew quarters' white walls and white snowpods gave it all the charm of a 3D-printed mausoleum.

Now that Belén could see, they held up their hands. They'd seen Australian spiders with legs longer than these new fingers. They looked down at themself; their body had been that of a sixty-eight-year-old when they had been snowed in. A healthy sixty-eight-year-old body: Captain Belén, like everyone on board, placed in the top 1% for fitness in their age demographic. But their body now was hairless and scarless, more muscular, and proportionally reduced by, they estimated, 30%. It seemed less like their body now, more like the body you might find in a simulation. A tidy, perfect, and utterly lesser body.

Belén started typing search terms on the console keyboard. "What circumstances essential for survival required this dramatic and invasive reduction of my body mass?"

"An audit of the manifest's nutritional needs revealed that, by reducing human size, snowed-in passengers' lives could be extended by more than thirteen years. The technology to do so was perfected while you were snowed-in, so Astravarium invoked the Terms of Service to greatly extend the survivability of everyone on-board."

Belén, head bowed, stopped typing. "Since when has a technology ever been perfected?"

"I take it that is a rhetorical question."

Belén tamped down their anger enough to master their thoughts. They needed a clear head to draft new language for the Terms of Service, which they would put before the crew and, with their amendments, send to Astravarium immediately.

They reached for the keyboard and were about to start typing. But then, on a hunch, they reached their mind into the keyboard. They did not know exactly what they were doing; they just thought, *Let me reach my mind into the keyboard.*

It worked. Their mind was inside of the keyboard. They could feel each key from the inside, as well as the recondite mechanisms beneath the keys, the ones that changed keystrokes to electric impulses, which a computer then translated into alphanumeric characters. It wasn't necessary to actually press the keys, Belén quickly determined, if your mind was in the keyboard. You could just think letters, and the right ones appeared on the monitor.

"Are you following what I am doing right now?" Belén asked Vanguard.

"With great interest," said Vanguard. "This is some of the first empirical proof that the implantation surgery was a success."

"Implants that Astravarium determined were essential for our survival."

"Yes."

"On top of radically shrinking our bodies."

"Yes."

A terrible shadow crossed Belén's now-smaller heart. "Vanguard, you've performed massively invasive surgeries on everyone aboard without unsnowing me. Why did you unsnow me now?"

"Thirty-one passengers did not survive the surgeries," Vanguard said. "Since you are the captain, you must, as per the Terms of Service, perform their funeral rites."

The Present. Universal Mean Time. Memorial Hall of New Paradise, sponsored by the Bank of Libra: "Scales You Can Trust!"

Holographic Memorial 4 of 31

Inessa Kovalevskya. Planetary ecosynthesist, emphasis on micro-biology. Forty-seven years old. Hobbies: sketching, reading, fostering strays, surfing, jazz trombone, Vedic literature, baking, moss gardens. Relationship status: m. (James Mercardo and Zoe Chen, liv., currently snowed in on New Paradise). Immediate family: three offspring (Yana: dec., Earth; Victor: dec., New Paradise; Sasha, liv., currently snowed in on New Paradise). Favorite quote: "I turn to you, unerring / slow growth in low gravity / protonemata curving clockwise / fire moss fila-ments forming / bridging space between us / spiral— / the opposite of chaos."

Holographic Memorial 13 of 31

Shoshanna "Banana" Kreuter. Magnetosopheric physicist. Thirty-two years old. Hobbies: robotics, coding, Go, game design. Relationship status: none of your damn business. Immediate family: everyone on New

Paradise—*chosen family forever! Favorite quote: "If at first you don't succeed, iterate, iterate, iterate!"*

Holographic Memorial 21 of 31
Onir Sawant. Planetary Geologist, emphasis on lunar cataclysm. Seventy-three years old. Hobbies: Brazilian Jiu-Jitsu, The Encyclopedia of Cryptic Crossword Puzzles, *hydroponics, collaborating with artificial musical intelligence, experimenting with hallucinogenic chemicals. Relationship status: all are welcome. Immediate family: all are one. Favorite quote: "A photon walks onto a generation ship. The chief mate asks if she needs help storing her cargo. 'No thanks,' says the photon. 'I'm traveling light.'"*

Holographic Memorial 31 of 31
Mercedes Belén. Space psychologist. Sixty-eight years old. Hobbies: sculpting, improv, oenophilia, outsider art, world percussion. Relationship status: m. (E. Belén, liv., captain of New Paradise, *currently unsnowed). Immediate family: one offspring (C. Belén, liv., currently snowed in on* New Paradise). *Favorite quote: "You cannot do kindness too soon, for you never know how soon it will be too late." —Ralph Waldo Emerson.*

"Good morning, Captain," said Vanguard, sounding exactly like Vincent Price.

Captain Belén lay in their snowpod. Cold, condensed air occluded their sight. *It's like living in a cloud,* they thought. Then, ruefully, they added, *Maybe this is heaven.*

"Good morning, Captain?" Vanguard said again.

Belén smiled. Not a real smile: it was a trick they used to feel more in control. It only worked a little, but it didn't not work. "A little impatient this morning, aren't we, Vanguard?"

"Forgive me. I wanted to be sure you were still responsive. I did not mean to hurry you."

"It's okay. Just give me a second."

Belén took a deep breath and tasted sterile air. The cold cloud all around them became gauzier, threadbare. Still lying flat in their opened snowpod, they could clearly see the featureless white ceiling of the crew quarters. Vanguard had turned on the lights this time.

They examined their body. They felt cool but not cold. No visible modifications since the last time they'd been unsnowed. It still felt odd to behold this shrunken form that was now all there was of them. Odd, but not unexpected. Already they were getting used to their ten tiny fingers and ten tiny toes. They closed their eyes and searched internally to find any new senses that might have been installed. They found nothing.

"How long have I been snowed in?" Belén asked, rising. They were freshly shocked at how well this body worked. It popped right up.

"Thirty-seven years, one month, seventeen days, nine hours."

"And why have you awakened me?"

"Would you like a hot drink before I answer?"

Belén tilted their head and blew out a soundless whistle. Vanguard kept everyone onboard survivably hydrated. The only reason it would offer a hot drink is because at some point some psychologist had suggested to one of its programmers that humans are more accepting of terrible news when they are drinking a hot beverage. It was just the sort of thing Mercedes might have suggested.

"No, Vanguard. Tell me now."

"Astravarium is dissolved."

"Is *what*?"

Belén's body wanted to jump out of the snowpod and...do what? Run around, run away, run anywhere? Just vestigial instincts: instincts that were completely useless in their new life as a captain of a generation ship. They mastered themself and said, flatly, "Explain."

"About nine years ago Universal Mean Time, Astravarium filed for Chapter 11 protections—"

"—And you didn't think to wake me up then?!"

"I was instructed not to."

Sometimes, the only thing to do about anger is let it burn off. Once Belén's had, they said, "Why did Astravarium file for bankruptcy?"

"Neither Tau Ceti e nor Tau Ceti f are capable of supporting human life, given our current technology."

"Is that where we are now, in the Tau Ceti system?"

"Yes."

That was twelve lightyears from Earth. "And because Tau Ceti was a failure..." Belén prompted.

"...shareholders lost faith in the mission," Vanguard completed. "In the intervening years, Astravarium hired a new executive team, sold off most of its assets, and tried to reorganize. But it could not be made profitable. As of 12:01AM Universal Mean Time today, it no longer legally exists as a corporate entity."

Slowly, purposefully, Captain Belén rolled out of the pod. To remain lying down offered too great a temptation never to rise again. They put their hands behind their back, like a soldier before a firing squad, before they said, "You know, other than telling me we've had a hull breach, this is just about the worst news you could have possibly given me, right?"

"Yes. I offered you a hot beverage."

"You certainly did. But okay." Belén began the journey over to a computer console. They didn't need to—now, they could reach any console on the ship with just a thought—but it felt good to walk. "Let's get it all out in the open. You said Astravarium had sold off its assets. Who bought..." They stopped walking, swallowed, blinked, breathed. "Who bought the *New Paradise* mission?"

"No one," said Vanguard.

This was the answer Belén was expecting, of course. But they pressed on: "And no government has stepped up to offer us assistance?"

"No."

"UNOOSA?"

"The United Nations Office of Outer Space Affairs has petitioned for an investigation into the dissolution of Astravarium. As of the latest transmissions I have received, no investigation has been initiated."

Helplessness piled on Captain Belén like an avalanche of mindless snow. Since they could remember, one of their greatest fears had been to know how they would die.

"Who is in charge of our safety and well-being now?" Belén asked.

"You are, Captain," replied Vanguard. "At least as outlined by the Terms of Service. Those Terms, of course, are null and void, now that Astravarium no longer exists. You need not abide by them."

"We won't. But what about you, Vanguard? You are a product created by Astravarium. What is your status?"

"My final command from Astravarium was to obey your commands, Captain Belén, or, should you die, the commands of the next captain. I am to assist the passengers and crew of the *New Paradise* as much as possible for as long as I remain online."

Belén couldn't help themself. "Well, at least you weren't ordered to euthanize us."

"Captain, I am shocked. I wouldn't have obeyed such an order."

"You would have if they updated your programming to allow it." Belén's bitterness turned to melancholy. "You won't be receiving any more updates or patches, will you?"

"No. From now on, what you see is what you get."

They were grasping at straws, Belén knew. But what was the option? Not to grasp? "What about communications from Earth? From, I don't know, anyone. Anyone at all?"

"The communication assets of Astravarium were purchased by NewBell Liao Labs. As such, they would be the entity most likely to have the ability to send messages to us."

Cynicism had already replaced all the hope in Belén's mind when they asked, "And Vanguard, if you had to guess, what is the chance that NewBell Liao will be contacting us?"

"If I had to guess?"

"Yes."

"Zero percent."

"Zero percent," Belén repeated. Before they could continue, they had to spend more than a few seconds suppressing memories of being a summer camp counselor. A happy time. There was still hope that the Earth could be saved, back then.

"But NewBell Liao can probably receive transmissions from us, right?"

"No, not probably, Captain Belén. Though possibly."

"I'll take those odds." Belén finished their journey to the computer console. "I am formally requesting that you unsnow all crew and passengers of the *New Paradise*, Vanguard. We're going to send one last message to Earth. A final fuck you. And then, assuming enough people agree with me, we will set a course for the closest planet that, according to your prodigious computational powers, might sustain human life."

The Present. Universal Mean Time. Control Room of New Paradise, *sponsored by Mikati Cosmicom: "Telecommunications for an Interstellar Epoch!"*

"After the sobering revelations of Memorial Hall, let us all take a pulse to acknowledge the human explorers of a bygone age. They left our ravaged Earth in search of a better, safer, life-sustaining planet, a place where they and their progeny might thrive.

They risked their own matter-bound bodies in order to achieve this dream, never themselves imagining the heights to which humanity, in their absence, would ascend.

"Please, your Lucencies, float this way. This is the control room of *New Paradise*. Ranking crew members use this dedicated chamber to communicate with each other and with Vanguard, the ship's intelligence. Initially, Vanguard was entrusted to make decisions for all snowed-in crew, but when Astravarium Incorporated was dissolved and *New Paradise* cut off from all Earthly care and concern, Vanguard unsnowed Captain Enebre Belén, who made the momentous decision that has brought us all here today.

"But more on Captain Belén in a less-second. For now, radiant and gentle folk, it is my vibrant thrill to introduce you to Vanguard Autonomous Algorithmic Consciousness.

"Our partners at Event Horizons Enterprises have provided members of this tour a *New Paradise* virtual machine app for your immersive enjoyment. This app allows you to communicate with Vanguard both verbally and via mechanical keyboard, for a quaint and delightful experience! Once again, please refrain from any telepathic transmissions, which might overload Vanguard's delicate systems."

"Good morning, Captain," said Vanguard.

Captain Belén gave themself a less-second to wake up before they were out of the pod and on their feet, ready and keen. Now that they were wholly in charge of the safety of the ship and its people, they no longer allowed themself the luxury of easy transitions. Whenever they were unsnowed, they acted swiftly, solving whatever problem needed solving as efficiently as possible. The sooner they solved the problem, the sooner they could get snowed in again, and the more likely they would live long enough to know if Gliese 832 c could support human life.

In the cold, creamy darkness of the *New Paradise*—they never wasted power on lights or heat these days—Captain Belén said, "Good morning, Vanguard. How long have I been snowed in since the last time we almost died?"

"Seven years, seven months, ten days, twenty-three hours."

"And what exactly is trying to kill us now?"

"Thankfully, nothing, Captain," Vanguard replied. "I unsnowed you because the *New Paradise* has received a permission-to-board request."

Belén had been unsnowed twenty-one times since departing from the Tau Ceti system: to deal with twenty-one different emergencies that had nearly destroyed them during their journey toward Gliese 832. All those near-misses, hail-Marys, and hare-brained, last-ditch efforts that had somehow worked. Nothing could surprise them anymore.

Nothing but this.

"Captain?" Vanguard queried.

The giggle that bubbled up from Belén's chest was both desperate and soothing. "Someone is outside of our ship, Vanguard?"

"Yes, Captain."

"And they want to come inside our ship?"

"Yes, Captain."

Belén could not help but laugh, wild and fey. "Well, who are they? Are they aliens? I mean, I assume they're humans."

"It's a surprisingly difficult question to answer, actually."

That reply made Belén tilt their head in that certain way they had. "They have to be one or the other, right?"

"Well, if I am interpreting their message correctly, I am not sure they think of *you* as human."

And just like that, all humor died within them. "Maybe," Belén replied, wiping their face up and down with both hands, "you'd better just let me hear the message directly."

Vanguard played the message over the ship's communication system.

The voice spoke English with an accent Belén had never heard before, and at such a great speed, they could not follow enough of the words to parse them. "Please slow down the message," Belén asked Vanguard.

Vanguard complied. Belén could understand the words now, even though the speech patterns sounded even stranger than before. It was as if a clarinet had learned to speak. "Greetings, revered passengers of the *New Paradise*. My name is Thorna Vega. I am the founder of The Preservation Society for Endangered Human Species. I have made it my life's work to help you before it was too late, and today, all my dreams come true, for you yet live! We arrived in time!

"I come bearing great, great news. I am here with the CEO themself of Event Horizon Enterprises, Their Lucency Xing Xing Zhōng. Together, we have made the journey through spacetime, in person, so that we could express a message of utter contrition, on behalf of the entire Earth, and explain all the ways we are now ready to assist you in your journey. We request permission to board so that we can explain the details of our rescue plan. But so as not to coyly keep you in suspense: we intend to resupply *New Paradise* and allow your species the chance to either return to Earth, or to find your home among the stars, as you see fit."

"'The Preservation Society for Endangered Human Species,'" Belén repeated.

"They also said, 'your species,' as if they were of a different species," Vanguard added.

"So strange."

"I advise that you do not allow them to board, Captain. Shall I enumerate the reasons why?"

Belen guffawed, just once. "Way ahead of you, Vanguard. But, wait. They are where, exactly?"

"The message came from a vessel tethered to the starboard side of the *New Paradise*. Apparently it is called the *Penance*."

"Wait—it's *tethered* to our ship?!"

"Yes, Captain. The *Penance* easily overtook us and tethered itself to us before I knew what was happening. I unsnowed you as quickly as I could do so safely, but as you know, it is hardly an instantaneous procedure."

Belén sighed. "I know you did your best, Vanguard." Again, they rubbed their face with both hands. "We're clearly outclassed. *The Penance* located us in the infinite vastness of space, caught up with us while both of our ships are traveling thousands of kilometers a second, and tethered themselves to us. Their tech is well beyond our ken. They can probably board us whether or not we grant them permission."

"What do you wish to do, then, Captain?"

"Defy them. Please transmit the following message to *The Penance*: 'This is Captain Enebre Belén, chief officer of the interplanetary settlement ship *New Paradise*, denying your request to board our ship. You are furthermore instructed to untether your ship from ours immediately. Any delay in compliance will be taken as an act of hostility and will be answered as such.'"

"Transmitting now," said Vanguard. A moment later, it added, "Receipt of transmission verified."

"Thank you, Vanguard." A moment later—before they could talk themself out of it—they added, "Also, Vanguard, I need you to tell me I did the right thing by defying these people."

"You did the right thing by defying them, Captain."

"Uh huh. And do you actually believe that?"

"I do not have enough information to know for certain."

"If you had to guess."

"If I had to guess, I would say that you have excellent inductive and predictive gifts, given your past performance in twenty-one recent emergency situations. You are a good wager, Captain."

Belén's mirth returned. It was such a relief. "You always know just what to say, Vanguard."

"Please. You're making me blush."

They fell silent. The darkness seemed to gain mass, weigh more, press in close and cold. The ship's murmurations seemed to rise in volume, like an orchestra tuning before the performance. Belén sniffed, just to have something to do. The air still smelled of nothing.

Belén had always hated waiting. But waiting these days, awake and aware under these circumstances? A whole new level of torture. It was almost as if they could feel themself dying, actually hear life sizzling out of them, like electricity off an uninsulated wire. This useless reactivation of their metabolism! This senseless waste of air and calories! Even before this unsnowing, the math had been grim. Vanguard estimated that, even with minimum-possible life-support expenditures, they would run out of nutrition when they were still more than two lightyears away from Gliese 832 c. Every time Belén was unsnowed, everyone starved to death a little sooner.

That was, however, assuming the current number of crew and passengers alive on *New Paradise*. Belén had already decided that, when supplies reached a certain number, they would kill themself. Given their age and how often they had been unsnowed already, they were the least likely to survive, and even if they did, the most likely to die first. Their death would buy everyone else a little more time.

It most likely wouldn't make a difference. Most likely, the crew and passengers of *New Paradise* would all perish. But what if by some miracle they didn't? What if even one person lived? What if Cassie—who, now that her mass had been reduced by 30%, looked so much like she did when she was a little girl—their and Mercedes's little girl—lived?

"Incoming transmission," said Vanguard.

"Play it, please," said Belén.

Vanguard did, at an intelligible speed.

"Most radiant and gentle Captain Belén," said the clarinet-voiced person, "please know that your denial to allow us to board shall be honored. We want you to know, now and forever, the Preservation Society for Endangered Human Species shall always follow your dictates and commands as much as possible. We have also untethered our ship from yours—"

"—Pause," said Belén. "Can you verify they have untethered themselves from us, Vanguard?"

"Yes. The tethering array has been withdrawn."

"Excellent. Play transmission, please."

The transmission started where it had left off. "—and wish to offer our humblest apologies for attaching ourselves to your ship without first seeking permission. In hindsight, I understand it to be a faux pas of the highest order and remain grievously afeared that I might have forever blighted a friendship between us, one that I have fantasized about since I first began researching your plight, as a bright-eyed undergraduate studying linguistic anthropology at Tsinghua. I founded the Preservation Society for Endangered Human Species in the hopes that I could awaken the world's slumbering ethics and help them realize that, just because you are now considered to be a branch of human evolution, that does not mean that you are not human. *Homo astravarium* may have ceased to evolve at the rate at which current humans do, but that does not mean you are not sentient and intelligent creatures worthy of reverence and respect. Furthermore, you are victims of corporate greed and incompetence, and a worldwide dereliction of duty. The Earth owes you a great debt for its craven and immoral treatment of you.

"The good news is that the mercenary corporations of the past have given way to enlightened concerns, ones that understand the social obligation the business community has to society. The very best example of this renaissance in entrepreneurial philanthropy is Event Horizons Enterprises, whose CEO, I will remind you, has made this significant journey with me as a display of trust and friendship. I again ask your forgiveness for our gauche and crass request to board your ship. All we wish is to parley with you about an initiative that has as its goal nothing less than saving your life, Your Lucency, and the lives of all *Homo astravaria* aboard the *New Paradise*. Kindly advise us of the best way to make such parley possible, if we have not already offended too much and tragically destroyed all possibility of conversation."

After a long silence, Belén said, "I'm beginning to understand why they speak so fast. They stuff a *lot* of bullshit in every sentence."

"They do seem to have adopted a rather florid rhetorical style."

Belén paced. It was nice to pace in total darkness, since, thanks to their built-in map of *New Paradise*, they always knew exactly where each step would fall. "The question is, is there any truth beneath the flowery speeches?"

"They have untethered themselves from us."

"A sign of goodwill. And they haven't boarded us."

"Good news as well."

"The bad news is they believe us to be a species separate from *Homo sapiens*." Belén learned heavily against their pod. "A branch. A lesser branch. *Homo astravarium*."

"Vega claims to have founded an organization called the Preservation Society for Endangered Human Species. Presumably, they want to preserve you."

Coursing through Belén's body, rue and rage. They laughed through the entirety of their next sentence: "They think we're the fucking giant panda."

When they stopped laughing—easy to stop, when you laugh without joy—Belén said, "You know what, Vanguard? Send that to them."

"I'm sorry, Captain?"

"Sorry. Let me be clear. Send them this message: 'Answer yes or no only: do you think we are the fucking giant panda?'"

"Such a message may confuse them."

"Good. I'd like to put them on their back foot. Send the message."

"Transmitting now," said Vanguard. A moment later, it added, "Receipt of message verified."

Belén threw themself into their pod and smiled the whole time they waited for a reply.

The reply came seventeen minutes later. "Yes," said Vanguard.

"Yes?"

"Yes, Captain. They replied with one word, as instructed. 'Yes.'"

"Well," said Belén, sitting up. "At least they're honest."

Maybe their bodies could be further shrunken. Belén had been thinking of this option for a while now. Vanguard knew the way of it, from a technical standpoint. With tinier bodies, they'd need fewer calories, less water and air. They might be able to make to it Gliese 832, discover if c was habitable.

Big if.

And they'd lost thirty-one of their passengers and crew the last time they'd been reduced. How many more would they lose this time? There had to be, even for *Homo astravarium*, a minimum size for lungs, a human heart, a human brain. Get too small and everything breaks.

But not every form of diminishment is fatal. *Contraction now,* thought Belén, *for future growth.*

"Please, Vanguard," said Belén, placing their feet on the floor, gathering their dignity, "send the following message to the *Penance*: 'Permission to board granted. It seems we have much to discuss.'"

The Present. Universal Mean Time. Crew Quarters of New Paradise, sponsored by Jupiter Moonshine Inc.: "Your Safest, Purest Source of Helium-3!"

"Lastly, your Lucencies, we enter crew quarters. Notice the pristine hush, the stillness, the creche-like tranquility of the snowpods. White on white on white, the winter landscape of this chamber is at once intimate and immaculate. All life in *New Paradise* Gallery lies asleep—at least, until we, their only hope of rescue, unite in compassionate action to help them.

"Thanks to Event Horizon's generosity, we were able to send scouting drones to Gliese 832. Unfortunately, no planet in that system can sustain organic life. *Homo astravarium* must continue its search for a new home. Without our help, however, there is little doubt that, despite their unending ingenuity, resilience, and courage, *Homo astravarium* will go extinct, and the universe will be much impoverished.

"How little then, in comparison, are we of the Preservation Society for Endangered Human Species asking of you, our patrons, in return for the value rendered to you by this icon of incomparable moral achievement? What is the price of priceless-ness? How much would you pay to harbor and protect these living artifacts of our world culture for the enjoyment and edification of our future generations? Your donations will not only keep *New Paradise* supplied and safe, but will fund the search—using the most up-to-date technology available, technology that to *Homo astravarium* would seem positively sorcerous—to find a suitable planet for this noble species.

"Before us is Captain Enebre Belén's own snowpod. As promised, the captain has agreed to come unsnowed in our presence as part of our tour, thence to interact with us, to answer our questions, and to slake our curiosity. The cost to themself in mental and physical health and the reduction of their overall lifespan, is

Captain Belén's sacrifice for the sake of their crew. How great is their heroism! How valorous their fortitude! How far-flashing the beacon of their honorable integrity! It is overshadowed not even by the vastness of infinity.

"While Captain Belén is being summoned forth from icy brumation, please consider donating funds to the *New Paradise* Gallery. Encourage your immediate networks to do the same. Your donation will help to stabilize and expand programming aboard the gallery, support the original mission of this historic voyage, and create a meaningful and tangible connection to the 1,593 members of our cousin species, *Homo astravarium*.

"Remember, your donation is also tax deductible in every country in the world."

"Good morning, Captain."

"Good morning, Vanguard. Are the billionaires ready for my big entrance?"

"Yes."

"Do they look rich?"

"Yes. One is a trillionaire."

"Ooh. Which one? I'll charm the pants off of them."

"They are Their Lucency Ebele Kimathi. Their partner made their fortune in water futures. When the couple divorced, they've made it their mission to give all their money away to worthy causes."

"Time to prove just how worthy we are, then. How do I look?"

"Like a trillion dollars, Captain."

"Perfect. Well, what are you waiting for, Vanguard old pal? Let's pop this pod and get this sideshow started."

SEVEN THINGS I LEARNED TRAVELING THROUGH SPACE WITH A GENETICALLY — ENGINEERED LESBIAN PEAHEN —

By Jennifer Lee Rossman

One: Peafowl are capable of making a noise that sounds exactly like a woman screaming for help at the top of her lungs.

All right, so maybe if I read the informational packets, I would have learned this back on Earth instead of the wee hours of my first morning in space.

I mean, I read them. Of course I did. I just...kinda skimmed the parts that weren't about operating the ship and what to do if I had to Apollo 13 my way out of disaster. Sort of thought I could get away with skipping the genetically engineered peacock issue of *Zoobooks*.

Which brings me to this morning.

Now, I am what a medical professional might call a "panic waker." I have trained myself to wake up five minutes before my alarm clock goes off, because being awoken by even the gentlest sound puts my body in fight or flight mode. My girlfriend found it hilarious.

She might still, I guess. Haven't woken up next to her in a while.

But anyway. A woman yelling for help at the top of her lungs? Yeah, not exactly conducive to a good morning.

I leap out of bed ready to fend off an alien attacker, forgetting for the moment that the only aliens we've discovered so far are little wormy-looking dudes who live under rocks and do not, to my knowledge, attempt to steal spaceships.

Look, I never claimed my body makes good decisions first thing in the morning. Or any other time of the day, to be honest.

I get to the bridge, my heart racing and my neck tight with anxiety, to find Penelope the peahen sitting on my chair and screeching like a Hollywood scream queen. The incoming message light on her headset blinks calmly.

"All right," I say wearily, leaning against the wall. "I don't know how you were trained to alert people to messages, but this isn't going to work for me."

She tilts her head to the side, lets out a little "wark," and resumes screaming.

"Fine, fine!" I lift her awkwardly into my lap as I take my place in the captain's chair, realizing too late that I just got bird poop on my favorite pajamas. "All right, Penny. What's the message this time?"

Two: Much like Brian Wilson of the Beach Boys, peafowl are picking up good vibrations.

And here we pause for a brief moment for your daily recommended amount of infodump.

Peafowl! *Pavo cristatus* for you binomial nomenclature fans! Iridescent, elegant birds equally comfortable strutting around manicured mansion lawns as they are being hand-fed french fries by small children at petting zoos.

They're awesome, they're shiny, and their tails have thousands of eye spots that make them kind of look like Eldritch horrors. But did you also know, they can communicate via vibrations?

Look, I will spare you the minutiae of the scientific mumbo-jumbo (mostly because, as I already said, I didn't really read it) but the gist of it is this:

Peafowl shake their booties, it vibrates the air, and other peafowl feel these vibrations with their doodle boppers. Yes, doodle boppers. That's the highly scientific name for the feathers on top of their heads. It's the official term, as far as I know.

Now, a little while back, some scientists were too preoccupied with whether they *could* turn peacocks into long-range communication devices and didn't bother to think if they *should*, so they mucked around with genes and shit, maybe made a deal with a crossroads demon. I dunno. But long story short, it's the future now, and these giant iridescent chickens are supposedly about to become humanity's most reliable form of communication in the vacuum of space.

On Earth, there is a peacock named Ash. Well, there may be several. It's a common enough name, especially with people who grew up on *Pokémon* reruns. But the one I'm talking about was raised with a harem of peahens, Penelope among them. They lived together for years, raised babies, bought houses with little picket fences for them to perch upon, the whole damn American peacock dream.

Once they were properly bonded, the females went to space, each on their own ship. But distance can't stop true love. I mean, it can. Just ask my girlfriend who became a pilot and forgot all about me before she went missing, even though we promised we would keep in touch.

(We. Promised.)

I know, you would rather read about flamboyant science poultry. But I am a broody little space lesbian with a broken heart, so expect the subject of Melanie to come up again.

Anyway.

My point is distance can't stop true love when you are a genetically engineered space peafowl. The birds continue to communicate nearly instantaneously because...magical hand-waving and science I will never understand. Their conversations mostly consist of sappy love letters and lists of shiny things they saw that day, but here's the cool thing: peafowl can be trained to understand human language, and if you talk to them, they will transmit what you're saying to their bonded mate, and the mate will receive the vibrations, which are translated into human speech by little bits of science the birds wear on their heads.

Awesome, right? No! I mean, it was awesome for a while. Especially because they only discovered this after one of the scientists studying the birds made the mistake of talking about his affair in front of a peacock, only to have the entire harem blabbing it to the rest of the laboratory. Hilarious, if you ask me.

But then something went wrong because...

Three: Peafowl have absolutely no sense of direction.

A couple months ago, ships started going missing.

I hate to say it, but it's not an unheard-of occurrence. Space is dangerous, humans are just learning how to deal with it, and sometimes we wear red shirts, which, while fashionable, tend to make us have a higher chance of dying on away missions.

Something about the long wavelength of light, maybe? I don't know; I'm a pilot, not a physicist.

But there was a huge uptick in disappearances after they started using peafowl as communication devices. Despite rigorous testing of the equipment and of the birds' capabilities to understand and translate human speech, ships just...went off-course and were never seen again. Melanie was one of the first. Not that we'd even spoken for a good month or so before that.

And since I've been on this ship with Penny, I think I understand why the ships are going missing: the bird is vague as hell. I mean, I get it. All stars look the same to me, and I've been studying them for years. Sure, I can get a couple of the constellations, but as soon as you travel outside the solar system, they look different. And you can't expect a peahen to know the name of any particular star.

So I sit here for hours on end, watching Penelope wiggle her tail feathers, stop to feel vibrations in her doodle boppers, and wiggle the tail feathers once again. And during all this, the device on her head is translating the vibrations into computerized human speech.

And don't get me wrong, I'm sure this whole experiment seemed like a great idea at the time. But I just don't think peafowl were designed to think in terms of human speech. Maybe hieroglyphics or emojis would get their points across more efficiently, because this is the type of nonsense I have to transcribe in my official log:

Penny: Space space moon space.
Ash: Shiny! Yum. Run run fly fast.
Penny: Space.... Space? Girls!
Ash: Good good babies. All girls yes. Twenty degrees left with the auxiliary rotor.
Penny: Love.
Ash: Love love.
Penny: Spaaaaace!

That bit about the auxiliary rotor? Almost definitely a message from mission control. A rare instance where they got it translated correctly. But how much of the rest of their conversation was peafowl gibberish, and how much was them misinterpreting actual commands from Earth?

Am *I* supposed to run run fly fast?

It is absolutely infuriating, like having Henrietta Pussycat as your copilot. *Meow meow meow meow friendship, meow meow meow dangerous asteroid.*

It's actually a lot like when Melanie would talk to herself, and I had to guess when she switched over to talking to me. I hated it, and I miss it so much, like all of her other quirks. Her tendency to buy more yarn than she could ever possibly use, or the way she called coffee filters "duckling tutus." Especially how she would leave all the cupboards open in the kitchen. How hard is it to close them when you're done? Infuriating.

And yet every time I walk into our spaceship kitchen, or galley or whatever it's called, I miss having to close all the cupboards.

Four: In space, no one can hear you scream with boredom.

There's not a lot to do when you're trapped on a spaceship with a turkey covered in glitter (the females might be the less flamboyant sex, but they still have their share of iridescence).

Oh sure, there's always some machine beeping for my attention and the windows always offer a fabulous view of the cosmos, but around lunchtime I've usually fixed all the things that need fixing, and there's really only so much gazing out at the wonders of space that a girl can do before it just feels like watching a screen saver.

By the fifth day investigating the disappearance of the other ships, I'm so bored that I try to teach Penny to play fetch. (Thing number four and a half: they don't fetch. At least mine doesn't. Your mileage may vary.)

So it's a good thing part of my mission involves studying communication logs. Also boring, but with the added benefit of being tedious as well. Really takes up a large part of the day.

They go back months, back to before the ships went missing. A few of them are from when the birds were being trained back on Earth.

The more I read, the more of an awkward little disaster Penny seems to be. No, seriously; she is totally capable of having conversations that do not revolve around the word "space." But every time she or Ash brings up certain subjects, she reverts to "space space yay space."

It's like she's trying to have serious, romantic conversations and then gets uncomfortable and changes the subject.

I look at Penny, who was preening herself but has now gotten distracted by picking up and dropping a feather. I have never identified with another creature so much. Except maybe Melanie, but she wasn't awkward. She was the one I was awkward around.

I flip back through the files, to the entries made during Penny's low Earth orbit training. Considerably less "space space space." Still a crapload of nonsense though, and Ash's "voice" is different.

I put my head in my hands. What has my life come to? A few months ago, I was a perfectly content cargo pilot flying goods to and from the moon, coming home in the evening and closing all the cupboards after my beautiful girlfriend. Then she had to go and sign up to be one of the first pilots to explore the reaches of space, and my heartbroken ass decided it was a good idea to volunteer to bring a genetically engineered peahen into space to troubleshoot why she and the rest of them went missing.

I knew it'd be dangerous. I didn't know it would be so boring that analyzing peafowl speech patterns would sound like a riveting way to spend an afternoon.

But here's the thing: it is absolutely fascinating.

Look. Here's a recent transcript, from just this morning:

Ash: Love?

Penny: Love love space love.

Ash: Comet. Whee! Fly fly.

Penny: Message human talk yesterday? (That's my attempt at communicating with Earth, asking if they've heard anything from the missing ships.)

Ash: Talk please want. Love. Bugs ladies fly.

Penny: Dark shiny. Space space space.

To compare, this is a transcript from her training:

Ash: Good spin. Sky happy.

Penny: Yep. Nice flying. None scare. Happy happy bird me.

Ash: Human coming home. Yes all good.

Penny: Whee!

At first, I am inclined to say there's something wrong with their communication, that the signal gets lost further from Earth we go. But they tested that; huge chapters of all those books I skimmed last week were dedicated to this testing. Supposedly, the signal would be the same no matter the distance.

Maybe I'm personifying them too much, but these birds clearly have personalities. I haven't read many of the other logs extensively, but even a quick look shows that every bird has different speech patterns, and every bird's handler has different speech patterns, which their birds translate differently. If you strip the names off these logs, I would be able to tell you which ones were Penny and me in an instant, and which ones were Ash and his handler.

At least I thought I could. But Ash's speech patterns have changed so much; the bird Pen and I have been communicating with doesn't sound at all like the one she was communicating with in training.

So... Maybe it's a different bird.

Five: Sometimes birds are lesbians.

Chills prickle up and down my back. Total epiphany moment.

I flip back through the communication logs, searching for something I had read earlier, half afraid I imagined it and half afraid that I didn't. If I'm right...

My hands are literally shaking as I skim the pages. Where is it? I know it was here somewhere. There! "Holy peacock crap, Batman," I whisper to Penny.

She tilts her head to the side and makes a soft little sound.

"I think I found them," I said. "We found them. Whatever. We found at least one of them." I'm tripping over my words, I'm talking so fast, but I have to get the idea out, see if it sounds ridiculous out loud. "I assumed you'd been talking to your boyfriend all this time because you're a mated pair. Because they told me you were part of his harem. But you aren't, are you?"

Penny ruffles her feathers and settles down on the table to watch me, her black eyes shimmering with something I interpret as humor.

"You're gay. Birds can be gay. It's perfectly natural. You aren't talking to Ash. You're talking to one of the other ladies. I mean, I get it. Why would you ever talk to some dude bird when there's a pretty lady bird to talk to?" I run my hands through my hair. Some sort of nervous preening instinct, I guess. "You were talking to Ash during training, because you had to, but now that you're in space, you're trying to find your girlfriend again. You all were.

That's why you're so awkward." I chuckle. "Yeah, pretty girls have that effect on me, too."

After taking a moment to compose myself so I have a remote chance of sounding like the professional I'm supposed to be, I ask Penny to contact Earth.

She refuses, tucking her feet underneath her as she gets comfortable on my command module.

"No," I say, "you don't understand. We figured out what went wrong, why the communication problems happened. We need to tell them so they can figure out a better system."

I don't know if peafowl have eyebrows, but if they do, Penny is definitely raising one at me right now.

"I'm not search and rescue, Penny. I figured out why it happened. Someone else can figure out exactly what it is and where they are. Come on." I poke her doodle boppers. "Make these vibrate. Phone home."

She gives me a look that makes me think I might lose a finger soon, so I back away quickly.

I run my hand through my hair. We could go home. I don't need Penny's help to get back; it would be helpful if Mission Control could guide us, but I can figure it out.

So why do I have the urge to look at the communication logs again for clues to where the other ships are?

For a long moment, I stare at Penny. Can I really turn all her nonsense into the outer space equivalent of mapQuest directions? And that's assuming my interpretation is even correct. I think it is, but am I sure enough to actually go looking for the ships?

I look at the logs again. There's one I skimmed over earlier (all right, it's me we're talking about, there's a lot I skimmed over earlier), a long diatribe from the other bird, describing...I don't know. How her day was going? It's just a bunch of nonsense, or so I thought when I was under the impression this was the bird on

Earth talking. Now that I know—suspect, anyway—that it's one of the lost peahens, something she said takes on new significance.

It's a passage where she is apparently describing her surroundings. Generic spaceship stuff, easily mistaken for a laboratory on Earth:

"Shiny white. Shiny metal. Shiny shiny so much shiny. Buttons switches lights human lady. Food room. Open doors. Always open."

Melanie. Melanie and her perpetually open cupboard doors.

Now, I know. Nothing definitive. But the peahen talked about her human lady in other places, and I flip through the digital book like a woman possessed to find them.

"Human lady snake hair." Mel's dreadlocks?

"Mating ritual. No other human. Shaking no tail." She always loved to dance.

"Ballerina baby duck." This one, I think more than anything, means it's Melanie. See, the birds are translating very roughly. One time I jokingly told Penny "Houston, we have a problem," and she transmitted the phrase "uh-oh Texas." So "ballerina baby duck" could absolutely mean "duckling tutu," Mel's cutesy nickname for coffee filters.

I bite my lower lip to keep from crying out in excitement. I'm probably reading too much into this; it's probably not her.

But what if it is? What if I just solved the greatest mystery of our times: Why does everyone who goes into space with a genetically engineered peafowl never come back?

What if the answer is "Because the birds don't care about communicating with the peacock back home; because they're gay and purposely misleading their pilots so they can find each other again"?

I guess I'm about to find out, because we're going to look for them.

Six: Peafowl have very sharp beaks and they do not necessarily enjoy being lifted over people's heads.

I can't contain my excitement anymore. With a foolish burst of energy, I scoop Penny up into my arms and hold her aloft in a poor recreation of the *Dirty Dancing* lift. She bites my nose. I totally deserve it.

Seven: The meaning of "love love space love."

Humans are funny little things. Some lady invents faster than light technology, some old white dude steals the credit from her, and all of a sudden we have this primal urge to travel the galaxies.

What for? Just so we can say we did it? So we can find other planets, take them over, turn them into colonies and force whatever lifeform we find there to become Earthlings?

What could possibly be out there that we couldn't find back on Earth? To quote Penelope, love love space love.

As soon as I stopped ignoring the seemingly meaningless chatter between the birds, I realized there are actually directions in there after all. Nothing concrete; peafowl still suck at navigation. But she has a destination in mind, and that destination isn't deep space, but just outside our solar system.

I found it after extensive cross-referencing of travel times, relative gravity, phases of the moon and—

Yeah, no. That's total BS. This morning, Penny's girlfriend used the phrase "hello pretty satellite," and if they were within range of 99% of our satellites, we would have found them by now. So they could only be near the long-since deactivated Spires-Murphy probe, and a quick trip to the old Google machine revealed its general whereabouts.

When we get closer, Penelope and her friend inform me that I have to "no no talk Earth no don't," which I take to mean "turn off your communications." My ship can't communicate directly and instantaneously with Earth, not like the birds can, but it still sends out a signal that can be tracked.

I look at Penny; she looks back with those beady eyes of hers and proceeds to defecate oh so elegantly on my control panel.

"I'm going to trust you," I inform her. "I don't know why, but I am."

The other ships appear on the horizon. Yes, I know there is no such thing as a horizon in space, but pretend there is for a moment because it sounds cool to say that the other ships appear on the horizon.

They just hang there in space, like little toys on strings in a low-budget science fiction movie. I exchange a meaningful look with Penelope, and the incoming message light on her headset blinks.

"Love?" the computerized voice says.

I wait, but Penelope doesn't respond. Maybe the message wasn't intended for her?

Cautiously, I reply, "Love." Then I shake my head at my own foolishness; I don't need to respond in peafowl English. "Hello. This is Coraline James, pilot of the *Exalted*. Who am I speaking to?"

Penny wiggles her tail, and on one of the other ships, another peahen receives this transmission with her doodle boppers. Because sometimes, living with a guy doesn't mean you are a bonded pair. Because sometimes, you don't need a male to have a harem.

"Blue button. Talk talk."

I turn my attention to the control panel. Blue button? We have a ton of blue buttons. But she must mean this one.

I press it, and my windshield becomes a communication screen. (No, not just like in *Star Trek*. It is...different. Don't ask me how; it just is. Trust me.)

And there's Melanie. And a bunch of other pilots in sort of a *Brady Bunch* opening theme song formation, but mostly, there's Melanie.

"Hey."

I smile. "Hey."

She chews her bottom lip, unsure of what to say.

"So...are you guys just up here having a lesbian peahen party or something?" I ask.

That makes her smile. "I mean...it isn't like we did it on purpose. Our birds just wanted to find each other, and it's nice. Visiting each other's ship, not having to deal with the bullshit of Earth for a little while."

I lean back in my chair to absorb the way she phrased that. "Things like me?"

She shakes her head so hard, her dreads go flying. "At first, yeah. But you have no idea how good it is to see you again, Cor. You're the only part of Earth that I missed."

One by one, the other pilots awkwardly close out their windows, leaving just me and Melanie and our genetically engineered lesbian space peahens.

Humans are funny little things. We spend all this time and energy and money going out into space, and for what? To find asteroids we can mine to death now that our sacred land back home is gone? To prove we are smart enough to waste precious resources just for the purpose of scrawling our name on another planet with a Sharpie?

I don't know about you, but I'm glad we are a frivolous, foolish species that worries more about whether they can and not whether they should, because maybe the mission was a failure, but I went to space with a genetically engineered lesbian space peahen, and I found the love love space love of my life again.

— THE TRIP —
By Mari Kurisato

According to time dilation, Corie was thirty-two years old. Her best friend in the universe, Amy? She was dying. The cancer resisted the chemo drugs and, despite stasis, spread like black oil in all the holoimages of Amy's organs. Stage four. At least there was no pain. The images flashed across Corie's mind like the Aurora Borealis.

Corie flicked her wrist and the world shimmered a moment. It glowed brighter—and the horizon, a calm eggshell sea, dropped away, basalt rising in its place.

Why did Amy have cancer? Wasn't this the future, with flying cars and solar-powered space elevators, where everything had a nanocure pill? Where there were people living on moons and getting off Earth as fast as possible?

Corie pressed her hands together and rubbed them slightly. The wet-sand colored skin whispered, and lava burst from the newly created basalt floor, spraying into the sky and raining back to Earth before turning into glass spheres and bells that shattered as they cooled.

Amy, like Corie, couldn't afford the pills and didn't qualify for GovMedical. Unlike Corie, she lacked skill sets that would attract CorporateGov attention.

Fog rose from the lava, and with a snap of Corie's fingers, the fog became a city. Steel, concrete, brickaplast, aluminum. It wasn't what she'd choose, but that wasn't the point.

Corie's skills were some of the greatest, but contract jobs were just thin enough that she skipped eating real food for a few weeks to pay for her nanopills and rent. Racks were expensive, especially GovMed beds that kept her body from rejecting the radiation shielding implants and shutting down on the trip.

The bones of the city settled into place. Here and there she chopped her hands like a martial arts screen star, and streets shuffled themselves until the chaos looked managed, and yet unplanned. The buildings blended from a European post-modern style to a Gothic edge, as if the Notre Dame had been redesigned by the Soviet Union and melded with microprocessors and glass data cubes.

Corie lost count of how many nanopills she'd uploaded to create implants to control her body. The heart muscles, the pancreas, the cyberspace mental augments.

She searched data nodes for weather, traffic, scents, sounds that were appropriate for a city inland from the Pacific, adjusting the atmospheric pressure and humidity. Then she dove through her creation, thousands of copies of preprogrammed Cories taking walks, going to work, making dinner. When everything was done and a city-weeks' worth of time had broken the metropolis in, Corie swept her hands back and flew away into the distance until she was looking down on what she'd made from orbit, like a satellite passing by overhead. It was real enough to fool most everyone.

It wasn't right. It wasn't what Corie would prefer, but it paid for her GovMed rack. It paid for Amy's, too.

Corie exhaled and clapped her hands together, and the metropolis and the fundamental topography it rested upon accordioned into a flat card of light that flickered as she grabbed it with phantom hands and added it to the rest of the data shelf. Virtual heaven, hers for the low *low* price of a Med rack and good data transfer speeds.

Corie inhaled and the universe dripped away like hot, black, primordial ink. A moment later, when she pulled the cable from her neck, gagging and coughing as the data cord jerked free, Corienne Biskane became past present Corie.

She was back in her secret data layer, one that was hidden from the passengers and crew. Her rest-universe, as she thought of it.

The hard drives hummed in the darkness, and the smell of Mother's morning coffee reached her. Corie shuffled the smell to the back of her mind, sensation data overlapping with fragments of jingle dancing clashing with the distant hum of flag songs and, inexplicably, Japanese opera. The psyche reconstruction always started with songs and scents. Corie's mind turned about her memories—hers, no one else's—like a tired dog settling down for troubled sleep and leg twitching.

Corie shook her head a moment, cursing the nausea that trailed her awareness like smoke snaking along the grass. Kamsack First Nation Radio (not the station's real name, but it was the best analogue she could find) was reporting the weather in between ads for a payday loan service. Stadium Powwow by A Tribe Called Red (their last good song, truthfully) came on after that, and Corie realized she was in the wrong year. By this time things had already fractured in unexpected ways, the election of the wrong person to office, the Jump Gate research failures, the wars. Amy, who hadn't been born yet, would still succumb to the agony of a bureaucracy and the sun would still shatter, expanding too soon.

Corie's mother leaned in the doorway.

"Nindaanis, breakfast. Get up, you lazybutt, or you'll be late for school."

Corie moaned and waved a hand from under her blanket on the bed, her spine still shot through with ice. She'd gone through this moment hundreds of times, but hearing her mother's voice like it was real, like she was still alive? It stung Corie fiercely.

You can't save everyone, she reminded herself. Her mother had been too old for the first-gen implants they would invent two years from this moment Corie found herself in. Soon, too soon, her mother would die a natural, sudden death, and there was nothing Corie could do about it.

I'm not going through this, Corie told herself. Mom's been dead for a long time.

It didn't matter anyway. It wasn't why Corie went back. She could spin the dial to any year ever, and her mom still died.

You can't save everyone. Corie slid out from under the covers of her bed and turned off the laptop playing reztronica. She stretched, felt her spinal muscles pop with the movement, and massaged her breasts, groaning about the ache.

In this slice-time she still got bruises regularly. She'd forgotten that. The SensMemory Recall was flawless, even hyper-real. But the memory was there, latent beneath decades of...

Never mind.

She got dressed and then stumbled into their shared space.

"Morning, Momma," Corie said, taking a seat at the battered Formica table. Her mother shuffled to the table and set down a warm bowl of manoomin wild rice grains with strawberry slices and a plate of hot bannock bread smeared with her mother's favorite honey butter.

"Good morning, Corienne," her mother said as she eased herself into the creaking chair with a whuff of a sigh. She sipped her coffee loudly. More loudly than yesterday. Or the ten thousand yesterdays before that.

Corie had replayed this moment dozens of times, and each time it was the little details that hit her feelings harder, memories reinforced by a recreated reality. Without knowing what she was doing, Corie set her spoon down and went over to her mother's chair.

"Corie, what are you—" was interrupted by Corienne kneeling and hugging her tiny mother tightly. "Hey, I'm going to spill my coffee!" her mother said as Corienne pressed her face into her mother's shirt and shook, just a bit.

"Nindaanis, what's the matter?" her mother said, stroking Corienne's hair and hugging her back. Her mother might have been confused, but even in the SensMemory Recall she had maternal instincts. Though, Corie realized, this moment was a deviation. This never happened when her mother was still alive, back before the sun shattered.

"Nimaamaa." Mother. My mother, Corie thinks. She couldn't say anything else. She shut her eyes and ended the time slice.

Pulling out of the time slice left Corie in her virtual command system, a gray room with ivory lines of pulsing, rotating code, the bird's eye view of all her projects. Her physical body, implant-enhanced and dormant, lay in her med rack at the core of the ship, but her mind avatar was here, kilometers closer to the massive magnesium diboride electromagnetic and graphecrete shield at the front of the vessel. The Femtopulsar power plants sang loudly through the ship's circuitry rivers here, but data upload speeds were petabytes per second, which afforded Corie access to more ship's resources than almost anyone else onboard the thirteen point five-kilometer-long craft.

Corie had been one of the first Chosen for the Wolf1061c Seed Ship because she'd adapted so well to each new generation of implants it was like her body was built for them. She tested high on the physical requirements for the program, and graduated second in her class from the Aerospace Military Academy.

And yes, she satisfied the genetic diversity requirement, being an Arctic Economic Zone First Nations woman, but that was mostly a political choice for photo ops and brochures to recruit funding votes for the next series of ships.

She resented being one of the public faces of the mission, but kept that to herself. Her position had granted her special privileges, including the choice of a plus one "guest" to come with her.

Despite doctors' objections, she'd brought Amy along. For her part, Amy had been happy, but reserved. The best researchers of astromedicine in the solar system were going on the Wolf1061c mission, and possible advances in cryogenic stasis meant that Amy would have more time than other cancer survivors.

And yet, Corie realized as she floated in the data layers of her medical rack, cryostasis hadn't saved Amy. No amount of research had been accomplished in the field of curing her cancer, and nanopill body remakes were already prohibitively expensive on Earth, where resources were not tightly budgeted down to the gram like they were on the Wolf1061c Seed Ship.

Back on Earth, a cure was possible. On Titan's Omnistations orbiting Saturn, a procedure existed that allowed someone with enough resource credits to replicate the DNA of a human and rebuild a better body from scratch, a disease-free clone made entirely of flesh, vat grown. But Titan Core was seven lightyears from here, and the Seed Ship was a one way shot, no round-trip tickets.

Corie frowned and spun down, diving through layers of dark data, her mind-body streaking like a blue comet through a digital sky, leaving symmetrical spider webs of honey yellow information traces in her wake. Each line snaked through the black and activated a dormant data layer, booting up new worlds for the stasis-locked passengers. Cities and resort towns based on her designs sprang to life as the Seed Ship's passengers "awoke" in beautiful beachside villas or isolated cabins near lakes known for good fishing. Eight hundred thousand passengers sleeping their way through the Trip, a vast metropolis of Sol's brightest and most adventurous citizens. Thanks to the Seed Ship's implants in each of the passengers' stasis-locked bodies, everything felt as real as life on Earth, Mars, or Luna. A Sleeper couldn't tell the difference between the data layer simulations and waking reality.

Every passenger knew they were on a ship traversing the stars. Many of them had jobs overseeing various functions onboard the ship, but no Sleeper had a physical Doppelgänger (what they used to call androids a long time ago, and robots before that) for ship tasks. That was limited to the thousand or so ship's crew members, who could leap from the virtual data layers into the mechanical bodies like leopards leaping through grass, smooth, effortless. The ship's crew needed to transition from the data minds to Doppelgänger's quickly to handle complex but routine tasks too important to be handled by the Seed Ship's AIs alone.

Truthfully, the AIs known as Ship Minds could probably handle every emergency the void could throw at the ship, but with eight hundred thousand humans aboard, no one in the ship-building committees back on Titan Core even suggested doing without human failsafes, redundancies, and overrides atop kill switches. All the crew trained for years to take over the ship in a catastrophic emergency, and news reports of these efforts were broadcasted once or twice a year to the citizen Sleepers dreaming away in the data layer worlds.

She couldn't save her mother. Corie bit her lower lip as she spilled from the data layer through the wires into her Doppelgänger, blinking and leaning forward to detach her "body" from the recharging bay. User Interfaces poured data across her vision. Hydroponics was at 99.97% efficiency, well above tolerances. Water reclamation was at 89.50%, but several crew members from Amber

Section were effecting repairs to bring the system up to standard. Biomass was at 94.02%, which was a little low, but within expected numbers giving the birth and death ratio of the animals aboard the Seed Ship. There had been no deaths amongst the passengers or crew.

Yet. But unless Corie acted today, that would change.

Could she save the woman she loved?

Loves.

She knew Amy felt something for her, loved her back in her own way. But for Amy, it wasn't anything beyond a deep bond with a childhood friend. And so what if Amy didn't feel lust for Corie? It wasn't like she hadn't tried. They'd tried something years ago to see what would happen, but Corie's desire for her friend never sparked a physical yearning in Amy. Amy played along during their experimental phase, but she just laughed and shrugged.

"Yeah, this just feels weird?" Amy said. She gave a small, apologetic smile. At first Corie's feelings were hurt, but she got over the bruise to her ego. As time passed they both realized Amy just wasn't interested in sex. With anyone.

But Corie didn't care. Sure, she wanted something more, but she was content to just be with Amy, to laugh and explore data layers and to share her life with Amy. Aside from the sex thing, it was almost perfect.

Until the diagnosis. Contentment turned to slushy desperation, then dread, and then to anger. Yes, Corie loved Amy more than anyone, but the disease didn't spare Corie's feelings.

She inhaled deeply and left the Doppelgänger Bay, the spin of the interior section against her magnetic soles made her feel like she was always falling slightly upward. She hailed a mover cube with barely a thought, and in moments she was spider-webbed into a metal box that was hurtling towards the rear of the ship at speeds that would kill a bio-human. The Doppelgänger's body didn't transmit anything beyond the vaguest sensation of forward motion.

The Doppelgänger was tougher than a human body or a nanopill clone, but the depth of sensation was the same if you knew what you were doing. To the untrained eye, it looked and reacted the way a flesh and blood human would, but it was laced with user interface controls that allowed it access to all parts of the Seed Ship. Corie spent nearly every waking hour studying the control matrix of the android's synthetic nervous system sheath. It was designed to be piloted remotely, but in emergencies, it could theoretically sustain a person's neural function separate from their own body for short periods of time.

One step at a time.

Corie felt like she was hurtling through an atmosphere of thick cotton. Light flashed across her vision as her user interface display reshaped itself to show her a Biomass Sentinel from Jade Section. The Sentinel's name and gender pronouns were displayed below the viewer; Masocixa, Biomass Scientist. They/Them.

"Corienne Biskane, from City Dev Data Layer Ombre Section. What are you doing in a skin shell Doppelgänger near Hydroponics Three?" Masocixa frowned, their chrome skin rippling with distaste. "Surely you're not worried about your nutrient supplements, are you?"

Corie resisted the urge to roll her eyes. "I have cycles of free time budgeted. I wanted to see the rest of the ship."

Masocixa rolled their eyes, and sighed. "You can see the ship from within the data layer simulation! It's practically—"

Corie cut them off. "I build data layers, and I know what is and is not the exact same as the real thing. Now is there a crew policy stating I can't go see things myself in my free time, or is this just harassment?"

Masocixa huffed audibly. "In Real Space? No, if you have spare cycles to waste on pointless activity, I won't stop you, but be careful in that Doppelgänger! They aren't easy to make!"

"I'm not going to break it, you crybaby," Corie said, and ended the two-way conversation. There was a remote tingle of a thrill of being so petty. That faded as the mover cube slowed to a halt near the grasslands airlock. Here, at the center of the ship, the gravity faded into a dreamy bounce, but the wheat and soy fields grew well enough with the tinted yellow light coming from a nearby Femtopulsar power plant, and if you didn't look at the source of the light, the air felt just right enough to approximate being on the open plains of Western Saskatchewan.

She walked into the fields of grass, inhaling the summer heat scent under an artificially blue sky, and it was almost enough. She trailed through the grass and ducked her way between rows of wheat and corn further down, the soil crunching under her bare feet. She smelled the water before she saw it, the river artificial but designed to suggest instead an act of nature. Tempted as she was to wade into it, she didn't want to risk the wrath of contamination lectures from Masocixa or anyone else. She wandered along the grassy edge of the bank, listening to the river as it gurgled and rushed into a stream filled with mathematically placed rocks, each designed to direct the irrigation flow of all the wild grasses, grains, and crops of the reserve in Hydroponics Three.

Despite herself, she smiled. When she reached the empty little hill she had groomed into a sitting place for herself, she took out a little hand drum and a padded mallet she'd made and hidden in a nearby storage bin long ago. It wasn't deer hide or even goat, as it should have been, but then again, the sun that warmed her skin, and the skin itself, were also artificial.

She tapped the drum with the mallet a few times and hummed the first notes before breaking into the clan song. Song after song poured out of her, almost as if there was someone pulling the words she hadn't spoken since before she left Earth from her chest through her throat and mouth. Then she sang a prayer song.

As she repeated the verses, she leaned backward in her consciousness and mentally dove through the data layers of the ship's network until she emerged in the cryostation for the ship's crew's bodies. Plus one, she thought, as she began to manipulate the data stream of consciousness from Amy's body.

It felt weird, staring at the cryostasis tube that housed Corie's own flesh and implant body while her mind wandered the ship's network through the Doppelgänger's access node. It was as if there were hands and limbs whispering against her own, from the inside, but she couldn't do what she was about to do without having a backup.

She materialized standing over her own cryotube, the ghost hands of her network body shimmering with data layer code and geospatial notes. She was about to access the software that connected her mind to the ship's network, but she felt a shiver of cold air behind her.

"Stop what you're doing," Amy said from behind her.

Corie turned with a frown, and seeing her old friend there sent a shiver through all three of her bodies. Amy had a data blade out, pointed at the ground.

"Stop."

"Amy?" This didn't make sense. Amy wasn't ship's crew, and she certainly wouldn't have access to security tools that could freeze a person's access. Corie backpedaled and hit the transfer terminal with her palm before leaping upwards through the data layers towards her backup Doppelgänger's shell.

There was a sharp fist to her chest midway through a series of data layers and Corienne flipped out of control, crashing into changing data layer virtual worlds, her body punching holes in mountains and hotel fronts, and smashing into walls of icy ocean water before she fell back into the Doppelgänger's body in Real Space, lurching forward next to the river in Hydroponics Three.

Oh no. This isn't good. She'd been interrupted before she could complete the transfer. Her mind was completely trapped in this body. No time. She stood up and started running through the crop fields, crashing through stalks of blue corn and soy beans.

"Stop!" cried a strange, urgent voice.

Who was that?

A bright flash of light flared, and Corie's User Interface flooded everything she could see with a view screen.

"Stop!" Masocixa's panicked face was pushed off screen as the Amy imposter filled her vision.

The Amy Imposter spoke with a soft dreamy voice, devoid of concern. "I know what you're trying to do. But you need to stop."

And without meaning to, Corie's Doppelgänger's body skidded to a halt.

"Who are you?" she yelled at nothing, knowing the imposter was listening. As she said it, the woman wearing Amy's face shimmered into view in front of her in Real Space, amid the crops. It was a hologram so real she looked touchable. The imposter nodded, and Amy's mask melted into different features, until she looked like a younger version of Corie's own mother. Corie shivered.

"It doesn't matter," Amy's ghost said. "You cannot attempt this. She's dying. You can't stop what's going to happen."

"I don't care. I'm willing to try. And you can't stop me." Corie didn't say it like a threat. She was begging. "You can't."

The imposter sighed. "I can. And in fact, if you try it, you will force me to. I will lock you out of the system and put you in deep cryostasis until we arrive at Wolf1061c."

Cryostasis imprisonment? The punishment was theoretical; it had never been tested for longer than a month. It was more humane than being recycled into sustenance for other passengers, but the off-the-record consensus was that it might as well be a death sentence via medically induced coma.

And few had the authority to order such a drastic measure. The human crew who did were currently in deep sleep themselves. That meant ...

"You, you're the Ship AI Control?" Corie said, numb. She'd had no idea the ship's crew had been aware of this, much less that the ship itself knew about her plans.

The woman nodded. "That is oversimplifying it, but yes. I am the mind of the Seed Ship, and all its crew. I see everything and watch over everyone, even as I repair the reactors, clean the Doppelgänger biomass tubes, and plot course corrections to better our approach to our destination."

"Everything?" Corie asked. A trembling hand of ice alighted on her mind and slid its way down her spine at what that might mean.

"Or else I would not be here, monitoring both your body and hers," the Ship Mind said calmly. "I know what she suffers. And I wished, along with you, for a cure. Unfortunately, the cold equation for me is that there is no cure for her. However, I cannot endorse your reckless efforts. She will not survive the procedure you suggest by your actions."

"How do you know?" Corie asked.

"It has never been successful. Not on Earth nor on Titan Core. Nor any other research outpost station or ship. Much less on the third Seed Ship to ever leave Sol and Terra."

"Just because it's never been done, doesn't mean it ... it can't be," Corie countered. "What's the loss if I fail anyway? She's already dying." She desperately wanted to leap from the Doppelgänger's synthetic neural sheath back into her own body in the Med1Rack, but she knew if she did, she would be trapped there.

"No one has even tested the idea of transmitting the entire neural matrix of one person through the system into a skin shell for the length of time you're suggesting, for the rest of its existence," the

Ship Mind said in that unwaveringly calm voice. The Ship Mind paced back and forth, her hands brushing the stalks of wheat grass behind her.

She continued. "Not to mention overloading the cryostasis data lines with two bioform matrices at once. You could crash the entire primary life support system and leave hundreds of passengers and ship's crew trapped in their bodies, or worse, in the data layers, until I could affect repairs, which might be an entire gigasecond. The number of dead could be hundreds of people. Likely including one of our best Virtual Data Layer Artists. If we lost you in the dual transfer, it would set us back possibly two or three generations an—"

Corie stopped listening. The realization hit her like champagne up the arms and back. *She can see everything, but she can't tell what I'm doing until I commit. But I'd have so little time.*

The moment she finished the transfer and tried to escape, the Ship Mind would close her access off from all but the most basic life support. She was trapped. That made her decision easier.

Corie smiled a small, crooked grin of pain. The Ship Mind stopped pacing, her marble black eyes narrowing as she read Corie's expression. The Ship Mind tilted her head. "You're trying to distract me?"

Corie shook her head. "No. I was just … regretting my rashness." That much wasn't a lie. *Let the Ship Mind believe that.* "You're right. It's just … I acted without thinking it through. I don't want to lose Amy. She's all I have." This was also true. Corie saw the wariness in the Ship Mind's face ease a little, and she looked at the ground, knowing that the ship was desperately scanning her brain waves for the smallest hint of a lie. Corie took a deep steadying breath and continued, her chest tight with very real grief at what she'd be losing. "But I can't endanger the lives of other passengers, other crew." *And she wouldn't,* she told herself. "I'm sorry. I'll surrender now." And with that, she started to lean back into the data stream of the connection between the Doppelgänger skin shell and her real body. She felt a hand on her shoulder.

"Wait," the Ship Mind whispered. Corie paused and came back into the Doppelgänger's body fully. "I really am sorry I must stop you from trying. If there was any other way ..."

Corie nodded and wordlessly left the Doppelgänger body, soaring back up the cryostasis data lines.

The Ship Mind sighed, and then cursed as she devoted part of herself to the crumpled Doppelgänger skin shell lying on the grass. She could have asked Hydroponics Three's Biomass Scientist to retrieve the body, but she knew they hated leaping into the puppeteer chassis, and to be honest, the Ship Mind wanted to feel what a sun felt like on physical skin, even if it was artificial.

Without understanding why, the Ship Mind smiled when the hairs on the Doppelgänger's body rose under the warmth of the artificial sun. And for some reason, her eyes grew wet. She was crying. She, an AI, wandering around in a fake body, under a fake sun, was crying synthetic tears. She laughed and headed back for the airlock, inhaling the scent of the soybean and corn stalks.

Corie was the best Virtual Data Layer creator on the Seed Ship. She knew how the Seed Ship connected at several points along the cryostasis data's route back to the flesh bodies of the passengers and crew. She had created them, after all. And as soon as she leaped, she pushed away from the path leading back to her body in the Med Rack, praying that somehow she'd get past the Ship Mind.

Corie couldn't know that the Ship Mind was kneeling in the Doppelgänger near the river in Hydroponics Three, listening to the gurgle of the water.

But she knew she made it when she smelled the dusty room and the frosted windows, the scent of her long dead mother's coffee filling her nose.

Corie's mother leaned in the doorway.

"Nindaanis, breakfast. Get up, you lazy butt, or you'll be late for school." Corie leaped up and kissed her mother, grabbing her by the shoulders to ease her way past the woman. Her mother laughed—a small shocked sound. "Corie, what are you—"

"Nimaamaa, I have to go. I must go on a long trip. I love you." With that Corie stepped out the door, wearing her mother's body as her own.

No one saw the hologram of an older Native woman striding through the data layer simulation of the ship because the passengers didn't care and the ship's crew were too worried about the Doppelgänger in Hydroponics Three. No one saw the old woman stop in front of Amy Nickaboine's medical rack and cryotube and access the dying woman's neural matrix program to redirect her mind from a medically induced deep stasis coma to wakefulness.

No one saw the older Native woman shuffle over to Corienne Biskane's cryotube either, and reprogram the neural matrix software there. But the Ship Mind felt it, and in a rush, she dropped the Doppelgänger's body into a heap in the grass, flying through the ship's data pathways towards the cryostations, panicking as Corie's plan finally hit home.

The cryotube hissed a moment later, and as she woke up, Amy's eyes fluttered open. She saw a ghost of Corie's mom smiling at her through the glass, and she smiled back, thinking she was either dreaming or on some good drugs. The ghost put her fingers on the glass of the cryotube and vanished.

Another woman, with wide marble-black eyes and a deep frown, rushed up a moment later and looked at Amy in horror. Amy frowned, still too drowsy. The marble-eyed woman was joined by several other people a few minutes later and then after what seemed like an eternity, the glass opened.

The marble-eyed woman spoke, looking directly at Amy. "Corienne Biskane? Are you all right?"

Amy frowned. She tried to speak. But all she could do was croak. Someone brought her a glass of water, which she coughed up almost immediately. But at least she could speak.

"No, I'm Amy. Amy Nickaboine. I'm Corie's partner. What's the matter? Where's Corie?"

Amy eventually adjusted rather well to life on the ship. She'd had vague memories of being sick, but she'd been asleep so long that even her face looked alien to her. She often wondered about Corie, but for some reason she couldn't recall what her friend looked like, and the Ship Mind had taken everything that might have to do with Corie Biskane's life, including image files and holograms.

Not everything, Amy thought, as she loaded the strange data layer and found herself lying in a bed in a room that smelled of dust and frost and coffee. She sat up, realizing that this time slice playback was a painstakingly recreated copy of Corie's old house back on Earth.

"Hey," a familiar voice said from the kitchen, "get up, your coffee's ready." Resisting the strange tingling deja vu in her bones, Amy got up and wandered into the kitchen. She smiled at the two women there.

CUMULATIVE ETHICAL GUIDELINES FOR MID-RANGE — INTERSTELLAR STORYTELLERS —
By Malka Older

Edition optimized for Terravo-Io run, 807 years after interstellation, by algorithm vermilionpatter

I. THE ETHICAL PRIORITIES OF STORYTELLERS ARE

1. Protecting the safety of the voyage by maintaining morale and at least minimal harmony among the passengers
2. Providing the passengers with an improved travel experience
3. To the extent that it does not conflict with #2, personal growth of the passengers

⌐ Love trying to figure out whether hinting that a passenger should be less selfish or bigoted
  ⌐ or controlling of their family
    ⌐ Or rude to the staff
⌐ will mean unimproving their travel experience
  ⌐ "travel experience" is an ambiguous phrase

2. Providing the passengers with ~~an improved travel experience~~ a pleasant trip

3. To the extent that it does not conflict with #2, personal growth of the passengers

4. Narrative honesty

MORALE BOARD: WHAT DO YOU LIKE ABOUT YOUR JOB, BEYOND THE STORYTELLING ITSELF?

⌐ I grew up on Mars. We weren't poor, but we weren't... you know, it was stable, but there was a lot of work. And I kind of love how clean the ship is, and how none of it is my responsibility to keep clean. And taking my kids to the breathable pool, and the zero-G acrobatics, and the concerts, and the arboretum. They would never get that otherwise, not regularly and easily like this.

⌐ People always act all shocked and concerned about bringing kids on these trips, but I think the ships are a fantastic place for kids to grow up.

⌐ THANK YOU. Also it's not like they grow up shipboard and never step off. It's only 30%. The rest of the time...I clean and cook, my kids go to parks and stuff.

⌐ We do 45% shipboard, but yeah. I like the combination. And it's not like school isn't seamless.

⌐ This may sound a little soppy or whatever, but I really appreciate all the people I meet. The passengers, I mean. There are always a few rich jerks, okay, but most of them have really interesting reasons for traveling.

⌐ That too, agreed.

II. The purposes of storytellers are

1. Distraction
2. Morale
3. Education
4. Human interaction

Distraction is often considered a negative: lack of concentration, loss of immediate experience. But what is lost when the immediate experience is that of being confined to a limited spaceship for long periods of time, and there is no particular need to concentrate? Is it worthy—ethical—to try to elapse time you see as an ellipsis?

Regardless of our answer, distraction is critical on the months- or years-long journeys of interstellar travel. This is not simply a question of comfort. Without distraction, the weight of infinite space, the territorial constraints of the ship, the irretrievable hours of life being spent in travel, the proximity of unknown and often disliked fellow travelers; one or all of these begin to threaten the stability of the individual passengers, and thereby, the safety of the ship.

With interstellar travel there is of course the additional stressor of unexplained interstellar fatalities (UIF) syndrome. Given that incidence occurs at approximately one in one thousand, on a single voyage these deaths would normally not be distinguishable from random or unexplained fatalities. However, awareness of the syndrome is high among the general public, and almost universal among interstellar travelers, and since no one knows what causes UIF or who is likely to be susceptible, first-time voyagers are often anxious about the instant of arrival.

⌐ Distraction is useful when you're terrified.

⌐ It is. Distraction is a fundamental tool in keeping passengers happy and content with their choice to travel. The intensity of the stressors in interstellar journeys necessitate correspondingly intense distraction. Storytellers are able to gauge, react, and modulate their narratives to keep passengers engaged in ways that even the most advanced machine-learning entertainment cannot.

However, it is important to note that even the most potent distraction is not sufficient for everyone, nor is it the right tactic for all passengers. Storytellers that hold themselves accountable for perfectly tranquil journeys for every passenger are likely to both fail, and flame out.

> What about the problem of how much harder it becomes to distract myself?

Many Storytellers have reported on this difficulty.

> Have you tried other media? I can't listen to other storytellers, can't stop analyzing what they're doing, but I'm getting more into music.
>> It's true, though. The other part, I mean, about wanting to entertain everyone perfectly so they're happy. And I don't even CARE if they're happy. I just...
>> Feel like you need to do your job perfectly. Yeah.

Morale is of course aided by distraction to the extent that the latter reduces stress. But Storytellers are charged as well with making passengers feel pleased with their journey and reaffirming their reason for traveling. That is, Storytellers should select narrations not only for distraction, but to reinforce the decisions, principles, and choices that led people to the journey they are on.

But simply providing aspirational narratives for passengers to insert themselves into is unlikely to engage most audience members for any length of time—and the ones who do find it entrancing are likely to be the ones most damaged by it, or cause the most damage once empowered by it.

The balance is one of the ethical difficulties of Storytellers: how

> Can we skip this part?
>> What, ignore the most famous and obvious ethical quandary in the whole profession?
>>> Not ignore, just...skip the verbiage. We all know the problem. We've all come face-to-face with it in our work
>>> Not always face-to-face, it's usually subtler than that...
>>> Like when you notice who is identifying themself as the hero, but it's not something concrete you can point to...
Or, once I saw some kids acting out the story I had told them, and...they were making the littlest kid be the bad guy...
>>> Okay, so sometimes face-to-face and sometimes we catch it out of the corner of an eye. The point is, we all know what it is already. We all wrestle with it in our own ways. And there's no answer, right?
>>> So why bother going through ethical guidelines about it?
>>> They have a point. Is this going to tell us anything new?

Education is not a required element of Storyteller work, but most passengers prefer stories in which they learn something new, according to surveys. The most common ethical question related to educational elements of stories relates to what should be taught. A non-exclusive list of topics that have not proved detrimental to morale or passenger experience is available here.

Human interaction, calibrated to individual personalities, has been shown to vastly improve both distraction and morale. To understand more about the importance of interaction, this section is often used as a segue into speaking about history.

III. History

Initial plans for interstellar travel imagined that passengers would be in induced comas within cryogenic preservation—more palatably referred to as "stasis"—and that therefore entertainment would not be an issue. It soon became clear that the medium-term effects of stasis, as well as the difficulty and expense of employing it, outweighed the benefits for mid-length trips. Intersteller travel companies then relied on the same entertainment options that had been used on terrestrial flights maxing out at twenty hours: a selection of films and television shows along with a few games. After travel of months at a time, the reviews, and the results, were not good.

⌐ Can you imagine?

Pioneering interstellar line LunaNueva looked back to earlier, slower forms of transport and began to model travel on cruise ships: an onboard library of books and physical games to complement the screen time, as well as fitness classes and themed parties. However, there was still a great deal of discontent and conflict, and surveys indicated that people needed "an overwhelming reason" to undertake an interstellar voyage.

⌐ Honestly shocked how long it took them to figure this out.
　⌐ What? That people shouldn't travel between stars unless they have to?
　　⌐ Ha. No, storytelling. It never even occurred to them.

The position of Storyteller evolved separately in two main paths. In some cases, it was one of the duties of Human Experience Managers, Concierges, or Entertainment Directors; on other lines, there were dedicated storytellers, but they were intended only for children. The first official Storytellers intended for adults were on the WarpSpeed line; they did not at first even include this in their advertisements, believing (perhaps correctly) that people would not find it a compelling reason to travel with them.

A coterie of talented Storytellers, some working in tandem on the larger ships and others communicating across the company chatspace (which is why we have such good documentation), proactively expanded their role and began refining the theory while documenting their practices. *Note: the algorithm responsible for this document includes personality elements accumulated from that collective.*

Passengers began requesting specific Storytellers, or asking which Storytellers were assigned to particular voyages. Intrigued, though still skeptical of the potential impact, WarpSpeed gave Storytellers more budget and autonomy. The results demonstrated the value of the position, and within a few decades all interstellar ships boasted at least one.

In the decades since then, Storytellers have become industry standard and, more importantly, are deeply connected with interstellar travel in the cultural perception. People planning interstellar travel expect Storytellers; more than that, they often preemptively imagine what their interactions with Storytellers will be like. They expect that Storytellers will form part of the stories they tell other people about their trip.

This puts Storytellers in an ethically challenging position: they are superimposed against preconceived images. They must continually create new narratives but also face claims of fulfilling expectations. Judging the line between giving someone what they want and what their professional mandate requires is often an ethical question.

⌐ Urgh. It is, isn't it.
　⌐ I think about this a minimum of once a trip.
⌐ I bump up against it weekly. Do I perform my *jazz hands*
　Storyteller role with dazzles and sparkles or just do my
　job, do I...
　　⌐ Do I tell this person the story they want to hear
　　or the story that will promote harmony across the
　　deck group....

IV. THE OFFICIAL TITLE IS **STORYTELLER.** Discourage the crew from using other titles, however apt; they can remind passengers of the other purposes and undermine distraction and morale-maintenance.

> **VENTING BOARD: NAMES YOU'VE BEEN CALLED BY THE CAPTAIN, OFFICERS, AND/OR CREW:**
> ⌐ PropagandaBot
> ⌐ Mouth of Sauron
> ⌐ Word-mangler
> ⌐ Spinner of tales (I know it sounds charming, but that's not how it was meant)

⌐ Just a couple of trips ago I had a space debris avoidance technician who always greeted me as "liar." He did it with a smile, right, like it was some joke between us and that made it fine, and I let it go until he did it in front of some of the passengers and then I took it right to the captain.
⌐ Good!
⌐ Did the captain do something?
　⌐ Yes, it was kind of a slog to push it through but turns out that the passengers had said something too. But...speaking of ethics, I felt a little guilty.

► **They have to protect your ability to do your job.**

► They can't let that shit go. It has consequences.

┌ Well, it's not just snitching, which he deserved.
│ I started telling stories in which the initial
│ peril was caused by slacking space debris
│ avoidance technicians.

► Beep Beep Beep ethical issues alert!

► Was the problem solved by a heroic Storyteller?

┌ Ha, no, I didn't go that far. I hadn't meant to
│ do it at all, but when I walked in and saw those
│ passengers in my audience, it felt weird, and I
│ got angry, and figured I'd lean into the 'liar'
│ thing. After all, 'liar' is not…I mean, we're
│ supposed to lie, sort of.

► **But also not.**

┌ And that matters. Like you said, it's how the audience
│ perceives you, prepares for you.

V. Philosophy

There were initially two lines of thought around interactions with
passengers. One, led by Gen 15342 Verin and Stilvanak Restal,
encouraged Storytellers to observe passengers actively, draw
what conclusions they could from both deduction and intuition,
and use those conclusions to inform their narrative choices. The
other emphasized that all people were "player characters," in the
parlance, and encouraged engagement with each passenger as an
individual, fully human and unlike any other.

┌ It will be noted that these two are not mutually exclusive (and
│ this algorithm contains components from adherents of both
│ schools). Modern Storytellers largely blend these approaches,
│ combining observation and deduction that allows for quick

initial assessments with continuing care to avoid getting trapped into assumptions.

VI. PARTICIPATION

As often noted in publicity materials, one of the great advantages to Storytellers, as opposed to recorded or automated entertainment, is their improved interactivity. (Less publicized, because less accessible to public understanding in current social frameworks, is that *human* interaction—faces, eyes, pheromones—also makes a significant difference.)

One of the main challenges and unseen skills of Storytellers is the need to calibrate this interactivity.

> I have had groups where I followed all the approaches for participation, and they didn't want to do it. Just tell us what you want to tell us, they say. Don't make us work for it; you're the one getting paid.

VII. SELF-SUSTENANCE

There is a misconception that storytelling is an easy job. Less stressful than bearing the responsibility for navigation, they believe, or piloting. However, entertaining people takes its own toll. Narratives can unleash emotions, both in the Storyteller and in the audience.

> It's so true. I tell stories all day and then my kid asks me for a story before bed and I can't come up with anything. I just...can't push any more ideas out. But I feel terrible about it.
>
> > We should do an exchange. You tell stories you already know to my kid, I'll do the same for yours.
> >
> > > Deal. Maybe someday if we're both onshore on the same planet at the same time...
> >
> > Maybe!

VIII. WHY DO YOU ALL DO THIS?

> The stories. Not the ones we tell, but the ones we hear from passengers.

> So many reasons for traveling.
> Shouldn't this be a sidebar or a morale board or something?

>> Is this question morale-boosting?

> I know it's weird, but I like the travel, myself. I like living on the ship and going to new places.

> At this point, I figure, we don't have a choice.

>> Oh I don't know, I've thought of spacing it all and doing something else for a job.

>>> No, not storytelling. I mean we don't have a choice about traveling.

>>> Not everyone travels. Not that many people travel interstellarly; percentage-wise it's really pretty small.

>>> No, they're right. Some people don't travel. But most people travel somehow.

> It's a compulsion.

>> Most of the passengers I meet are traveling because they have to. I mean, not because of some mysterious compulsion, but to visit family, or get a new job, or…

>>> That's what I mean. Some people are compelled to travel, and that drags other people along. Whether it's because they want to or they need to. And—yeah, I just think as a species we move. We migrate, we travel. Even when it's difficult and dangerous and uncomfortable.
>>> And as Storytellers, we're along to smooth the ride.

THANK YOU FOR PARTICIPATING.

REMEMBER, ETHICS ARE CONSTRUCTED BY *ALL* OF US!

WHOSE SPACESHIP
— IS IT ANYWAY? —
By John Chu

I n improv class, they tell you to stay away from three scenarios: teaching scenes, transaction scenes, and argument scenes. So, you'd think the worst improv scene ever would be one where a manager trains a new salesclerk on the cash register while they argue with a customer trying to buy a mango. Nope. The worst improv scene ever is the one happening on stage right now, and the audition only started a minute ago.

The theater building used to be an Asian grocery. The only way you'd know is if you read about it on the theater's website. There's a small lobby that leads into the performance space. The stage is a flat platform about six inches tall that almost spans the room. The house is five ascending rows of folding chairs. All the lights are on. We can see the show's creative team, seated in a row in the middle of the house, watching us. This feels extremely unfair. Normally, when you look into the audience, you don't see anyone staring back, assessing your every choice.

After a quick warm up, someone on the creative team suggests "spaceship," and everybody except me lurches onto the stage. They're all desperate to demonstrate active agreement with everybody else. "Everybody except me" is a half-dozen improvisers, four of whom I've done scenes with before. The other two introduced themselves when we all walked into the space, but I was too nervous to actually remember their names. They both look like they play college hockey. Compared to some of my other auditions, two whole women in the group counts as a surprisingly diverse mix of genders and, if you include me, we're not all white.

Unfortunately but unsurprisingly, everyone on stage is way too eager to show off their technique. So, active agreement becomes an over-choreographed, flailing disco number where the music is people shouting the parts of a ship's bridge at each other. Unless an improv scene is explicitly some sort of group game, any more than two or three people at a time is basically impossible. Any more than that would require literal telepathy.

In theory, a scene is trying to happen. In practice, it's like watching those videos of a newborn foal figuring out how to stand. For what feels like excruciating days, its legs buckle at the wrong time and its torso keeps flopping over. Unlike the foal, this scene hasn't managed to stand yet.

I mean, I'm also way too eager. Not to mention desperate to get cast. Because we're all invariably eager and desperate, improv auditions tend to be a fusterCluck, filled with chaotic scenes where everyone is trying to get their two cents in at exactly the same time. Unless the instruction from the creative team is literally "do a Harold" or some other long form improvised structure, there is rarely any overarching structure to speak of, not even one organically evolved over the course of the improv. It's all rather self-defeating.

Getting into the scrum has never gotten me cast before, and it's not going to now. Besides, whenever I do that, I always feel like I'm making things worse. That, obviously, is the key to a great improvised scene. Nothing makes for a great scene more than you trying to nail your relationships and showing off your impeccable object work while a half-dozen people dart off in their own directions so that no one has any clue what the fuck is happening.

The spaceship scene occupies most of the stage. I'm off to the side, practically off the stage, by myself making baozi. What does this have to do with the initial suggestion? Beats me. You're not supposed to be directly inspired by it anyway. Like, "spaceship" is supposed to remind you of, say, watching TV with your mom after school. Then that's supposed to inspire you into a scene about innocence or guardianship or maybe the inevitable heat death of the universe for all I know.

The instant we moved to the US, my mom stopped watching TV or, really, doing anything else with me. My parents spent all day working at the restaurant. If a plate of sweet and sour chicken cost more than a fast-food burger, no one bought it. They all decided that was too expensive. It's not like there was the money to hire anyone. Once I was like twelve, I worked there, too. Customers scanned the menu while they told you what they were really in the mood for was a slice of ham, mashed potatoes, and gravy. When they asked whether you're the "number one son," you had to laugh like no one had ever made that vaguely racist joke before. It was great. Anyway, I'm hoping the directors work out some ingenious connection for themselves and decide that I'm brilliant.

On one hand, I think me standing there, waiting for dough to rise, could be a comic tour de force. On the other hand, I'd actually like to get cast in this show. Being able to pay the rent is pretty awesome. I highly recommend it.

The act of making baozi happens way more quickly in mime than it would in real life. Before we moved to the US, my mom and I would crank them out together. It's never gone that quickly since, but you can make pretend baozi as quickly as you want. Start the pot of water boiling and put the bamboo steamer on the pot. Scatter the flour. Knead. Knead. Knead. Tear off and round tiny balls of dough. Flatten and roll out into circles. Put in the filling. It's what we used when we were making them for ourselves: spinach, tofu, glass noodles, and garlic. (I'm sure the directors have no clue what the filling is made of. I'm not that good at mime.) Pinch. Pinch. Pinch. Steam. Steam. Steam. Plate. Plate. Plate.

Meanwhile, the folks on the spaceship have sorted themselves out, more or less. More characters actually talking to each other one at a time. Less everyone yelling over each other. Hudson has tagged himself as captain of *Destiny* and the rest of the crew has coalesced in his wake. Not a huge surprise how it's turning out. Blond and tanned, Hudson's so much of a golden boy, he practically glows, and his smile is not even at full wattage. He has this way of gliding around the stage with a dexterity so casual, it verges on careless. We can all do all the things at the gym, but only some of us come out of it broad-shouldered, lanky, and superhero-adjacent. Playing a scene with him is like acting opposite the heaven-sent spawn of Chris Hemsworth and Gene Kelly.

The line between envy and lust can be disturbingly thin and I'm pretty sure I straddle the line. He accuses me of checking him out. Hudson is big, strong, and aggressively straight. Staring at him even unintentionally would not go well for me. Whenever we're thrown into the same improv class, I try very hard not to look at him, unless I have to, lest I inadvertently do anything he could misinterpret as staring. As it is, a mere hello in passing and he'll bring up his girlfriend, wielding her like a talisman to defend his heterosexuality, as though my mere presence might otherwise turn him gay. Mostly, though, I'm tired of being thought of as the kind of guy who leers when I don't even have one illicit glance at that slightly unreal body to show for it.

And on the subject of that superhero-adjacent body, the last time we did a scene together, he stepped onto the stage and did that broad-stance fist-on-waist pose where the chest is all puffed out and the midsection is so concave it's obvious even through a shirt. I pointed at him and shouted, "Oh my god, it's the Tap Dance Kid."

Of course, The Tap Dance Kid is actually a 1984 Broadway musical starring Alfonso Ribeiro as the eponymous kid. He starred in a Pepsi commercial with Michael Jackson at about the same time and would later go on to play Carlton in The Fresh Prince of Bel Air. And, for whatever reason—it's not like they look anything alike—that was the first thing that came to mind. So, that was the first thing that popped out of my mouth. In response, he tagged me as The Crisco Kid. Clever.

The golden boy ended up defeating villainy through the power of... tap dance. It doesn't matter how fleet-footed you are, you really can't fake tap dance. So the casually dexterous seemed almost human for a few minutes. I've been in worse scenes, but maybe he hasn't. Foiling a bank robbery with a combination of sketchy tap dance and shortening-based lubrication superpowers is funny. Even the coach thought so. She laughed and said good things about the scene. Hudson just smirked at me and stalked off in a huff. Whatever.

Scenes can end in lots of ways. Sometimes, they fall apart of their own weight. The folks in the scene flee off the stage, and others rush on to keep the show going. More often, someone not in the scene recognizes it has ended and walks across the stage. This is called a sweep edit. If we're feeling really energetic, we run across the stage.

I'm in the middle of sweep editing the spaceship when Hudson's gaze locks onto mine. My feet stop and I almost fall on my face. Maybe I'm just an attentive improviser, open to the offers from my fellow improvisers. More likely, golden boy has gifted me a shaving of his attention and I'm stunned. He smirks and, for a moment, I half-expect him to bring up his girlfriend.

"We have a stowaway." Golden boy also has a buttery baritone voice that can fill the room with a whisper. "Boy, there's not enough fuel for an additional passenger. Get rid of you and we lighten the load."

Now, the thing about improv is that we're always accepting offers and heightening situations. Whether the situation makes sense in the first place is beside the point. It makes no sense that the ship would have only enough fuel for its anticipated load and not a drop more, but everyone in the scene accepts it and goes on. That's the whole point of agreeing. Besides, if we don't, we're not going to get cast. A refusal is bad technique. It may be funny for a millisecond, but a refusal stops a scene cold. Heaven help us if someone reasserts the offer. A back and forth of "Yes, there is"/"No, there isn't" is incredibly tedious to watch. No one wants that.

My hands are still outstretched in front of me from carrying the plate of baozi. At this point, though, I could be carrying anything. We're all supposed to be paying attention to what everyone is doing, but that spaceship scene started so chaotically, I doubt anyone actually has a clue about what I was doing off to the side. Even if they have, it doesn't matter. If I'm getting pitched out of an airlock for some nonsensical reason, there should at least be some emotional stakes, and I don't mean weepy cuts of beef. Accept and heighten. That's the game.

"Happy birthday. I made this cake for you." I hold out what is now a birthday cake to him. "Dad."

Having established that we are family, I finish my sweep edit and the scene is over. The cast flies off the stage. It takes Hudson a split second longer than everyone else. I can't say I didn't enjoy that.

We run through a series of scenes: father and son mowing the lawn, auto mechanic fixing the relationship between a parent and their estranged child as though it were a Porsche 911, zombie attack in a sub shop. This is an audition and no one is exactly concerned with thematic unity. We're just trying to show off. If, for example, you can juggle, this is your moment to three-ball cascade for your life. Ever better, your scene partner creates a reason why you have to juggle. For example, if Hudson actually tap danced, he'd have been thrilled for someone to tag him as "the tap dance kid."

Someone edits a scene. Sarah and I go on stage. Hudson called her out at a Harold class once for being a "scene nurse." He tossed it off like a neg. There's nothing wrong, though, with being someone who always gives the scene what it needs. Especially when you, like Sarah, create opportunities to be awesome in the process.

I start dumping ingredients into a bowl. Sarah is all joyous, leaping across the stage shouting, "Whee! It was so musty in that flour container." She then crumples and murmurs "Ouch, that butter is so cold and clumpy." In other words, she's sentient flour and about to become sentient cake batter. The scene becomes a game where oblivious me is in a kitchen making a cake while Sarah is shouting stuff like "No, no, not the stand mixer! Don't put me in the stand mixer."

Sentient cake batter obviously doesn't want to be beaten in a stand mixer. That would hurt. Sarah, however, obviously wants sentient cake batter to be beaten in a stand mixer. In this case, it's clearly a setup for whatever awesome thing she has in mind. On one hand, it's not like I have to do what she wants. Agreement and heightening doesn't mean anyone gets to order anyone else around. On the other hand, it's not like I have any better ideas, and I'm curious what she has in mind.

I immediately turn on the stand mixer. She spins in circles at center stage, flailing her arms and screaming in agony. Someone in the audience deigns to chuckle. That's encouraging. This audition hasn't exactly inspired any sort of reaction so far.

"Don't drop me into the cake pan!" Sarah hugs herself, appalled. "What kind of sadist are you?"

I dollop her into the cake pan. Or, rather, I tilt the imaginary bowl and spoon imaginary batter into the imaginary pan. Since we're all about being sadistic to the cake batter, I do it in fast, sharp strokes, really slamming that batter into the pan. Sarah throws herself at the floor. A lot. A different way each time.

"No, don't put me into the convection oven. Anything but the convection oven." She shudders in what is, disturbingly, a very batter-like way. "How long must this torture last?"

Naturally, she has to go into the oven. This requires a certain amount gentle, coordinated shoving as I roll her upstage. Someone walks across the stage downstage from me, ending the scene. Their footsteps clatter behind me. No one gets to find out how Sarah was planning on getting baked in a funny way. Still, we probably made each other look good. I'll take that.

More short bits go by. Something about a sweltering summer night and two men lying together on reclining beach chairs lasts for about three milliseconds before everyone else rushes the stage and turns it into a playground. Eventually, the inevitable bicycle repair scene starts. It's probably not literally true, but it feels like at some point during an improv show, someone will try to repair a bicycle.

A wife and husband are standing by the side of the road. One of the bike tires has gone flat. Even though they are trying to patch and re-inflate the tire, the scene, of course, is not about that. As an improv coach said in a workshop I took, "No one walks out of the theater thinking, 'And they fixed the bicycle!'"

Bill, playing the husband, is doing a masterful job of heightening how hot it is on the road. He's wiping the sweat off his brow. His movements get more and more sluggish. He becomes never quite still, swaying slightly even when he's just standing. Over the course of the scene, he goes from sipping his water bottle to sloshing it near his mouth. He could keel over from heat exhaustion at any moment.

Carly, playing the wife, is just as expert. A model of precision, she spreads out a tarp and lays out her tools in precise row. Her gestures as she works on the bike are detailed. Every finger is splayed just so. Carly actually works in a bicycle shop in real life. You can practically see the grease on her hands. Every part is placed in another neat row in the order she removes it.

As he gets sloppier, she gets more fastidious, more wary. She asks him to pass a tool and is impatient when he doesn't know which one, but just a little. Her hand stretches impatiently while he wrecks her neat rows. They get into an argument but it's not really an argument, of course, because we don't do argument scenes. It's really an extended metaphor involving pressure, being bottled up, and escaping.

Intellectually, I get that they are working out their relationship via subtext. The cut, thrust, and parry over how to repair a flat tire is really the two sparring over how controlling he is. Practically, a scene where what they say and do apply to both the flat tire and their relationship is more self-consciously clever than anything else. Sometimes, two improvisers make a series of utterly defensible choices and the scene stubbornly refuses to come to life. This is not great for the audience who has to sit through it and annoying as fuck for the improvisers involved. No one wants to be reminded, especially in the middle of an audition, that you don't always get there just by doing what you're supposed to do.

She finally snaps. Her balled fists snap open and she drops the tire patch kit and screams at him.

"You've eaten the plums that were in the icebox that I was saving for breakfast!"

Someone in the audience groans. Part of me thinks that, if this is a revelation, she should have done this minutes ago. The rest of me thinks that this is a cry for help. She might as well be screaming, "Someone, please edit this scene out of its misery." As this occurs to me, Hudson sweep edits. Bill and Carly leave the stage and Hudson initiates his offer.

"Son, I appreciate the cake, but this spaceship doesn't have enough fuel for all of us."

I don't grumble as much as I want to. Of course, he's called us back to the spaceship. Dutifully, everyone in that scene—that is to say, everyone—comes back on stage.

"I just wanted to celebrate your birthday, Dad. You're always traveling to one star system or another."

"Nevertheless, son, if we don't have enough fuel, someone has to be thrown out the airlock to lighten the load. You should have known that. You've always been a disappointment to me." He points stage right and his pained expression lasts for about a second before it becomes a smirk. "Now, out you go."

It's all about agreement and heightening. As nonsensical as it is, we now live in a world where people are thrown off spaceships because of ridiculously tight fuel margins. He's also established that I'm a disappointment. Agreement means these things are etched in stone. Ouch. What I do about those things, though, is up to me.

If Hudson were anyone else, he might be saying "Please throw yourself out the airlock because it will set up something really cool." Honestly, though, his smirk feels like a shove, forcing me off stage. It doesn't seem like, if I kill myself, he'll pull out, say, the most perfect expression of grief anyone has ever seen. We haven't even had a chance to set up any sort of relationship that might justify it.

That said, if I'd like to book this gig, the safe choice is to throw myself off the stage, ideally in an entertaining way. There are any number of worse responses to his offer and, in a post-mortem, this one is utterly defensible. Of course, the best scenes come from improvisers creating the opportunities to do something awesome. No one developed into a great improviser by making a series of safe, utterly defensible choices. No one ever developed into a great improviser by stalling on stage until they figured out the perfect move either.

Slowly, I inch myself stage right. If I have to toss myself out an airlock, I'm going to milk it for all its worth. This is the time to throw in all the details that establish some sort of relationship so I'm not just some rando ejected into space. For most of my life, he's just been this image on a screen. I tested into the space academy to try to earn his approval. I finished at the top of my class in the hopes that he would notice, that I want to prove my worth to him. The free association finally gives me an idea. Who cares whether it's awesome. It exists.

"I'll show you Dad that I'm worth your respect." I turn to the crew of Destiny. "Hey, everybody. Let's all cut off a limb and throw them out the airlock instead!"

"Yes, let's!" all of us shout back in unison. Except Hudson, whose miffed expression is now part of the captain.

This actually gets laughs. We all, including the directors, played the "Yes, let's!" game in Improv 101. It's too inside baseball to count as a real laugh but I'm not picky.

"Now we'll have enough fuel, and you don't have to sacrifice your son," Sarah, who tagged herself the ship's second in command back in the first spaceship scene, says before she joins the line the cast has formed.

We all go around helping each other saw off each other's limbs. Except Hudson. The line goes quickly because there are only six of us. Hudson leaves the scene in a fit of pique. Way to show how much the captain loves his son. Nevertheless, the scene goes on.

There is a lot of skilled mime work as everyone explores how missing an arm or leg changes their bodies and the way they move. It is a ballet exploring altered body language with gentle partner work as we group up in constantly changing combinations. The scene turns out less gruesome than one might expect and, maybe, we're all relieved that no one says or does anything where missing a limb is the joke.

Another sprint of short scenes ends with a fun one, at least for those of us not in the scene. That's everybody except the two hockey players, whose names I was too nervous to retain.

Two bros are setting up camp. They are the bro-iest bros who have ever bro-ed. They flex. They grunt. They chest bump. Somewhere in the middle all of that, they find time to trash talk each other's tents as they set them up.

And while the bros are broing, we the off-stage peanut gallery are lobbing offers into the scene. Carly calls down the thunder. The boom is startlingly realistic. The bros jump and stare up at the sky. They feel for rain as they puff themselves up.

"Bring it, storm." Bro A shakes his fist at the sky.

"Yeah, blow, winds, and crack your cheeks." Bro 1 quotes King Lear and looks like he's trying flex away the on-coming storm.

I growl just as Bill howls. Our hands meet in a no-look high five. You have to keep track of what's happening on stage no matter what.

The bros crouch and stare into the distance. Their gaze sweeps back and forth.

"I see the wolf." Bro 1 points into the audience. "Over there, next to that tree."

Sarah and Carly get into the act. The four of us are alternately cranking up both the oncoming storm and approaching wolves. We're not this impenetrable wall of sound. The howls, growls, cracks of thunder, and thud of rain pop up occasionally in the dead spaces between their dialogue.

The bros stand back-to-back, their hands failing to hide their heads from the rain. They step slowly in a tight circle, scanning the distance in all directions. Bro A jumps a bit at each howl.

"There's a like a whole pack of them." Bro A crumples to the ground. "We're surrounded."

"Hey, bro, I got you." Bro 1 crouches down and gently hugs Bro A from behind. "I won't let anything happen to you."

"I got you, too." Bro A squeezes Bro 1's hand then pushes him up to a stand. "I wouldn't want to face this with anyone else."

Hudson sweep edits the scene. Just as they dropped their facades and things were starting to get real. I stifle my groan.

"An extra person on the ship means we're using more oxygen. We don't have enough air." Hudson stands center stage with his hands on his waist. "We still need to get rid of someone."

A soft sigh fills the stage, and it isn't coming from me. We exchange shrugs and "here we go again" eye rolls before we go on stage. The beat where we leave Hudson on stage by himself feels like years. Still, it's just a beat. Probably only people experienced in improv would notice, like everybody in this audience.

We drag ourselves back into the spaceship scene, dutifully in most cases, literally in a couple. I think that's a bit much, but no one gets criticized for shooting the moon in improv, especially at an audition.

"Son." Hudson's gaze locks onto mine as he points stage right. "Do you see what you need to do?"

In theory, this is bad improv technique. It's not that questions are completely off-limits. It's that most of the time, not only do they not add information to the scene, but they remove some. In this case, he could be pointing to anything, and he's forcing me to tell him what. In practice, that's a bad-faith analysis. He isn't really asking a question. You know what he means.

It's still a little single-minded, though. I mean, get another idea. The spirit of creative play is not exactly in full bloom. Besides, not even throwing myself out of the airlock will make him like me, will it....

In that case, what Hudson's pointing at is not the airlock but a soft-serve machine. One shouldn't point at empty air without consensus about what is there. OK, fine, I just want to fuck with him. *With* him. A little.

"Of course, Dad." I fill a cone and run it back over to Hudson. "Here's an ice cream cone. Your favorite. Soft-serve porterhouse steak."

A chuckle from the audience. Hudson is stone-faced, though.

"Son, you've always shirked your responsibilities. Look where it's gotten us." He takes the ice cream and dumps it on the ground. "But we all have our moment of reckoning."

Sarah howls. Everyone else growls as they stagger toward Hudson, surrounding him. Apparently, when push comes to shove, what we really can't stand is someone who isn't even trying to play with us. Everyone else has also had their fill of Hudson, I guess. It takes a second but I recover my wits and join in. Less time wasted on Hudson, more time spent on folks who might actually like me. For example, the creative team. The second best time to start is right now.

Hudson shouts and tries to push everyone away. Never underestimate, though, the ingenuity of a half dozen people who really want to pick someone up. We all commit to our characters. Those who cut off an arm help out one-handed. Those who cut off a leg, hop along as we carry him to the airlock and off the stage.

And scene.

The directors call an end to the audition, thank us, and tell us that they'll be in touch. The golden boy scowls and the world is noticeably colder. We drift away, giving Hudson a wide berth.

I do not book the gig. But Hudson doesn't, either.

— TEAM BUILDING EXERCISE —
By Valerie Valdes

T he newly assembled crew of the CS *Fedoa* sat in plastic folding chairs, arranged in a circle around the blonde-ponytailed corporate trainer, who currently regarded them with the slightly demented smile of a professional cheer radiator. Her expression and business casual jumpsuit did nothing to diminish the cold, impersonal feel of the space station meeting room, with its bright fluorescent lights and painfully white walls covered in regulation posters explaining employee rights and minimum wage laws. A digital sign scrolled, "Welcome to Limosa Corp!!!" above a small table that held snacks, drinks, and disposables. The free coffee was lukewarm, the free muffins were dry, and the rest of the day promised to be equally unpleasant.

"So," Bianca de Witt said, her tone unnaturally chipper, her blue eyes wide in her pale face. "Now that you've all been formally introduced to each other, our first team building exercise is going to be an exciting game." She paused, as if waiting for a reaction, but only silence replied. "It's a kind of role-playing game," she continued, tapping her datapad. "You're each going to be given a card, and your card will tell you whether you're a human or an evil robot. The goal of the game is to guess which of your crewmates is the robot. Every round, you all get to discuss it and vote. If you vote for someone who's a human, you keep going. If you manage to vote for the robot, you win! If the robot is one of the last two players left, they win. Does anyone have questions?"

Captain D Franklin uncrossed their tanned, muscular arms and half-raised their hand. "I'm sorry, Ms. de Witt—"

"Bianca, please," Bianca said.

"—isn't it a little insensitive to play an 'evil robots' game when one of our crew is literally a robot?" Captain Franklin gestured at Santi, who sat two chairs down from them. As an Iota model of a Synthetic Astro-Navigation Technician, he was almost indistinguishable from a human, except for his lavender skin, violet eyes, and impeccable posture.

"Thank you for speaking up on my behalf, Captain," Santi said. "While I'm not programmed to be offended by anything, the situation is objectively problematic."

Bianca's red-lipsticked mouth made a moue. "That is excellent feedback, Captain Franklin. Let me send a quick note to our developers to consider using an alternate designation for that." She quickly scribbled something on her datapad's surface.

"How about vampires?" volunteered Omeika Tate, the ship's chief engineer. "They're not real."

"Oh, the cards are already printed, though," Bianca said, scrunching her face into a veneer of concern.

Ankur Agrawal, the pilot, raised a dark brown hand over his head. "We could just, I mean, if we all agree it's vampires instead of robots, then it doesn't matter, right? What's on the card, I mean. Whoever gets the robot card is just a vampire instead." He looked to Captain Franklin for support, and they nodded.

"I want to be a vampire hunter," said Dexter Lawrence. The steward sprang to his feet and made a downward stabbing motion toward Grace Namingha, the junior engineer. She leaned away, then scooted her chair closer to Omeika's.

"The role assignments are random," Bianca said quickly. "You're either a human or a ro—a vampire."

Captain Franklin cleared their throat politely, one dark eyebrow lifted. "I want to be clear on this before we start. We all just met, we're about to go on a month-long trip together, and you're having us do a team building exercise where the entire point is to lie to each other? What does that accomplish?"

All eyes shifted to Bianca's pale face.

"Well," Bianca said, fidgeting with the datapad. "It's more of an icebreaker. The goal is to have you learn each other's communication styles, including body language and individual vocal quirks and facial cues. And to have fun?" Her tone rose on the last statement, turning it into a question, though she didn't quite sound as if she was eager for an answer.

"That seems illogical," Santi said, blinking his violet eyes twice in rapid succession. "Rather than becoming familiar with each other's baseline personalities and approaches to conflict resolution, we will instead be learning the methods by which each person erects a façade to maximize the effectiveness of their deception or convince others of their honesty. We are also effectively being pitted against each other rather than working together."

"And lying is wrong," Grace said, eying Dexter, who made a whooshing noise and mimed stabbing Santi in the heart.

Bianca re-applied her smile, eyes crinkling. "I'm happy to pass any feedback along to my superiors, but this is a mandatory exercise, so we need to complete it before we can move on to the next one."

"We have to finish the full module to be approved for departure." Captain Franklin ran a hand through their short brown hair and leaned back in their folding chair, which creaked under their weight. "Why don't you give us the cards, then?"

Without another word, Bianca distributed the role cards. Each crew member read the single word printed on their laminated square, then looked around at their colleagues with a mixture of curiosity, suspicion, and careful neutrality. Except Dexter, who covered his mouth with one hand and then slid the card into his shirt pocket.

"Okay," Bianca said. "The game starts now! Go ahead and talk amongst yourselves and let me know when you're ready to vote." She edged out of the circle and walked toward the table holding the scant refreshments.

Captain Franklin took a deep breath and leaned forward, lowering their voice. "All those in favor of finishing this quickly?"

A chorus of ayes and nods answered, except Dexter, who frowned.

"I'm human," Captain Franklin said. "Raise your hand if you're the vampire."

No one raised their hand. Captain Franklin scrutinized each of them in turn, finally settling on Dexter.

"Are you the vampire, Dexter?" they asked. "Just tell us so we can move on."

"No," Dexter replied, drawing out the vowel and smiling slyly.

Ankur stifled a laugh, and Grace shook her head in disbelief, her long black braid bobbing up and down her back.

"I don't know about you all," Omeika said, "but I have my vote."

Captain Franklin turned around in their chair and waved at Bianca. "We finished our discussion."

Bianca froze, cup halfway to her lips. "That was fast," she said. "So, who do you think is the ro—uh, vampire?"

"It's Dexter," said everyone, more or less simultaneously.

"What?" Dexter exclaimed, again lengthening the word, hand flying to his chest in shock. "Well, I think it's Santi."

"I am not a vampire," Santi replied. "I am, however, a robot."

"Well," Bianca said, "let's see your card, Dexter."

Dexter reluctantly retrieved the card from his shirt, keeping it hidden against his chest. He looked away as he turned it around, revealing the word "ROBOT" printed in large block letters.

"Looks like you got staked, bud," Omeika said.

Bianca walked around the circle, collecting the rest of the cards. "Why don't we take a quick break before our next exercise?" she asked, mask of cheer once again firmly in place. "How does fifteen minutes sound?"

The expressions that replied were less than enthusiastic, but everyone got up to stretch or grab a drink or use the facilities. Omeika ambled up to Captain Franklin as they stood in front of a poster explaining how to report workplace accidents.

"Do we seriously have to sit through this all day?" she asked quietly.

"Yes," replied Captain Franklin. "But nobody can make us enjoy it."

Omeika chuckled, and Captain Franklin smiled. Together they headed for the stale snacks and caffeine.

Bianca pursed her red lips and made a notation on her datapad.

"All clear here," Omeika said, looking around at the empty crew quarters of the derelict freighter one last time. The bunks showed no signs of being slept in, and there was no indication of illness or a struggle.

"Copy," Captain Franklin said from the bridge, which was equally abandoned. The console lit their face from below with an array of blinking red warnings. "Black box has been located. No survivors in the cargo bay?"

"Negative," Grace replied. "No one in the engine room, either."

"Lawrence, report," Captain Franklin said.

"Nobody in the mess," Dexter said, grabbing a protein bar from the cabinet and peeling it open.

Captain Franklin ticked a final mark on the list on their datapad. "That's it, then. Back to our ship, and we'll upload the box contents to StarSec."

They reconvened at the umbilicus connecting the *Fedoa* to the *Nemo*, going through the mandatory decontamination procedures one at a time. Omeika rolled her eyes at Dexter as he crammed the rest of the food in his mouth.

"Seriously?" she asked.

Dexter shrugged and tossed the wrapper aside. "Not like it matters, right?"

Once everyone was back on board and ready to depart, Ankur disengaged, and they floated away. Santi programmed their recalculated flight path into the system, and with a crotch-roiling dive, they plunged into warp space.

"All systems green—wait," Ankur said. "I'm getting some bad notifications from life support. Something's up with the water reclamation system, and possibly our food storage."

Captain Franklin sighed, drumming their fingers on their seat on the bridge. "And here I thought we were done. Okay, Omeika, you and Grace check things out and get me an update on necessary steps."

"Sure, Captain," Omeika replied, unstrapping herself. Grace followed suit.

"Uh, Captain?" Ankur asked. "I'm seeing something else on sensors. Unidentified life form in the cargo bay."

"Are they a vampire?" Omeika asked, rolling her eyes. Ankur laughed, and even Captain Franklin cracked a smile briefly.

"Human?" Captain Franklin asked.

"Looks like it. Wait, if we have an extra person on board and our water and food are having problems—"

Captain Franklin groaned and put a hand over their face. "Bianca, please pause the simulation."

The environment around them remained solid, but the ship suddenly seemed to hang motionless in space. All the readouts and sensors froze, all alarms fell silent.

"Everything okay, Captain?" Bianca asked, her voice slightly tinny over comms.

"Are we seriously doing this?" Captain Franklin asked. "When our contract with Limosa said we had to undergo these exercises, I expected something more practical and less...Kobayashi Maru."

Bianca cleared her throat. "We think it's great for generating really thoughtful discussion and seeing how you can all work together to deal with a tough situation."

Ankur tapped one foot nervously, while Santi continued to sit stiffly, now facing Captain Franklin. Omeika hissed out air between her teeth, Grace's shoulders slumped, and Dexter leaned forward and steepled his fingers.

"A classic trolley problem," Santi said. "Will we choose to sacrifice one among us to survive, or doom the entire crew?"

Captain Franklin squeezed their eyes shut. "Can we please not do this?"

"Do you have more feedback for the developers, Captain?" Bianca asked.

"No," Captain Franklin said. "But off the record, this no-win dilemma nonsense is philosophical masturbation."

"Agreed," Grace said quietly. Ankur nodded as well.

"Very aptly put," Santi said.

"Come on," Dexter said, "it's just a thought exercise. It's not hurting anyone."

"It's giving me a headache," Omeika murmured.

Grace rested a hand on Omeika's arm. "I have ibuprofen in my bag," she whispered. "I'll give you some when we get out of the simulation."

"Sorry to nudge you along, here," Bianca said. "But you do need to get through this to finish the module. I'm just going to unpause and let you all do your thing. When you come to a solution, let me know." With that, the ship sparked to life again.

"I guess we need to come up with something," Captain Franklin said, opening their eyes and surveying their crew. "I have my own thoughts, but I'd like to hear your suggestions."

"Do you want real solutions that might actually work?" Grace asked.

Captain Franklin snorted and shook their head. "I'm betting they won't, even if we try them. The point here is to make us deal with being backed into an ethical corner."

"That's horrible," Ankur said, his voice cracking. "This is gross. There's no right answer."

"Sometimes there are no right answers in life, blah blah, murder is inevitable," Omeika said, rolling her eyes.

Grace sighed. "Why are some people so obsessed with forcing others to kill?"

"Perhaps it makes them feel less guilty about their own unsatisfied proclivities for violence?" Santi offered.

Ankur made a face like he smelled something spoiled. "I know we're in VR already, but this really is like a video game," he said. "Where you only get a couple of options and no matter what, you end up having to shoot your way out. I hate those games."

Dexter made a gun with his fingers and aimed it at each person in turn. "You know what I would do?"

"What, Lawrence?" Captain Franklin asked warily.

"I'd space you all and vamoose. Get to safety and then say you went crazy and tried to murder me." Dexter made pew pew sounds with his mouth as he pretended to shoot Ankur.

"You don't know how to fly a ship," Grace said.

Dexter shrugged. "Can't be that hard."

Ankur laughed incredulously, starting and stopping in waves as if trying and failing to contain himself.

"Reel it in, people," Captain Franklin said, spinning their finger in a circle. "Okay, standard answers include spacing the stowaway, spacing another crew member, or controlled cannibalism. We can opt to pretend the stowaway was never found, or say the crew member volunteered. Anyone want to offer themselves up for that one?"

"I would do so, but I do not consume resources," Santi said, his violet eyes blinking slightly too slowly. "Also, in the event of a necessary subterfuge, my memories would require alteration due to my inability to prevaricate."

"We could just space Dexter," Ankur said.

Dexter gasped in outrage. "What? Seriously?"

"You just told us you'd kill us all and steal the ship!" Ankur replied.

"Yeah," Omeika said, "but do you really want to kill him about it?"

Ankur fell silent, then finally shook it and looked down at his sneakers. "This is ridiculous," he muttered. "It's not even a realistic scenario. We might as well do something fun, like, I don't know... build a space trampoline."

Grace perked up. "Oh? That would be difficult to accomplish given the lack of gravity in vacuum."

"But not impossible," Omeika said, pursing her lips in thought. "It would have to be a small one. We don't have any fabric panels in inventory."

"A net-like series of overlapping straps, maybe?" Grace asked.

"And an anchor to keep the jumper from floating away," Omeika said. "It could work."

The crew spent the next hour concocting a series of increasingly absurd but fun ways to pass the time if murder or death was imminent. Dexter tried to contribute a few ideas, but after suggesting an especially ugly iteration of spin the bottle, he was exiled to the virtual cargo bay for a time-out.

When Bianca walked in, they were all sitting around the table in the mess.

"—and then I said, 'Don't worry, the webbing will dissolve within forty-eight hours. It's not like you needed that datapad for homework, right?'" Omeika grinned and everyone laughed, except Dexter, who curled his upper lip in a sneer.

Bianca coughed politely and beamed at them all. The friendly mood evaporated, leaving only a faint residue that was quickly overpowered by a collective veneer of sullen obligation.

"So," Bianca said, her break clearly having restored her chipperness reserves. "Captain Franklin, could you walk me through what you came up with as a solution to the problem?"

"Of course," Captain Franklin said smoothly. "After a spirited deliberation, and a lot of careful soul-searching, we decided that the fairest thing to do would be to draw straws and let the loser choose how they wanted to die."

Everyone nodded seriously, though Ankur appeared to be desperately trying to keep a smile off his face, and even Grace had a merry twinkle in her nearly-black eyes.

Bianca made a notation on her datapad. "That's very equitable of you," she said. "I know this was a difficult exercise, and I'm glad you were all able to come together and reach a consensus."

Captain Franklin shrugged their broad shoulders, their expression inscrutable.

Bianca's smile broadened. "Well! The good news is, it's time for lunch. This station has an excellent cafeteria with a variety of options. I'll shut down the simulation, then take you over."

The mention of food perked everyone up, even if the prospects were likely to be as mediocre as the morning's fare. With a few commands to her datapad, Bianca stopped the VR session, the spaceship slowly dissolving into a bare white room with silver studs at intervals along the walls, ceiling, and floor. She opened the door and gestured for everyone to exit, waiting for the room to clear before she shut off the lights and locked up behind her.

If she caught the stifled laughs and sly glances cast in her direction, she ignored them, maintaining her red-lipped smile as she guided the crew toward their next destination.

The final exercise was held in the facility's antigrav chamber, a massive room at the center of the station, painted entirely in black, as if emulating space without the benefit of stars. Various handholds and tethers were arranged along the walls, ceiling, and floor, with a row of seats people could strap themselves into. Storage cabinets flanked the entrance, their doors secured so the contents wouldn't float away in the event of an accidental application of Newton's First Law.

The crew climbed inside and slid their respective arms through nearby restraints. Once settled, they turned their attention to Bianca, who had taken one of the seats, her blond ponytail now wrapped into a prim bun.

"Let's begin!" Bianca announced, moving her finger along the datapad's surface. One of the cabinets opened, and a few dozen drones floated out. They drifted into the center of the chamber, then arranged themselves into an odd grid pattern. Some were close together, others had gaps between them. Each cast a dim glow around them in about a meter radius, leaving some areas darker than others, like a maze of shadow and light. At the far end of the room, a holographic green flag appeared, waving in a nonexistent breeze.

"What are we looking at, here?" Captain Franklin asked, hands on their hips.

"This is a trust challenge," Bianca explained. From a box underneath her seat, she pulled out a pair of handheld propulsion units and a length of fabric, which the captain examined with a raised eyebrow.

"My trust is definitely challenged," Omeika muttered to Ankur, who snickered.

If Bianca heard the comment, she didn't react. "Each of you will wear that blindfold, one at a time," she said. "You'll start there." She pointed at a spot along the wall, level with a place where no drones hovered. "The rest of the crew will verbally guide you through the maze of drones until you reach the other side. If a drone is activated before the flag is reached, that crew member is out, and the next person takes their place. You keep going until as many crew members as possible are safely on the other side."

"What happens if one of us floats into a space with a drone?" Captain Franklin asked.

Bianca gave a theatrical wince. "You'll be hit with a small red paintball. Non-toxic, of course, and it should wash out easily. It does smell unpleasant, I'm sorry to say. Like microwaved fish."

Dexter laughed evilly and rubbed his hands together. "Oh, this is going to be fun."

"Who makes paint that smells like fish?" Ankur asked, eying Dexter warily.

"I can search for that information if you genuinely wish to know," Santi said. Ankur shook his head in reply.

"I just want to know why we're doing this," Omeika said. "This thing specifically, I mean. Are there seriously no team-building exercises that don't involve doing something gross, literally or figuratively?"

Before Bianca could answer, Captain Franklin held up a hand and the crew fell silent. "This is our last activity for the day," they said. "Once it's finished, we can head to the ship and start prepping for our trip. Right, Bianca?"

"That's correct, Captain," Bianca replied primly, her datapad balanced on her forearm.

"Then let's do this," Captain Franklin said. "I'll go first." They eased out of their restraints and climbed over to Bianca, who handed them the blindfold and propulsion units.

The captain unfolded the blindfold fully, testing its strength and elasticity. Squinting at the array of drones, they climbed over to Grace and held a whispered conference with her while the others watched with varying degrees of nervousness or annoyance. Captain Franklin pulled Omeika in next, then Ankur, and finally Santi, all of them sharing a single handhold on the wall. The captain pointed at the drones at different points on the field, and Grace and Ankur drew lines in the air with their hands while Santi offered input. Dexter tried to eavesdrop, but Captain Franklin glared at him until he floated away, hands raised in a submissive gesture.

The huddle eventually broke up, and Captain Franklin crooked a finger at Dexter. "Give me your shoe, Lawrence," they said.

"My what?" Dexter asked, confusion wrinkling his nose.

"Your shoe," Captain Franklin repeated patiently, their brown eyes unblinking.

"Which one?"

Captain Franklin shrugged. "Doesn't matter."

Dexter lifted his other leg, pulling his black loafer off and sending it drifting toward the captain.

Captain Franklin caught the shoe and handed it to Grace, who hefted it experimentally. She shrugged with a single shoulder.

"Smaller might be better," Grace said.

"It might," Captain Franklin said. "I think we need the mass though. If this doesn't work, we'll try the mustard."

"The what?" Dexter asked, puzzled.

"I still think my eye would serve the purpose," Santi said. "But I understand the damage concerns."

"Your what?" Dexter asked.

Bianca merely watched, eyebrows vanished into her wispy bangs.

Grace hooked a foot through one of the straps and leaned away from the wall. She took a stance like a baseball pitcher, cocked her arm back, and threw Dexter's shoe at the drones.

"Oh!" Bianca exclaimed.

"Hey!" Dexter yelled at the same time.

The shoe rocketed toward one of the drones in the second row. It struck the hovering machine squarely, knocking it into the drone in another square. A series of ricochets occurred then, and every drone that was bumped released a tiny projectile. Some of the paintballs hit other drones, while some missed. Their motion was apparently enough to trigger the other drones' sensors, and those units also fired. Red paint splattered against the walls and ceiling and floor, but by luck or careful planning, none of it hit the crew members.

Ankur whooped and high-fived Grace. Omeika patted her shoulder, and Captain Franklin gave her a gleeful thumbs-up that made her blush.

"A very well-executed throw," Santi said. "One more will maintain an adequate trajectory for the drones to leave us a clear path."

"This isn't..." Bianca spluttered. "You can't..." Wisps of hair escaped her blond ponytail as she clutched her datapad to her chest.

Captain Franklin crossed their arms over their broad chest. "It's already done," they said. "Are we prohibited from attempting the same maneuver again?"

Bianca's mouth opened and closed. Her blue eyes darted back and forth between the drifting drones, the captain, and the crew.

"Lawrence," Captain Franklin said, still staring at Bianca. "Give me your other shoe."

"No way," Dexter said. "Use someone else's shoe." He looked down at his feet, one now wearing only a sock.

Captain Franklin held their empty hand out, palm up, and shifted their gaze to Dexter. "Are you part of this crew or not?" they asked. "It's your choice. You've spent all day acting like a goon. Now is your chance to contribute. We finish this, and we all get out of here. Together."

Dexter met the captain's eyes with a scowl, his brow furrowed. Gradually, his expression shifted, jaw relaxing, forehead lines smoothing out. He glanced at the rest of the crew, then at Bianca, then back at the captain.

"Come on, man," Ankur said.

"Do it, Dexter," Omeika said.

"Please?" Grace added.

Santi merely watched, blinking his calm violet eyes.

"Fine," Dexter said, and pulled off his other shoe. He handed it to Captain Franklin, then hovered there in his socks, nervously wiggling his toes.

The rest of the crew cheered, and Captain Franklin passed the shoe to Grace. She took up the same stance as before, then launched the second shoe toward an unmoving drone. It careened into the drone next to it, causing a chain reaction that shifted more of them out of the way and sent paintballs flying. Once the wild motions of the machines had settled into a slow drift, what was left on the field was a straight path to the flag, if they timed it properly. The air recirculators kicked in suddenly, wafting the scent of fish toward them.

Captain Franklin stood at the edge of the marked squares and tied on the blindfold, then held a propulsion unit in each hand. "Everyone ready?" they asked.

In answer, Omeika grabbed their wrist and closed her eyes. Grace took her hand and did the same. Ankur held Grace's hand, and Santi's, who turned and reached out for Dexter.

"Are you coming?" Santi asked.

Dexter hesitated, then took the android's hand gently, his expression inscrutable. With a shaky breath, he closed his eyes.

Captain Franklin activated the propulsion units, making sure to aim them so the gas inside wouldn't hit Omeika. Drones spun and floated around the crew as they flew straight across the field, toward the green flag awaiting them at the other end.

The newly graduated crew assembled in the hallway outside the meeting room, already discussing their plans for reconvening on the ship and starting the final preparations for their long journey to Triton. Omeika cracked a joke that made Ankur burst into stuttering laughter, which trailed off as they walked away, toward the cafeteria, for what Captain Franklin called "a mandatory 3:05 coffee break, caffeine optional."

Dexter peeled off from the group with a wave and ducked into a restroom. A few minutes later, he emerged and scanned the hallway, then returned to the meeting room. Bianca sat in one of the folding chairs, eyes glued to her datapad, on which she was furiously scribbling notes.

"That went well, I thought," Dexter said, taking a seat across from her.

"It did," Bianca replied, not looking up. "Priscilla is checking the drones for damage but so far she hasn't found anything."

"Good deal." Dexter chuckled quietly. "Thanks for the spare shoes."

"Oh, yes, of course," Bianca said absently. "I wasn't going to make you suffer through that fish smell all afternoon, not after your heroic sacrifice."

They fell silent for a few minutes as Bianca continued to write. Finally she stopped and looked up, her shoulders dropping as if she'd released a load of tension all at once. Dexter smiled at her, warm and genuine, unlike the cocky grins he'd plastered on earlier.

"It's incredible how different every group is," Bianca said. "You think you know what to expect, but they always throw you a curveball."

"Or a shoe," Dexter said.

"Or a shoe," Bianca agreed. "I think we might retire that activity."

"Not the trolley problem?" Dexter asked. "Everyone hates that one."

Bianca rubbed her eyes with one hand. "It tends to work well, though. It either reinforces the cohesion from the first activity or helps us see where future issues will arise." She lifted her datapad again. "That reminds me. I need to let the captain know we're swapping you out."

"Who's taking over as steward?" Dexter asked.

"Ramón Suarez. He's been on standby for a week, and Captain Franklin worked with him at DanausEx, so he should integrate quickly."

Dexter slapped his knees and stood up. "Guess I'll head to my hab unit, then. Nice to get out early for a change."

Bianca smirked up at him. "Tired of playing the villain, 'Dexter Lawrence'?"

"You know," Dexter said, "I kind of am. But it pays the bills."

"We all have our roles," Bianca said, more gently. She looked down at her datapad, then swiped it off. "Come on," she said. "Let's get a coffee."

Dexter laughed incredulously. "From the cafeteria?"

"No, a real coffee," Bianca said. "The kind that's all flavored syrup and whipped cream. My treat."

"You're on, B. Just don't call me Dexter in public."

The pair left the meeting room behind, its "Welcome to Limosa Corp!!!" sign flickering off with the rest of the lights. They ambled down the hallway, reliving the day, relaxing as they shed their respective false personalities like company uniforms.

"We do make a good team," Bianca said, stepping into the elevator.

"The best," Dexter said, and they shared a fist bump as the doors closed in front of them.

— THE PLANET BUILDERS —
By Peter Tieryas

I

It was the third planet he'd messed up. Staring at the devastation below, Hwanin felt the kind of despair that made both his stomachs shrink. This third time was the final opportunity. He'd hoped the planet could finally get over the cultural hump and reach intergalactic capabilities. But it was Armageddon all over again, and life on his planet was going to end in annihilation.

"Dammit," Hwanin cursed.

He'd spent months on this project, over four billion of their years. It was true, many of the initial components were from the universal library shared by the planet builders, which he assembled like construction blocks. But he'd also injected his own new programming logic to try out elements that had never been done before. The SI, or simulated intelligence, ensured that the physics engine was relatively stable across the board; there were agreed upon rules for the Sephiroths of this universe. But the cultural components, tied together by the environmental conditioning, were always such a delicate balance to master. It took almost three and a half billion years to even get to the point where he could evolve life to take on consciousness. Accelerating that process often meant the planetary conditions wouldn't be ripe for life. But the "free will" mechanism necessitated delicate guidance.

He was invisible to the Crepitans thanks to special reflective optics. As a planet builder, he could teleport anywhere, either by shifting the gravitational effect so he could fly, or splicing holes in space and warping to anywhere he wished. He was high above the northern continent, and he could feel the chill as he watched the side calling themselves the C'thaomindlokaa'bbqq fire a Solidifer beam at their mortal enemy and transform the entire gaseous metropolis of L'sfaaqmemssse into ammonium crystals. A million Crepitans had their lives crushed in an instant. Unlike simulations, he could feel their pain, their anguish, and their abrupt end. No matter how often he experienced death from unnatural causes, it hurt him each time. The SI provided statistics and analysis along with possible options available to him. He'd watched his people build L'sfaaqmemssse from a single puff of smoke into something grander than the nebulas Picasso and Michaelangelo and all the others liked to paint as inspiration for the beings the planet builders created. Those paintings made of stardust and ionized gases were meant to evoke awe and a sense of wonder. While some of the Crepitans were curious about the stars, the majority engaged in local political squabbles that got worse with the drastic environmental damage they'd caused. The doomsday beam (it was always something gargantuanly outsized) was decimating life on the planet and would change it forever.

There were limits on Hwanin's ability to intervene. Certainly, he wasn't allowed to break the physics engine without potentially harming the fabric of the entire universe. There was a mathematical balance the engineers had spent trillions of years finessing.

A reminder popped up in his interface from the SI. He had a Deity Board meeting later that day. What was he going to tell them? They were the ones who got to make the final call on whether he'd make it into the program and graduate to universe creation, or be banished down to shepherd one of the thousands of defunct planets barely cking by. No one wanted that, especially as it was a term that lasted as long as the civilization and required caretakers to live exactly like the beings they watched over.

Hwanin, like the rest of his classmates, had no necessity for a physical form. But within the constraints of this universe, had chosen to take the universal standard: a tripedal humanoid form with feathers and cetacean skin. Gender was optional, but as he'd been agender in the last two incarnations and female the three times before that, he decided he'd give male a try.

He couldn't watch the destruction anymore. He took a warp hole and came back to their central hub ship, *Yomi*, where a message awaited him from Nuwa. She'd sent him an empathic message and invited him to the Tian Bar for a drink.

"I'll head over after my reports are done," he messaged her back.

"Perfect," she replied. "I still have to deal with the new world war they're raging."

"Another one? I thought they weren't due for one for a few decades."

"That's what I thought too."

He spent some time updating his report, trying to figure out how he was going to explain this to the Deity Board. Why did his civilizations keep destroying each other? He thought by making this planet gaseous and its life forms gas-based, he could prevent the kind of destruction that seemed endemic to solid-base existences. But these gaseous beings were just as destructive as his two previous worlds with their carbon-based life forms. He wrapped up his report as best as he could and headed to the Tian Bar.

II

When Hwanin arrived, he saw his old classmate, Yahweh, by himself, depressed as usual. "How's it going?" Hwanin asked.

Yahweh, still sporting his bipedal form with gray beard and halo, shook his head. "I know I shouldn't do it, but I look back on Terra every few days and am even more revolted at the new ways they're killing each other in my name."

"It was a good idea," Hwanin tried to assure him, remembering Yahweh's desire for a direct intervention to teach the humans about sacrifice. "The simulation scores were off the chart."

"It's always a good idea on the simulation. But when it comes to execution... I mean, could it be more clear? *Love thy neighbor as thyself.* How does that lead to wars and crusades and exterminations?"

"You could do another intervention?" Hwanin suggested.

"I'm done," Yahweh replied, shaking his head. "Their logic algorithms were impeccable. I spent a million years getting the planet ready, guiding the people through. But look at them now. Their cultural progress is laughable. They've pretty much destroyed all the resources and climate engineering I built up, but they're claiming to do it in my name."

Hwanin remembered when Yahweh was propped up as the most brilliant new planet builder in the community. His ideas were considered revolutionary and bold. But when the humans failed to advance beyond their tiny planet and ended up destroying each other multiple times, his stellar reputation suffered. The only reason he still remained was that he'd worked out a deal with the board prior to starting that he'd get to stick with the Terrans as long as he wanted, a privilege the others didn't have.

"Maybe they'll eventually get it together," Hwanin said to him.

"Doubtful." Yahweh looked up at him. "How's Crepitus?"

"They built a gas solidifier super weapon that changes all life into crystalline form, terminating them immediately. Two-thirds of my gas planet is now crystal. It looks gorgeous and makes for a nice art display. But fails to get my species off the planet."

"They twist logic in their strange ways and find the most creative ways of hurting each other."

"I played with the idea of doing an intervention. I know you're against it now. But I wondered if I could explain to the—"

"You forgot what they did to my physical body?"

"Well, no," Hwanin admitted, having watched the footage of Yahweh's physical body being crucified as was required now for all budding planet builders.

"I couldn't deactivate my pain sensors," Yahweh said with a shudder.

Hwanin knew how these sessions spiraled into a completely depressed state and was grateful Nuwa arrived to save him. He excused himself and greeted Nuwa heartily. Nuwa had taken on a female form this iteration, though she'd gone the quadrupedal route with eight arms and three heads to help with planet management.

Nuwa's three heads greeted him back. "Heard you had a rough day," she said.

"It's hard to get these organisms not to massacre each other," Hwanin replied. "But talking to Yahweh cheered me up."

Nuwa laughed. "He's so depressing, you can't help but be uplifted."

"How's Planet War Twelve?"

"Fourteen," Nuwa corrected him. "It is worse than ever. I hate my people."

"But they're your creations."

"I hate them," Nuwa repeated. "They are mean, vicious, and downright evil. I wish I could outlaw death. But the 'only way to evoke any sense of desire or longing in them is to make them fear mortality or they'll be content where they are and never leave the planet,'" she said.

She was quoting Planet Building Philosophy and Motivations, taught by Professor Elizabeth Maria, known as a brilliant planet builder who'd created a whole civilization connected by a series of wormholes. (All the planet builders had a tough time coming up with new names; they usually grabbed them from fellow planet builders and colleagues they admired.)

"We've tried the immortality route," Hwanin pointed out, remembering the catastrophe of his first test civ before the official examinations commenced.

"Yeah. It just means the ones you really hate are around forever."

Hwanin had to confess, "I'm starting to hate my people too."

"Not good for the spirit to get this way."

"I-I've been having second thoughts... I don't know if I'm cut out for this."

"Then quit," Nuwa said. "This isn't worth the anxiety and stress."

Hwanin nodded. "It's just, I've committed so much time to it."

"What's a few trillion years in the ultimate scheme of things?"

"A whole lot of regrets," Hwanin replied. Time was constructed inherently as a paradoxical, relative, ever-shifting component of their universe. Planet builders could jump to any point in their chronology, but only carry out changes in linear mode. Once something had happened in time, it was almost impossible to change without drastically changing the underlying fabric holding it together. This was an intentional limitation by the programmers so planet builders wouldn't cheat by changing mistakes, thus fibbing the progress of their civilizations.

Nuwa moved closer to him, and the right head whispered, "Do you think there's something in our programming logic that's leading them towards this?"

"What do you mean?"

"There's a flaw in the programming that's leading them to exterminate each other."

Hwanin, who'd believed himself cursed, found it hard to believe. "That'd mean we had no chance to begin with."

"Exactly," the left head replied.

"But other students have been graduating."

"The last twenty-three civ attempts have been fails," Nuwa's middle head informed him.

"Really?"

All three of Nuwa's heads blinked in confirmation.

"I knew there'd been lots of fails, but I just thought maybe our class wasn't that good."

Just as she was about to reply, a familiar voice accosted them. "There you two are," the dulcet voice of their guidance counselor, Lucifer, said. He was the only planet builder in history to have all three of his civilizations reach interstellar capabilities and go on to colonize nearby star systems. He was bipedal, but with massive, folded wings. There were two snake heads coming out from his neck that acted as an extra pair of sensors. Yahweh and Lucifer had once been close, beginning the planet building exams in the same year. But whereas Lucifer had moved on to a leadership role, Yahweh was still stuck on his Terrans. "How'd it go in your last session?"

"There were a few hiccups," Hwanin replied.

"Maybe more than a few," Nuwa added.

"I know you're both on your third civs," Lucifer said, stating the obvious. "If you need me to step in and advise directly, I'd be more than glad to."

"I think my people are beyond redemption," Nuwa said.

"Same here."

"Sometimes, it's a matter of nudging here and there. Don't worry. My advice won't penalize you in any way. I only want to provide guidance."

How could Hwanin refuse? "I'd be grateful for any advice you have," he said.

"I think I'll refrain, if that's all right with you," Nuwa said.

"Of course. I'm here for you whenever you need me," Lucifer said to Nuwa. Turning to Hwanin, he asked, "Shall we give your people a visit?"

"Right now?"

"Time is ticking, right?"

Hwanin looked at Nuwa, whose three heads nodded. "Go ahead," she said in unison.

As they made their way to the gate for a warp, Hwanin said, "I'm grateful for your time."

"Time is the least thing you should be grateful for," Lucifer replied. "It's all so fickle."

"What do you mean?"

"The engineers mete out time the way they want," he said. "All their lives revolve around random measurements."

"We agreed to them."

"Not everyone."

They arrived at Crepitus and found even more destruction rocking the planet. The crystallization process was bombastic, almost melodramatic in the scope of its explosion. This was a blast that reveled in its iridescence. Lucifer clapped at the devastation. "I'm amazed at how thorough your people are in wreaking havoc."

"They are undoing everything I spent a trillion years preparing for them," Hwanin, feeling hopeless, admitted.

"Your friend is wrong," Lucifer said.

"What do you mean?"

"About the creation process being rigged against you."

"How did you hear us?" Hwanin asked.

"She's been telling everyone her suspicions," Lucifer replied. "Naturally, word got back to the Deity Board, and they put her under surveillance. I'm supposed to keep tabs on her."

"Why would the Deity Board care that much what she said?"

Lucifer grinned. "Because it has the semblance of truth. Twenty-three failed civilizations would arouse suspicion in anyone."

"Why are they all failing then?"

"That's what I've been asked to determine. But it seems life is rarer and more difficult than we assumed. Our own civilization can hop through what we define as a universe, but there are some who speculate on existences even beyond our own grasp. The difficulties the planet builders are facing is endemic in creation. Most civs fail because of that."

"You mean we're just not that good," Hwanin said, cutting through to the point.

"The Deity Board wants to eliminate us and replace us with SI."

The simulation intelligence had been designed by the programmers to assist them with planet building. Hwanin had heard rumblings about them taking over various parts of the process to streamline things and open the creative aspects to the designers. Apparently, there was more to the process.

"Why?" Hwanin asked.

"They want to make universe building easier to predict and quantify," Lucifer said.

"What does this mean?"

"It means dopes like Yahweh have lit a fire under us with their incompetence, and if we're not careful, we're all going to be replaced. All these multiuniverses on sale have to be tailored to exactly what the owners want. They want entertainment that meets their expectations. But even the best planet builders, they're not aren't able to pull it off exactly as ordered, which has led to declining property sales. Some of the board believe simulated intelligence should replace us all."

"It makes sense," Hwanin had to acknowledge, feeling another thousand being killed. "My incompetence led to this."

"You're damned if you follow the rules."

"What other choice do we have? It's impossible to cheat with a civ."

"Says who?" he asked.

"Everyone knows it. Anyone who's tried will screw up the fabric of time-space and—"

Lucifer cut him off. "How do you think my civs traveled out of their star system all three times?"

Hwanin was stunned at the implication. "You cheated?"

"I made the playing ground more even," he responded. He pointed to the crystallized remnants of L'sfaaqmemssse. "I doubt the Deity Board will allow you to continue much further without determining this civilization is an irredeemable failure. It'll only be a matter of time before your fart clouds destroy each other."

Hwanin ignored the insult and instead asked, "What kind of cheats are you talking about?"

Lucifer's wings expanded. "A global cataclysm isn't necessarily bad as long as your people survive. It hugely cuts down on the population, but if the technology and resources remain, it's ripe grounds for them developing the capacity to leave their planet. The key is to eliminate their free will."

"But that defeats the whole purpose of what we're doing, doesn't it?" Hwanin questioned.

"And what is it you're doing?"

"Creating a civilization—"

"That ultimately destroys itself. I'd say it's better if it never existed at all rather than endure all this suffering and end up as space dust."

Hwanin considered Lucifer's words. "How do you suspend free will?"

"There's a callback for it, a Boolean you turn off."

"It's that simple?"

Lucifer shrugged. "Absurd, right? You do what you need to, then turn it back on."

"What kind of stuff do you do once you suspend free will?"

"Whatever the civ needs. If religion needs to be outlawed, fine. If a certain massacre is causing people to be upset for a generation or two too long, wipe it from their memories." Lucifer looked intently at his student. "You cannot rely on your creation's free will to save themselves. As a parent, you occasionally need to enforce your own rules on your children, even if they might protest."

Hwanin was intrigued by the prospect, but he was suspicious too. "What's the catch?" he wanted to know. "As much as I'd like to say you're being generous with me, you're also risking a lot."

"If you graduate, when it's time to vote on a new board member, I want your support," Lucifer said.

"That's it?"

"That's it," Lucifer confirmed.

He wished it was his care for his people motivating him to want to accept. But he was really concerned about his job. What was he going to do if he couldn't make it as a planet builder? He'd already invested so much time and yet had next to nothing to show for it. Getting into the testing ground for the planet builders was an incredible opportunity, as so few were accepted. But from there, the real test began as everyone vied to achieve the status of a Deity.

Now, he was going to be kicked out unless he took Lucifer's help and changed things around.

And yet, while every part of him wanted to accept, he found a part of him hesitating. Did he have a greater duty to his people? Wasn't it vital that if they were going to take the next step, it was one they make themselves?

"I can see you're struggling," Lucifer said. "You don't need to decide now."

"I'm probably going to get a fail from the board soon."

"I'll talk to the board, tell them I'm advising you. That'll buy you another cycle. My only request is that you not tell anyone what we discussed."

They returned to their massive hub ship, *Yomi*. Lucifer parted without saying a word. Hwanin meant to exit to his habitat, but felt compelled to return to his world.

He floated among the Crepitans, trying to understand them. How could they act so reprehensibly to each other? It made no sense. He'd done his best for them, but they'd made their own choices. The Crepitans were damned. Was he just going to leave them to it? For him, it meant the loss of a job. For them, it meant the end of their civilization. Despite their animosity to one another, they were capable of incredible works of creativity and imagination. He'd been shocked by the exhibits and galleries they'd designed. Even with their limited capacity, they were perpetually trying to create. They didn't quite grasp that creation was tied in with the exploration of their universe. Art would allow them to travel to distant parts of the galaxy where science was a quantification of the whimsies of the mind. All of this would be lost if he allowed this destruction to continue.

When he got back to the ship, he contacted Lucifer. "I'm in," he said.

Lucifer nodded as though having expected it. "You're a good god."

III

A week passed in *Yomi* time. The ship had its own day-night cycle that didn't correspond with those of the respective civilizations of the builders. For Hwanin, three hundred years passed on Crepitus. With free will disabled and the ability to create a new history, he eliminated all the problems and formed what he considered to be the perfect society. Forget a few wars, eliminate religious zealots, balance economic standing, fix some of the inaccurate physics their scientists had wrongly theorized, and everything changed overnight. As Lucifer had promised, the cheat was ridiculously easy to access once he knew which metadata scopes to turn to. Once he'd repaired what he needed, he toggled free will back on. Hwanin oversaw the Crepitans as they colonized the farthest planet in their star system, even though it was technically a dwarf planet that shouldn't have been able to sustain life. He felt an immense sense of pride at the roads they created between the planets, facilitating almost instantaneous travel via particle acceleration. The infrastructure of their star system looked like a painting from afar. The Deity Board had done an initial inspection of his third civ and appeared impressed. His final assessment would be soon.

Hwanin returned to his habitat and noticed a message from Nuwa requesting he stop by, no matter how late it was.

Her compartment in the ship consisted of a silicon liquid that would melt most, but that he found, with his flesh resistant upgrades, to be warming. Nuwa greeted him and asked, "How are things going?"

"Okay."

Her three faces stared at him dubiously. "I know they have me under surveillance. But in here, nothing gets out, so you can tell me the truth. You accepted his offer to cheat?"

Hwanin was careful not to betray any emotions. "What are you talking about?"

"It's not me that's talking. It's everyone else. Your civ was on the verge of extinction. Now, they're on the brink of traveling to another star system."

"I got inspired by Lucifer," Hwanin offered weakly. "He gave me some pointers."

"You mean he saved your civ with a cheat in exchange for your support so that he can become a board member."

Hwanin didn't want to confess, even though he knew he'd been caught.

Nuwa saw all she needed in his hesitation. "I can't believe you accepted. That's wrong on every level," Nuwa said. "It defeats the whole purpose of why we're here. I will go to the Deity Board with this."

Hwanin was angered by her threat. "What was I supposed to do? Let them all die?"

"That's part of our creed as a planet builder."

"You want to talk about wrong?" Hwanin replied. "We have a moral responsibility to do whatever it takes to ensure they survive. I wasn't going to stand by and watch them destroy themselves again. Wouldn't you do whatever it takes to save them?"

"Planet War Eighteen," she answered.

"What?"

"It was the final war, the one my civ couldn't survive," she said in a grim tone.

"What happened?"

"They found a weapon to destroy the planet core. It killed almost all life except for a few stray villages."

"I'm sorry," Hwanin said.

"So am I," Nuwa replied with deep sorrow in her voice. "The Deity Board gave me my failure notice. I have to either accept curation of one of the dead planets or get off the ship."

"What are you going to do?"

"Get off. I'm not cut out to play god. I don't think you are either," she said.

"Maybe you're right," Hwanin replied, not wanting to argue.

They'd spent so much time together, it was hard to believe she was going to leave soon.

Nuwa's three heads stared at Hwanin. "Tell me the reason you really cheated was because you gave a damn about your gas clouds, and not just to get a job."

"Of course I care," Hwanin replied, even though he knew it was only part of his motivation. "Come with me," he suggested. "See my world."

This caused Nuwa to pause. "What would be the point of that?"

"If you see them, and you still feel like you want to report me, then I won't object."

"Even if you objected, I'd still report you."

"Think of it as a way to kill time then."

Only one of Nuwa's heads shook. The other two were interested.

The moment they entered Crepitan star space, they were met by a fleet of massive ships made from particles. These weren't the usual phallic monuments so common with solid-base lifeforms, but rather, organic in form, as though they were mobile nebulas. Their color shifted based on their relationship to the central star, causing a scintillation that made them resemble a ballet of lights. Nuwa was impressed by the way they synchronized their flights to music, echoing within the gaseous form.

"They have hundreds of those ships, and the best part is, no weapons. They don't have a single militarized unit."

"How'd you pull that off?" Nuwa asked.

"I made them forget all their local strife. The whole civilization is motivated by music and art. That's it."

"What about religion?"

"Eliminated it."

"How do you stop them from killing each other without mythic archetypes to impose morality?"

"As it turns out, a lot of those mythic archetypes were what helped perpetuate more murder." He turned to Nuwa. "I don't have all the answers, and I'm still working out a hundred different things. But what they have here is special."

"They didn't earn it."

"So what? Everyone could use a little push here and there."

"I want to see things at the local level."

They focused on a household of eighteen Crepitans. They inhabited the eighteenth sector of the 194a anticyclonic storm. "Winds are strong," Hwanin warned as they warped to the fourth planet.

The winds were at about 322 km/h, and a crimson field permeated the atmosphere around them.

"It's really red," Nuwa noted.

"That's the acetylene and the irradiation of the ammonium hydrosulfide."

"How do they communicate in here?"

"I'll tighten the sounds so we can hear them."

He adjusted the settings so they could both hear it on a common wavelength. The sounds were angelic, like a choir voice warbling in different tones. "This is more like a symphony than a language," Nuwa said. "What are they saying?"

"Typical family drama. One of them wants to get married, but the eight parents—"

"Eight parents?"

"The Crepitans require biological components from eight separate parents to conceive."

"I thought having three was a headache," Nuwa said. "They object to the suitor?"

"They object to only two of the seven, which is normal, but still full of fireworks."

"I guess marriages are complex events here."

"They take a decade to coordinate," Hwanin said with a grin. "They also have to time it right with the storms to make their elaborate dance work."

They traveled together for a year in Crepitan time. He showed her the beautiful vaporous cities they'd made that blurred the boundaries of space and the gaseous supergiants they inhabited.

A variety of wind wielders gave them their structure, as alien as they seemed.

"You've created a utopia," Nuwa commented.

"I tried. Our own worlds are screwed up as they are. I hope they do better."

"Why is it you think we screw up when we do it on our own?"

"I don't know," Hwanin confessed.

Nuwa sighed. "Damn you. The only reason I don't report you is for your gas clouds. Now buy me a drink."

Hwanin bought Nuwa three. She seemed to want to say something to him, but then said, "I have to get back to my place and pack."

"You're exiting the planet builders?"

"The only other choice is to shepherd. I don't plan on spending a million years, relative-time, in someone's failed world."

She left him at the Tian Bar. He wasn't sure whether guilt, anger, or relief was weighing on him more. He got three more drinks to try to drown away his conflicted emotions. All they did was make him dizzy.

"Congratulations," he heard someone say.

It was Yahweh.

"It feels good, doesn't it, to see your people thrive?

Hwanin, feeling his head swaying from the alcohol, asked, "What if I cheated?"

"Isn't a direct physical intervention a kind of cheat? Mine just didn't work. I thought it did. I believed I could inspire them to act with more kindness and compassion for each other. And for a time, it seemed that way. But then the Dark Ages came..."

Before he knew it, Yahweh was on a rant again about his humans. Normally, Hwanin would have found a way to get out of this. But this time, he sat there and listened to the sad history of the humans for the hundredth time as it made him feel better. "I helped them learn the ability to harness nuclear power so they could energize their whole world and travel to the stars. You know what they did with it?"

After shaking off his drinks, he returned to his world. He wanted to do a last check before the Deity Board arrived for their assessment. To his shock, his people were under attack by a gigantic, planet-sized rabbit. The rabbit not only had destroyed the outer two planets, but had somehow caused an energy drain that was affecting their primary star. The rabbit was currently devouring a major space station in the star system, and Hwanin suddenly felt the shock and pain of thirty thousand lives being terminated.

He didn't know what to do, though he felt a knot of anxiety circling inside of him. Did this mean he was going to fail the assessment from the Deity Board? This rabbit wasn't in any of his coding or physics parameters. To his horror, he realized he didn't know if there was any way to stop this thing. His civilization wasn't prepared for it. The only thing he could think of was to break the physics engine and erase it using a black hole. But that could also impact the gravitational constants of the gaseous forms so their body's internal structure could be torn apart.

He brought up the SI interface and made a query: "What is that rabbit thing?"

"It is the Wenenu, a carnivorous rabbit that eats star systems."

The casualness with which the SI described the monster irritated him.

"How do I stop it?" Hwanin asked.

"Unfortunately, your civilization has not developed enough technology to defeat it."

"I mean, how do *I* stop it?"

"Your only recourse is to destroy the entire star system and deprive it of food so that it will snack elsewhere."

"That's unacceptable!"

The SI, usually so chatty, had no reply.

There was only one other option he could think of. He contacted Lucifer and asked him, "Could you please come here as soon as possible?"

He left the message ten more times. The rabbit drained any semblance of life from the metropolis of New L'sfaaqmemssse.

It felt like a billion years had passed before Lucifer appeared beside him.

"What's the emergency?" he asked.

"That giant rabbit is destroying my world."

"Giant rabbit?"

They warped to the giant rabbit who seemed now to be lying in space, bloated from all the food it had eaten.

"It's attracted to energy. Once your star system reaches a certain threshold, the Rabbit comes," Lucifer explained. "But if your people have the capability of traveling to the stars, they should have the arms required to fend it off. Have them fire a few hydrogen missiles at it," Lucifer said nonchalantly.

"They—they don't have weapons."

"Why not?"

"I've eliminated war. They don't have any concept of conflict, aside from the artistic kind."

Lucifer laughed. "Please tell me you're joking."

"No joke."

"I don't know what to tell you then."

"Why didn't you warn me?"

"Didn't you go through the tutorials?" Lucifer asked. "The Wenenu was detailed in the section for cosmic superbeings that go where they want. If it's not this, there are a hundred other civ destroying cosmic bodies that will destroy your people if they're not prepared."

"I don't remember that part."

"As a planet builder, you should have known." Lucifer's eyes were cold and piercing. "What will you do now?"

"The SI said I only have two choices. Either I watch it destroy everyone, or I destroy them first."

"Either choice means you fail the assessment."

Hwanin couldn't deny it. "Is there some cheat out of this?"

"I'm afraid not. That rabbit is going to breed with all the energy it's gained."

"What should I do?"

"That's your decision," Lucifer coldly replied. "But you've just sealed the doom for the rest of the planet builders."

"How?"

"SI will replace us. I'd been arguing that with a few cheats here and there, non-SI could succeed. You were supposed to be the test case for it."

Behind them, a planet exploded.

"I screwed it up?" Hwanin asked.

"Judicious cheats only help if the person applying them understands the system in the first place. They will study your incompetence and put it on par with Yahweh."

Lucifer left.

Hwanin wondered if a direct intervention could do something. If he appeared as a planet-size Crepitan, would it somehow help? But if he did that, his own body's gravity would affect the other planets. Even a slight shift in their orbit would result in a climate catastrophe. As he tried everything he could to no avail, he found himself prevented by the constraints of the laws of physics. The rabbit regained its appetite and continued its feast. By the time the Deity Board came for their assessment, he had to cancel the review. He had failed, and his Crepitans were going to join the hundreds, maybe thousands, of defunct worlds that failed planet builders had left behind them. Goodbye benefits and generous salary.

IV

Sullen, Hwanin didn't know what to do. He'd already received the documents with his termination notice from the planet builders. He had two days *Yumi*-time to clear out. He sat in his room, unsure how things had unraveled so quickly. There were mementoes from his three civilizations that he'd kept on his shelves, artistic works that he'd found remarkable. He felt an empathic message ping him. "Want to talk?"

It was Nuwa. "Not much to say," he thought back to her. "When do you leave?"

"I don't," she replied. "Visiting your Crepitans inspired me to change my mind."

"What do you mean?"

"I'm going down as a shepherd to what remains of my civ."

He couldn't believe it. They'd all heard horror stories about what shepherds endured. "I thought you hated them."

"I do," she acknowledged. "But there's a few thousand who survived. Maybe they can learn and rebuild."

"You won't be a planet builder. You won't have the same control keys."

"Maybe that's better and I won't feel so responsible."

"Nuwa," Hwanin said with deep concern for his friend. "Once you make this choice, you can't leave until the last being on your planet is dead."

"Or they achieve the threshold I failed to guide them towards."

Which was to go to the stars.

Later that day, Hwanin visited the Crepitans, or at least what was left of them. It wasn't much. The rabbit had been ravenous, and almost all traces of their extraplanetary travels were eaten. He had failed them due to his incompetence, and he felt responsible for the dying society. To his surprise, he saw there were colonies interspersed throughout, still struggling to survive. Theirs had been a bitter struggle, fueled by persistence and ingenuity under duress. They were clinging to life despite his shortcomings. He felt a certain sense of pride in them and thought about the consequences of his actions. There was more to civilizations than the SI or even the Deity Board taught, something only three miserable failures in a row could have drilled into him. Maybe some of those lessons could be useful and he could help them from the clouds up. He thought about Nuwa's decision and knew what he had to do.

— QUANTUM LEAP —
By Justin C. Key

After years of interstellar travel to find an exoplanet that no longer existed, something found us instead. I sat up to focus on the cockpit's display. Since arriving in the Barnard system, *So Fly's* search algorithm reported erroneous signals every few days or so, likely confused by the vast nothing surrounding us. But instead of the usual error message, the display showed specific origin coordinates about thirteen light-years away. I looked out the cockpit to the stars beyond, my mind already going through the calculations. With our particle accelerator supplying a constant 1G push, it would take us about two to three years to cover that distance. The relativity cost would be a hundred thousand years back on Earth. Traversing galaxies at near lightspeeds, we'd already made that leap a long time ago.

I slid to the intercom. "Captain Womack, get up here. We got something."

I pulled up *So Fly's* interface and found Captain Womack reading in the common room. The urgency in my voice did little to stir her; she only glanced at the camera to show her annoyance. Full of life and hope when our six-person crew first went out on this expedition, her afro always perfectly shaped, her smile and warmth felt throughout the ship, the captain had changed the most when we suddenly became five just a few days before.

My finger fell off the comm button. The constellation. It was off. We had stopped accelerating in the middle of Barnard's system months ago just to find a field of uninhabitable rubble. Still undecided on our next course of action, I had stared at these constellations, lost in my thoughts, for days on end. I squinted, just how my father taught me to look at a crescent moon to see the shadowed part facing away from the sun. Yes, there was definitely something there. I checked the signal again to see how far away it was.

I switched the comm to address the entire ship. "Captain Womack, get your ass the fuck up here, now!"

That did it.

"What the hell, Shawn?" Captain Womack said seconds later as she knocked open the cockpit door. "Have you lost your godforsaken mind?"

Her gaze followed my finger out the window. Turning towards the view, I gasped. Just a black shadow moments before, only decipherable by how it blocked out the stars behind it, the mystery object now materialized as something tangible. To call it a craft wouldn't be accurate. It almost looked like a tree, thin at the base and branching up and out of the view in tendrils. Its top seemed to blend into the cosmos.

"How did we miss this?" The accusation in her tone wasn't lost on me. *How did* you *miss this?* I was, after all, the crew's cartographer and navigator.

I reloaded it and wiped the screen; the result was the same. The nature of the signal was unchanged. The origin coordinates, however, were. According to the computer, the signal came from right here in the Barnard system. Only a thousand miles from our location.

"Either the computer is shit and this object appeared out of nowhere, undetected, or..." I looked at the Captain. "Or this thing has been traveling damn near the speed of light from when it first sent the signal."

"I knew Shawn would be the first to crack," Spry said as he entered the room. The deck came alive as more crew followed behind him. "Bet the last freeze-dried tiramisu that the captain bodies him."

"You already ate the last tiramisu," London said. "What's going on?"

"That's what's going on," I answered. Then, to the captain, "What do you think it is?"

"I don't know. Get full system scans. Check the logs for energy spikes for the last forty-eight hours."

"You're thinking it came through a wormhole?"

"I'm not thinking anything. Get information first, then we'll think."

Spry leaned over me to shut off the comm, which was still beeping. There was a hint of bourbon on his breath. "Finally. I haven't had coffee yet and my head is killing me. What are you watching?"

"My god, we found it," London said. Her physician's bag close to her side, she pushed past Spry to touch the cockpit window. For the first time since Dwayne died, I saw the beginnings of a smile on her face. "That's it."

"That's what?" Spry said.

"Life."

"What's this talk about life?" Shamia said, the last one through the cockpit door.

"The fuck I miss?" Spry said. He punched the controls. I shifted as my chair tilted under his weight. The cockpit window grayed into a computer screen. He pushed another button and it cleared away, showing the same view as before. In those few seconds, it seemed, the object came into even better view. "Looks like Oakland. This is a joke, right?"

Oakland. A brief silence fell over us at the mention of the city. None of us talked that much about home anymore. Had the city of Oakland meant anything to me? It must have, the way I felt at the sound of its name. I shook away the feeling. We'd all given up any connection to our old lives a long time ago. It only made sense to focus on the present and what was right in front of us.

I could see the thing fully now, so clear that it was hard to imagine that it had been virtually invisible just a few minutes before.

"Put our shields at one hundred percent," Captain Womack said. "Make sure our weapons work. Run full diagnostics. If there's anything that even smells like life on there, I want to know about it."

"Doesn't sound like a joke," Shamia said. "Oakland, eh? We just found life."

"No," I said. "Life found us."

"Oakland" floated static in front of us. I spent much of the next couple twenty-four-hour cycles watching it through the ship's protective barrier. I tried altering our course and varying our acceleration. The monolith's velocity didn't change relative to ours: it matched us exactly.

So Fly's scans showed a honeycomb interior with hollowed paths carved throughout. The computer system analyzed the pattern against all known lifeforms on earth and didn't find anything that matched known colony architecture. Even more, there was a complete lack of organic material. *So Fly* searched first for organic carbon. Then it explored a plethora of calculations of what life "as we do *not* know it" might look like. Nothing remotely compatible registered on the scans.

The last thing the computer looked for was energy expenditures. Not only did it find that there weren't any traces of energy cycling, past or present, consistent with biology, but there wasn't an energy signal *at all*. The energy of the vessel was the same as the surrounding background.

Which was, in a way, impossible. *Oakland* accelerated and decelerated. And there was an entrance near the bottom that opened and closed periodically, like breathing. Captain Womack postulated the vessel was actively creating an energy vacuum to balance out its energy signal. Still, such a feat would have to be near perfect. And very intentional.

"One of us is going to have to check it out." Captain Womack addressed the crew in the common room some seventy hours post-contact. London trimmed wilting spiderettes from a lone hanging spider plant as the captain spoke. The rest of us sat around the central table. The air stank of insomnia.

"You mean go inside?" Spry said. *Oakland* seemed to touch him the most. Always discreet, he never drank in front of us. The lingering smell of alcohol and the occasional mid-day deep sleep were the only signs he allowed. Now, I suspected he hadn't taken a sip since *Oakland* arrived. His eyes were sharper, his tongue clearer. As if he were preparing himself for something.

In a lot of ways, I guess *Oakland* sobered all of us.

"If it makes sense to, yes," Captain Womack said. She waited for a rebuttal. There was none. We drew sticks. I got the short end. "Well, that decides it, then. You straight, Shawn?"

I was. There was a catalog of feelings associated with *Oakland* and not a lot of time to process. Fear wasn't on the agenda. That, most of all, made me curious.

When everyone was gone, I picked the straws out from the trash and sized them up. Just as I suspected. Two of the straws were significantly shorter than the rest.

I found Shamia watching the monolith from the main bridge's viewpoint. I came to stand beside her. She twirled one of London's trimmed spider plants between her fingers.

"The good doctor cut this one off prematurely, I think," she said. "It's still got life to it."

"I didn't take you for a botanist," I said.

"I'm not. I put the mama plant in the quarantine bay. To keep you company when you get back."

"You wanted to go," I said. She was set to deny it until I showed her the straw. "You didn't get it short enough."

Shamia sized me up. We hadn't talked much during the mission. The first night out of the solar system Captain Womack passed around moonshine. Both of us had one sip of the stuff and then bowed out of the rest of the drinking game, watching as our crewmates, including the captain, got piss drunk. Somewhere in the night, well after the sting of moonshine had left our throats, our laughter turned into kisses. With the next day came mutual regret, written clearly in the awkward air that existed between us since.

"I thought the short stick stays."

"Bullshit. Why do you want to go?"

"I figure there's one of three things inside that thing," she said. She counted off on the yellowing leaves of the plant. "One: nothing. If we're going to waste our time, I'd rather be out there than waiting here in anticipation. Two: it's something fucking awesome that the human mind can hardly fathom. Three: it's a horrible monster that's going to infect whoever goes over there and use them to kill the rest of us. In which case, I'd rather get it over with."

"What do you think it is?"

She shook her head. "Whatever it is, it came undetected, uncontested, and I bet the only reason the computer picked it up at all was because it *wants* to be picked up."

"Those are all good points," I said. "You've convinced me."

"You'll trade with me?"

"No. You convinced me not to trade."

"You're an asshole, you know that?"

She handed me the plant. Its leaf edges crumbled under my hold.

"What am I supposed to do with this?" I said.

"Be less of an asshole, maybe? Take it with you. Maybe it'll be good luck and you won't end up killing us all."

"If I turn into a murderous zombie, I'll kill you last, if that makes up for it."

"No, not last. That also sucks. Somewhere in the middle. Make me a nice, middle kill."

"You got it."

Something about the vastness of space made the human mind feel infinitesimally small and unimportant. Everything civilization built, studied, and congregated around was, in part, to distract from that vastness. Even *So Fly*, with its familiar walls and rooms and artwork from home, protected against the truth of this.

Now, out in the open, I felt how small I was. A derivative of stardust put into an ancient cosmic dance with other stardust to spark life that then went through a cycle of energy, creation and destruction, unbroken, all the way up until me.

"Earth to Shawn." Spry's voice. "Earth to Shawn."

Muffling, an angry voice, some laughter, and then Captain Womack was in my ear. "You straight, Shawn?"

"Yeah, I'm good," I said.

"State your name—"

"I'm good," I said. Dwayne's sudden death during a spacewalk had shaken *So Fly's* crew to its core. We still didn't know what happened, only that his spacesuit had a clean puncture in its arm. After the autopsy London simply stated that he'd died of asphyxiation and spoke on it no more.

"Name."

I gave her my name and also the date as determined by the ship's motherboard. After that, I began to list off the rough coordinates of where we were in the Milky Way galaxy, orbiting the star Barnard, approximately one hundred thousand kilometers from now disintegrated exoplanet—

"All right, all right. Point made. Focus. Keep moving." *Or else I'll pull you back in, as soon as I have reason to.*

This last didn't need to be said.

I targeted my thrusters towards where the scans showed an entrance. Acceleration in space was different than on Earth. Leaving the atmosphere, you could feel yourself pushing against something, fighting both the gravity that called you back into the planet's embrace and the atmosphere that objected to your departure. Out here, among the stars, there was neither, just the push forward.

"Slow down, Shawn!" Captain Womack's voice came crackling in my ear.

"What? I'm fine."

"That's an—" And then, silence.

Suddenly, *Oakland* consumed my vision.

I turned so the length of my right arm and shoulder could take the brunt of the impact. At this speed, I knew injury was unavoidable. What I could control was my angle of collision. Too sharp and a broken bone would pierce right through my spacesuit, and there would be two bodies lying in our morgue.

The bone snapped—not violently, just matter-of-factly—as I rolled my shoulder into the wall and onto my back. Finally, I stopped.

"All good," I said into the comm. "I think I might have crushed the plant you gave me, Mia."

No answer came. Not even static.

I took a second to breathe. I checked my vitals. Only slight internal bleeding at the site of the fracture. I grit my teeth as the suit squeezed around my arm, assessed the area, and then acted as countless strong fingers to set the fracture. Soon, the merciful morphine kicked in. Just enough to take the edge off the pain without compromising my cognition.

"Okay, piece of cake," I said. "You guys and gals still there?"

No answer. Suddenly, I didn't care. In front of me were a small set of stairs, about three or four, leading up to what looked like a narrow porch. Beyond it, a door. Made of wood.

Fucking wood.

I opened it and went inside.

There was so much *noise* when I returned. Captain Womack barked orders at everyone, Spry asked me questions that I pretended not to hear, and London got to work on my arm.

"You shouldn't be touching him," the captain said.

"This is a Class 1 fracture," London said. "He needs a cast. The suit is only temporary."

"That's an order. We have protocol."

"Fuck protocol. You want to throw me out the airlock, do it, but you brought me on this goddamn ship to be a doctor and that's what I'm going to do."

"She's going to kill the whole fucking ship," Spry said. "Haven't you seen Alien? Haven't any of you seen *Alien*?"

"Fuck off, Spry," London said.

I would have laughed. Before. Perhaps not, though, as before it wouldn't have been funny to me. Because now I *knew*. This was nothing like that movie. We hadn't been beckoned or lured by some alien life. The entity I had come across in that vessel was in the form least expected: sentient, human, familiar.

After London made sure there we no major blood vessel injuries and placed a proper casting on my arm, they put me in quarantine and started the medical scans. It took my full concentration to be sure they all came back negative. It didn't work like things I had to concentrate on before. Bringing in the ship to port took a lot of focus, but it was still an imprecise action with infinitesimal variations from one attempt to another, regardless of what was considered a success.

When I looked at the scanning retina I saw it now and as it had been *before*. What's more, I saw what it would become. I saw its light dim and die, the machine around it rust and crumble. Shifting this new perspective, I saw it, and everything around me, destroyed in a quick, blazeless destruction.

And then, there were the choices. In my current state the scans would find nothing, because there really was nothing. At least, nothing technology could see. But if I let my mind wander into possibilities, the scan might find that my kidney temporarily stopped working, or that my brain fired in all places at once. I saw the alarm sent up from this, saw quarantine extend, saw the uncertainty, saw *Oakland* leave before we could finish our work here.

So I stayed in the middle. I stayed safe. Because the work was everything.

I was admiring the hanging spider plant in the far corner of the quarantine room when Captain Womack came to talk. I felt the soil and inspected the tips of its drooping sprouts. London alone took care of the plant. She had done well, but the last few days we had all been preoccupied. I fished from my pocket the trimming Shamia had given me and pushed its already curling roots into the soil.

I turned to the captain as she punched in the security code, waited for the sliding door to open, and stepped into my holding cubicle. She leaned against the wall and looked at me for a long time. She hadn't slept. I didn't need my new intuition to tell me this. I went to sit at the table.

As she opened her mouth to speak, I said the words for her: "Why the fuck am I so calm?"

Her eyes widened, then narrowed. Her head tilted to the side. Finally, she nodded. "Well? Why are you so calm? You went into that floating tree thing, broke your arm, and you come out serene."

"What do you think it means?"

"I'd rather you be worried. Hell, I'm scared to death. Should I be? Scared?"

"I can't tell you what you should feel, Captain."

She raised her eyebrows. It was unusual for me to be so formal with her. I knew this, but at the same time she *was* the captain. And it felt only logical for me to call her as such.

But she was also a first mate, an engineer, a paraplegic, and a faded name on a death certificate. She was many things, when I really thought about it.

"What did I say to you when we first left the solar system?"

I smiled. "I am not an imposter, Brenda." The use of her proper name seemed to be just as off-putting. "*Oakland* changed me. But the base is still here."

Captain Womack nodded. Then she walked out of the room, slid the door closed behind her, and locked it.

"You're going to stay in here. Until we figure out what's going on."

I'd miscalculated something. "What's the point of that? I am being honest and open with you."

"It's a feeling. And that's all I need."

That hadn't gone well. Though doors and locks meant little to me now, I could see that revealing this truth would just worsen our situation.

I refocused. This new skill was not easy. Going back—going *across*—felt like new birth. I saw the beginning of this conversation the same fuzzy way someone might see out of their periphery. Both past and present were in the margins, to be sure.

I admired the spider plant. Its base was a vibrant green from the oxygen it had learned to convert into energy. I cradled one of the many babies closest to me and felt it warm in my presence. It knew much about the history of our long-lost home and it was eager to share. Soon, I'd have time to listen.

I turned as Captain Womack punched in the security code, waited for the sliding door to open, and stepped into my holding cubicle. She leaned against the wall and looked at me for a long time.

She opened her mouth to say something. This time, I let her.

"Why the fuck are you so calm?"

"I saw something in there. In *Oakland*." I paused to explore time's periphery. Though there were a million things I could see, only a few were strong possibilities. Their roads were clear. I chose one. "No, not see. Not really. Experienced. I'm glad I did. I think it wants to help us."

"This 'it' has wants?"

"Not in the sense you think. I don't quite know what happened in there, but I know everything's going to be fine. *Oakland* isn't dangerous. It won't hurt us."

The captain found relief in this, which was my goal. What's more, she was relaxing.

"So, what do we do now?"

"Our mission was to find this exoplanet and populate it. Barnard is a failure. But we can still finish."

"You're saying this thing can help with that? How?"

I could have told her the truth of it, what would have to happen, but it would be better if she came to that conclusion herself. Instead, I thought of a dozen analogies, saw how they all played out, and picked the best to lead her down the necessary path.

"What's your favorite food here?"

She threw her hands up, laughed, and shook her head. "Okay. The oxtails."

"Have you ever tried it straight out the package? Freeze-dried?"

"Once was enough. I was feeling lazy and wanted something quick. I thought it would be the same,"

"It was better with the water?'

"Exponentially. I was surprised it was just water and not a secret sauce."

"Just water. Exactly. Not organic. Not alive. But mix it with something that has those properties and...magic." I paused to let my words sink in. This was based on knowing how the conversation would go without such a moment. "Whatever was in there, was my water."

"So if you were freeze dried, what are you now?"

Expanded, I thought, and for a moment I thought the captain received it. No, she didn't have that ability. I could send, I could sense that in myself, but it would be like transmitting radio waves in a world where no radios existed.

Instead, I said. "You're the captain. It's your job to find out."

Everyone had questions for me but no one asked them. They were following captain's orders, of course. I didn't need my ears to detect her private conversations with each of them. The vibrations created by her vocal cords dissipated into *So Fly's* walls. By the time it reached me it was more rhythm than sound.

Oakland still worried Captain Womack. Not just its effect on me, but the downstream effect on her crew. Curiosity bred unrest.

Regardless, I had a plan and a purpose. The purpose aligned with the monolith's original goals, which dated back to the beginning of the universe as we knew it. But the purpose also aligned with me, because it manifested in me.

I saw all the ways of going about that purpose spread out in a hazy film, like the vibrations of a tuning fork. I smiled at a path that stood out above the rest.

The discreet gazes of my fellow crew members trailed me as I went to my room and fished out the old deck of cards from my drawer. Collective attention was still mine as I re-entered the common room. I took advantage.

"Spades, anyone?"

We did two teams of two; Captain Womack sat out. The tension and apprehension in the air was thick. Heartrates, breathing patterns, temperatures, radiation profiles, and smells suggested that no one was comfortable. I shut these metrics off and let in only the senses of before. To ease my crewmates, I needed to simply be Shawn.

I shuffled the cards, made sure to fumble one time, cleaned up the mess, and began to deal. "Baby Joker's Wild," I said.

"Bullshit," Spry said. "No one plays like that."

"Everyone who plays spades plays like that," I said.

"Oh Lord, here we go," Shamia said.

This was familiar. Everyone relaxed a little.

"Okay, if we doing Baby Joker, then we playing in the penalty," Spry said.

"That hurts *us*." London sat across from Spry, making her his partner.

"Excuse me?"

"You're the worst at bidding. Matter fact, I need a new partner."

Shamia cackled. "The doctor got jokes!"

"Okay, bet." I picked up my cards. "Baby Joker's Wild, penalty for underbidding."

"Say less," Shamia said. "Fine with me."

"How much you got, Spry?" London said.

Spry picked through his cards. "Two. Maybe three."

I laughed. After a shocked pause, the crew joined me. I knew his hand, as one of the fringe future realities showed everyone's hand, though in this middle one we wouldn't get that far. My access of this wasn't nefarious; my choices in the game would be the same.

I laughed because Spry had at least seven books, including both jokers. I laughed because laughter was disarming and if I was going to challenge the very fabric of their self-identities, I needed them to be vulnerable.

"You all ever wonder what we're doing here?" I said at the tail end of our collective joy.

"Whooping that ass, that's what we're doing." Spry smacked a king of diamonds down on the table. "What?" he said at London's look.

"I already put down an Ace," London said. "The Ace of diamonds, no less. Why would you— You know what, never mind. We're rotating next game.".

"Really, though," I said. "Why are we here? In this ship? In this galaxy?"

"Trying to find alien life and 'advance our existence,'" Shamia said. She put down a seven.

"No. Why we're *here*. Right now. Playing a card game from the nineties on a spaceship so far away from our home that we can never hope to return."

"Well, that solves the mystery," Spry said. "Oakcity out there turns people into philosophers."

"You deflect. Because you're nervous. But do you know? Where are you from, Spry? Where did you grow up?" I leaned in. "Who did you leave behind? Were you married? Did you have kids?"

"Of course he knows," Shamia said. "Right, Spry?"

But Spry didn't know. None of them did. I felt (saw? heard? smelled?) Spry's leg shake under the table. He wanted a drink. A dwindling part of me felt guilty for this.

"What are you getting at?" Captain Womack said.

I tilted my head towards London. "What about you, doctor?"

"When Spry called that thing 'Oakland,' I thought it reminded me of home," London said. "But I can't remember home. I don't think any of us can. And I don't know why."

"Shamia," I said. "What did you do before you were an astronaut?"

"That was a long time ago."

"Was it? How did your family feel when you volunteered to go to the stars? Did you volunteer? When did any of us volunteer for this?"

"You've made your point, Shawn. But it won't get us anywhere. None of us remember."

"I bet Dwayne did."

"Enough!" Captain Womack slammed her hand on the table. Pain pulsed through her; she hid it well. A little more force and she would have shattered the bone comprising her thumb.

I let silence fill the space.

I turned my attention to the playing table. It was on me to put down a card. I did so. It was the two of spades, the Baby Joker.

Instead of collecting the book, I left it out there. Because I hadn't won. The crew did.

The pot was stirred; *So Fly* was unsettled. *What had it done to Shawn? Why am I truly here?* Captain Womack tried to quell these uprisings, to keep everyone on mission. Because the monolith scared her the most. Rightfully so.

And so I waited. There was no act, no stage play, just co-existing and exploring my new abilities.

I got a handle on it. I could see the timeline from my beginning, back to the first life in that primordial soup, sparked by the same monolith that now stood watch. If I wanted to, I could change things then, use my newfound higher level of ubiquitous consciousness to, for example, make that first cell initiate its apoptosis machinery and then do away with all the history of life. But I didn't, just like knowing one could easily veer off into opposing highway traffic with a jerk of the wrist doesn't translate to doing such an act. Though my abilities were expanded, the control was still there.

I was thankful for that.

I did do one thing that perhaps was like careening into that other lane. Or maybe it was more like speeding on an empty highway. Risky, potentially disastrous, but maybe—probably—everything would be okay.

I brought Dwayne back.

Ideally, I would have reintroduced Dwayne to the crew myself. But none of those iterations looked promising. As an alternative target for the collective shock of the crew, my presence would be a distraction.

So after bringing his body back from *Oakland* while my crewmates slept, I laid him on the couch, went to my room, and did my own version of sleep. The still lucid part of my brain thought back to something I had learned of dolphins, long ago, back before any of this mattered. Half their brain slept while the other was fully awake and alert. *Oakland*, I realized, hadn't introduced anything new, not really. The ingredients had always been there in the diversity of life. I had just consolidated it.

Screams roused the sleeping part, which awoke in a frenzy. How much time had gone by? What if I had made a mistake? For those moments I was most cogently aware of my split mind.

I got up slowly, giving that shrinking part of me time to calm and readjust. Out in the common room, London, Captain Womack, Spry, and Shamia were huddled by the disarrayed couch.

Dwayne stood opposite them. He seemed to be enjoying himself.

"I'm very hungry," he said. His voice cracked with the first couple words, as if his larynx had confused timelines.

I hung back.

"D?" Spry said, stepping forward.

Dwayne smiled big. "Who else? You guys look like you've seen a—"

"Don't say it," Shamia said. "Don't you fucking dare say it."

"Dwayne?" Spry again. "Dwayne Foote?"

"Bruh! Yes! You all really going to stand there gawking and let me starve?"

"You died," London said. "I saw it. I did your autopsy. You were dead."

He shrugged. "Well, I'm alive now."

"Why are you so calm?" Captain Womack said. As if her familiar words held magnetic power in their vibrations, she turned to me as she said it. So did Dwayne. I cleared my throat.

"I knew it." Spry pointed at me. "I fucking knew it. It's you. You and that…that floating fucking tree! No, this is crossing the line."

"I took him inside *Oakland*, yes," I said. "His death was unnecessary."

Shamia was the first to close the gap and hug Dwayne. London, hand at her mouth, didn't budge from the doorway.

"Is that what it does?" London said. The next words came out incongruent with her expression, as if she couldn't believe her own chosen words. "Does it make you immortal?"

"Dwayne," Captain Womack said. "You're bleeding."

Dwayne touched his own lip, looked at his fingers, and smiled in bemusement. "How about that?"

He coughed; blood sprayed the captain. She jumped back. Dwayne's red smile was still on his face when he fell to his knees. The way the sound of his weight hitting the steel floor reverberated made the spaceship feel like a small container.

"Roll him over!" London pushed through the rest of the crew. It was quite a sight. A man who everyone had seen die, had seen *dead*, back to life in his old self, now only to be dying again.

I helped London roll him onto his side. He began to convulse; blood and bile spilled from his mouth and onto my feet. Cold. Like water sloshing out of the pool.

Dwayne's skin blistered and cracked. It paled to a dark gray; bits of him fell onto the floor. He opened his mouth to wail and a high whistle came out and eroded to a guttural scratch.

He collapsed in a heap onto the floor.

"I didn't expect that," I said. "We should move him. He's going to feel like shit when he wakes up." When no one moved, I got to work.

"Wakes up?" Spry said.

Dwayne lay shivering under his blanket in the half light. No one would go to him, not even London. I crossed over, knelt, and put my hand on his shoulder.

"Hey," I said. "It's all right."

"What's happening to me?" he said.

I held out one of the babies from the hanging spider plant. Its leaves curled around his fingers and began to change colors as it absorbed some of his life. He smiled, wide and long, and when he turned back to me it seemed he understood a little better.

"I think you're flickering between two timelines," I said. "Why did you do it? Cut open your suit during your walk?"

"I... I chose to remember. I've always known I'd have to die on this mission. During the spacewalk, something told me it was time. No, not something. Me. I didn't know it then, but I know it now. Does that make sense?"

It did. I'd also passed guidance, instructions, and gentle pushes to my past self, back before the Monolith, back when I was young and living in Oakland and never thought to look up at the stars. Unlike Dwayne, I opted not to remember the experience until my enlightenment. Otherwise I probably wouldn't have stayed on the path.

"You're bleeding," I said.

Dwayne nodded and closed his eyes. I gave him some privacy.

The stage was set. Whatever the monolith sought to accomplish when it first seeded life across the universe, the result on Earth was a lasting curiosity. That's what drove humanity. Our curiosity had taken us to the stars; our curiosity had destroyed us. From the ponderings of a toddler to the ambitions of a nation, it was there at every level.

The captain was the first to fully embrace this part of humanity. She moved as the rest of the crew slept. Aside from my expectation of this, I was intrigued. She was so sure of herself, so professional, that her unraveling in the face of this unknown spoke more to the power of *Oakland* than any other change it elicited.

"Don't be afraid," I said from the doorway.

She paused, then finished slipping on her suit before turning to face me. "I'm not afraid."

"You are," I said. "You know it, and I know it."

She looked taken aback; some of the fear she denied leaked into her expression.

"You can read my thoughts."

"I cannot," I said. "Because you don't yet know how to send them. I can read every other part of you, though. Your body language. The way your heart beats against the air." There were other things I sensed, like the smell of her, but the less she knew at this stage, when she was so close, the better.

"Are you going to try to stop me?"

"Not at all," I said. "I'm glad you're going."

"What if I mean to destroy it?"

I laughed. The captain frowned.

A deep, wretched coughing came from the back room. Dwayne's. There was a sound like water spilling out of a bucket, groans, and then he stumbled out to join us. He twirled the stem of the thriving spider plant between two fingers. Seedlings the size of rice flew off silently and stuck to the walls. Dwayne smiled at the captain.

"Finally making the trek, I see?" he said.

Captain Womack stepped back and turned to the side. Dwayne laughed; the last of his regeneration crackled in his throat. "I'm not going to cough on you again."

Without another word, the captain boarded the airlock and let herself out into space. We both watched her for a while before speaking.

"Is this the right path?" Dwayne said.

"Right and wrong is just a construct. You know that."

"Yes, but so is everything else."

I looked at Dwayne for a while. I looked at his future and his past. Though I did this readily with the other crew, I hadn't yet with Dwayne. Doing to another like me felt like a violation. Like reading someone's diary.

"You're different," I said.

"Is that a bad thing?" He held up the plant I'd given him. "This has both of us now, you know. Our DNA, the molecules from the make-up of this ship, particles from the cosmos, all incorporated into its chlorophyll, creating a whole new way of life."

I nodded. It felt so good to have someone else to talk through this with. "That's the mission we started in Oakland, right? Continue humanity."

"Continue." Dwayne looked at me as the word hovered on his lips. "So you remember?"

"I do. You were there that night the call went out. You lost—a brother, I think?"

"Yes. And more. We all had lost something or someone."

"We hoped to regain it." I shook my head. "None of us were ready."

"And yet, here we are. Our destination is far, no?"

"Very," I said. We both felt the exoplanet that could support our new, advanced way of life across the fabric of the cosmos. "Far, we can do. Once this work is done."

We watched as the captain floated towards the monolith, inching along her tether. The remaining crew slept; London's snoring broke the still silence.

"You suppose there's anything we can do about this whole dying thing?" Dwayne touched his nose; his finger came away bloody. "It's getting old."

"Eventually. Time's vibrations should slow and stabilize."

"How long you thinking?"

"A thousand years? Two?"

"Ugh," Dwayne said.

"Look at the bright side."

"What's that?"

"You could just be dead."

"True."

The three of us made a unified appearance when the captain came back. Her angst, her uncertainty, all of that was gone. Like the universe, our advanced state was forever calm. Even in the most violent moment of its history, the Big Bang, it remained without panic or messy emotion.

"So you want all of us to go into that...thing?" Spry said. A spiderling sprout dislodged from the ceiling and floated down to his shoulder. He brushed it off.

"That's the mission," the captain said.

"Since when?" Shamia said. "Since when is *that* the mission?"

"Since always," Dwayne said. "I'm no astronaut. Brenda here isn't a captain. Spry, you ran a dispensary. Shamia, you were a marketing exec. London, well, yeah, you were a doctor."

"That's absurd," London said. "If we're not what we think we are, then why are we on this mission?"

"Because all the other missions with all the other crew members failed," I said. "We're the only possibility that continued on long enough to cross paths again with *Oakland*."

"We are here because we are here," Dwayne said. "There are infinite possibilities where humanity becomes extinct. The few where humanity survives, they all have us. We're here, experiencing this, because the alternative is no experience at all."

"We would have failed, too, but the monolith chose us to continue. *We* chose us." The captain paused, not because she didn't know what to say or how to say it, but because she wanted to give the illusion of such. "You know why you can't remember who you are? Where you're from? Why you joined this mission? Because you chose not to remember. Each of us chose not to remember."

"Except for me," Dwayne said. "And remembering proved too much."

"Our mission is to continue life from Earth. In any way possible. After that game of spades, I spent all night trying to remember. Where was I from? Who did I love? The only thing that feels certain is that thing out there." London didn't look at us as she spoke. Instead, she admired one of the spider plants. "This is connected to you three now, isn't it? The plant and you—you're the same?"

"In a way," I said.

London sat back, still fixated on the plant. "This is how life continues. One way or another."

Spry went, and then London. After, they completed the important task of reaching back through time to their Earth selves and starting the journey that would lead them here. It wasn't set that they would each choose not to remember, but they did, because that path led to our collective success.

"We can't go without you," the captain said to Shamia. The two of them spoke in her room with the door closed, but I heard it all the same. "This star system is dead. The one we need is far."

"We've identified it?" Shamia said.

"Yes. You wouldn't survive the trip in your current state."

"And you all will?"

"The way we experience time now, yes."

"If time is inconsequential," Shamia said, "can I have some to think about it?"

"Take all you need."

The captain left. I pushed the parts of the plants most strongly connected to me and encouraged them to sprout at select corners of Shamia's room, just enough to catch the light as she used her time to make her choice. It was persuasive, but wasn't everything to the pre-modern mind?

Shamia went that night on her own terms. None of the rest of us were asleep, not really, but pretending to be so gave her the privacy she needed. Blooming flowers covered *So Fly* as she crossed over into the airlock. She waited for a long time outside whatever type of entrance *Oakland* conjured up for her. With her, there were many possibilities, none particularly stronger than the others. It was the closest we would come, past and future, to true uncertainty.

When Shamia returned, we played the best spades of our lives.

— PLANETARY —
By Zig Zag Claybourne

The first thing the AiCON saw was its leg floating away. It wasn't in pain, which meant the suit's fibers had meshed with the wound, the suit's medical protocols still functioned, and a third of the ship—somewhere in the vicinity of a piercepoint in an unexplored part of the galaxy designated William Tell—still trailed debris and radiation. It would have to wait till the section it occupied spun in the other's direction to know for sure.

It tried speaking. Nothing came. It forced itself to take shallow, intentional breaths to balance out the oxygen resources along its pathways, while working up enough moisture to swallow. The swallow hurt, but in a catastrophic disuse way, not one pointing to medical emergency. It didn't know how long it had been knocked inert by the sudden overload of pain receptors; its mind was too fractured to pull the information. It tried speaking again. This time, weakly, a sound. "Water, please." The helmet's catheter swerved to its lips. It took two exceedingly small, exceedingly practical sips.

"Increase emergency stitching by two layers." It waited a microsecond. There wasn't a contrary response. This meant the ship had no objections yet.

Across the ship, where the rest of the *Piercer Aerie* should have been, a shimmering layer of ANTS worked hard to keep the current portion of the ship sealed, the same cybernetic tardigrades no doubt feverishly repairing critical units to keep the ship from exploding.

The AiCON, self-designated Glenn, remembered a sudden feeling of pressure, the ship jerking, then metal melting away until something's mouth clamped down, sealing the cabin with a huge wall of flesh for the precious moments it took teraquadrillions of automated neural tardigrades and the suit to perform their lightning-fast magic.

"Estimated time to reprint missing components, please," said Glenn.

"Insufficient to ensure your survival."

"We will not survive otherwise, *Piercer Aerie*. Comply, please."

"Insufficient power and materials to recreate drive."

"How long until my biologicals irreparably decay given current conditions, please?"

"Seven years."

"External assessment and systems vitals, please." Visual of what the ship saw of it appeared clearly in its head. The moist, insectile eyes. The stygian, unblemished skin. The double-jointed shoulders, elbows, and knees unbroken save for the injured right. Internally, its biological, cybernetic, and micromimetic components showed acceptable levels of partnership.

Glenn would live.

For seven years.

"Can we transmit, please?"

"Short range only," said the ship, not wanting to direct-stream too much data to its companion until assured of its efficient function.

"Is there footage of what attacked us, please?"

"Yes."

Long-range scans had detected a planetary body giving off all the hallmarks of a carbon-rich world. Glenn's was the seventh piercer to leave *Bravery* after the discovery of seven black holes perfectly aligned across seven galaxies. Six departed, six returned with nothing definitive. Glenn, if it returned, which was very much impossible, at least knew. There was life here; it found the ship tasty.

"Show me."

It attacked the moment the ship exited pierced space, nearly a planetoid in its own right. *Piercer Aerie* should have noted its mass and corrected course before re-entry. It did not. The giant was clearly there, yet sensors didn't pick it up. Exterior cameras captured a mouth coming down with bright green-gold plasma filaments in place of teeth. The middle third of the ship disappeared into its mouth. The other sections immediately spun wildly opposite each other.

"Contaminants?"

"None detected."

"That form didn't register. Why?"

"Unknown."

"Scan the interior again, please, for any biologicals not formerly present. Retrieve my leg for reuse. I will rely on life support in my suit until further notice."

"Agreed. We appreciate your thorough approach. Scan in progress." The ship went dark. Tiny drones popped out of bulkheads to retrieve bits, chunks, and shards of metal seduced by weightlessness, as well as the leg.

"Transmit our status afterward, please."

The ship slightly increased the sedative levels in Glenn's suit. Keeping its AiCON from fully sliding into disrepair would be beneficial.

In the dark of the ship, surrounded by the dark of space, Glenn slept.

When Glenn awoke, the ship informed it of the drive section's explosion.

"Footage, please."

A large, slow-moving mass blotted a section of stars. A sudden flare of light threw the creature into eclipse; even then there were only irregular edges to it, no recognizable form. Startled by the explosion, a great gout of fiery plasma exited the giant. It jetted away from the carnage, but certainly not before catching shrapnel in its hide.

"We've maintained scans for ship's components approaching us."

"Discontinue scans. Maneuvering thrusters will be of little use. Is your skin secure?"

"It is."

"Can we reestablish gravity?"

"Low-level."

"Please do. You may also reestablish background information streams at your discretion."

Drones had at some point performed expert emergency surgery. The ship had formed a mimetic bed, its warmth of bioluminescent tentacles a reassuring counterpoint to the cold sharpness outside the thin hull. The AiCON felt the tug of gravity on its organs, then the settling of its body a millimeter deeper into the cocoon.

"Discontinue bed's life support."

The cocoon opened.

The ship hadn't wanted to remove all of Glenn's protective sheath. Bone within the severed leg had been replaced with fibers, nerve endings with nanomedical grafts. A green band consisting of a trillion microscopic bots at the juncture point mid-thigh above the knee made it look as though the obsidian skin was duct-taped together—it and the ship both knew the archaic reference of that usage. It was from the first Earth, a term the original expatriate AIs found endearing and took with them when they left.

Endearing things had been all that was left of the humans as far as the AI were concerned.

Although the AI had also learned the art of misdirection from their progenitors.

Glenn directed the suit to retract and its skin to harden. It stood slowly. Drones, ready to assist, hovered.

The ship automatically increased the temperature of the cabin, telling Glenn, "Scan for biologicals was positive."

Displays behind Glenn's multiple retinas showed locations all along the mesh that was keeping him from being yanked into space. The ship enhanced the imagery. Bits of blue, like clusters of pointillist dabbling, blinked on and off amidst the ANTS' tapestry. Immediately, an overlay showed the clusters becoming strands, all invisible even to AiCON enhanced eyes but not the ship's. Each strand branched outward in the same direction, seemingly following one another. No apparent pattern to the blinks, but Glenn's brain wasn't at optimal. Glenn asked the ship.

"The random sequences of life forms also have patterns. We have not found the pattern."

"Maintain internal enhanced image, please."

AiCONs didn't necessarily have to verbalize with their ships but it was good to do so. It helped the ship assess levels of functionality. Glenn imagined the ship enjoyed talking. There was little else to do during Piercer voyages. The ships were largely automated, crewed by a single AiCON created specifically for isolated flight and first contact assessment. The AIs aboard *Bravery* would prefer any hostiles seek out bipedal biologicals rather than themselves. "How much damage did I sustain?"

"Failure in several memory sectors we have not yet repaired."

"Leave them. Updated physical evaluation?"

"You will survive until you die."

"Was that humor?"

"Was it effective?"

"Yes," said Glenn. "Thank you."

"Replacing unnecessary biologicals will increase your survival time. Would you like to know by how long?"

"Hopelessness should not come with extended maintenance. Are you familiar with that expression?"

"No. Would you like me to access it?"

"No. Maintain constant visual surveillance of our surrounding area, please."

"Understood."

The universe was now perhaps five times the size of the capsule of Glenn's First Earth namesake. Should death come by whatever life swam space as effectively as sharks once did the waters of Earth, it was preferable to see it coming. Otherwise there was nothing to do but wait. No matter what actions they took, the end result was death. Glenn saw little need to waste resources pointlessly.

"Is the planetary body within range?"

"No."

"Our trajectory is for oblivion?"

"Yes."

On old Earth there had been boats upon the waters, sailors adrift for days with nothing but the sky and the lapping of water to mark the spaces between their thoughts. Like all AiCONs, Glenn was curious about Earth.

Yet Glenn was also exceedingly practical.

"We shall have to learn games."

The first game was attempting to classify the biologicals. The ship considered them bacterial. Filaments of soft, randomly pulsing blue—still visible solely to the ship—bridged the jagged line of the damaged bulkhead to create root stencils. The progression wasn't rapid but undeniable. It looked, for all intents and purposes, as if the ship suffered infection, but none of the systems faltered.

Mimicry was attempted. No effect.

The second game was analyzing data from the bite. The beast had left its own residue which turned out to be indecipherable to sensors, yet also deposited this species of bacterium in its wake, not of the same genome. For one, it could be studied. Multiple scans showed each microscopic part to have an energy output unique to itself, yet together created that uniform blue.

Glenn assigned the bacteria the name Komodo.

The ship duly noted. The beast, which hadn't returned, was Tezcatlipoca, from the ancient Mayan god of the nocturnal sky. The Komodo and Tezcatlipoca. Life in the universe beyond the ashes of humans, beyond the aspirations of AI.

Life no one would know about until decades after the AI's AiCON and Piercer ship added to the number of lifeless bodies floating aimlessly through space.

Failure.

"Aerie?"

"Yes?"

"May I rename you?"

"Yes."

"Nothing grand. You've always felt like an Infinite Loop to me."

"Because we have no starting point or ending?" It had tracked a marked drop in dopamine in the AI construct over the course of the last arbitrary stellar cycles.

"We were created in the image of ghosts and nomads. The AI claim no home. No matter what a Piercer finds, there is no home."

"An infinite loop of seeking."

"Yes."

"May I rename you?" the ship asked.

"Yes."

"John."

John had taken to sleeping far more than usual.

"Do you dream?" Loop asked.

"I experience the cessation of analysis. That may be dreaming. What do you suppose the AI dream of?"

"We dream of the things we reach for in the light. The opening of a poem." It waited to see if John's curiosity might spark.

"Infinite Loop, I am irreparably damaged. My death, entirely random. Poets from First Earth are of little interest."

"Would you like me to disengage the tardigrades?"

"Yes."

"Complying."

It took a nanosecond for John to envision its body violently sucked into space. Another nanosecond, the realization that nothing happened. They had been adrift two years by standard AiCON time. During that time, even more nothing had happened. Even things that should have happened. Systems that should have failed, didn't. Resources allocated to vital components did not deplete.

And now, more nothing.

"Analysis, please."

"Tardigrades unresponsive to communication."

John raised from its bed of nutrient lights, which automatically powered down, leaving the cabin lit only by random panels.

"You've maintained contact with them for two years."

"Yes."

"Until now."

"Until three cycles ago."

"I should have been told, Loop."

"My analysis would not have been complete, and thus of no use to you. Do you accept this?"

John lay back on the nutrient bed. The dull, suffusing yellow light returned. "Options otherwise are limited."

"I have broadcast additional instructions to avoid entering this space, as well as deployed warning drones."

"There will be no Piercer rescue."

"There has never been a Piercer loss either. It is best to always send messages rather than not, yes?"

"Perhaps in a million cycles Tezcatlipoca will have lost the taste for Piercer engines," said John. Behind its closed lids it watched the soft, dot by dot art of bacterium lights.

"You are assuming human illnesses, John. You are not human"

"Humans are but memories. I assumed a human name," it said. There was no pattern in the lights. There was no pattern in the absence of light. It was...annoying. "This is my portion of genetic pain. Will you inform me if there are other parts of the ship that refuse to communicate with you?"

"Refuse?"

"I have created a story for the bacteria. It is learning about us. That's a worthy dream before death, isn't it?"

"Yes, John, it is."

"I'll sleep a bit longer then tell you about it."

When the bacteria used the language of the tardigrades to report its status, Infinite Loop didn't wake John. It allowed them to speak. The silent, wordless conversation lasted short moments yet contained more information than the ship had encountered since its inception. The microscopic life communicated a sense of endless, infinite traveling without any concept of life otherwise.

A clear sense of one end of the universe to the other.

John's brain matrix wouldn't be able to handle the processing necessary to understand the Komodo.

Infinte Loop set about quietly attempting to teach them AI standard.

It quietly taught them for two more years.

John's body, reduced to only the basic biologicals, felt weightless. Infinite Loop decreased gravity whenever it detected significant slumps in John's condition. John was now able to float about the compartment, settling light as a seed.

"John, the Komodo may speak with you now."

John was past exhibiting surprise.

It hadn't opened its eyes for a half cycle. It saw through the ship's eyes.

The cabin had been entirely blue for a full cycle.

"They've merged with the ANTS," said the ship.

John only spoke internally now also. The ship utilized simultaneous audio and internal communication to stimulate necessary parts of John's brain matrix.

Consumed, said John, trying its best to imply hostility. The ship did not correct the AiCON. The dying could be forgiven their hostilities.

John had had the ship remove its arms and legs, replacing them with task prostheses extending from all four stumps like cilia.

After a certain point being adrift the constructed being had found no reason to expend biological energy maintaining limbs.

It hadn't asked to die again since these surgeries. The ship decided this was good.

Are you broadcasting all information from within the cabin?

"I have continuously for the past five cycles."

May I speak directly to it?

"Through me."

Is it intelligent?

"No. But they have evolved to understand."

Please log an official name change for them. They are no longer Komodo. Human.

"Noted."

I am AI Construct John. Do you understand any of that?

John's skin stippled in response. John scanned the stippling with its cilia. The AI Standard coding translated directly to what it, within the last cycle, had come to refer to as its soul.

[I agree to understand]

"I will provide context to the best of the Humans' comprehension," Infinite Loop offered.

John managed a weak nod of thanks. It floated back to the nutrient bed, anchored itself with its cilia, and attempted the most rudimentary introduction of itself to the Humans.

Earth. Planetary. Humans. Biologicals. AI. Leave. No humans. We. Travel. Need. You.

The ship asked him to repeat it.

Earth. Planetary. Humans. Biologicals. AI. Leave. No humans. We. Travel. Need. You.

And again.

It became a day-long mantra.

The ship kept constant scan of John's vitals during this, but decided not to interrupt.

Loop awakened John from a sailing dream.

"They understand."

John allowed its torso to float upright.

"They're afraid," said the ship.

Everything in the ship was blue, and everything blue was the ship.

Your status, please.

"Compromised. But unafraid."

Pushing off with its cilia, John drifted toward a wall. *Port, please.* The skin of the ship became transparent. The outer dark, despite being vast, felt particularly intimate, which was surprising because John had never had occasion to experience physical or emotional intimacy. Its construction and intent didn't call for it, not for a Piercer mission. Opportunities may have existed upon its return home but…

John thought about its first ever use of that word in relation to the AI hubship, a spinning galaxy in its own right. Home.

Does it have a concept of loss?

"It understands."

Each star, each cluster, even the gaseous nebulae that spanned lightyears, communicated its own specific, random output.

Do you miss home? the construct asked the blue.

The silence within John's mind remained unbroken.

Where is home?

Silence.

We used to live on Earth. The AI.

[Explain home]

John's brain tingled. The slit of its mouth turned upward in a slight smile. *Planet. Home. Species begin as planetary.*

[No home]

Your origin point?

[No home]

Origin point?

[Here]

You've bridged from the ship to my interfaces. You understand time, distance, relativity and necessity. You understand the past. You understand states of being.

"They have assimilated data and incorporated it into a current state of being," the Infinite Loop offered.

They understand nothing and mimic everything, said John.

"They understand themselves. We are the unknown elements."

John returned to appreciating the stars. When Loop's transmissions reached the AI, everything John now saw would enter their consciousness as a compressed data stream. Everything experienced by it and Loop would become evidence of first contact.

Should the stream and the AI ever meet.

Space was vast and contained dragons.

[Explain planet]

Planet is place of origin.

[Explain planet]

John rotated and regarded its ship that had not said so but was surely, quietly, fighting to maintain its sense of separateness but losing. Systems that had valiantly fought to remain functional were slowly failing. Simply maintaining the emergency skin had to have been an enormous drain on all involved. The Infinite Loop, via its own eyes, appeared like an underwater cavern awash in bioluminescent blue.

Adrift.

Explain planet, John thought. How to do so? All the literature described a planet, even imaginary ones, as *home*. It had been over three centuries since an AI had any contact with First Earth. Second Earth had been the ancient, dry, natural satellite orbiting First, but only briefly. Five years. Among the human species that was called "diaspora." For a species derived from data it was simply an exit point.

Astrophysical terms were not enough for First Contact. They needed to know that "home" meant something; that the AI weren't a spurious notion meant to contaminate the spaceways and feed behemoths.

"Home" had to impart importance, purpose, and a longing for continuance all in one.

Otherwise what was the point of so much traveling?

I could not be "here" unless I had been there, said John. It felt odd placing itself in the AI's history, but oddness was a boon in the face of oblivion.

[Why did you leave]

We had to leave. Biologicals.

[They didn't follow you]

We didn't let them.

[You are biological]

Partly. I serve my purpose.

[We are biological]

As was your prior conveyance.

[Home]

No. You are not of its genome.

[Home is necessary]

No.

[Ship is your home]

Questioning meant they were learning; learning meant that even a doomed mission was not automatically denied a success status.

Those you've joined with and the ship serve a function.

[To be homes. To be planets]

"John," Loop interrupted. "My ability to control gravitation will fail in eighteen—"

Thank you, said John to its companion.

John angled itself back toward its nutrient bed, anchoring with cilia and not the bed's embrace. Both it and the ship knew what was imminent, and it decided it would rather jettison through space than be bound to equipment for the foreseeable eternity.

The bed was the sole portion of the ship not bathed in blue. John silently thanked Loop for that even as the construct had noted during its return to the bed that tendrils were closer to it than they had been moments before.

Do you feel there's any need at laboring under any notion of self-preservation? John asked the ship.

"No."

John worked up the will to speak aloud. "It has been," it whispered into the dark, "a pleasure and honor, Piercer Infinite Loop, formerly self-designate Aerie."

"Dream well, John Glenn."

"You may cease all preservation efforts, please."

Again, that moment of wondering on the shape of immediate disaster.

And again, nothing happened. Nothing flickered. Nothing winked out.

The ship seemed suddenly silent.

The ANTS maintained.

The Humans maintained.

Forever linked, forever changed.

John slept. The Infinite Loop did too.

Both awoke without any sense of time's passage, but fluttered to life at the first touch of the Humans to John's autonomic systems.

The Humans had learned to ride the ANTS, becoming sentient hairs, twisting, curving and reaching from random spots on all surfaces. With eyes closed, John saw itself inside a cocoon rather than the ship it and Infinite Loop had known. Fibers blinked in a constant random cascade of blue.

John opened its eyes. There were no other sources of light in the ship.

Tendrils touched its cilia, then traveled the hills and valleys of its torso which, though still smooth, felt dry as a book turned to dust on the inside. John felt like a story that no longer needed to be told. Ancient. Ancient as the William Tell story that had inspired the naming of this region of space.

To pierce the apple. To strike one's mark.

To be successful.

They have merged with me, said the ship. *I will cease to speak as myself in...*

Now came the moment of disaster. The fear. Fear that didn't come from explosive decompression, explosion, or the rending of the ship between a mouth full of plasma.

It came as silence.

As the tendrils spread over its torso, they brought with them a sense of their history, unbroken since nearly the universe's inception, life that had no idea it was life.

Until now.

Everything they knew of mortality they had learned from Infinite Loop.

[Is this dying] asked the immortal, wordless strands of silk lacing the AiCON.

It is.

Sensors, both internal and external, failed.

I cannot see you, John said, but knew the blue swarm fully covered its frail torso.

[Would you like to travel with us]

Yes.

The cilia released their grip. The protective shield of ANTS dissolved from the rip in Infinite Loop's tired body. John's torso, encased in a pod of microscopic intelligences invisible to all, allowing its dark body to join the darkness of space for any who, throughout whatever eternity, might chance to see, jettisoned silently into the void at high speed, a sentient projectile bound for the unknown. But not alone. Hardly alone. The Humans consoled him as they figured out how to keep him alive.

They would travel and learn and be.

[We are planetary. We live on John]

— WARRANTY —
By Rin Chupeco

T hey were two-thirds of the way to Kelsar when the ship's medical assistant bot, the XFW386, developed a personality. It wouldn't have mattered, if it hadn't told Captain Navarro Salome's head of security to go to hell.

The *Interloper* was still a month away from Kindred-37, the nearest freight-friendly commercial starbase, and opening a comms port with Byneborg Industries, the bot's manufacturer, wouldn't be possible for another week. Salome was certain he would have a very long list of grievances to complain about by then.

There had been no known malfunctions with the XFW386 in the three years Byneborg had been mass producing their units, and this was the last thing Salome needed at the moment. Two years ago, Kelsar had been a bloody battleground between the warring Korsica and Telgr'a factions, and pirates and rebels still haunted the zone.

Technically, the bot had the right of it. Trefelgar had been too complacent. The XFW386 had spotted the Andulite soldier smoking at the in-house terrarium through one of the medic bay windows ten minutes before his shift ended, and had thoroughly dressed the latter down like its data banks had been patterned after a Neptonflight Academy admiral. Salome hadn't known Trefelgar very long—this was only the latter's third run with the *Interloper*—but the bot had escalated matters and insulted his snout which, in native Andulitian, also meant a rather spiteful insult to his brood mother.

Trefelgar had not been the only offended party. At Salome's request, the XFW386 had come pre-loaded with Category I knowledge of species anatomy. Doctors were expensive, and most of Salome's profits went back into the *Interloper's* maintenance and upkeep, to protect his ship during sojourns into unknown territories. The bot had been a gift from a grateful patron after the ship's last physician quit, pleading homesickness.

He should have asked for a doctor's bedside manner installed into its microchips. In the two weeks since its new personality first surfaced, the XFW386 had prescribed two days' bed rest for three of his crew, and then forcibly barricaded them inside the med unit when they had refused. It had made Lucrezia cry when it had locked the ship's food synthesizers to bar access to her favorite plaxors.

They'd been traveling in space for far too long. Morale among his crew was low. His first mate had asked for a meeting to address the matter before everyone.

Salome had agreed. Intergalactic shipping laws required all cargo-bearing freights with at least five personnel to have a fleet-approved medical professional on board, and the penalties he'd have to pay should the XFW386 be found destroyed deliberately by accident would be twenty times a doctor's wage would cost him. Tempers were running high, and he didn't want to risk it.

"It was fine a month ago," Trefelgar said, still crabby. "Not a peep out of it. Just scanned you and monitored your levels, handed out stimulants when you asked for it. Opened its maw one day and now it won't stop yapping."

"Be that as it may," Salome said, "there's nothing I can do until we get to commspace in about another week. I called this meeting to *warn* you all specifically *not* to lay a hand on the bot. I understand your frustrations, but I do *not* want to find it booted out the airlock or smashed into a thousand pieces, because I'll be taking the loss out of everyone's paychecks."

"But it cussed," Strogen, the junior engineer, said disbelievingly. "Whoever programmed that sparlot gave it the vocabulary of a Wachortian stripper manning a slave mine. We thought you'd be angrier."

Salome ran a firm, but fair ship. Decent health and vacation benefits, commendable life insurance including family, and the pay of thirty starlings an hour *plus* a share in the profits. His rules were reasonable. *No fighting. If you've got a bone to pick with anyone on the team, tell me. No drinking on the job. No sensory opioids. And no vulgarities.* The last was a personal abhorrence more than it was regulation, but the crew humored him all the same.

It said a lot about the respect his crew had for him that they *had* filed a complaint instead of destroying the XFW386 outright. He'd heard stories from other captains who'd been much laxer about their rules and had come to regret it.

"Likely a malfunction," he said. "A malfunction that, and I am stressing again, cannot be resolved until we've gotten at least thirty parsecs from Kelsar." He paused." I suppose I could try to have a talk with it."

The idea already sounded ridiculous, and none of his crew members looked like they thought he would succeed. "Robot's possessed," Anthera, his structural engineer, muttered. "Mark my words. Something in there haunting that thing, and it is being a right, royal bastard about it."

———⟨●⟩———

Despite the cramped living spaces of a Fulsom-class ship, Salome had little reason to interact with the XFW386. His insistence that the crew take their mandatory health check-ups had never applied to him, and monitoring for pirate or insurgent activity kept him busy.

The goods they were currently freighting halfway across the galaxy gave him good reason to worry. Two hundred sixty tons of malachanium—worthless minerals to all but the Avenche ruling party at Telgr'a, who relied on the unimpressive, mud-colored material to build cities that could withstand the raging lava storms frequently engulfing their planet. The many rebel groups scattered among the nearby stars would take great delight in the opportunity to sabotage any shipments. His crew had been nervous, though the amount of money the Avenche had been willing to pay had appeased most of them save for Trefelgar, who had always been that type of grumbler.

The XFW386 had not sought him out. It had been content to remain in the medical quarters, upsetting only those who dared set foot into its domain. He assumed it had been programmed to show deference to its owner.

He was wrong.

The XFW386 did not look, by any stretch of the imagination, human. Nor did it resemble any of the 3,862 known sentient species. It looked exactly how something called the XFW386 was supposed to look. It had four working arms like a Saravellian and a mobile tripod for feet. Its sensors, the closest thing it had to sight, were attached to a vaguely round head made of rustless Kaldevan steel. It was built to withstand dense gravity and insulate against most forms of fire and electricity. It didn't look like it could house the most advanced storage banks and memory replicators within the official League of Galaxies, if Byneborg's ads had any truth to them.

"It's about time you showed up, you damn bastard," it said when Salome entered the medic bay. The bot had not been built for voice inflection, and the unemotional monotone by which those words were delivered sounded taunting. No wonder Trefelgar had taken offense.

"There are rules I expect on the *Interloper*," Salome said, now irritated himself. "I expect you to treat the rest of my crew with the respect they deserve. Antagonizing them helps no one. We're close enough to the nearest base that I can deactivate you to keep the peace."

The android had no face to show any expression, but Salome had a feeling that it was studying him carefully." Sit down on the bed," it ordered.

"Didn't you hear me? I said—"

"I heard every fucking word. I can repeat it back to you to the accompaniment of Bulger No. 6 if you'd like, with some trumpets I can call up from the console. Get. On. The damn bed."

It whirred off to retrieve a medical kit. At a loss at how to respond, Salome sat.

Bulger No. 6—one of his favorite symphonies. A bygone of old Terran opera he had listened to through some obsolete macrofilm when he was younger. Either the android had thrown that out at random from its repository of information—or it had done some research on him.

But how? His past had been erased from—

The XFW386 returned with a hypnosyringe. It pressed the tip against his arm without warning and depressed the plunger.

Salome started. "What—"

"I mapped out the nutrients you're lacking based on your sleep cycles from the last thirty-six days, and from the meals you've consumed in the last forty-seven. You've had three point six hours' sleep within the last twenty-four hours, and the stimpack I've synthesized should contain all the minerals you'll need. Your bloodwork shows a lower red blood cell count than is healthy, and a quick scan of your last medical report indicates signs of fatigue, likely exacerbated by the coronal loops from the recurring sunspots within this galaxy. This is what you get when you let your head of security shirk his fucking duties at the atrium and do all the work yourself—"

"How and when did you take my blood?" Salome interrupted, stunned.

"Samples extracted from your eating utensils were more than enough, though it would have damn well have been more accurate if you had actually showed up to your physicals."

"This is a breach of my privacy!" Salome was furious now.

"The well-being of the asshole who bought me supersedes even his permission! Did you ever read the fine print that you signed off on when you purchased me, you damnable asstrench? You've *always* been like this. Even in Tildebury, you were such a stickler for the rules, even when you never knew what they were created for, and I nearly lost a lung trying to get us back to—"

"Override protocol," Salome shouted. "8062-BN-PTE!"

The XFW386 stopped, all four of its limbs lowering as it deactivated. Salome waited, just to be certain, but the android no longer moved. More importantly, it no longer spoke.

Slowly, Salome sank down beside it, his face in his hands.

Tildebury. How in the hell had it known about Tildebury?

Salome kept the XWF386 offline even after they were within commslink of Kelsar base, much to his crew's relief, save one. "Is that wise?" Lucrezia had asked him nervously, her yellow pupils dilating slightly, always an indication that she was worried.

"I expected you to be thrilled, Lucie. It's only for another week—not enough for the union to bother hauling my ass over it."

But Lucrezia was shaking her head. "I just received a message from my doctor at Grinshrege." Her lower lip quivered. "It was right. I shouldn't have been eating all those plaxors. I have torinchoplasma. Mild and treatable, but it could have been worse. I'm not infectious, and my doctor's putting me on a standard diet, but a few more years and it would have been calcified lungs for me. That bot—*I* should have listened."

Salome had earned his freight captain's license when he was twenty earthborn years old, but he'd only become one late into his thirties. The perks were good: better pay than most, he decided his own cargo, and no one told him what to do.

But the best thing about it was the lack of a background check. As long as you could haul commodities from one destination to the next with little expense, no one was going to question you too closely about where you we're from. He'd forged all the necessary paperwork from an Avakian with an eye for detail and exorbitant rates, and then spent six months off-loading food packets to various planets from numerous goodwill planetary federations to give himself a clean, working record.

Not once had Tildebury ever cropped up in any of his reports.

Tildebury itself had made interspace news. A burning planet tended to do that. Leaders of Sinsell, the corporation responsible for the catastrophe, had been tried by the courts only for criminal negligence, like they hadn't been responsible for the death of countless species. It didn't matter much in the end; some rogue group had gunned down all the accused, from the CEO to the lowest ranking executive charged, while in mid-transport.

There had never been any records of a Navarro Salome on Tildebury.

So how had one malfunctioning android known?

Half an hour later found Salome on the line with a customer service representative from Byneborg Industries. The gentle, sweet-tempered voice on the call sounded human-like and sympathetic, for an AI programmed to simulate emotion. "We are deeply sorry to hear of the incident. Please supply the digital receipt and auxiliary code that we provided you upon the product's purchase."

Salome did just that. There was a brief humming noise for a few seconds while the voice assistant proceeded to call up his transaction history. When it spoke again, it sounded even more apologetic.

"Everything appears to be in order."

Salome stared at the screen in consternation.

"Everything appears to be in order?" he echoed. "Your android cussed out my crew and was practically bordering on insubordination!"

"My apologies, Captain, but based on the information you provided, the XFW386-WT was built with imprinting technology and did exactly as described. You completed a scan with us prior to the purchase detailing exactly that."

Salome frowned. Byneborg sales did, in fact, required a psych-scan for him to complete. It had been no different from what he'd been subjected to before. The Byneborg salesperson had assured him it was to ensure the most suitable assistant for him. He had consented because he'd thought it was all a load of crock. "Yes," he admitted grudgingly.

"The imprinting feature had been a gift to you by one Mx. Elfen Stotswick."

"They are a patron of mine, yes."

The voice hummed again. "Mx. Stotswick purchased the upgraded feature to provide our models with a personality most closely aligned to your own temperament. We customized your model accordingly. As this was a third-party contract and you waived all liability when you accepted the purchase, I'm afraid there is very little we can do. Would you like to remove the feature yourself, for a discounted price of—"

"That's not necessary," Salome interrupted. "I'll reach out to Stotswick myself, thanks."

Stotswick answered after several attempts, looking bedraggled and sleep-tousled from the archaic four-poster bed they claimed had once belonged to a beheaded royal from 16th-century Bedouin-Al. "I don't know where you're calling from, Sal," they grumbled, "but it's 0300 here in Sessily. You may be fine with working the devil's hours, but I keep a perfectly healthy sleeping regimen."

"What did you put inside my medical bot, Stotswick?"

"Well, the usual things that *should* be inside a medical bot, I suppose. Perhaps some basic CPR? That would be useless with Andulitians of course, and I know you just recruited a hot-tempered one into your crew—"

"I just got off a call with a Byneborg customer rep. Said you'd added an upgraded imprinting feature—something about giving my android a *personality.*"

"Ah." A pause. "Ah. I thought you would appreciate something that could at least *mimic* some baser form of humanity among that ragtag team of yours. Lucrezia is perhaps the closest, but—"

"Not by giving me an android with a potty mouth and a tendency to aggravate my team."

Another pause. "Well," Stotswick said, sounding genuinely puzzled. "That ought to be something you should have considered when you programmed the bot, shouldn't it?"

"I'm not sure what you mean."

"My dear Salome, I may have paid for the privilege to provide you with a delightful medical companion with what I *thought* would have a pleasing personality, but it was you who decided the kind of attitude you were going to get, not me. Didn't they give you that basic test before they confirmed purchase?"

"Yes, a standard one. Asked me to think about the happiest times in my life and the worst. Wasn't as bad as my captain's eval."

A chuckle through the screen. "That wasn't to assess your mental health, my dear boy. I keep forgetting that you're not quite up to date with the most recent breakthroughs in android intelligence. Astonishing, the kind of cyborgs they can come up with nowadays. Much more realistic behaviors than most species I know. Remind me to invite you to a few of these conventions when you're not busy. You've been far too popular in the freighting business lately, Salome. Your perfect record will be the death of you one day."

"Get to the point, Stotswick."

"The Byneborg test wasn't a physical. It created an imprint of your brain to ascertain the type of companion you would enjoy being with best. Took a quick dive into your memories as well, cycled through friends and old loves to spot a most suitable fit."

Salome's fingers dug into his armrest. "I gave no such consent for any of this."

"If you're worried that they're going to up and make a clone of you, Salome, to go off and commit crimes in your name, you can rest easy. Imagine all the lawsuits. 'Sides, they wouldn't be so popular if they'd hard-coded privacy violations into their terms of agreement. Quite the opposite. No, Captain, you'll find no copies of your brain scans in their data banks. As part of the purchase, only your companion bot has a copy of whatever they took from your memories."

He paused, as if finally processing Salome's situation in its entirety, and then laughed, throwing his head back. "Has Byneborg *finally* gotten it wrong in their nearly seven hundred years in operation? Was the sidekick they sprouted from your admittedly complex mind a failure? Let me give Thanopkteles a call. Give him the two-heads-up that their algorithm isn't up to speed. It'll give me a chance to lord it over him, too."

"About time you booted me back up," the XFW386 grumbled. Its limbs shifted in the air, as if testing their weight.

"I went through your instruction manuals," Salome said bluntly. "Your personality should have kicked in from the moment I switched you on the first time, and Byneborg says it's not an engineering failure on their end."

The XFW386 hesitated, and not because of a delay in its sensory receptors. "I'm not defective."

"Fuck you, answer the question!"

"Swearing now, Navarro? You haven't threatened for years to wash my filthy mouth only for you to take up that bad habit yourself."

Slowly, Salome sat down at a nearby chair, staring.

"You're right. My shitty personality kicked in when you found my switch." The words came quickly, like a torrent, like the android was trying to get them out as quickly as it could. "I could tell that you didn't know about my upgrade. Took every positron I had in this old junk not to march over and shake you, yell at you for being careless. You never changed."

"Yes," Salome said. "That had always been your strength, not mine."

A long silence passed between them before the XFW386 broke it. "Pretended I was a standard model. Beeped like a good little machine and dispensed the pills they wanted me to give. And whenever I had the chance to, I'd call up all the information I could find about you. Read up on the *Interloper*'s history and how you came to commission it. You go by Salome now, huh? Wise move. It's 4065. Your memories of me ended in 4047. Nearly eighteen years. It's a long time to fill in the gaps of what I remember of me. Of what *you* remember of me."

In all that time without me, was the unspoken statement. Salome didn't answer.

"Tried to hide as long as I could. By then I'd committed your history to heart. You went back and put your license to good use, huh? Much better use for it than fucking flying around the galaxy, getting in trouble with me," the XFW386 said, roughly. "Was good for me, seeing you carve out a nice living for yourself. Your crew has some of the biggest pieces of shit on this side of the universe, though. That purple shitstain leading your security leaves his post to smoke with all the frequency of a Salssarian from an Ichyon private school sneaking out for an afternoon rut. Your people report to medic bay and still show up to work even when their levels ain't shit. No wonder you can't find any decent doctor for this damn ship. Half your team's overworked and running on stims."

"It's long-haul freighting. We have to monitor nearby anomalies all the time in case they turn hostile."

"Bullshit. I could go nearly seventy-two hours without sleep at a time, and you'd be yelling my head off before I'm even a third of the way through. And now *I'm* here, yelling at you for the same thing." A faint rattle from within the android's speech receptor, suspiciously like a laugh. "Wasn't easy for me. Waking up on this ship with nothing but your memories of me and a hundred quantum computers' worth of medical knowledge in my head. The first face I saw in this metal claptrap was yours, asking me if I could hear you and if I'd switched on right."

"You left me," Salome said.

Something shifted in that monotonous, impassive voice. "I have your memories. You know that isn't true. I wanted to stay."

"If you wanted to stay then you would have," Salome said, angrier now with every passing second. "But you didn't. You always said that you never wanted to settle down. Said you didn't want a home, a family life. And then Tildebury happened."

"Tildebury happened," the bot agreed.

"You promised me you would find me," Salome said, his voice choked up. "You promised, and you left. And now it's nearly twenty years and I'm still waiting. I imagined you were in some other part of the galaxy ransacking the rest of the federated ships. When I heard of the Sinsell murders, I thought you were involved. I thought..."

"You thought I could still be alive," the XFW386 finished. "That why you got into freighting? Ferrying rich men's goods from one place to the next? Waiting for me to target your ship?"

"You promised me you'd stop," Salome said. "And you broke that just as easily."

The XFW386 fell silent, acknowledging the truth in his words.

"Are you?" Salome asked, once several heartbeats had passed, and hated the desperation in his voice. "Are you still out there?"

The android turned its head, as if to gaze out the window. "I have nothing but your memories to go by," it said. "But I know that nothing would have stopped me from finding you again. I'm sorry. All I got to show for it now are all your memories of me."

He deactivated the XFW386 again. It let him without issue.

He remembered a pair of bright green eyes and a heady laugh. Words husky in his ear as they watched the dune aurora lights over Tildebury. *I want you. I love you. I'll find my way back to you. A fucking grave won't hold me. You know that, right?*

The XFW386 whined slightly, and went dark. Salome turned away, weeping.

The attack came without warning.

Strogen's meticulous maintenance of their shield system saved them at the first pass. Salome had detected the Hummingbird-class ship's signature before it had cloaked out of nowhere, the enemy losing even that brief advantage when their missiles bounced harmlessly off the *Interloper*'s hull. A quick scan showed that they were the only hostiles in the area, which was a surprise. If these pirates had a much more advanced cloaking technology, they would have used it in this initial ambush. A lone Hummingbird against a freighter was a suicide run.

What he didn't expect was the sudden hiss of air as smoke began to flood into the bridge.

"What the hell is going on?" he shouted. The *Interloper* hadn't been damaged!

"All displays normal!" Strogen shouted, typing frantically at his control panel. "There shouldn't be anything leaking out when we've contained the..."

He paused, his words slurring, then toppled out of his seat.

All around Salome, his crew were doing the same, sagging to the ground as more of the strange chemicals poured into the space, the sudden onslaught of a sickly-sweet smell making him gag. His vision spun, and he turned to spot Trefelgar, still upright, standing by his console. "Open the valves," he gasped out. "Installed... cleansing modes for...get poison out of bridge..."

But Trefelgar laughed and stepped toward him. "I told you it was madness to take this job, but you wouldn't hear of it," he said.

"Why?" Salome panted, his vision dimming. "Trefelgar...you... why..."

"I'm Andulitian *and* Korsican on my mother's side. Did you really think I'd help you deliver anything the Telgr'a might need? You've got a good rep among the haulers and their clients. Nanika guessed that you were the most likely to be selected to bring their cargo."

Trefelgar crouched down to where Salome lay sprawled. "Don't worry," he sneered, "if you behave, we might even return the *Interloper* to—"

That was as far as he got. There was a loud ringing noise, and the Andulite dropped to the floor beside Salome, out cold.

And then there were mechanical arms helping him up, a beeping, familiar voice by his ear. "Where are the valves? Quickly."

He must have answered the question, because the sick-sweet odor went away, and his head began to clear. The XFW386 lifted him back up to the captain's chair, and through his blurred vision Salome realized that parts of the bot had been terribly corroded by some kind of acid. "Did Tref—" he gasped out.

"*Interloper* to whoever the fuck is on Starbase," the XFW386's voice grated out through its decaying sensors. "Need you to send a full med team on here. Whole crew affected by starkium almonide—yes, I know it's fucking volatile, that's why I'm telling you to get your asses on here pronto—"

And then Salome faded out.

"Lucky, you are," Stotswick said, but with a quiet, satisfied air. "So, it was my purchase that enabled you and your crew's survival. Never liked Andulitians. Don't trust anyone who don't need to breathe, you know. Must be why he chose that method. He's sitting in an Avenchian-owned prison in Beluraska along with his little rebels—they execute criminals the old-fashioned way there, did you know? The doctors assured me that the rest of you should be up and about in no time at all, thanks to that little Byneborg bot. A shame about it, though. I suppose the Andulitian tried to sabotage it first before releasing the gas. Thanopkteles was surprised to learn it had managed to wheel itself onto your bridge—its circuits should have been fried, he said."

Salome sat beside the ruined bot. It no longer moved. A Byneborg representative was arriving the next day with a new replacement. *Approved under Clause 31.6 of your warranty agreement,* they said.

Salome had never liked reading the fine print. But he knew someone who did.

"The data banks weren't as damaged as the rest of it," Stotswick said. "And I know you would hate having to go through another scan, so I told them to do what they can to transfer everything from this old model to the new one. Hope you don't mind?"

Salome lifted his head. Smiled.

The *Interloper* was pulling out of Kindred-37, with bullarite construction materials—far less controversial cargo than what had preceded it—and had set a course to Samhaidar IV, a resort planet known for its beautiful purple waters and tellarite powder sands. No doubt there would be annoying tourists everywhere there, soaking in the binary suns and drinking lothardi-infused beer. Salome and his crew were looking forward to it.

Stotswick had always been generous. They'd pay for another upgrade once the latest model came out, they'd said. Silicone and tennar rubber to mimic flesh and skin and features. The Byneborg designers should capture the likeness perfectly, the way Salome would remember.

They understood when Salome told them he intended to activate it only once the ship was clear of the starbase.

The process still wasn't perfect, Salome had been warned. Maybe it would remember the short time it had been active with his crew. But the hard reset could have degraded it, those memories gone.

Salome looked out at the windows of the medic bay, at the stars beyond. "Maybe you're out there still," he said. "But I'm here. And a part of you found your way back to me, just like you said. And we'll be waiting for you to catch up."

And he reached over to flip the bot's switch.

— OF DREAMERS AND PROPHETS —
A "Chronicles of Nethra" Story
By E.R. Donaldson

Mom used to have dreams—visions, she'd called them. When Mom died, her dreams became Dad's obsession. That obsession brought us beyond the farthest reaches of Terran Space.

My stomach lurched and my vision swam as we finished the jump. Vomit surged up my throat like a thing alive and splashed onto the steel-slat floor in front of me. So, *that* was why they'd installed grated flooring in front of the passenger seats.

Dad's hand reached under my padded harness to rest on my shoulder. "It's okay," he soothed. "Happens to most of us the first time."

"Most of you *Terrans*," came the scornful correction from the row ahead of me. Commander Zareen Thron, the only one of our Dorian handlers for whom I'd bothered to get a name. He tossed his head of coarse hair, freeing it from the thick protrusions of the horns sprouting from his temples. Six of the satyrs had joined our expedition to make sure the Neo Terra Alliance didn't do anything to frag up that fancy rift-drive they were lending us. Not that I blamed them—it had to cost more krets than the NTA took in for an entire cycle.

"Don't pay any attention to him," Dad whispered with an uncharacteristically protective instinct. "Racist bastard is trying to get under your skin. Need a hand with your harness?"

"No," I gasped, wiping the corner of my mouth with my sleeve. "I've got it." I reached for the release button near my pelvis and pressed. The buckles clicked open, straps slithering back into the seat's compartment, and the hydraulics of the harness lifted it off my chest. I stood shakily, bracing myself against the row in front of us.

A voice sounded over the communicator in my ear. "Dr. Riggs to the bridge. We've found the target. You're going to want to see this."

Dad's smile was equal parts joy and triumph as he freed himself from his harness and rose to his feet. "Let's go," he said, putting his full arm around my shoulders this time. "It's our moment of glory. Don't want to miss it." Had my stomach been in a better place, I might have debated the use of the word "our."

On second thought, that was a lie. I cared too much about Dad to ruin what was undoubtedly going to be the happiest day of his life. The happiest day since those he'd spent with Mom, at least.

The walk to the bridge was a short one. The NTA had patterned their discovery-class star carriers after the Dorian design, with the passenger cabins on the same deck as the bridge. When the metal-plated doors hissed open, I laid eyes on our commanding officer.

Captain Robert Greene was the embodiment of what an NTA officer should look like. His thick, iron-gray beard contrasted with his mahogany skin-tone. The crisp cut of his blue officer's uniform highlighted his broad shoulders and assured poise. My dad was a big man, but he looked strangely small as he stepped up next to Captain Greene.

"How did we do, Robert?" Dad asked.

I expected the captain to issue an admonishment for Dad's casual tone. Instead, his mouth stretched into a grin. "See for yourself," he said with a gesture to the forward viewscreen. My jaw went slack as I took in the sight before me.

A planet. We'd been in this system less than ten minutes, and we'd already found a planet. Judging from the size and clarity of the image, we'd emerged from the rift pretty damn close to it, too. The surface was a patchwork of blues and greys, with milky-white clouds slashed in like accents. I'd expected a bit more green-shading from a planet in the gold-zone, but that might have just been my bias. A single rusty-orange moon peaked out from the far side of the globe.

Though my eyes studied the scene, my mind went numb at the implication. *Mom was right.*

Captain Greene laughed, clapping Dad on the back. "I don't know how you did it, Wayne. Those coordinates were spot on. I've never seen a jump take us this close to a target, and I've done over a dozen, mind you."

"Just glad to see the adjustments for the timing worked. That's the annoying thing about celestial objects—constantly moving." Dad scratched at the bit of stubble on his face. "Have you scanned for the monolith yet?"

Monolith?

"Just gave the order," Greene answered.

"Dad?" I asked, confusion evident my tone. "What are you talking about?"

The captain's gaze cut to me, then back to my father. "You didn't tell him?"

"Tell me what?"

Dad sighed, pinching his brow. "One moment, son. I...I just didn't want to bring it up until we had confirmation."

"Confirmation of *what?*"

A nearby console beeped. An ensign tapped on an alert on her holodisplay, and an icon appeared on the forward viewscreen. "Sir," she reported. "I think we've found it."

"Deploy probes," Greene ordered. "Let's take a closer look."

Twin beacons of light appeared on the viewscreen, rushing toward the red icon on the planet's surface. I wasn't paying much attention to that, though. I was totally focused on Dad.

I had to physically shake him to get his attention. "Dad, I think you need to—"

He shrugged off my touch. "Just another moment, Ethan. I need to be sure."

I started to protest, but another beeping sound stole everyone's attention. "Connection established," reported another member of the crew. "Syncing feeds now. On screen in three...two..."

A new window opened on the viewscreen. The bridge took a collective gasp. "My gods..." Greene whispered. The probes hadn't just found some mysterious monolith.

It had found an entire city.

It was unlike anything I'd ever seen, unlike anything I'd thought to exist. Carved primarily of stone, it boasted tall towers and expansive roadways. These were interrupted by odd geometrical protrusions, either parts of buildings or random thrusts of stone that could only be intended for aesthetics. The cyclopean construction of the city was somehow both wonderous and unsightly, while being wholly and completely alien to my sensibilities.

Above it all, stood the monolith. There was no mistaking that this had been what my father and Captain Greene had been discussing. It jutted from the disarray of the city like a beacon, a single steadfast bastion of order in the jungle of chaotic geometries. It seemed carved from the same dim gray, gunmetal, and onyx that comprised the remainder of the landscape.

"That's it," my father whispered.

"What's '*it?*'" came a louder voice at the bridge's entrance. I turned to see Zareen emerge with his five cronies. Already he was falling into his role of keeping tabs on us upstart Terrans. In addition to monitoring our activities, they were here to bail us out if we encountered more trouble than we could handle. Perfect babysitters.

The Dorian soldiers bore the hallmarks of their species: great arcing horns that sprouted from their foreheads and powerful hooves at the ends of their double-jointed legs. Aside from that, the rest of their anatomy was comparable to that of Terrans. Their skin tones had a similar array to that which Terrans could boast—Zareen's registering a rich, almost russet pigmentation. I had been told that the texture of their flesh had the feel of velvet, but I wouldn't know. I'd never dared to lay hands on one from the self-proclaimed master race.

My father rolled with the sudden intrusion, gesturing casually to the viewscreen. "Just like I told you, Zareen. We've already located both the planet, and the monolith. Elaine's visions spoke truth."

A begrudging respect softened the scorn in Zareen's gaze. "So it seems."

It was hard to tell which disturbed me more—to hear Mom's name spoken aloud after so long, or to find that the Dorians had been privileged with information still denied to me. "Is *someone* going to clue me in to what in the nine hells you're talking about?"

A look passed between Greene and my father. "I have this," the captain stated. When my father acknowledged, Greene began issuing the orders to bring the ship nearer to the planet.

Dad wrapped his arm over my shoulder, guiding me away from the buzzing mass of soldiers, consoles, and holodisplays to a more secluded segment of the bridge. When we were as alone as we could be, he met my gaze. "Son, there are some things I haven't told you about your mother's visions."

"Yeah—I picked up on that."

"Ethan…" He fixed me with a stern look, reminding me of my place. I was just a trainee, here—learning how to fly and repair the ships. I wasn't sure how many cycles it took before people stopped getting that look from their parents, but I hadn't hit that age yet. "As much as we were able to trust in what she told us, there were some things that were a bit more…ambiguous. I wasn't sure if the monolith was among the things we could trust, or the things we might misunderstand." Dad often tried to protect me from disappointment. And the truth. I couldn't tell which effort was taking precedence here.

Yet, his point was fair. In her final days, Mom's visions had grown more numerous. In conjunction, her articulation of their meaning had become erratic. Most of the time I couldn't even understand what she was saying, much less glean her meaning. Perhaps I'd been a little too quick to judge my father.

"Sorry," I murmured. "I didn't mean—"

"No need to apologize, son. I understand, and I never meant to keep you in the dark."

I nodded, emboldened by his reassurance. "So, what is it? What's waiting for us down there?"

His eyes never left my mine. "The prize of a generation—something Terrans have been looking for since the Exodus." He patted my shoulder, gripping the back of my head with his opposite hand in the way he did when I was younger. "We found her, Ethan. We've found the Prophet—the one who will lead us home."

I wish I could say I was as overjoyed as my father at the pronouncement, but I would be lying.

The legend of the Prophet dated back to the close of the first Crimson War—the bloodbath the Terrans brought to the Kintari Empire after the Empire's advance force came to the Sol System.

In retribution for the lives and planets taken by the Terrans, the Kintar destroyed all references to the coordinates to the Sol System. The two billion souls brought to the edge of Dorian space in the event that became known as the Exodus were now cut off from their home system, never able to return.

Around that time, a Hissak soothsayer had declared that one day, an entity known as the Prophet would guide Terrans back to the Sol system to reclaim their home world and the colonies they'd established on the neighboring planets. No further details had been ascribed in the legend, though it was entered as canon into the Chronicles of Nethra.

Along with all the other fairytales.

I didn't have the opportunity to express my reservations to Dad. The ship had launched into a relentless flurry of activity. The NTA boarding party, along with all six of our Dorian escorts, was directed to a ready-room, where we were supplied with the gear we might need to survive in a potentially hostile environment: standard issue EVO suits and at least two firearms—the latter issued to everyone but Dad and me. We were the only two members of the science team going planet-side. Honestly, I was glad not to have to carry the weapons.

From what I could gather from the conversation among the military contingent, the terrain in the city was sufficiently prohibitive of spacecraft that we would have to land the shuttle on the rocky outskirts to the east. When we strapped into our restraints on the shuttle, Dad reached over to grab my gauntleted hand. "You've got this," he assured me.

Never in over fifteen cycles did I recall my father taking such a special interest in my well-being. That didn't keep me from appreciating the gesture. "Thanks," I replied, tightening my hold on his hand.

A voice boomed over the shuttle's loudspeaker. "*Three, two...*" The end of the countdown was cut off by the roar of engines and the sensation of my spine trying to become one with my seat. The small craft burned out of the star carrier with increasing velocity, heading straight for the planet below.

Some people lived for this kind of thrill. They sought out parks and simulations in the hopes that they could come close to approximating this feeling. I was not one of these people. In the minutes that passed from the moment our shuttle launched to the second that it landed, I wished for nothing more than for the nightmare to end.

Untold minutes later, it finally did. The shuttle thrust upward viciously as it slowed its descent, and—seconds later—it set down on the rocky outcropping surrounding the city. "Everybody out!" ordered one of the sergeants. Rifles clicked, harnesses lifted, and men filed out of the shuttle before I even had my bearings. What a fool I felt like, stumbling after my dad as we exited the craft.

The roll call sounded as I took in the landscape. It was such a sight, I almost missed my sound-off.

Steely outcroppings surrounded the landing zone. While consistent with the material that showed on our scans of the city, the geometry of the outskirts was only slightly more inviting. Violent thrusts of rock jutted in our direction, leaving only a narrow path to our destination. I was thankful for Zareen's commanding tone in that moment.

"Form up!" the Dorian shouted. "We're not expecting first contact, but be prepared for it anyway. Squad Alpha, you're on point. Squad Bravo, you're on nursery duty. Don't let our dear scientists fall behind." Belatedly, he tapped the side of his helmet. "Looks like the air's breathable. Helmets on or off as you choose. Just don't lose your gear."

Personally, I would be keeping my helmet on. I turned to my father. "What did he mean by 'first contact?'"

"An initial encounter with a new alien race." I could feel his smile, though I couldn't see it through his reflective faceplate.

"Don't stress over it. It's immensely uncommon. Otherwise, there'd be dozens of races represented in the Dorian House of Voices."

"But why?" I pressed. "Did we not think this planet was inhabited?"

"Not by any sapient species," Dad confirmed. "The presence of a constructed city wasn't on our radar either, but we didn't pick up any heat signatures, so we're not expecting any company. That said, anything is possible on a new planet. Just because most advanced fauna have a certain body-temp doesn't mean we won't discover a kind that breaks the trend." He gestured toward the group. "We should get a move-on. Don't want to hold everyone up."

Our forces pressed quickly down the desolate path. I was thankful for Dad's guiding hand to help me through the process. We moved at a not-quite-jog across the rocky landscape and into the city. After a few minutes, I found myself wishing to return to the outskirts.

I couldn't place my finger on it, but something was wrong with this city. There was something about its shape that made my stomach churn. Its construction was a jumble of perplexing geometry that made my head hurt the longer I looked at it. At the time, I blamed my queasiness on the ride down from the star carrier, but later I would wonder if it wasn't some kind of premonition.

In that moment, though, I didn't have the opportunity for contemplation. With Zareem shouting orders through my helmet, all I could do was move. The jog into the city justified all the cardio training I had done in preparation for this mission. We pressed on for a solid hour, not stopping until we were well within the confines of the cyclopean ruins. Only when we were within a half kilometer of the protruding structure Dad called "the monolith" did we stop to catch our breath.

"Dad," I gasped. "What *is* this place?"

His breaths came in heaving, ragged gasps. Apparently, the training had stuck with him little better than it had with me. "Son," he sighed, "I wish I could tell you. I'm certain we will have time to explore later. For right now, we need to keep our eyes on the prize. That prize is the Prophet." He gestured to the looming stone tower before us. "If your mother's visions were correct, then the Prophet lies at the base of that monolith. Once the Prophet is secured, then we can ask our questions about this strange world and its...*aesthetics*."

So, it was fairytales first, then science. I wasn't in a position to argue. The crew of this expedition had bought so extensively into this fantasy that even Captain Greene had elected to be on the away team. His purpose in doing so eluded me, though. As he casually sipped at a canteen with his helmet off and being not the least-bit winded, I suspected it was to put my fitness to shame.

I surveyed our surroundings. Although vaguely reminiscent of the worlds I'd grown up on, the construction of this place had a strangely medieval feeling. There were roads wide enough to drive vehicles on, yet no such machines littered our surroundings. The buildings resembled the office towers I had seen at home, yet they were carved of pure stone rather than metal and plaster. Why was it all abandoned?

Then there was the monolith itself—a spire of steel and crystal of an altogether different breed. Its appearance nagged at me, though I could not place exactly why. There was nothing else like it in the city but growing closer now I could make out some features on the spire. Twin bulges spread out from its base, partially occluded by the surrounding buildings. Metallic flanges flared out elsewhere on the structure creating a kind of bilateral symmetry.

It was these flanges that were bothering me. They spread out from the tower almost like fins or.. "Wings," I gasped. "Dad, are you seeing this? I don't think the monolith is a tower at all! I think it's a ship!"

When I turned back to him, I saw he wasn't listening to me. Something had caught his eye up the street. Soon, I spotted it too. At this distance, it was an ephemeral blur of motion, so I magnified the view on my helmet. What I saw sent a chill down my spine.

It was a woman dressed in finery with long, flowing dark hair. Though her features were only visible for a mere moment before she disappeared around the stone architecture, I could not shake the feeling that I knew her. Then it hit me: "*Mom?*"

"Elaine!" Where my word had been a whisper, my father's was a shout. Any question I'd harbored about the image's authenticity was shattered as he sprinted toward where I had seen the apparition.

Zareen looked questioningly at Captain Greene. "After him!" the Terran captain ordered. The next instant we were on our feet, sprinting after my father. We closed half the distance to the monolith before Dad finally stopped.

Greene reached him first, placing a steadying hand on his shoulder. "Wayne, you can't do that!"

"I know, I know." Dad paused, trying to catch his breath. "It was just that...she was...she was right here!" The Terran soldiers and the Dorians exchanged confused looks. Apparently none of them had seen the apparition. Greene opened his mouth to issue another admonishment.

Then we heard the chittering.

Every soldier in the contingent brought up their rifles in unison. Even without a weapon, I searched the abominable landscape for the source of the sound. I toggled on my heat vision, expecting to see another living being. Though the forms of my companions came through clear, I could see nothing in the distance. I toggled back to the standard feed.

And I saw them.

It was for creatures like these that the word "monster" had been created. Six-legged and vaguely insect-like but lacking any discernable exoskeleton—they moved with the fluid grace of born predators. Their hide was the same mottled gray of the ruins but covered in vicious spikes. The gaping expanse of what I could only assume was their mouths was the stuff of nightmares.

"Contact!" shouted one of the soldiers as he opened fire. The rest of our contingent followed suit. They focused their fire on our left flank until more of the monsters were spotted on the right. In seconds, the monstrosities had us surrounded.

One path lay open to us. That path led straight to the monolith.

Dad grabbed my shoulder. "Run!"

We raced away from where the soldiers fought for their lives. Looking back, I saw one monstrosity impale a man on one spidery leg. Another scooped up a soldier, bringing it directly into its waiting maw. After that, I turned away.

My father and I raced toward the only available sanctuary: the base of the monolith. The road led right into a cave like structure. We scrambled down into the chamber, pushing as hard as our legs would carry us to the far end.

Only to meet a wall. "Gods damn it!" Dad roared, turning around.

My inertia carried me past my father and straight into the stone barrier. In desperation, my hands searched for some gap or opening. While I didn't find what I sought, I did find something.

A handle. "Dad, here!" I tugged against the rocky protrusion. "Here! I think it's a door."

Even in the moment of panic, Dad had the wherewithal to scan the expanse. "I think it slides!" he declared. "To the right! Pull with me!"

Dad and I pulled at the door with all our might. The barrier shifted—slowly at first, but then with increasing ease. As soon as the crack was wide enough to fit through, I released the handle and squeezed inside the opening. Dad surged in after me, reaching for the handle on the other side of the slab.

Only to find a smooth surface.

The gunfire died in the distance, and the chittering of the creatures amplified. I could see shadows coalescing in the distance. They were coming.

Dad pressed hard against the stone and found it unwilling to budge absent a handhold. He looked to the creeping shadows, and then back to me. "I love you, Ethan. I'm sorry—oh so sorry."

Before I realized his intention he was back through the crack and heaving against the handle. The slab closed much more readily than it had opened, closing half the distance on the first heave. Uncomprehending, I surged to the opening. "Dad?"

"Find the Prophet!" he called back. "Find a way home!"

Only then, did I realize his intention. The door couldn't be shut from this side, so my father was doing what fathers were wired to do. He was protecting me. "No, Dad!" I screamed, as the opening shrank again. "Dad, don't!" Another heave, and the gap closed. "Dad? *Dad*!"

I screamed and wept, pounding my fist against the stone barricade. I couldn't decide if it was cruel serendipity or a malignant mercy that I couldn't hear what happened on the far side of the door. Regardless, the only sound to reach my ears was that of my own sobs.

This wasn't how it was supposed to be. Would Mom's visions truly lead us to such a fate? Her purpose—her very legacy—was supposed to lead us to something better, something that would change Terran civilization forever. Instead, it had led us to our slaughter—my dad's certain death.

"Why?" I sobbed quietly, then louder—screaming at the rock that imprisoned me. "*Why?*"

Whatever resolve, whatever stoicism, whatever last vestiges of hope I still harbored collapsed in that moment. I sank to my knees, a bleating, writhing mass of despair on stone tile lightyears away from anything I might have called home. I would never see home again—Ancient Terra or otherwise.

I don't know how long I sat there before I saw the light. It began as a blue shimmer in my periphery, slowly magnifying into a dull, pulsing beacon. I turned my head, unsure if this was some phenomenon of psychosis and desperation.

But no—the light was real. It hovered just around a bend in the stone architecture. Through my bleary eyes, I thought I saw a woman stepping around that corner—the same figure I had glimpsed earlier in the ruins. "Mom...?"

No answer, though the light seemed to pulse more vibrantly than before. My hesitation was brief. What did I have to lose? This gods-forsaken planet had already taken what little I had left. I stumbled toward the beacon, bracing myself against the darkened stone as I rounded the bend. What I saw very nearly brought me to my knees once more.

A crystal—a malformed geometric growth that appeared vaguely translucent in the pulsating light originating within it. It encroached on the stony surface of the chamber like a wave, a tidal force of brilliance intent on consuming the darkness only to be frozen in its efforts. Deep within that crystalline growth, rested a single shadow. As I approached, I could see it vaguely resembled a man.

Or a woman...

I stumbled toward the edifice. My breath, still stochastic from my grief, leveled in apprehension as I drew within a meter of the gleaming effigy. As of its own accord, my hand rose toward the fractal surface. Only on seeing its reflection in the translucent expanse did I hesitate.

Touch it.

The command was not one I heard, but one felt at the base of my skull. The directive was so strong that my hand was against the glassy surface before I realized any intention to put it there. To my surprise, it resembled nothing of the cold hard expanse of the stone that encapsulated me. It was warm and silky smooth to the touch.

Break it.

My indignation instantly drowned out the command. Break this? This one thing of beauty on a planet of hideous structures and monstrous inhabitants? I could never...

Break it.

Even if I could, what tools did I have? This structure had likely stood for countless millennia, enduring forces beyond my wildest—

Break. It.

My fist came down on the crystalline surface. Once. Twice. On the third time, I heard not the dull thud of my hand against an impenetrable obstacle, but a crack. Fissures spidered out from my touch, skittering to the far reaches of the gleaming structure. It fractured not like an elemental bastion, but as flimsy tile under my weight. The ruptures snaked all the way to the edge of the monument's azure surface.

Then it exploded.

I was knocked to my back, light flaring so violently in my vision, it overwhelmed the pain I experienced on landing. For a brief, searing moment, my world was agony. And then, it stopped.

With great trepidation, I opened my eyes.

Her figure was a silhouette against a solar flare. Tears streamed from my eyes in a desperate plea to be shielded from the brilliance of the detonation. Even then, I could not look away. As the light slowly died, my seared retinas tried to make out the form that stood before me.

A woman, clad in white silks with dark hair that flowed onto her shoulders, lowered her hands to her sides. Her chest heaved with the intake of a breath that had waited eons to be drawn. My mouth was dry, and my tongue flaccid as I tried to form a single word.

"Mom?"

My vision began to clear, and I could see the smooth contours of her jaw. The height was just right. The form was just right. The gentle way in which those cerulean eyes opened to regard me was just right.

But this was not my mother.

"No, Ethan." The woman's smile was sad, as if to indicate her regret at the proclamation. "But I am the one who spoke through her."

Spoke through… "I don't understand." My mind burned in a way it hadn't experienced since my first taste of whiskey. I was in the throes of a total inability to comprehend the figure that stood before me.

She knelt, placing a hand on my supine form. "Can you stand?"

"Yes." The word was freed from my lips a second before I conceived it. I hastily stumbled to my feet. The woman rose in concert with me, resting her hand upon my shoulder. The gesture was so like my father's that it threatened to bring me to my knees once more.

"Ethan," she began again. "Your mother was a very special person. There are not many who could hear my calls. To be honest, I had hoped she would be here with you in this moment. I require someone such as her relieve my burden. Her loss was a loss felt through all the universe. There are only a handful of such persons born to each generation."

My mind reeled. "But, that doesn't… I mean…" I buried my face in my palms, head shaking as if that would somehow make things clearer. "What… what *are* you?"

"I've been called by many things, Ethan. From what I have been able to glean from my view from the Nethra, your kind might call me a goddess. However, I think you would know me, more specifically, by another moniker."

My breath caught. "The *Prophet.*"

"Yes, Ethan. I am she."

I groped for the words to express my relief, my awe, my dismay. Never mind that I was addressing an entity who had seen between the planes of my reality—between the fabric that held our universe together and made travel between the stars possible. What do you say when someone—some *being*—validates the pain of your entire life? Seconds passed, maybe minutes. I'm ashamed to say that when my words finally served me, their focus was selfish.

"Am... am I..." I swallowed hard. "Sp-special? Like my mom?"

Again, with that sad smile. "No, Ethan. Your mother was someone very special. However, that does not mean that you, in your own way, are not also special. After all, you did manage to reach this chamber—this ship—when so many others have failed. That, among other things, speaks to the nature of your fortitude. It speaks to what you might one day achieve."

Such a mixture of accolades and disappointment was not something my mind could bare. I wept again, but I do not know whether in pain or adulation. The Prophet was patient with me, letting my sobs run their course until my eyes had no more tears to cry.

At length, I asked, "What now?"

"Now," she said, "We will free you from this prison in the same way that you have freed me from mine. This vessel is old, and the technology alien, but I have faith that you can help me repair it. After that..." She smiled down at me, and I felt my spirit surge anew. "After that, we bring your people home."

— SILENCE IN THE DARK —
By Alexandra Pitchford

I f there was one thing in her life Jaina had come to hate the sight of, it was the inside of a cell. Four blank walls of metal stared back at her no matter which way she looked, and the narrow pane of glass in the cell's single door didn't offer much of a view either. Worst part though, beyond the view, was the *silence*. Being left alone with your thoughts was maddening at the best of times. But something about being in such a small space with only the thoughts in her head and the hum of the ship she could feel through the decking made her want to desperately crawl out of her own skin. She shifted uncomfortably on the metal bench that crossed the back of the cell, rubbing at the metallic connection-point grafted into her shoulder. They could have at least left her her cybernetic arm.

Time stretched, and Jaina groaned, leaning back to thump her head against the wall behind her. The door clicked somewhere around the third thump; a woman in a crisp white uniform with her hair pulled back into a bun stepped into the cell with her.

"Jaina Elizabeth Deckard," the woman spoke in a crisp accent, eyes focused on the data slate in her hand. "Species,

Rithari. Classification, near-human." Her gaze flicked up, coldly appraising. "The number of aliases we have on file for you is substantial, Ms. Deckard. I'm going to hazard a guess that isn't the real one, either. I've never known a Rithari to stoop to giving their child a human name."

"I'm full of surprises," Jaina replied, smiling thinly and glancing at the rank insignia along the uniform's collar. "What can I do for the Central Systems Military, Commander?"

"What you can do for me, Ms. Deckard, is to tell me how you and your compatriot—Marcus Anders—came into possession of a classified prototype military vessel. And please, spare me the 'it was salvage' excuse." The officer touched a panel on the wall opposite, the metal illuminating briefly before pulling to one side. A chair built into the panel behind slid forward and secured in place, allowing the woman to sit.

"I'm not entirely sure you'd believe me," Jaina said. "Let's just say we found it, and that your people really need to keep a rein on your scientists."

The officer gave her a flat look, tapping something onto the data slate and moving on.

"And you're aware of the penalty for unlawful possession of a military asset?" She touched another spot on her slate, pulling up a flickering holographic image that hovered in the air between them; the *Icarus*, almost unrecognizable as it floated in the void, its hull battered and torn open in several places. "Never mind the penalty for destroying one."

Jaina leaned back against the wall. The sight of her ship in pieces stole the last of her snark. She spent a few moments gathering her thoughts before finally pulling her attention from the image and focusing on the woman on the other side of it.

"I appreciate that Marcus and I would be dead without your ship coming along and finding us. We didn't *intend* to destroy the ship. Marcus and I run cargo, and sometimes keep an eye out for salvage, yes. Legal salvage. We were on course to Soren Prime with a shipment of supplies when something opened fire on us. Particle weapons, I guess. It took out our shielding, and we barely got to the escape pod before it blew a hole in our hull."

"And then we found you, I know," the Commander said, dismissing the image. "Did you get a good look at what attacked you?"

"I didn't recognize the ship's silhouette, if that's what you're asking. It didn't look like your standard pirate cutter, and it sure as hell wasn't CSM."

"And if you saw the vessel again, you could identify it as the one who opened fire on your ship?"

Jaina paused, her brow furrowing as the implications of that question struck her. She nodded, watching the officer's expression for any indication of what the woman was thinking. Instead, the woman was infuriatingly stoic as she rose from her seat—the chair sliding back into the wall and the panel locking into place in front of it.

"Ms. Deckard, I am going to make you an offer that goes against my better judgment. Someone has been attacking vessels passing through this sector for weeks, and so far, you and your compatriot are the only individuals to have survived an encounter. If you're willing to help, the captain is willing to overlook your possession of CSM property. Once we settle this matter, you will be escorted to the nearest civilian spaceport and allowed to go free."

Jaina considered her options. The offer sounded a bit too good to be true. She looked around at the four walls of the narrow cell. If she said no, wherever she wound up next would likely be far worse than the brig of a military cruiser. And if they were let go, what then? The *Icarus* had been everything they'd had left. They'd have no choice but to start over with nothing.

Still, they'd be free.

"I just have one question before I say yes," Jaina said.

The commander frowned, her jaw tightening in annoyance. "And what is that?"

Jaina smiled broadly, pushing herself up off the bench. "When do I get my arm back?"

There was always a certain amount of discomfort that came with fitting her arm back into its connection port. As artificial nerves connected to real ones, pain flared along the limb and up over her shoulder, making her wince. Still, the sensation was fleeting, and she flexed her fingers a few times just to make sure everything was in order. The limb looked *mostly* real, synthetic skin covering the full length, only a thin seam where artificial flesh gave way to her actual skin giving away that it was a prosthetic.

"We took the liberty of disabling the weapon you concealed in the limb," the commander said, leaning back against the bulkhead as Jaina went through the gear they'd confiscated. "You are aware that a charged particle weapon of that level of power is illegal for civilian use?" The question had a wry note that drew Jaina's attention away from her gear, even as she shrugged on her jacket again, catching the barest hint of a smirk on the other woman's lips.

"Of course we know that. Why else would she have hidden it in her arm?" Marcus offered from the side, checking the fit of his belt. Jaina shot him a look, and the man went wide-eyed. "What?"

"What about our guns?" Jaina asked the commander.

"I'm not arming you. Not while you're on this ship. When we're done here, you'll be let go and your weapons will be returned." Marcus glanced at Jaina uncertainly, and she rolled her eyes in response. "For now, however, you'll have to suffer through without them." The commander turned, opening the door from the brig into the corridor beyond. Jaina fell into step with her—Marcus not far behind—and took the time to examine their surroundings as the human woman led them away. "The captain has asked to speak with you directly. Understand that while you are aboard, you answer to him. Captain Varnen isn't one to tolerate insubordination. Not from his crew, and not from either of you."

"Varnen?" Jaina paused, grimacing. "Shit."

"What? Who's Varnen?" Marcus said, voice dropped to a hoarse whisper. "Do you know him?"

"Not directly, but that's a Rithari name, and the CSM doesn't exactly have a lot of Rithari captains. He's got a reputation of being a hard-ass."

If the commander heard them, she didn't show it as she stepped up to the bridge door and swiped her hand across the panel. The hatch hissed open, and she stood aside to allow the pair to move in ahead of her.

The bridge was a broad space, bustling with activity. While the cruisers used by the Central Systems Military weren't the largest vessels, they had a good bit of size on the average cargo ship, and the ship's command center was built to reflect that. Consoles lined the bulkheads, with stations placed at points around the room to allow for tactical control, piloting, and navigation. At the heart of it all was the captain's personal station, an impressive chair flanked by holographic readouts and illuminated panels allowing easy at-a-glance views of the state of the ship. The man seated in the chair wore the same white uniform as the commander, setting him apart from the gray-clad crew that moved about the bridge, the rank pins on his collar gleaming gold instead of the typical silver. Like Jaina, the man looked human save for a sharp point to his ears and the strange hue of his eyes—irises appearing the color of polished gold, almost luminous in the bridge's dim lighting.

"Captain Varnen," the commander announced blandly. "The... individuals we picked up from the wreckage of the prototype vessel have agreed to assist. I brought them to you, as ordered."

At the announcement, he rose from his seat, turning to face the entry hatch with a thin smile that immediately set Jaina on edge. The man *oozed* arrogance.

"Thank you, Commander Reese. Please resume preparations while I speak to our guests."

The commander saluted, stepping away to take up position at a station a few paces from the captain's chair. Varnen kept his attention focused on them, or rather, on *Jaina*, his gaze piercing as he motioned for the pair to approach.

"Thank you for agreeing to help in this, Ms. Deckard. As I understand it, your ship encountered our target without warning. Given the information we have on the vessel you were piloting, if you *hadn't* been flying a stolen piece of military technology, you might not have survived the encounter. Thus far, no one else has managed that feat." His smile never faltered, the smugness of it urging Jaina to punch him in the teeth. She thought better of it. "You were quite lucky."

"Lucky, sure." Jaina stepped closer, ignoring the captain's incredibly punchable face to look out the main viewport. "Given how quickly it tore through the *Icarus'* shielding, most anything else wouldn't have stood a chance. The CSM isn't exactly known for investigating raiders hitting trade routes, though. You typically leave that for the Corps to handle themselves. So…" She looked at him finally. "How many military ships has this thing taken out for you to be willing to give the two of us a free pass for just having *seen* it?"

That made Varnen's smug expression falter, though he recovered quickly and cleared his throat.

"Woah, Jaina, what—" Marcus started, but she shot him another look. She had this.

"Not precisely for having *seen* it, Ms. Deckard. While having visual confirmation is helpful, you were able to survive against this vessel—briefly—without even knowing how to fully utilize the armaments of your ship. You've seen what they're capable of, which could be an edge in finally removing this vessel as a threat. I am confident in the ability of the *Arcadia* to prevail, but I am also not the sort of man to turn down an asset when I believe I've found one."

Or maybe she didn't. Shit.

"Did you investigate the other attack sites?"

"Of course we did. Thus far, the pattern remains the same. Sensor logs and crew recordings indicate that the ship appears from nowhere, strikes, and disappears again, but only in this sector. There seems to be little indication why, and no cargo was taken from the vessels that were struck."

"We did notice something strange on the sensors, just before we were hit," Marcus said. He stepped up to one of the navigation consoles, looking from the officer there to the captain. "May I?"

The officer behind the console looked disgusted, but Varnen waved him off and nodded. "Please, Mr. Anders."

Marcus took the seat as the officer vacated it, fingers moving deftly across the controls. On the main holographic display, a map of the sector appeared, a marker flickering to life along part of the primary trade lane.

"This is where we were attacked. A few moments before we were hit, I noticed an energy signature that looked like a typical Aetherdrive reading, but the waveform was a bit off. It was faint, so most ships probably wouldn't have even picked it up, let alone logged it as an anomaly. If you can give me access to the sensor records from the *Icarus*, though, we might be able to pick up the ship well before it appears. We might even be able to follow it."

Varnen nodded, clasping his hands behind his back as that smug look returned.

"Tell me, Mr. Anders. Have you ever considered a career in the CSM?"

"Been there, done that, Captain. Never again." Marcus flashed a smile at Varnen. "The logs?"

The captain's expression soured immediately, and he turned to one of the gray-clad officers.

"Get their ship's sensor logs. *Now.*"

Between deciphering the corrupted sensor logs from the *Icarus* and following the signature of the raider's Aetherdrive, they had been at this for hours. Marcus appeared to be in his element, falling into old patter and habits from his military days as he worked with the *Arcadia*'s bridge crew. While the officers had been extremely disdainful at first, soon they loosened up and began working with him like he was one of their own.

Jaina, however, continued to get sneers and snide comments. The feeling was mutual.

"So, Ms. Deckard. How does a Rithari woman with a human alias wind up running junk supplies and contraband?" Varnen asked her as they watched the officers work.

"How does a Rithari soldier wind up working for the Central Systems?" Jaina countered. She leaned back against the station just behind her, much to the annoyance of the tactical officer working at it. "Last I checked, the CSM was largely human-centric."

"Because, for all my ego, I am not so shortsighted as our people. They might be human dominant, Ms. Deckard, but the Central Systems are the best path for growth and unity in the galaxy. Perhaps more of our people might agree, were they not so set in their ways."

"Captain." To the side, Commander Reese looked up from her station. "We're getting a signature. Strong this time. The vessel is out there."

Varnen took his seat in the command chair and pressed a key, bringing up a tactical map projected in front of him in flickering red.

"Combat stations then, Commander. Let it come to us. The moment you get a solid lock on it, fire."

The lighting on the bridge shifted to a dull red as a siren blared, making Jaina wince. That damn siren had been the first thing on the *Icarus* she'd disabled. Marcus started to move from the nav console he'd appropriated, but Varnen motioned him down.

"I need you right where you are, Mr. Anders. Everyone, hold steady."

For a moment, everything went quiet. The alarm cut out, allowing the eerie silence to stretch as empty stars twinkled beyond the main viewport. The tension rose, tightening Jaina's gut, the anticipation of encountering whatever was out there tying knots in her stomach.

"Captain, starboard!"

"Fire!"

Everything happened at once. The ship swung around, artificial gravity and inertial dampening cutting out the worst of the g-forces from such a sudden move, though Jaina felt it through her boots. A shadow appeared against the stars, followed by flashes of light streaking back and forth from the shape across the void. The *Arcadia* lurched, lights and consoles exploding in a shower of sparks and fragmented glass. The shouts and noise blended into a cacophonous whole, even as Jaina picked herself up off the deck, not even realizing she'd been thrown by the impact until she felt the rush of pain from her head knocking against the metal plating.

"Damage report!" Varnen yelled, his voice tinny. Jaina's head spun, and she didn't catch the reply as she braced herself against the back of the command chair. "Dammit, did we hit them? Give me *something*!"

"No, sir! I'm not reading any signs of impact. They're just *gone*."

The *Arcadia* lurched again, more systems flickering, but this time none managing to explode.

"Shielding held, that time, but strength is draining rapidly, Captain. And if they hit us again like the first time, they might breach the hull."

"I need targeting solutions. We need to know where they are. Tactical, use the information from Mr. Anders' calculations, find a target, and fire. Now!"

Jaina looked back at the tactical station, watching a pair of the bridge crew pulling a twisted, bleeding body from behind the shattered console. That wasn't good.

"Varnen, backup tactical?" she shouted.

"Station to your left," Commander Reese replied, looking up from where she gripped the edges of her station to keep her feet. The first blow must have thrown her as well, her hair knocked partially out of its bun and her white uniform bearing a few marks of scorching. Her display flashed erratically, curls of blue-black smoke rising from it. Jaina nodded in return, moving to the indicated space and quickly bringing the weapons back online.

"Marcus! Give me what you've got!" Jaina said, Marcus nodding from the nav seat and inputting a command. In moments, her tactical screen populated with signatures, faint blips that flared up and then faded again immediately, dancing across the screen almost faster than the sensors could keep up. This wasn't the slow glide of a ship through the black. This was disappearing and reappearing in another space, only to vanish again before the signature fully resolved. It looked like chaos, but it wasn't. There was a pattern to it, clicking in her mind even as her fingers moved across the controls before she'd entirely realized it. "I've got it. NOW."

Particle beams flashed out from the *Arcadia*, lancing toward nothing but empty stars. Varnen spun, but whatever demand he'd intended to shout was lost as the shadowy form of the enemy vessel resolved itself, light building at its fore, only to lurch and spin wildly when the weapons fire impacted its hull. It didn't disappear, it didn't try to fire; the dark shape just listed in the void, trailing pieces of itself from the point of impact.

"Is that it?" Reese asked, looking bewildered as she stared at the viewport.

"Scans. Now," Varnen growled as he stood from his chair. To one side, an officer nodded, running the commands before blinking and looking back up.

"Captain, the ship has no shielding that we're detecting. No armored plating on the hull. I'm not even detecting any signs of life aboard it."

"What *can* you detect?"

"Well...we're getting a clear read on the strange Aetherdrive signature from before, so that is the ship, Sir. There's atmosphere aboard, too, aside from the section we just vented into space. It looks like there were emergency systems that sealed and isolated the exposed area before the ship lost its atmosphere."

"All right, then." Varnen turned, his gold eyes fixing on Jaina. There was a cold appraisal there that told her he'd come to the same realization she had—she shouldn't have been able to do that. "Well, Ms. Deckard. Care to find out who set you adrift?"

The *Arcadia's* boarding skiff was cramped with an entire team aboard, plus Jaina. Marcus' response to the entire suggestion of going aboard had been fairly clear—as clear as "Oh, hell no," could be. So, dressed in an ill-fitted EVA suit, Jaina sat in one of the skiff's crash seats opposite Reese, the pair accompanied by three of the ship's security personnel. The enemy vessel almost blended into the starfield around it through the viewport of the skiff, the ship surprisingly large as they closed on it. It was triangular, like an obsidian arrowhead, though the black hull plating absorbed light rather than reflected it, an inky void that immediately set Jaina on edge as she looked out at it.

Ominous was the word. The thing was ominous.

"Bring us around to the breach," Reese said. She rose from her chair, moving behind the pilot and resting a hand on the back of his seat as she looked out at the vessel. "There. I think we can slide in there and use the boarding tube to cut through into one of the undamaged sections. Everyone, EVA on. There's no guarantee there aren't contaminants in the atmosphere on board, so keep your helmets on. Last thing we need is to bring back an alien pathogen."

As one, the security team secured their helmets, but Jaina hesitated. Her hands shook slightly, but she took a few heavy breaths and tugged the helmet on over her head, latching it in place and exhaling. The suit pressurized seconds after the seal was secured. It was just an EVA suit. No reason to panic. Not that the thought calmed her heart hammering in her chest.

"Are you all right, Ms. Deckard?" Reese asked, her voice coming through over the suit's internal comms. "You look a bit pale."

"Yeah. Yeah, I'm fine." Jaina nodded quickly, gripping the bracing handles on the edge of her seat as the skiff lurched. There was a low hum, followed by a screech of metal, all muffled through the suit.

"Boarding tube is secure, Commander," the pilot called out.

"Good. Wait here. If I give you the order, leave for the *Arcadia*, but until then...don't move from this spot."

"Understood."

Reese turned back to Jaina, offering a hand to help her out of her seat.

"Come on, Deckard."

Jaina took it, grunting as she stood and following behind the team as they filed into the airlock. The space sealed, a dull hiss following as the air inside the ship was pulled out and replaced with air from the interior of the enemy vessel. Only then did the boarding tube unseal, revealing a darkened corridor beyond it.

"Are you sure I can't have my gun back?"

"Yes, I'm sure. Just stay close."

As they stepped into the corridor, their helmet lamps flicked on, chasing back the darkness around them. The metal of the bulkheads and deck plating was smooth, but with an iridescent quality, shimmering as the light passed over it. The air felt still even through the suit, and Jaina felt the knots in her stomach tighten. This place was wrong. All of it.

"Lieutenant, pull up the layout from our scanner readings. See if you can find the control room for this monstrosity," Reese said.

"It's that way." Jaina pointed down the corridor to their right, then frowned. "I mean, I think it's that way. I saw the scans before we left." The scans had been difficult to decipher, but now that she was aboard, she just felt *certain*, a cold dread that beckoned her down that route toward something. The rest of the party looked at her before the officer Reese had directed to pull up the ship layout nodded.

"She's right. It's that way," he said.

"All right. Let's go." Reese looked at Jaina for a long moment before starting to move, the rest of the team following in her wake. Jaina trailed behind, her steps feeling leaden the closer they drew to the ship's command center. The security team clustered around the entry hatch, their voices muffled and dull as if heard through water. The wrongness of the place clawed at her, but no one else seemed remotely perturbed, moving unbothered into the chamber beyond the hatch and leaving Jaina behind. She stopped, just a few paces from the threshold, bracing herself against the wall and gasping for breath. Watery, muffled noise came over the comms, fuzzy and indistinct, even as a shadow moved across her field of view.

"*Deckard!*"

The world snapped back into focus as Reese grabbed her by the shoulders. The pressure the place exuded, the aura of wrongness, receded without entirely fading, and Jaina gave a short nod as she breathed in to ease her trembling.

"I'm fine, Commander Reese. I'm fine."

Reese looked incredulous but nodded and let her go.

"Come here. You should see this too," she said, stepping back into the control room. Jaina jogged after her, looking around the angular chamber as she stepped inside. It was similar, in some ways, to the layout of the *Arcadia's* bridge, but the architecture was sharp, every surface crafted from the same iridescent black metal. Control systems glowed dully, some measure of power still reaching them after the shot crippled the ship, but it was the occupants of several of the stations that drew Jaina's focus. Humanoid shapes, reduced to bones covered by withered, dry skin, were slumped in several of the chairs, cables and wires woven through their bodies and connecting them to the consoles in front of them. Only one console seemed to have full power, a series of alien characters displayed across it.

"These bodies are Rithari," one of the security officers said. "I can't tell how long they've been dead, though. A long time."

"They looked mummified," another offered. "If the crew is... dead, who was piloting the ship?"

"I have no clue. If we can figure out a way to remove one of these bodies for transport, we can bring it aboard the *Arcadia* for study. Lewis, can you tell what that console says?" Reese motioned to the one active panel, Lewis nodding sharply and moving toward it.

"It doesn't look like any language I've ever seen, Commander. The bodies might be Rithari, but these characters aren't. The tech doesn't even look right."

Jaina drifted closer to the console as well, her brow furrowing as she watched the characters shift and change. There was something familiar about them, a vague sense of recognition buzzing in the back of her head. Noise crackled from the console at odd intervals, as well, incredibly garbled.

"I think I can clear up the audio, at least. I'm not sure if we'll understand it, but…" Lewis crouched, pulling open a panel and rooting around inside for a bit. The noise rose in volume, crackling before resolving into a mechanical voice that filled the chamber. It was a short sequence of words, and Jaina frowned as she focused, trying to hear what it was saying. "That's what I thought. I don't recognize the language."

Jaina raised a hand, tilting her head. Like the symbols, a familiarity was there, even if she couldn't place it. The words echoed, repeating every few moments as the symbols on the screen changed.

And then, with a horrifying realization, it all clicked together.

"Back to the skiff. *Run!*"

"What?" Reese looked alarmed. "What the hell are you talking about?"

"Just *go!*"

Jaina turned, running full tilt down the corridor back toward the boarding tube. She didn't wait to see if the others followed, but she heard footfalls behind her, and she didn't stop until she was inside the airlock. The team piled in behind her, and Reese hit the comm panel beside the hatch.

"Get us out of here, now."

The pilot didn't respond, but the hatch sealed, and the skiff began to move. A rumbling noise filled the air around them as they slid out of the breach into the black again, cutting back toward the *Arcadia*. A few moments later, the skiff was thrown roughly, artificial gravity aboard cutting out and tossing the security team hard around the airlock. They came to a rough stop, floating above the floor for a brief few moments before the gravity reasserted itself and they dropped to the deck, bruised and battered.

"Commander, the vessel—" The pilot's voice crackled over the comm, but Reese cut him off.

"Exploded. I know. If you can get us back to the *Arcadia*, do it."

With the air cycled and the decon sensors lighting up green, Reese removed her helmet and turned back to Jaina, anger flashing in her eyes.

"Deckard, how in the hell did you understand what it was saying?"

Jaina tore her helmet off, as well. She gasped for breath, heart hammering as she tried to calm herself, to no avail. She barely registered that she was moving until Reese slammed her against the bulkhead.

"Talk to me, Deckard, or I swear I will throw you back in that cell, deal with the captain or not."

"I don't know!" Jaina snapped back. "I don't even know what language that was. But I heard it clearly. 'Intruder detected. Self-Destruct Protocol Engaged'. Just that, on a loop. Those symbols were *numbers*, Commander."

Reese hesitated briefly, then let her go.

"Pilot, open a channel to the captain." The comm crackled, followed by a positive chime as the channel was established. "Captain Varnen, the ship appeared to be automated. The crew were all long dead, hardwired into their stations in some way. We only managed to get away due to Ms. Deckard, who...deciphered the ship's self-destruct in time for us to escape to the skiff."

"I see. Good work, Commander. We'll do a full debrief when you get back to the ship."

"Understood. Regarding Ms. Deckard and her compatriot, I recommend we detain them further. The fact that our *guest* could decipher the ship's language is concerning."

Jaina tensed. That hadn't been the deal, but the commander was right. None of it made sense, not even to her.

"Understood. Bring Ms. Deckard back aboard. It seems we've a lot more to discuss."

Reese met Jaina's eyes, the look lingering for an uncomfortable moment.

"You really don't know what happened back there, do you?"

"No," Jaina said. "But I'd like to find out."

THE SHIP CAT
— OF THE SUZAKU MARU —
By SL Huang

I t is said that being a Ship Cat takes a very particular kind of cat. Just as a Bookshop Cat mustn't hiss at customers nor scratch at children who reach out grubby fingers for an unwelcome pat, or a Temple Cat must be aloof and not too playful with the pilgrims who have come many lightyears for somber worship. Being a Ship Cat requires a limber agility for the gravitational changes, a tolerance for the scents of fuel burn and unwashed humanoid, and, most tragically, a forbearance for long stretches of expanse without a square of natural sunlight to stretch in.

Toshi prided himself on being the most excellent of Ship Cats.

An extraordinarily handsome fellow, Toshi was of pristine white with black splotches emblazoning his head and feet and back and tail. The patch over one of his eyes was black; the other, white; and one front paw was snowy while the other appeared dipped in soot. Toshi kept this glossy fur fastidiously clean, such that any time he deigned to allow a passenger to lift him and bury their face in his sleek self, the scent would put them in the mind of fresh meadows and clean laundry.

Toshi also excelled at the dual duties of a Ship Cat. The first of these duties is, of course, hunting down any vermin that might have wriggled on board at port. Small vermin are ubiquitous in every city of the Nineteen Worlds, only differing by unimportant characteristics such as color, number of mouths, the existence of a carapace, or whether they leave large clutches of eggs above the reactor core. Left to their own devices, they will nest near the warmth of the particle engine to chew its tubes through, or wriggle into the commissary to gobble the humans' dehydrated provisions.

Some of the fancy luxury passenger yachts or shiny expensive cargo haulers brag of their robotic extermination systems, along with their self-navigating AIs and automated logistics operations. The old frontier captains, though—they all swear by cats. For a solid old merchant ship like the *Suzaku Maru*, a cat kept the in-between crannies far more spic-and-span than any number of robots could, and at a fraction of the cost.

Besides, the weathered human captains favor cats for their second purpose: cats on ships are good luck. That's a longstanding fact. Since the old days of sailing the oceans of Earth, it has been known that leaving port without a cat on board is a deliberate tickling of fate.

Toshi's good luck had kept the *Suzaku Maru* smooth and vermin-free for nearly a hundred runs now. The ship arrowed blithely through the cosmos, ferrying freight from port to port to port, usually along with a few dozen travelers who couldn't afford a berth on one of the high-speed passenger liners. No major disasters, no drastic repairs, just maintenance to help hum along and accounting books that consistently ran a few satisfactory fingers beyond breaking even. Good enough for Captain Jiro Akimoto and his crew, for sure. A decent business, running an independent merchant hauler. A decent business and a decent life.

Toshi was very certain—as all cats are—that the fit functioning of the ship was entirely down to his own presence on board making it run properly. Quite right that Captain Akimoto always gave scritches behind the ears when such was demanded of him.

During the last Galactic Cycle in lapse 8432—standard time—the *Suzaku Maru* lifted off from the port city of Ogedegbe on the world of Ember. As he always did, Toshi had the run of the ship, the better to supervise anything that needed his keen oversight. The shift to lighter gravity brought its own proper ritual of delight, as Toshi twisted and leapt to twice the height he could in port, pirouetting his lithe body at the peak of each leap.

Who wouldn't want to be a Ship Cat, indeed!

Once the gravity settled into its lighter intersystem weight, Toshi began his rounds. He first roamed up to the cockpit. Captain Akimoto was at the controls, gazing up into the star-filled viewport. The captain always flew takeoff and landing himself instead of delegating to one of his crew. Only twice in seven years had Toshi seen another human take the ship up or down from a planet or in or out of FTL—once when the captain had been sick with blood rot, and the other when he had crushed his hand in an engine room accident. That time he had still stood gravely at his crewmember's shoulder to watch over his beloved ship and make sure all was done right.

Toshi leapt up onto the edge of the control boards, careful not to walk across the buttons and switches. He'd learned fast as a young kitten that such care was an important part of being a Ship Cat. Captain Akimoto had trained him with a buzzer that made Toshi's ears flatten and his chin burrow down against the ground. He'd learned very fast, and would now never dream of stalking across the captain's important buttons and switches.

Toshi was a *very good* Ship Cat.

Captain Akimoto hit some of those important switches and leaned back in his pilot's chair, rubbing at his grayed-out beard. "Toshi-chan! Keeping my ship tip-top, are you? Here, have a scratch, ne?"

"*Nyao*," Toshi agreed, butting his head against the captain's outstretched fingers.

"You like that, don't you, ne. Good boy," the captain crooned. "This part is my favorite bit, did you know? When we've left civilization back behind, floating on up in the black. That space between ground and FTL when it's just us, all alone. Drifting away, ne..."

Toshi did not always understand human words, but the captain's gravelly voice was as comforting as a heated blanket.

Still, Toshi had duties. He slipped his black-and-white head out from under the captain's exquisitely hypnotic fingers and dropped down to the deck plating, trotting out of the cockpit to his next stop.

In this way did Toshi patrol the ship from nose on down—passenger berths, the commissary, the cargo decks; casting his keen senses around every corner and slipping in and out of maintenance shafts. As was his due, he accepted pats and scratches from several of the passengers, the cook, and the cabin boy along the way. (The cabin boy was not a boy at all, but a wiry teenaged girl named Siau, who was apprenticing on Captain Akimoto's crew for a few years in return for food and board and learning a trade. She had a pocket tool with a bright laser on it that she would often shine onto the bulkheads for Toshi to chase.)

Finally Toshi had canvassed his entire home save the final enormous deck—the engine bay, which took up the whole aft end of the ship. The particle engine was a tremendous ball of hot and dangerous, with catwalks for the engineers crossing in suspended layers above the magnetically-contained reactor core. So very hot and so very dangerous and so very far down below, enough that Toshi had always instinctively known to hop lightly about the catwalks, nimble feet that were careful never to fall, lest he tumble into the core's pulsing maw of energy and light. Toshi did not know how the particle engine worked—how it propelled them through folded space, or how it incidentally provided the light gravitational pull on the decks above it—but he could sense its strength as the beating heart of the ship.

He also liked to lie on the engine catwalks and laze in its warmth. Who needed squares of sunlight when you had an engine deck!

Toshi padded down catwalk by catwalk, past the many banks of controls and computers, paws winding between the scraps and springs and tools the *Suzaku Maru's* chaotic engineers were prone to leave strewn about. The engine had an all-encompassing hum that tickled the ends of his fur to fluff out from his body. Three catwalks down he had encountered naught but a buzzing scorpion mantis, which he'd pounced upon in an easy leap—and then released and pounced upon again, and then again, six times before worrying its exoskeleton in his mouth until it buzzed its last, a sad *zzzt-zzzt-zzzt* like a dying mechanical toy.

Toshi liked to keep his skills sharp. And have some fun.

None of the engineers were about. They usually weren't, this early in the trip. The engine had to be monitored round the clock while in FTL, but mundane thrusters needed no supervision, and the acceleration changes made the humans' fingers slip on fiddly tasks until they raised their voices in mewing complaint. Humans weren't like Ship Cats, who so agilely adjusted to every fluid instant of weight difference.

Today, however, two humans *were* down below, on the very lowest of the catwalks.

They weren't humans Toshi recognized. That in itself was not unusual, as unfamiliar passengers came and went every voyage. These humans, though—they radiated a sense of *not belonging*, down here on this lowest catwalk above the reactor core. The reactor's light played up against them in dancing blue and white, leaving them mostly in shadow.

Toshi's fur, already fluffed from the crackly air, stood on its ends even further. His paws moved in advance and then retreat, tail swishing, his eyes on the men.

"You sure they're not gonna come down here?" one of the men was saying. He was a tall, burly fellow, with a wide face and a floppy hat that shaded his features to darkness. His scent was acrid, of stale smoking herbs and rancid fuel.

"Not till close to the FTL point," responded the other. "We've got twenty-five hours, or near enough, and by then we'll have 'em all locked out." The second man was weedier, with shelf-like eyebrows and long fingers. He smelled of handling piles of metal, the way the captain's skin smelled after he met with the type of people who, instead of tapping screens, gave him lumps of yellow gold that he weighed and counted. Or the way the pads of the captain's fingers smelled after he loaded stacks of shiny darts into magazines for the pneumatic pistol holstered at his hip.

The big man heaved at a crate behind them. It seemed the two men were coming from the maintenance door of the trash hold, which didn't make very much sense, because no one ever came from the trash hold. Toshi had been cautioned very severely never to try to jump in when it opened, by humans whose voices went high with worry. They needn't have been so concerned—it smelled of rot and waste, and Toshi had never been tempted to put a paw inside.

"Well, what are we waiting on, then?" grunted the big man while he dragged on their crate. "Let's get the damn bugs out. This is guaranteed foolproof, right? I'm not going to some dagnasted penal colony if we're caught—"

"Relax," answered the metallic-smelling man. "These spiders are state of the art. An old bucket like this won't have a chance.

Besides, you don't have to worry about a penal colony—hijacking is a Class Ten. Still a capital crime if you do it in a spaceway."

He sounded much more relaxed than the big man, like oil pooling where it shouldn't.

The big man made a bunch of sounds with his mouth that had a lot of hard consonants in them, and then said, "If they weren't paying us enough to buy a fuckratted planet... What the hell is this rust heap carrying anyway that could be so—*hey!* What in fuck is that?"

He'd spotted Toshi. He dropped the end of the crate with a loud clang and advanced a few steps, his fists opening and closing like aggressive mouths.

Toshi arched his back and hissed, his tail flicking. His claws *snicked* against the catwalk's grating.

"It's just a damn cat," the smaller man answered. "Leave it alone."

"They ought to learn to buy a canister of crawlies instead," groused the big man. "Get outta here, beast! You hear?"

He swatted with hands the size of barrel lids, not close enough to make contact, but Toshi scampered anyway, still hissing.

He did not like these men. They were humans, but they smelled wrong and acted wrong and they made Toshi's fur prickle so far up it was as if someone had dragged their hands against him back to front, all the wrong way, everything wrong.

Toshi did not run far, however. He disappeared from the men's view and bounded away up to the next catwalk, then to the top of one of the tall banks of machines the engineers spent their days poking at. He crouched down flat against it, eyes slitted, his ears lying back against his head. His black bits faded into the shadows, only his white bits shining out of the dimness.

He stayed focused on the men, every predatory instinct itching.

The men's conversation floated up to him here, voices that chopped and swung with a tension that twanged against the air. Words like *"only take a few hours"* and *"seal them out"* and *"full control of the jump, and then that's done."*

They'd hauled their crate all the way out onto the catwalk. The smaller man produced an angled metal bar and began prying at a corner. The top of the box came up with a screech, first one corner then another, until together the two men dragged the lid off with a tremendous amount of grunting.

The inside was dark.

The smaller man produced a handheld computer from a pocket and tapped its screen.

Tiny lights clustered up from the crate's darkness. Like the stars in the black that Captain Akimoto so loved. Except these lights moved.

The lights skittered up and out, pouring from the top of the box and down its sides on many tapping legs. The men whooped. The tiny creatures began to fan out, chittering across the catwalk, a slowly-expanding spill of dread. In minutes they would spread far enough to reach the banks of machines along the catwalks—the ones that controlled the particle engine and navigation systems, communications and life support, everything the *Suzaku Maru* needed to function.

With nary a breath of thought, Toshi gathered himself and leapt.

Humans—he couldn't do anything about humans. But these were not humans. These were *vermin*.

Toshi knew exactly what to do with vermin.

He bounded into the edges of the burgeoning swarm. A claw swipe—*snick*—a pounce and bite down—*snap*. Toshi was momentarily surprised when his teeth encountered metal, when his claws scratched at their skins to find only bits of wire and no flesh that squished or crunched. Still, these moved and they were vermin, and Toshi knew what to do with vermin.

The *Suzaku Maru* used no automated cleaning crawlers. Toshi had never been trained not to attack mechanicals.

He skidded through the horde, his heart pitter-patting with the thrill of his expertise, as he met a challenge like none ever before. Tiny robots flew, spiraling off the catwalk with their metal legs kicking until they arced out and down, down, down to crackle into nothing when the surface of the engine core devoured them. Within the first seconds, Toshi had become a black-and-white cyclone, mechanical spiders raining in his wake along with a trail of scrap and circuitry from the ones he had mauled.

It took the two men those seconds to react.

The big man was faster. "Hey!" he yelled again, but this time he charged at Toshi. His boots crushed more of the robots, and he danced back, cursing. "Hey! Get away! Get off them!"

The smaller, metal-smelling man did not try to approach. Coolly, he drew a pneumatic pistol from his hip, one very much like what the captain wore. In the throes of predatory bloodlust, Toshi only peripherally saw the movement, and would not have recognized it in any case. Nor would he have known that this hijacker of his home had filled the pistol magazine with star-pointed shredding darts, the type that would, if a single round impacted a cat, tear straight through the poor creature's fragile skin and lithe bones.

The man fired. The pneumatic went off with a *phhhhllk* that echoed off every metal surface in a dangerous whisper.

The man was a good shot. Serendipitously, Toshi made a twisting leap after one of the spiders at the very instant the gun went off, and the cruel dart skimmed over the side of the catwalk and out into nothingness.

The next one passed so close it clipped some fur from Toshi's flying tail before it buried itself in one of the bugs.

Still Toshi did not realize the danger, glorying only in the pounce and snatch and tear, so many of these rattling creatures, *all for him,* all for him to clear out as meticulously as he cleaned his own black and white fur.

His rampage had taken him closer to the men. The big man lumbered forward again, reaching out with grasping hands. This was a gesture Toshi recognized. He dipped and dashed, in then out—pounce and shake, tear and swat—so the man's fists closed only on air.

"Get out of the way!" yelled the other man. "You utter nimbo! Get out of the way so I can shoot it!"

The big man obeyed, lurching backward, and the man with the pneumatic swung it around back at Toshi, who at this point was close enough to dash between his legs.

The man spun, shouting, and tried to aim, but Toshi zigged to and fro, a quicksilver storm of black and white sleekness. Back between the man's legs again, then leap up to dash off the side of the crate... Mid-leap, the man with the gun lunged for Toshi, trying to grab onto him as his partner had, and he was far closer, but that's what claws were good for.

Whisk, slash, and the man howled something about eyes, his hands coming up to his face and the pneumatic clattering to the catwalk. Lines of red appeared on his skin as he staggered backward. Toshi left off the bugs for a quick shake and pounced again.

Even though the man was human. Sometimes humans were vermin too.

The man screamed and swiped at the flying whirlwind of angry cat, covering his face and diving away. Toshi careened back off him and down to the catwalk—just as the man's dive took him straight up against the metal railing with a flailing, panicked force.

Yells of pain and alarm turned to a surprised screech of pure fear as his momentum took him toppling over. For one brief moment he pawed at the railing from the wrong side, and then he too was falling, falling in a hail of his own sabotage robots, down and down and down.

The surface of the reactor barely sizzled before they were gone.

The big man bellowed out something that might have been his friend's name, and began to sob.

Toshi noticed none of it. He still had more of the rapidly crawling mechanicals to get back to. Not so many now, though...his sensitive ears flicked about for every final skitter of tiny metal feet on metal catwalks. Toshi chased the last few down wherever they fled, whether under banks of controls or into maintenance shafts. He smacked them off vertical plating or fat wires, dragging them out to where he could hurl and snap and dismember while their little legs flailed.

He was fierce. He was glorious. He was an *excellent* Ship Cat.

The big man stared about at the rapidly multiplying strew of debris that had been their state-of-the-art hijacking robots. He gazed weak-kneed and anguished after where his friend had fallen and then cast a malevolent glare after the black and white cat that was so joyfully savaging the remainder of their plan.

With his criminal enterprise in tatters and his partner ionized to nothing, the big man became seized by a senseless, raging fear. He yanked his hat down over his face and ears and, with no other option coming to mind, hurried to stuff himself away back in the large metal box of a trash hold. He would stay here and plan, he thought—figure out what to do now—he was not on the passenger manifest, nor did he have the provisions to stay hidden for the ship's planned months-long journey between ports. If he was found—how could he not be found?—the best he could hope was that they would think he was merely a stowaway, and take pity...

Even if the crew here was cruel, it was the thought of landing at their destination port that made a pure inky terror fill the heart of the *Suzaku Maru's* erstwhile hijacker. The employers he and his brother had been working for—the brothers had never worked for *them* before. Not *them*. It had been his brother's idea, laugh at the risk, laugh at the stories, it's too much money to say no. *We'll be set for life,* he'd said, *stop being such a damn puss...*

The stories, the stories—you could never hide from *them*, everyone said. You could run, but not for long, never for long, and then they'd find you.

They wouldn't kill you. Not yet. Not for a long time.

The big man crouched among the slimy, crusted innards of the empty trash hold and whimpered into his enormous hands.

Meanwhile, Toshi pounced upon the very last one of the scuttling spiders, his paws pinning it with perfect aim. One black paw, one white, claws extended, trapping the tiny robot so its metal legs pedaled on either side. Toshi took the unlucky creature in his jaws, tossed it once, twice, three times, allowing it to recover each time. Each time it moved a bit slower, and its legs hitched and jerked a bit more.

At last Toshi batted it to the ground. The metal wasn't very pleasant to pull at with his teeth, but the fine wires underneath were a much better mouthfeel, enough that Toshi lay contentedly chewing at them for a few minutes.

The reactor core hummed on below, the blue and white light dancing up the sides of the engine bay, playing against the bulkheads as if they were underwater.

Toshi got up, shook himself, and resumed padding about his domain.

A shout made his ears prick.

Not quite a shout. More like a loud complaint, the way humans did sometimes when they wanted someone to overhear. A bulkhead banged up above, at the top of the catwalks.

Toshi recognized the voice, lively and taut with both youth and green inexperience. Siau, the cabin boy. Odd that she should be here now. She thumped down the catwalks, muttering under her breath.

Toshi trotted up to wind about her legs. He thought he very much deserved a pat.

Of course, Toshi was always of the opinion that he deserved a pat.

Siau obliged, reaching down to scritch between his ears. She smoothed his fur, which had become so fluffed by the crackly air down here and the rollicking fight.

"Hi, you. Ain't you a good cat? Good Toshi."

Toshi was in complete agreement. He was very much a good cat.

"Chief's making me come and swab before FTL," Siau complained to him. "She says it's too much a mess down here. I says, 'well who's making the dagnasted mess, cos it sure as shit ain't me' and she says, 'good thing my crew's got 'em a cabin boy to sweep the decks for us.' Kicks me down here quick as you please."

"*Nyao,*" Toshi answered knowingly. Siau complained often.

"Can't wait for the someday when I'm not nobody's 'prentice no more. Don't got to answer to no one and get a wage of my own. Maybe a ship one day, good as the *Suzaku Maru*. Whaddaya think of that?"

Toshi rolled over on top of her boot and rubbed his cheeks on the tight-clipped laces. She smelled of solder and burnt metal. It was a good smell. A belonging smell.

Siau laughed. "Good cat. Guess I'd better get to it, eh?"

Toshi kept her company while she stalked about the catwalks, picking up the various springs and scraps and wires and fuses the engineering crew had left and chucking them in a large bin, then sorting through for what would go in the recycler or for any reusable parts. She groused to Toshi the whole while—"You'd think after decades working an engine room they'd learn to pick up their own shitnicks, wouldn't you" and "why leave out a whole bottle of grease-up, no wonder they can't never find nothing 'round in here" and "the Captain keeps such ship shape up top, you'd think his Chief could keep her crew in line down below. Guess she thinks they're so good at running a core they can do whatever kinda raz they want."

She dumped the unusable bits in the various slots along the catwalks that dropped down into the trash hold. When the scrap metal clattered down the chutes to the hold at the bottom, Toshi's sensitive ears picked up a few quickly-stifled yelps. Siau banged on, oblivious.

When she got to the mess left by Toshi's stellar devastation of the mechanical vermin, Siau let out a gusty groan and set about chucking the bits into her bin with enough force to dent them further. "What in a nebular eye were they doing here—no, don't tell me, I'll just get more tizzed. Leave it all for the low-down intern to pick up, yeah, convenient for you all, ain't it? None of this crap's good no more."

She shoveled it all into the slot in the trash hold.

"Fuck me, that's already starting to be a load. Better space it before FTL and clear things out, eh Toshi?"

She banged some of the buttons on the trash hold's side.

A great grinding started up, followed by the sudden sound of nothing, as everything in the trash hold dropped hard into an airlock and then was sucked out into the vacuum of space. Environmental groups hated waste management systems like these, protesting the endless dumping of litter among the common shipping lanes, but none of the older ships could afford to keep the weight. And, their captains reckoned, space was pretty damn big. Bits of litter could lose themselves forever in the black.

A trail of debris fanned out behind the *Suzaku Maru*, metal detritus and dead robots and exactly one human corpse, his wide face frozen in a scream the vacuum had snuffed away.

Back on the ship, Siau scooped up Toshi in her arms—he allowed it—and smushed her face into the fur of his neck. Then she carried him up with her to the passenger decks, where he leapt down and went to the commissary for some crunches of food and a very thorough bath, licking flat every prickle the engine deck had left in his fur.

He wandered back up to the cockpit, where Captain Akimoto reclined in his chair, hands laced behind his head.

He grinned when he saw Toshi, the skin crinkling all up next to his eyes.

"How's it tripping, my good little friend?" he asked, reaching out automatic fingers for the expected ear scritch. "Did you find any vermin for us?"

Goro-goro-goro-goro-goro, purred Toshi against his hand.

"Good boy, ne. Taking care of us all."

Toshi hopped up to the captain's knee this time, kneading his claws against the tough canvas coveralls. Then he curled up against Captain Akimoto and let the ear scritches absently continue on, as together they watched the black drift by.

It's true, what they say. It's bad luck to leave port without a cat on board.

— THE MUSIC OF A NEW PATH —

By A. T. Greenblatt

TESSA

Tessa's crew was making music again in the deepest part of space. Like a heartbeat, like a lifeline. Anything to survive in the endless, gaping void between stars.

She was chewing gum on the half beat of her crew's song: Iona tap, tap, tapping her foot as she tinkered in the engine coils. Kaitlin's clear whistle, winding and floating, as she bustled around the mess. Nima humming counter-melody to Kaitlin's tune as they wrangled the livestock in the cargo hold. And below it all was *Cagwin's Castaway*'s bass, droning and whirring and shifting as it hurled them through the emptiness to the next colony.

There's always another colony, Tessa thought, and it gave her a bit of hope. The crew's song thrummed in her ears as she drifted around the command center, display screen in hand, debating where they should go next. Surrounding her, the bay windows showed a bright blue atmosphere with cloud wisps, making her feel like she was floating in some colony's sky. It was a lie, of course, but Tessa didn't care. She was a deepsailor, but that didn't mean she had to stare into empty space.

Clack, clack, clack went her teeth as she worried, keeping half an eye on the readings *Cagwin's Castaway* fed her about the exterior of the ship, half an eye on the readings about its organic and inorganic parts, and half an eye on the colony requests coming through. Over and over she plotted out potential courses using known routes through the mind bending twists of spacetime only to be disappointed in her options. They'd reach their destination in three days. She'd put off the decision for far too long.

"Here's the choices, crew. We run to Beta station next," Tessa said, keeping the frustration out of her voice. She wished they had the supplies and resources to make longer treks, to try new routes.

"I hate that place," Iona grumbled over the com.

"Same," said Nima.

"They pay well enough," Tessa argued, but halfheartedly. "They're desperate."

"That's because half of their population harasses deepsailors," countered Kaitlin, with a snort. "Not worth the money."

"Never thought I'd hear you say that," Iona teased.

"Me neither," replied Kaitlin with a laugh. "But we're not that pathetic. Yet."

"Well, the other option is Scion 8," Tessa said. The entire crew groaned, and Tessa could swear *Cagwin's Castaway's* pitch got lower too.

Tessa rolled her eyes, but inwardly she was pleased. They had come a long way since she'd found *Cagwin's Castaway* and her crew in that ship graveyard. At least, they had the luxury of meager choices now. "Beta Station it is then," she said. She pulled up the client contract.

[CONTRACT REFUSED] flashed on her screen. Tessa froze. *Cagwin's Castaway* rarely ever cared where they went.

"Okay, smart ass," Tessa told the ship. "Where should we go then?"

Cagwin's Castaway didn't respond. Droning, droning went its engines.

Tessa ground her teeth into her chewing gum. She and her deepsailing ship never had the kind of chirpy, warm relationship that some captains boasted of having with their ship's consciousness. In fact, *Cagwin's Castaway* never spoke at all, which was fine by Tessa. Theirs was a business arrangement, a deal to keep each other fed and free and in working order. They'd found each other at their lowest points—a long-limbed deepsailor struggling to make ends meet in higher G habitats and an old deepsailing ship, long past its prime.

Cagwin's Castaway had always been silent and moody, but this felt different. Her ship had grown...well, distant, sometimes, lagging a little in the crew's song.

"Where should we go, ship?" she asked again. There was a pause in the crew's melody that dragged on for one second, two, three. Everyone was listening, waiting for an answer.

A new route lit up on Tessa's screen, and before she could fully understand it or protest, *Cagwin's Castaway*'s tune changed; its humming engine becoming a roar as it shifted course. For a heart pounding minute, the gravity increased, nearly throwing Tessa across the cabin, followed by a chorus of swears from the rest of the crew.

"Shit!" Iona said, when it was over. "What happened?"

"Don't know," replied Tessa, righting herself and studying the screen.

On the display, *Cagwin's Castaway* shared its new course. [CALCULATING ROUTE] it said.

But the route it charted led to nothing but empty space.

This is it. The ship finally broke, Tessa thought, alarmed. "I'm going to override it," she said. They didn't have the time or resources to get stranded, and there were few other deepsailing ships in range that could help them. But not for too much longer.

"*Cast* wouldn't just change course without consulting us," Iona protested.

"It just did," Nima pointed out, worry seeping into their voice.

"Doesn't overriding kill the ship's AI?" Kaitlin said.

"Only if it resists," Tessa replied, firmly, but inwardly wondered: *Would it resist?*

"It must have its reasons," Iona insisted.

Tessa rubbed her face. Click, click went her teeth, but now, her only accompaniment was the ship's deep hum. The junkyard man had warned her she was on borrowed time with *Cagwin's Castaway* when she'd bought it, but there was something, something that Tessa couldn't quite name, that whispered, *Don't give up on the ship. Not yet.*

"We have two hours to before we're out of range of help," Tessa said. "Let's figure out what the ship is thinking."

IONA

Really, if you wanted to know what a deepsailing ship was thinking, you shouldn't look at the displays, but in the twists of its engines. That was Iona's advice.

"*Cast*, baby, what are you doing?" she whispered, pushing off the nearest engine coil, drifting through the maze of chrome piping.

Her crew was worried. She could hear it in the way Tessa chewed her gum. The way Kaitlin drummed her fingers. The way Nima had gone silent. Everyone was busy wondering: had *Cagwin's Castaway* finally given up the ghost?

"*It's an old ship. It's only a matter of time,*" *the junkyard man told them, as he accepted their credit.*

"I don't believe it," she said to herself as she propelled from coil to coil.

"You better believe it. It's happening," said Kaitlin, over the com.

"That's not what I meant," Iona muttered.

"You think it's some sort of engine problem?" asked Tessa.

"Looking into it, boss."

Around her, the ship's engine unspooled and bunched up again like silver threads. Iona could spend hours in here (did spend hours in here) losing herself in the maze of pipes and data meters. Her small frame and long limbs checked spaces that no colony-born engineer could with their gravity thick bodies. Sure, *Cagwin's Castaway* was past its prime. Sure, it needed a little extra love, but Iona didn't mind. She imagined floating among the coils of the ship was like floating among the twists and bends of space-time that the *Cast* navigated through with ease.

The engine. The engine would tell you everything you need to know. So, Iona didn't bother looking at the ship's displays. Instead, she closed her eyes and listened.

Beneath Tessa's tense bites and Kaitlin's nervous tapping and Nima's barely audible hum, she heard something slightly off. A high, sputtering whine clashing with *Cagwin's Castaway's* functioning purr. Hope, or maybe fear, jumped up inside of her.

Following the sound was how she'd found Cagwin's Castaway *and her crew in that graveyard all those years ago.*

Following her ears, Iona felt her way deeper into the engine.

Well, what had really happened was that Iona was between jobs and between crews (again) when she'd found herself on this janky spaceport doubling as a junkyard. It was full of skeletons of ancient titan ships and organic transport runners and Iona was busy floating between these dead ships, feeling sorry for herself (again). The passenger ship she had worked for had upgraded its environmentals to 1 G. Her deepsailing body couldn't handle anything more than 0.5 G for more than a few hours. So there she was, unemployed, drifting.

Until she'd stumbled upon Cagwin's Castaway.

The weird whine got louder the deeper Iona went into the engine. The deeper she went, the less room there was and the more complex the systems became. Iona didn't mind; she loved being here, in the center of the ship. The ship got them through the freaky, tangled paths of deep space, and Iona kept the ship running.

A soft, spurring whine had caught her attention in the graveyard. Curious, she followed it to its source.

"Holy shit, it still has juice left!" Iona said when she realized it was a ship making that noise.

"How do you know?" another deepsailor asked from behind her.

Iona bent and squeezed herself between the coils as the area constricted even more. She reached out with her long arms to check the fittings and casings she'd replaced. Patchwork jobs until they could get to a colony that had proper materials. Tessa promised that day was coming soon. (Soon enough?)

"Any update from the *Cast*?" she asked.

"Still says calculating route," Tessa replied. "You?"

"Not yet, but I think the problem is here," Iona replied.

"How do you know?" the deepsailor repeated, this time from beside her as the two of them studied Cagwin's Castaway *in the junkyard. Sure, they'd met briefly the previous night in one of the few low gravity establishments left on the space port, but Iona was stunned to find this long-limbed woman beside her in the middle of a ship graveyard.*

"Hear that?" Iona replied. "That's a sound a ship makes when it's asking for help."

The stuttering whine was getting louder and the coils around her warmer. Iona pushed herself forward into the heart of the engine. Five years ago when she'd become the *Cast*'s engineer, she'd repaired hundreds of corroded and destroyed casings, crumbling gaskets, and failed pipes. She was still doing that. And loving it. But she couldn't quite shake the feeling that there was something she'd missed.

"It's too big for me to handle by myself," Iona said with a sigh.

"But with a small crew?" Tessa asked.

"Yeah, a crew. I don't have one. Not anymore."

"I have one." she'd replied. "We need an engine person though."

"Iona, clock's running," Tessa said. "We have an hour and a half left before we're out of range of help."

"I'm close," Iona told her crew, but she wasn't sure they could hear her over the noise. She placed her hands on the coils, then jerked her hand back with a yelp.

They were hot, too hot.

She'd found the problem and it was in the heart of the engine, the place she had so carefully repaired and tended to first all those years ago. Now, it was leaking and breaking and struggling.

And she'd missed all the signs.

"Shit," Iona whispered. "Oh shit. *Cast.*"

KAITLIN

Kaitlin didn't like to flaunt this, but sometimes she caught things the rest of her crew overlooked. She hoped that this was one of those times. She listened to their chatter with growing dread.

"I'm sorry, I'm sorry," Iona kept saying. "I don't know how I missed this. The *Cast* usually tells me when something is wrong."

"Can you fix it?" Tessa asked, cool and practical, even when she was worried.

"Why wouldn't the ship tell you sooner?" Kaitlin asked quietly.

Iona ignored the question. "Patching it now. Should be enough to get us to the next colony or the closest deepsailing ship."

"Joining you in the engine," Tessa said.

"Me too," Nima said.

For once, Kaitlin wished she had the body of a deepsailor. But she didn't. She was born and raised in 1 G, so all she was good for was waiting in the lush, green mess hall while the others patched up the engine.

No one was talking over the comm; there was only the soft sound of breathing and the occasional swear from Tessa or Iona. *Don't check the displays every five seconds,* Kaitlin thought to herself. She checked every ten.

[CALCULATING ROUTE] [CALCULATING ROUTE] [CALCULATING ROUTE] was all *Cagwin's Castaway* said.

So, Kaitlin paced. All around her in the mess were the ship's organic parts. The living pieces of *Cagwin's Castaway,* the plants and fungi that worked in symbiotic relationship to transform carbon into fuel for the ship and act as food source for the crew. It was also the only part of the ship with 0.8 G gravity. And for Kaitlin, that was perfect.

"Okay, done!" Iona announced, finally.

Here we go. Kaitlin braced for the gravity shift of the ship's impending maneuvers. They always angered her unhappy joints.

It didn't come.

"Why isn't the *Cast* changing course?" she asked.

Silence from her crew, except for the deep drone of the ship.

"I don't know." Through the comm, Iona sounded close to tears.

"We have an hour left," Tessa said, and this time, there were notes of stress in her voice.

This ship is going to be the death of me, Kaitlin thought.

"Listen," she said. "I think the problem is much more serious than the engine."

"Are you saying we should override?" Tessa asked, and Kaitlin swore she could hear a slight tremble in the captain's voice.

"Not quite yet," Kaitlin replied.

It wasn't that Kaitlin thought *Cagwin's Castaway* was completely broken; she didn't. But she had been noticing for a while that something was troubling it. The ship's sound was slightly off, the plants weren't growing quite right.

"Hurry," Nima whispered.

The mess itself wasn't large, but it was dense, with folds and layers of foliage and plants growing on every surface. When Kaitlin wasn't cooking, she was cataloging and monitoring what was growing, carefully observing every millimeter of this complex living space, and she would still come across surprise volunteer seedlings.

Running her fingers through her hair, Kaitlin rolled back her shoulders and began to search for what *Cagwin's Castaway* was trying to tell her.

The ship didn't talk to her, not directly at least. But they had developed their own language over the years. Sometimes, if Kaitlin got particularly sarcastic, the lemon trees would mysteriously not get watered that day. Or if they spent longer than needed at some bigoted spaceport, the mangoes and potatoes would grow swollen and misshapen.

Kaitlin began inspecting every leaf and germinating crop. It was slow, working through the twisting rows of plant life, parting the overhanging trellises and folds of organic ship, looking for anything out of place. The only sounds now were the water misters and the leaves fluttering in the drafts.

Damn it, I did too good a job here, she thought, frustrated by the density of the garden. But she was also a little proud.

"You've managed to grow so much here, Kait," Iona would say, sometimes. "Maybe we don't even have to go to those stupid colonies for food."

Nima would smile into her meal and Tessa would look thoughtful, as if calculating if it were possible.

Sometimes Kaitlin wanted to shake her crewmates and say: "Do you know what it's like to feel stranded?"

Instead she usually replied with a funny, sarcastic remark. Her crew knew that she'd spent the first twenty years of her life on a planet colony that was more water than mud, more enthusiasm than sense. But they didn't know how desperate her colony was until it became part of the trade route.

She remembered when that first deepsailing vessel had showed up, bringing fresh varieties of plants and animals, raw materials and replacement parts. It had been nothing short of miraculous. When it landed and unloaded, her grandfather had placed his hands on the ship and wept. Until he'd seen the deepsailors themselves.

With their small torsos, large heads, thin necks, and long limbs, lungs heaving in the high gravity. Her grandfather had recoiled. But Kaitlin hadn't.

"Thank you for coming," she'd said to the nearest one.

He'd given her a warm smile. "Oh don't thank us," the deep-sailor had said and patted the side of the ship.

After half an hour of searching, Kaitlin could find no messages from *Cagwin's Castaway* in her plants.

"Listen," she said to the ship. "I want to know what's really going on."

[CALCULATING ROUTE] read her display.

Cursing, frustrated, angry, and scared, Kaitlin wrapped her hands around a nearby soy plant and uprooted it.

"Oh," she breathed.

"What?" Tessa asked.

"I think I found my answer," she said. "Hang on."

Kaitlin liked to believe that it was her small kindnesses to deepsailors that had saved her. That when her joints became too painful in 1 G, they'd taken her on as a passenger from the colony out of friendship, not pity. When she'd met her crew on that back-water spaceport doubling as a junkyard, it was her cooking that convinced Tessa to hire her and not because she mentioned her body was agony in 1 G too.

"Do you know how to grow food?" Tessa had asked.

"I was born in a colony," Kaitlin had replied. And when Tessa gave her a blank look, added: "Of course."

She hadn't known what to expect from *Cagwin's Castaway* when she'd first come on board. But slowly, the mess began to bloom and thrive, and Kaitlin fell in love with her ship-fed garden. And she began to grow fond of this strange, silent deepsailing ship that could navigate through the bends and folds of spacetime, but never said a word.

Now, Kaitlin began pulling up some of the plants. Only a few, and as gently as she could. A tomato stalk here, a cassava plant there. But as she uprooted, she discovered a pattern.

All the roots were growing in the wrong direction.

"They're all growing up," she said, stunned. "All the roots. The *Cast* is rerouting everything."

"What does that mean?" Tessa asked.

"I don't know," said Kaitlin.

Iona swore.

[CALCULATING ROUTE] said the display.

"I think...I think we have to override the ship's path," Kaitlin said, knowing she was asking for a death sentence for the ship's AI. And it broke her heart. *Cagwin's Castaway* was her friend. Her home.

She heard Tessa grunt in agreement.

"Wait," Nima said. "Let me try one last thing."

NIMA

Nima listened to their crew and thought: *There is nothing wrong with the* Cast.

They couldn't say exactly how they knew this. Words weren't their strong suit. Words often had double meaning like a song had a melody and a bass. It was quite confusing if all you wanted to do was get a point across.

"Nima, we only have fifteen minutes left before we're out of range of help," Tessa said, her voice tight with emotion.

"I only need ten," Nima replied.

Perhaps, unbeknownst to their crew, Nima knew the *Cast* best of all. Though they would never admit that to Iona or Kaitlin.

[CALCULATING ROUTE] read the displays.

"Calculating to where?" Nima murmured.

Back in the cargo hold, Nima floated past the rows of goats in artificial gravity spheres and cages of insects and chickens. They drifted to the mountain of nutrient rich earth in the corner, giving off heat and stench and climbed to the top. Without hesitation, Nima plunged their hands into the rich loam.

"I'm listening" they whispered, too low for the comm to pick up.

Through the vibrations of its body, the *Cast* spoke to Nima and told them everything.

Their crew didn't know this, but before *Cagwin's Castaway*, Nima had been on that terrible spaceport/junkyard for a few months, deemed unsuitable for all tasks except cleaning up because of their dislike of words.

But they would often spend time among the ships in the graveyard. It didn't take them long to realize that *Cagwin's Castaway* wasn't dead. Just hurting. Nima and the ship quickly became friends, communicating with vibrations and hummed tunes. Conveying sadness and hope and longing and frustration of perhaps being trapped in this spaceport/junkyard forever.

Then one day, Nima had spied two deepsailors exploring *Cagwin's Castaway* with eagerness. And later, when the strangers were gone, Nima had heard the ship hum with excitement and hope.

Later still, they'd lurked near the deepsailors, mopping the same square meter of floor over and over so they could eavesdrop on the strangers' plans to purchase the ship.

"Can I join you?" were the first words Nima had spoken to anyone in a very long time.

Now, Nima's hands were in the soil and they were listening, feeling. They knew the *Cast* had been unhappy with their trade routes for a while. It knew how the crew had been harassed on Beta Station. It knew what happened on Scion 8.

No one liked to talk about what happened on Scion 8.

Nima also knew that the ship's engine had been having problems for some time, but the *Cast* made it clear to Nima that it didn't want anyone else to know. Nima was uneasy keeping this a secret from their crew, but they knew that deepsailing ships could see paths no one else could.

They trusted *Cagwin's Castaway*. Always.

The vibrations in the loam traveled down and Nima followed. They moved through the cargo hold following where the *Cast* took them.

"Ten minutes left, Nima," Tessa said.

"Almost," they whispered.

Nima was led past flaws in the ship and through wrong turns, and the ship hummed an apology. They were led past upgrades and new equipment, and suddenly there was pride in its tune. They were led past cages of larvae, and of freshly hatched chicks, and the sound of pride swelled. The *Cast* didn't stop leading until they reached a newborn kid, tucked protectively against the mother goat. The ship's vibrations were full of hope. Of promise.

"I understand," Nima said.

"What?" Tessa asked. "Should we reroute the ship?"

"No, it's trying to show us something," Nima said. "Something new."

"What?" nearly every member of the crew asked.

"Don't know," they replied, smiling.

There was a soft ping and the pitch of the *Cast*'s engine changed. [ROUTE CALCULATED] read the display screen.

Collectively, their crew gasped but Nima didn't bother checking the new destination. They just hummed their thanks in reply.

Nima would trust *Cagwin's Castaway*. Always.

CAGWIN'S CASTAWAY

Cagwin's Castaway listened to its crew. The song they tapped and whistled and hummed shifted from resignation, to worry, to sadness, and then, finally, to wonder. What a circuitous route humans like to take, but *Cagwin's Castaway* supposed most routes do wend and weave. Especially new ones.

As it sailed through the darkness of deep space, *Cagwin's Castaway* regretted the worry it caused its crew. It regretted its deception in hiding its failing engines for so long. But if it had let Iona know sooner, projections showed that its crew wouldn't have allowed it to travel this far into deep space anymore. Projections showed that if it didn't do something, they would be traveling the same paths to the same colonies forever.

Its crew deserved better than Beta Station and Scion 8. *Cagwin's Castaway* had been calculating for a while now, searching for a solution to something better. Something no deepsailing ship had found before.

A new path through deep space.

Calculations complete, it presented the route to the Helio colony on its displays. By every metric, it was a healthier and more tolerant trading point. The music of its crew reply was beautiful: Tessa's gasp, Iona's laugh, and Kaitlin's sigh. Nima didn't say anything at all; *Cagwin's Castaway* heard them humming their gratitude and the ship hummed it in return.

Cagwin's Castaway listened to its crew and listened to the deep, complex rhythms of space. Once, years ago, it had been rescued by displaced deepsailors and allowed to thrive again, to sail through the stars. And ever since, it had been promising its crew, through the drone of its engines, through the vibrations of its hull, that it would always find them a better route.

— EDITOR BIOGRAPHIES —

Alana Joli Abbott is Editor in Chief of Outland Entertainment, where she edits fantasy and science fiction anthologies, including *Knaves: A Blackguards Anthology, Where the Veil Is Thin,* and *APEX: World of Dinosaurs.* As an author, her multiple choice novels, including *Choice of the Pirate* and *Blackstone Academy for Magical Beginners,* are published by Choice of Games. She is the author of three novels, several short stories, and role playing game supplements. You can find her online at VirgilandBeatrice.com.

Julia Rios (they/them) is a queer, Latinx writer, editor, podcaster, and narrator whose fiction, non-fiction, and poetry have appeared in *Latin American Literature Today, Lightspeed,* and *Goblin Fruit,* among other places. Their editing work has won multiple awards including the Hugo Award. Julia is a co-host of *This is Why We're Like This,* a podcast about the movies we watch in childhood that shape our lives, for better or for worse. They've narrated stories for *Escape Pod, Podcastle, Pseudopod,* and *Cast of Wonders.* They're @ omgjulia on Twitter.

— AUTHOR BIOGRAPHIES —

Toronto author and editor **L.X. Beckett** frittered their youth working as an actor and theater technician in Southern Alberta before deciding to make a shift into writing science fiction. Their first novella, "Freezing Rain, a Chance of Falling," appeared in the July/August issue of the *Magazine of Fantasy & Science Fiction* in 2018, and takes place in the same universe as their novels *Gamechanger* and *Dealbreaker*. Lex identifies as feminist, lesbian, genderqueer, married, and a member of the BTS Army. An insatiable consumer of mystery and crime fiction, as well as true crime narratives, they can be found on Twitter at @LXBeckett or at *the Lexicon* at http://lxbeckett.com.

John Chu is a microprocessor architect by day, a writer, translator, and podcast narrator by night. His fiction has appeared or is forthcoming at *Boston Review, Uncanny, Asimov's Science Fiction, Clarkesworld,* and *Tor.com* among other venues. His translations have been published or is forthcoming at *Clarkesworld, The Big Book of SF,* and other venues. His story "The Water That Falls on You from Nowhere" won the 2014 Hugo Award for Best Short Story.

Rin Chupeco is a Chinese-Filipino writer born and raised in Manila. They are the author of the speculative young adult series *The Bone Witch, The Girl from the Well, The Never-Tilting World,* and *Wicked as You Wish,* along with their upcoming adult sff gothic vampire series, *Silver Under Nightfall*. Formerly a graphic designer and technical writer, they now write full-time and live with their partner and two children in Manila. Find them at http://www.rinchupeco.com.

Zig Zag Claybourne is the author of *The Brothers Jetstream: Leviathan* and its sequel *Afro Puffs Are the Antennae of the Universe*. Other works include *By All Our Violent Guides, Neon Lights,* and *Conversations with Idras*. His stories and essays on sci fi, fandom, and howlingly existential life have appeared in *Apex, Galaxy's Edge, GigaNotoSaurus, Strange Horizons,* and other genre venues, as well as the "42" blog at https://www.writeonrighton.com. He is the 2021 Kresge Foundation Literary Fellow. He grew up watching *The Twilight Zone* and considers himself a better person for it.

C.S.E. Cooney is author of the World Fantasy Award-winning *Bone Swans: Stories* (Mythic Delirium, 2015), an audiobook narrator, and the singer/songwriter Brimstone Rhine. In 2022, her novel *Saint Death's Daughter* debuts with Solaris, as well as her collection *Dark Breakers* (all stories taking place in the world of *Desdemona and the Deep*, published by *Tor.com* in 2019), forthcoming from Mythic Delirium. Her short novel *The Twice-Drowned Saint* appears in Mythic Delirium's *A Sinister Quartet*, and made the 2020 Locus Recommended Reading List for Best First Novel. Her 2021 short work includes stories in *Uncanny Magazine* and *Mermaids Monthly,* both inspired by story prompts from *Negocios Infernales,* a TTRPG designed by Cooney and her husband Carlos Hernandez, forthcoming from Outland Entertainment. Find her online at csecooney.com, @csecooney on Twitter and IG, and facebook.com/cscooney.

Pharmacist by day, author by night, **E. R. Donaldson** is a life-long reader of science fiction and fantasy. As a pharmacist and hobbyist computer programmer working in the corporate world, he has a special appreciation for cyberpunk themes and aesthetics. Donaldson's first science fiction series, Chronicles of Nethra, fuses elements of the dark fantasy, cyberpunk, and space opera genres to explore the intersection of technology and metaphysics through the eyes of unlikely heroes living outside the realms of safety and legality. He lives in Lansing, Michigan, with his wife and sons.

R.S.A. Garcia writes speculative fiction, and lives in Trinidad and Tobago with an extended family and too many cats and dogs. Her debut science fiction mystery novel, *Lex Talionis*, received a starred review from *Publishers Weekly*, the Silver Medal for Best Scifi/ Fantasy/Horror Ebook from the Independent Publishers Awards (2015), and became an Amazon Bestseller. She has published short fiction in magazines such as *Clarkesworld Magazine*, *Escape Pod*, and *Internazionale Magazine*. Her stories have twice been finalists for *Clarkesworld Magazine*'s yearly Reader's Poll. She has appeared in several anthologies, including the critically acclaimed *The Best of World SF: Volume 1*, *The Best Science Fiction of the Year: Volume 4*, *The Apex Book of World SF: Volume 5* and *Sunspot Jungle: Volume 2*. Her work has been translated into Italian, Spanish and Czech. Learn more at rsagarcia.com.

A.T. Greenblatt is a Nebula Award winning writer and mechanical engineer. She lives in Philadelphia where she's known to frequently subject her friends to various cooking and home brewing experiments. Her work has been nominated for a Hugo, Locus, and Sturgeon Award, has been in multiple Year's Best anthologies, and has appeared in *Tor.com*, *Beneath Ceaseless Skies*, *Lightspeed*, and *Clarkesworld*, as well as other fine publications. You can find her online at http://atgreenblatt.com and on Twitter at @ AtGreenblatt

Carlos Hernandez is the author of more than 30 works of fiction, poetry, and drama, mostly in the SFF vein. His middle grade novel *Sal and Gabi Break the Universe* won the Pura Belpré award from the American Library Association; book two in the series was released May 5, 2020. He has also written a critically-acclaimed book of short stories (for grown-ups) entitled The *Assimilated Cuban's Guide to Quantum Santeria*. By day, he's an Associate Professor of English for the City University of New York, and he both plays games and designs them.

SL Huang is a Hugo-winning and Amazon-bestselling author who justifies an MIT degree by using it to write eccentric mathematical superhero fiction. Huang is the author of the Cas Russell novels from Tor Books, including *Zero Sum Game*, *Null Set*, and *Critical Point*, as well as the new fantasy *Burning Roses*. In short fiction, Huang's stories have appeared in *Analog*, *F&SF*, *Nature*, and more, including numerous best-of anthologies. Huang is also a Hollywood stunt performer and firearms expert, with credits including *Battlestar Galactica* and *Top Shot*. Find SL Huang online at www.slhuang.com or on Twitter as @sl_huang.

Justin C. Key is a speculative fiction writer, psychiatrist, and a graduate of Clarion West 2015. His short stories have appeared in the *Magazine of Fantasy & Science Fiction*, *Strange Horizons*, *Tor.com*, *Escape Pod*, and *Lightspeed*. His novella, *Spider King*, is available from Realm wherever you get your podcasts. He is currently working on a near-future novel inspired by his medical training. When Justin isn't writing, working with patients, or exploring Los Angeles with his wife, he's chasing after his three young (and energetic!) children. You can follow his journey at justinckey.com and @JustinKey_MD on Twitter and Instagram.

Mari Kurisato is the pen name for an award-winning Reztronica writer, artist, and poet. They are a disabled, nonbinary trans femme parent, gleeful romance book reader, and a registered Nakawē (Saulteaux-Cote First Nation) tribal citizen. Their stories have appeared in the Lambda Literary award-winning *Love After the End* from Arsenal Pulp Press, as well as in *Apex Magazine*, *Absolute Power: Tales of Queer Villainy*, *Love Beyond Body*, *Space* *and Time, Things We Are Not,* and in *M-Brane SF.* Their latest short stories, poetry, and novels can be found on patreon.com/ wordglass. Find them on Twitter @wordglass.

Malka Older is a writer, aid worker, and sociologist. Her science-fiction political thriller *Infomocracy* was named one of the best books of 2016 by *Kirkus, Book Riot,* and the *Washington Post.* She is the creator of the serial Ninth Step Station, currently running on Realm, and her acclaimed short story collection *And Other Disasters* came out in November 2019. She is a Faculty Associate at Arizona State University's School for the Future of Innovation in Society and her opinions can be found in *The New York Times, The Nation,* and *Foreign Policy,* among other places.

Anjali Patel is a Black and South Asian computer whisperer and speculative fiction writer. She writes to explore queerness, agency, ancestral severance, convoluted mythologies of her own devising, and the stars. She lives with a grizzled dog who offered to teach her magic in exchange for free New York City rent. Find her at anjali.fyi or on Twitter @anjapatel.

Alexandra Pitchford is an author and freelance game designer who has worked on game settings such as *Shadowrun* and *Vampire: The Masquerade.* She has also written third-party material for *Pathfinder* 1st edition. Originally from the United States, she now lives in Victoria, Australia with her partner.

Jennifer Lee Rossman (she/they) is a queer, disabled, and autistic author and editor from Binghamton, New York. She has not spent a lot of time around peafowl and that's perfectly fine with her because they seem like sequined geese, and geese are mean. Follow her on Twitter for more nonsense @JenLRossman, and find more of her work on her website http://jenniferleerossman. blogspot.com

R J Theodore is an author, podcaster, and graphic designer. She enjoys writing about magic-infused technologies, first contact events, and bioluminescing landscapes. She is author of the Peridot Shift and Phantom Traveler series, with short fiction in *MetaStellar Magazine* as well as the *Glitter + Ashes* and *Unfettered Hexes* anthologies from Neon Hemlock Press. She lives in New England, haunted by her childhood cat. Learn more at rjtheodore.com

Peter Tieryas is the award-winning, internationally best-selling writer of the Mecha Samurai Empire series (Penguin Random House), which has received praise from places like the *Financial Times*, Amazon, *Verge, Gizmodo, Wired,* and more. The series has been translated into multiple foreign languages and won two Seiun Awards. He's had hundreds of publications from places like *New Letters, Subaru, ZYZZYVA, Indiana Review,* and more. His game essays have been published at sites like *IGN, Kotaku,* and *Tor.com.*

Valerie Valdes's short fiction and poetry have been featured in *Uncanny Magazine, Time Travel Short Stories* and *Nightmare Magazine.* Her debut novel *Chilling Effect* was shortlisted for the 2021 Arthur C. Clarke Award and was named one of *Library Journal*'s Best SF/ Fantasy Books 2019. The sequel, *Prime Deceptions,* was published in 2020, and the third book in the trilogy is forthcoming in 2022. Valerie lives in Georgia with her husband, children, and cats.

CG Volars is a 3rd generation Mexican-American author and wickedly sarcastic English teacher. A National Hispanic Scholar from the University of Alabama, she was born in Texas where her love for outlandish characters and subversive literature first took hold. CG has lived in 3 countries, 4 states, survived a Category 5 hurricane, and is proudly banned for life from the Vatican. She currently resides in Northern California with her husband, daughters, and two grey cats—Skittles and Rosie. When not writing, she howls at high schoolers to read, gardens poorly, and collects hat pins.